TALLROCK

Farming Livia Book One

XANDER BOYCE

MOUNTAINDALE
PRESS

DEDICATION

This book was written in memory of Miranda and Kael, who left too early. And to every parent who has had to bury their baby.

CHAPTER ONE

Arrival 1

DAY 1

Matt sat, waiting for the download to finish. He considered reviewing some of the beta tester footage that had been released. But he had already pored over all of the available content and had made his decisions. Well, most of them, but the ones left were dependent on what options they had kept or added since they had closed the beta four weeks ago.

The game was Livia. The largest world ever created, having a playable landmass of 100 million square miles, larger than the surface of the Earth. That wasn't including the various underwater areas either. A paradise from before the industrial revolution. None of the skyscrapers and dirty air that had become ubiquitous on Earth. Livia was filled with life and magic straight out of fairytales. But, and perhaps most importantly for Matt, it also had a real money transfer system. Meaning he could transfer real-world money into in-game currency and back out.

The world was enormous and had been divided up into hundreds of Kingdoms, both large and small. There were benefits and drawbacks to every size. Of course, if he picked a powerful Kingdom, there would be plenty of quests and other activities to pursue. But also a lot more competition for the limited resources available to that area.

He began researching the various Kingdoms while he waited. A ping announced the install was finished, and his neural interface started a countdown for full immersion. Shifting from where he had been sitting on the couch to a more comfortable spot lying down, he mentally commanded the neural link to bypass the countdown, and he was in.

The world was dark. A thin line began approaching from the distance, discernible only because it was the sole light in the blackness. The line approached, and it resolved itself into a single word, 'Livia,' in a multitude of colors. They shifted and expanded, allowing him a top-down view of the entire world of Livia, which was in the shape of an Alderson disk. The sun in the center was much smaller than any real star could be, but still able to provide all the energy needed for the surface of the disc. The disk itself spun in a clockwise rotation.

Above a central landmass, three black airships appeared; they were somewhere between a blimp and an old age of sail galleon. Their hulls were festooned with bladders to provide lift while three masts proudly boasted red and black sails. The term 'windrunner' came to his mind, the data stream telling him what the ships were called. The foremost windrunner banked away from him, exposing its broadside cannons, which discharged a mass of magic and physical projectiles directly over his head. Instinctively ducking away from the bombardment, he turned to look at what their target was.

A dragon, brilliant red in the sunset, was caught full-on with the bombardment. Electrical magic crackled over its muscles, its wings stiffening and causing it to lose altitude. Then the physical projectiles hit it, tearing gaping holes in its wings. Still, the dragon pushed on, flapping slowly as it tried to regain its momentum. It crashed into the ship. Its claws carved deep furrows in the side of the vessel and popped a number of the bladders. The ship drifted, no longer able to maintain its course, into the path of another of the windrunners. The black sails shifted, and the second windrunner carved through the air away from its doomed companion. Exposing its own broadside, which unleashed another bombardment of hell on the ship and dragon alike.

The dragon screamed in rage and pain, shaking the air around Matt as the entire scene shrunk down until it disappeared over the central landmass, which was now labeled Middar.

The circle of the disk rotated counterclockwise and took Matt along with it, another scene appearing as it shifted to another continent. More black windrunners surged forward, carrying thousands of metal clad marines hanging from ropes ready to rapidly disembark.

Two armies fought on the ground below. Bursts of light lanced up from the land of the 'defending' force, singeing a hole most of the way through the windrunner and breaking the foremost mast. The ship responded in kind, it's broadside raining death down on the troops below even as it lost altitude.

Matt watched as the windrunner splintered into the ground, the marines disembarking even among the chaos of the crash. Bright flashes of light from handheld devices similar to guns struck the metal armor, bouncing off and creating a ricochet of light that bored holes into any non-reflective surfaces it hit.

Behind enemy lines, the marines fought to return to the front but were stopped by a shield of blue energy that appeared in the middle of the two armies, rising as far as the eye could see. The defending troops around the windrunner's marines all began shouting for joy. Even as Matt zoomed up and away, the blue wall was still visible and blocking off almost an entire continent, which was now labeled Thel'kan.

Other sections of the world had their own cutscenes, and Matt realized he was being shown the recent history of Livia. The black windrunners were often featured. He came to recognize the flag—a green, white, and black version of the Union Jack—that they were flying as the symbol of Pinnoc, the dominant power in much of the world. Although they were shown losing almost as often as they were shown winning.

Matt's understanding was that they were a power on the decline. Especially after the recent loss of the two full legions as they tried to cross the Spines of Aktrosha, a mountain range on a continent named Gogland. The windrunners that had been transporting them disappeared into the mist, leaving that section of the mountains shrouded in mystery.

"Welcome to Livia, where you control the future. Do you know where you would like to join our story?" With a nod of his head, Matt pointed at the last location. Gogland. The Alderson disk expanded until that was all he could see.

It was a large-ish continent, tapering on both sides towards the core while the rimward section expanded into an ice-encrusted mountain range that split the continent in two. The trailing half was filled with eight to nine hundred foot tall trees and was labeled Quel de Mitgar. There was a gap of uncontrolled territory in the mountain range now marked as the Spines of Aktrosha. To the trailing side was a stretch of unbroken forest, followed by a long plain that spread across thousands of miles before reaching the sea, which was labeled as the Alliance of Kiddesh. The entire leading side was dotted with small pocket states labeled Pinnoc.

"You've chosen to start in Gogland. There are three main playable factions in the region. Quel de Mitgar, the Alliance of Kiddesh, and Pinnoc." Around him three walls of text, one for each of the nations, were visible. Quel de Mitgar was easy to ignore. They were a highly militaristic nation of elf-like creatures that lived in cities high in the boughs of the redwood-like siccora trees that thrived on the trailing half of the continent. The Kiddeshans were also easy to discount, as they were nomadic hunter-gatherers, which didn't align with how he wanted to play the game.

Which, of course, left only Pinnoc. The flavor text described it as a strong empire dwindling in power. The childless High King grew old, and the various rulers of the core duchies each vied to be the next in line for the throne. Which confirmed what Matt had heard of the country. Pinnoc's population was so large that he could pick any of the playable races. But what really drew him was the idea of being a colonial pioneer in a mostly untamed wilderness. Even better if, when King Tasdel died in a few years, the colonies in Gogland could gain independence, removing the heavy taxation most goods currently experienced.

"I'd like to be a… Pinnocian?" He realized he had no idea what to call someone from Pinnoc, but the AI of the game seemed to understand him, and it immediately shifted to character generation.

Around him were seven pillars of light, and inside each were groupings of individuals that all seemed to be roughly the same race, although some of them varied wildly. Directly in front of him stood the humans, just like those that dwelled on Earth. Going around the circle, next to the humans were a group of short, hairless halflings called eiran, and a tall and slender race with pointed ears he recognized as elves but which the system labeled quinthan. Next, a race of muscular green-skinned humanoids with wild eyes and tusks called dragon tribesmen but which could have easily been fantasy orcs. A group of dwarves labeled cianese, anthropomorphic beastkin, and finally, a group of massive… well, dragon-men called draks.

Having read enough about the anti-nonhuman sentiment of Pinnoc from the beta testers, he ignored the other races. Although the draks were tempting, they didn't quite fit the role he wanted to play and had some severe disadvantages to compensate for their impressive physical characteristics. After selecting the human group, his perception zoomed forward and he was again surrounded by about a dozen different pillars of light, each showing several humans with various labels underneath them. This time they all appeared to be origins or ethnicities. Ranging from half quinthan or dragon tribe to Tua'tatian. After scanning over their descriptions to ensure they hadn't changed since the beta testers reported their attributes, he selected Pinnocian-Capital.

The Pinnocian-Capital subrace of humans gave him some mostly irrelevant bonuses and two important ones. One: a bonus to his starting wealth in the form of a king's writ, which allowed him to claim a portion of the new land as his own. And two: a bonus major affinity in any of the magical trees.

The next section of CharGen was avatar appearance customization. Some of the beta testers had made some rather horrific avatars, but he had no interest in having to see something like that when he looked in a mirror.

Selecting the option that modeled his avatar after himself, he frowned, considering his options. He decided to add a few inches of height to bump the avatar up to 6'1" and changed his curly hair to straight while giving himself a military crew cut. It wasn't easy to find a barber in the frontier, and he had no desire to look like some of the players at the end of the beta who had let their hair grow wild. He then gave himself a bronzed skin tone, as he didn't really want to experience a virtual sunburn.

Finally, he was down to stat and skill distribution. The system for Livia was very open-ended. There were no classes; character growth was unfettered by any restrictions except for the affinity system. Which was broken down into two parts, elemental affinity and skill affinity.

Elemental affinity consisted of four sliding bars. Earth and air, fire and water, light and darkness, and life and death. He selected his elemental affinities by picking a point on the bar. From the beta testers, he had learned that a balanced bar was, generally speaking, a bad idea, since your ability to use skills and spells with any elements was dependent on having a minimum affinity.

With a balanced bar, he would never be able to utilize anything more advanced than the mid-level abilities. Matt slid his elemental affinity bars to heavily favor earth, water, light, and life. He turned his attention to the other portion of the affinity bars.

Skill affinities didn't determine which skills he could acquire—that was just a matter of practice, or training—but it did determine how easily he could learn those skills, as well as how powerful they were. Two people with level 100 swordsmanship would have vastly different results if one had a major affinity while the other had no affinity or even a minor affinity.

As a human, he was able to select five major affinities and ten minor affinities. The Pinnocian-Capital subrace let him choose an additional free major magical affinity. The skills affinity list was daunting, and there had been some reports of people gaining extra skill affinity points as they advanced through quests. There were four skill trees for each of the four basic categories of skills. Martial, Magical, Crafting, and Gathering. These broad categories were further broken down into hundreds of individual skills. Many skills were built upon each other. For example, if someone wanted to become an armorsmith, they would need to earn skill ranks in: metalworking, blacksmithing, leatherworking, and armor crafting. Only after reaching a minimum proficiency in those would they unlock armorsmithing.

Major affinities placed in root trees would slowly trickle down. If someone got to rank 100 in blades, they could pick any of its sub-skills, like swords, to also get a major affinity. Although the time it took to master a single skill meant that even the most dedicated beta testers had only gotten two linked affinity gains.

Because of the complexity of the skills system, there were a number of the typical presets, things like fighter, druid, cleric, and ranger, as well as dozens of the less typical ones like witchdoctor, magitechnician, necromancer, shaman, and cavalier.

Matt ignored all of those and instead focused on his plan. He put his major affinities into water, earth, and bonding magic, as well as the husbandry skill. Those were the four most important ones. Next, he picked mana manipulation, as he intended to be doing a lot of magic and wanted to have as much mana as he could.

That left one last major affinity and the ten minor affinities. Frowning, Matt tapped his finger against his lower lip. "How much am I going to need to defend myself on the frontier?" he wondered aloud.

He was surprised when the AI responded, "That depends on how you want to live your life on Livia. From your selections, I assume you would like to become a Floramancer, is that correct?"

"Yes? Maybe, not sure what a Floramancer is, but I want to use magic to grow crops and farm," Matt responded while looking around for the source of the AI's voice, but it apparently did not have any representation in the interface currently.

Sensing his desire for something to talk to, a woman appeared next to him clad in a leafy green dress. Or at least he thought she was a human. As he looked closer, he realized that her hair was made of red maple leaves, and her skin had a tough, almost bark-like texture to it making her a dryad.

"What sort of farm were you thinking of?" The plant lady spoke with the voice of the AI from before, and Matt frowned.

"What do you mean?" he asked.

"There are many background options that would fit your desired playstyle. Do you want to farm with a collective? You could also farm with a mentor, or cut your own path." As the dryad spoke, three background options appeared in front of Matt.

Collective Farming

You are a member of a collective that pooled their resources together to purchase a more substantial portion of land. The members of the collective will each have individual responsibilities, which will allow for a more productive farm if properly managed.

Farming with a Mentor

You are assisting a more veteran farmer with their farm. They will teach you the ropes, and you will eventually inherit a portion of the farm when they have deemed you ready to farm on your own. During your training, you will receive a monthly allowance but no share of the profit.

Frontier Farmer

You have received a land grant from the king as an incentive to populate the trailing frontier. You will be on your own unless you decide to recruit more help on your farm. Your land will initially be completely undeveloped.

Matt started to open his mouth to say that he wanted the third option immediately.

The dryad spoke first. "I know that you came here determined to do the third option, but I must warn you. That path is by far the most difficult and the least likely to end in success. The other two options are far more likely to be a rewarding experience for you."

Matt paused, considering. He had been preparing to be a frontier farmer since he first heard about Gogland. The untamed wilderness described by the beta testers was everything he wanted in a game. But the warning worried him. This was basically the game telling him that he was picking an advanced option, and he probably wouldn't be successful at it. A lot was riding on his ability to make a living playing Livia, so he needed to make a profit.

Would he enjoy working in a collective? He had never been fond of group projects in school. There was always that one kid who ended up doing all the work while everyone else screwed around. That had always ended up being him growing up, and he didn't really like the idea of having to carry the dead weight. But, on the other hand, if he got hard-working people, it would allow them to specialize and create a built-in party for other content he might want to play. Also, it'd be useful to repel any attackers if there were multiple people.

"How many people would be in the collective?" Matt asked the dryad.

"There are no other unbound currently attempting to join a

collective farm. The number would be determined by location, but somewhere between ten and twenty individuals is usually recommended," the dryad answered.

Unbound was the game's term for the players. Which meant he would be saddled with a bunch of Non-Player Characters or NPCs if he chose the collective farm. That would mean they were more likely to do their share of the work, but he wouldn't have the built-in group that was the main draw of the collective.

Matt wished he would have pushed Dave a little harder into playing as a farmer. His friend was dead set on becoming an adventurer, saying the sale of loot was bound to be much better than any profits from farming. With a sigh, he dismissed Dave from his thoughts for now and focused on the second option.

"If I choose the mentor, how long would it take for me to have my own farm, and what would my salary be?"

"That depends on you, but four or five months at least. As for the salary, it would be enough for you to keep yourself fed and clothed, but not much beyond that."

Matt shook his head; there was no way he could afford to go months without making a profit in the game. Option two was out, which really only left number three.

"I'm going to pick Frontier Farmer, but I'm curious. Does its land grant stack with my king's writ?" Matt asked, and the dryad smiled at him nodding her head.

"It seemed likely you would, but I wanted to make sure you at least considered the other options. As for your question, they do indeed stack, and you will receive two tokens." She turned her head and gestured. "If you are going to pick that option, this is what I suggest you do with your affinities."

She pointed at the floating lines that represented Matt's choices, and they all shifted a little. His elemental affinities had stayed somewhat the same, still strong in water and earth, but light and dark had balanced out, and life and death had swapped.

His skill affinities, on the other hand, had changed quite a bit. Keeping the major affinities with water, earth, magic, as well as husbandry, but herbalism, assault, and death magic had joined the list while bonding had swapped to a minor affinity. For minor affinities, the dryad had also selected: physical fitness, imbue magic, mana manipulation, alchemy, leatherworking, condensing, ranching, skinning, and processing.

"I mean I guess I understand most of those, but why should I do death magic instead of life?" Matt asked.

"You will be alone in the wilderness; you will need a way to keep yourself safe. Death magic is by far the most potent type of attack spell; there are also many useful death spells for a budding farmer."

"Okay. What about all the crafting stuff?"

"You will need to be self-reliant to survive in the wilderness. Being able to produce your own clothing and shelter will greatly increase your comfort and safety. Alchemy will allow you to work longer and recover from any injuries you sustain. That is the same reason I suggest mana manipulation and physical fitness. These are skills that will allow you to work harder and longer than you normally would be able to. Additionally, all but the last two of these skills will allow you to produce sellable goods to supplement your income while your crops grow."

Matt tapped his finger against his lower lip as he considered the dryad's advice. "Okay, I get that, and you know this world better than me. If you think that's what is going to make me the most successful, I'll do it." He glanced over at the dryad. "What is your name anyway?"

The dryad smiled at him again. "I am Livia. It is a pleasure to meet you, Cycle Mage. By what name will you be known in Livia?"

Matt paused, thinking. "Call me Kastigan. Or just Kas for short."

Livia nodded. "Well, Kas, you're almost ready to start your journey. You just need to pick some starting equipment."

Kas nodded his head. "What would you recommend?"

"I'll put together a kit for you." Livia waved her hand, and he was suddenly surrounded by various racks of leather clothing. "Just say when you've picked an item, and it will move on to the next set on the list. I'll also put together a bag with the kits and tools you'll need that don't need you to pick a style."

Kas nodded his head and began trying on various items. Each of the items had the exact same stats, a modest boost to defense, but looked different to allow him to select something that fit his own aesthetic. He found a pair of fringed leather pants and a jacket he liked that made him look a lot like an early 19th-century mountain man.

He then picked up a couple daggers that appeared in various sheaths around his body as he selected them. A surprisingly comfortable pair of sturdy boots came next. He supposed the game had made some considerations for comfort over realism. He slipped a dagger into a concealed sheath in the boots, raising his total number of knives to three.

The jacket, boots, and pants all came with appropriate, if somewhat boring, underclothes and socks. Attire selected, Kas' next choice was a bit surprising to him. Wands. He had seen a few of the beta testers using a wand but had no idea what they had been using them for. "Wands?" he asked, and Livia answered from behind his shoulder.

"Yes, since a good portion of your magic is going to be performed out of combat, a wand will help focus and amplify it. I wouldn't recommend using it in combat until you get more accustomed to it, as that can cause miscasts. I've put out wands that will work best with earth and water magic. They will also work with the minor death magic spells you learn to help your farm. As well as the light and dark ones, but they won't give anywhere near the power boost you will get for your earth and water ones."

Nodding in understanding, Kas turned back to the table of wands, picking them up and giving them a shake before analyzing them to look at their stats.

Item Name: Beech Wand (Agate)
Combat Prerequisite: 10 skill ranks of Channel Wand

Description: A wand made of beech wood with an agate inset at one end. Greatly amplifies water and earth magic channeled through the wand. Moderately amplifies all other types of magic.

Item Name: Cherry Wand (Topaz)
Combat Prerequisite: 15 skill ranks of Channel Wand
Description: A wand made of cherry wood with a topaz inset at one end. Greatly amplifies water and earth magic channeled through the wand. Moderately amplifies all other types of magic.

Item Name: Holly Wand (Aquamarine)
Combat Prerequisite: 20 skill ranks of Channel Wand
Description: A wand made of holly wood with an aquamarine inset at one end. Greatly amplifies water and earth magic channeled through the wand. Moderately amplifies all other types of magic.

There were other variations, but the combat requirements weren't that important; Kas wasn't going to be in combat much. He decided that it didn't seem to matter much and picked the Holly and Aquamarine wand. Assuming that the higher-level channel wand meant it would be more potent, and less likely to need to be replaced.

He slid the wand into a pocket he discovered along his right thigh and turned around, realizing that there wasn't anything left for him to select. A large backpack sat next to his feet, a saw, axe, and bedroll visibly attached to it, and he leaned down to pick it up, wincing slightly at the weight.

"Well, it seems you're ready to go. Any last questions?" Livia asked as soon as he had the bag situated.

"This doesn't seem like it's big enough for everything that I need. What about seeds?"

"The bag, like most in Livia, is capable of carrying more than you are accustomed to. I've included a few seeds for basic crops; you'll be able to find more profitable seeds as you explore Livia."

Kas nodded his head as Dryad-Livia spoke, glad that the

game was sacrificing some realism in favor of convenience. "Hm, well, any advice for me?"

Livia smiled. "So few of you unbound ask me that. You all seem so eager to start your adventuring." She paused for a moment, scanning Kas up and down. "I think you'll do just fine. You've selected an unusual path, but I look forward to watching your exploits." She reached forward to kiss Kas on either cheek. "Just be yourself and work hard."

Blessing of Livia acquired. For the next week, all experience gained will be doubled. You took the time to ask Livia her opinion, and she has blessed you for your consideration. Remember, Livia is not just a game; it is a living world whose future you can help write.

"Good luck, Kastigan."

And with that, his perception was flying through the air. Zooming across Gogland until he stopped just before the oppressive mountain range he had seen in the introduction before. He looked down and saw an expansive forest stretching from the foot of the mountains trailward back towards the ocean.

At the base of the mountains, standing tall above the forest around him, was a mesa. Easily a mile across, with some buildings built upon its upper face. A merchant windrunner—designated as such by its colorful sails and hull—was docking at scaffolding near the center of the mesa.

Kas zoomed toward the windrunner, seeming to slow down a bit before landing on the deck of the ship. The sounds of people rushing to gather their belongings after the six-month trip from Pinnoc to Gogland nearly taking over the shouts of the Captain who called out from the poop deck, "Welcome to Tallrock! Now get off my ship!"

CHAPTER TWO

Arrival 2

Kas' position on the windrunner meant it would be some time before he could actually disembark, especially after some sort of commotion started at the gangplank. So, he took a moment to familiarize himself with the UI and his character sheet. The UI was standard; a thought would open up various menus or a GUI. He could also navigate around the UI with a thought. The neural interface was doing all the heavy lifting. He took a few minutes to toggle health bars and created a HUD to display his own mana, stamina, and health.

He then opened his character sheet.

Name: Kastigan *Race:* Human *Origin:* Pinnocian-Capital

HP: 50, *Mana:* 100, *Stamina:* 75

Level: 1, *XP:* 0, *XP TNL:* 100

Attributes:
Intelligence 10, Dexterity 10, Strength 10, Wisdom 10, Charisma 10, Constitution 10.

Regen Rates:

HP Regen: 60s, Stamina Regen: 10s, Mana Regen: 10s, Combat HP Regen: -, Combat S Regen: 20s, Combat M Regen: 14s.

Elemental Affinities:

Fire -------- | -- Water, Light ----- | ----- Dark, Earth -- | -------- Air, Life --------- | - Death

Nothing too outrageous here; as a human, his stats had started balanced. He was currently level one and had a ten in every stat. His health points or HP were at 50; in Livia, the number itself was an abstraction that helped him understand how much damage he could take before he died.

Livia was a realistic game; as he incurred injuries, he would also lose combat effectiveness. Meaning that if someone could cut off his arm, he wouldn't be able to use it until it was healed. Not to mention that it would hurt. Not as much as in real life, but the neural interface would ensure that he would experience some feedback when injured.

To test the pain levels, he pulled out a dagger and poked his finger. He felt a dull ache that eventually grew as he increased pressure on his finger until he drew a drop of blood. He knew that Livia, like most modern VR, only had a 5% pain setting, which made the prick feel about as bad as poking the corner of a Lego with your finger. Satisfied with how the pain 'felt,' he saw that his HP had dropped a single point. But that would regen in a minute, so he wasn't worried about it.

Intelligence and wisdom both affected his total mana pool in a 5:1 ratio, giving him a respectable mana pool of 100 points. Stamina was a little bit harder to compute. Every point of constitution gave him five points of stamina and every two points of strength did the same for a total of 75 stamina.

Regens—how fast all three pools came back—were half as fast in combat for mana and stamina and non-existent for HP. He wasn't entirely sure how the system determined if you were in combat or not. If you were stealthed waiting to ambush something, did that mean you were in combat? Was the person you were stalking in combat? He hadn't really paid much attention to what the beta testers had said about combat when he was doing his research, since it wasn't something that had interested him.

It took him a moment of staring at the elemental affinities before the numbers appeared over the lines. They were all rated on a scale of 100. So, he had 80 in water and earth but only 20 in fire and air. 50 in both light and dark, while death was at 90 and life—his lowest—was only 10. Unless they had changed the system around since the beta testers created characters, most of his learned spells would be on the fringe of his elemental affinity levels, which would mean his death spells would be more potent than any of his others.

Kas' next goal, as he investigated the interface, was to check out his skills. First were his physical skills. He only had ranks in three of them; physical fitness I and two of its children, endurance I and running I. Minor affinities gave you five levels in the root skill and two levels in two of its children. It wasn't much, but gaining the first rank of a skill cost money or a large amount of effort. Every skill also came in five different ranks labeled with Roman numerals from I to V. To upgrade a skill's rank, you had to be level 100 in the earlier rank and use a skill tome.

There was some speculation that a high enough scribe could also create skill tomes, but none of the beta testers had been able to do so. The earlier level skill tomes could be purchased from skill vendors, but the rank fours and fives could only be earned from quests or by getting them as 'drops' while using abilities or spells associated with that skill.

Kas' magical school tree was much more filled out. Nothing surprising there, there hadn't been any changes since the beta test. Although it seemed like he got the extra skills in random sub-skills for these too. He had been hoping for mana circulation I rather than mana projection I, but other than that he had gotten all the ones he needed, and the additional ones he wanted he should be able to learn in town. The same could be said of his other two groups as well. The only other disappointing subskill result was smelting from processing, since he didn't have any intention of getting into mining.

Next was the option on the HUD that he was most eager to explore, his abilities list.

Spell Name: Frostbolt
Prerequisites: 80 water affinity, Water Magic I 1, Assault Magic I 1, Chilling I 1
Damage: 9.9–19.8 water damage (average 14.8)
Range: 15m
Cost: 5 mana
Cooldown: 2.5 seconds
Description: Shoots a bolt of frost at the target, dealing 5–10 cold damage (bonus damage for affinity and high intelligence), and slows the target for 3 seconds.

Spell Name: Death Blast
Prerequisites: 90 death affinity, Death Magic I 1, Single Target I 1
Damage: 14.6–31.3 death damage (average 23)
Range: 30m
Cost: 5 mana
Cooldown: 2.5 seconds
Description: Shoots a blast of death magic that deals 7–15 death damage (bonus damage for affinity and high intelligence).

Spell Name: Rock Shard
Prerequisites: 80 earth affinity, Earth Magic I 1, Assault Magic I 1
Damage: 13.8–23.7 earth damage (average 19.3)
Range: 20m
Cost: 5 mana
Cooldown: 2.5 seconds
Description: Creates a sharp shard of rock that shoots towards the target, dealing 7–12 earth damage (bonus damage for affinity and high intelligence).

The first three were just the basic attack spells for their respective elements. Of course, they all got a few upgrades based on how much affinity Kas had with that element. The frostbolt was the weakest damage wise, but adding chilling to it made it a useful crowd control spell. Death blast was a very high-affinity version of the basic spell with a better range and damage to mana ratio. It also did considerably more damage than frostbolt but didn't have any secondary effects. Rock shard was the odd man out, with a lower range and damage than death blast. Aside from otherwise empty rotation slots and trying to level earth magic, he didn't see himself casting it often.

Spell Name: Shape Earth
Prerequisites: 80 earth affinity, Earth Magic I 10, Bonding Magic I 5
Cost: 10 mana
Cooldown: 1 minute
Description: Manipulate earth in a targeted area with a radius of 3 meters.

Spell Name: Water Spray
Prerequisites: 80 water affinity, Flowing I 5, Attraction I 5, Area of Effect I 5
Damage: 9.9–29.7 water damage (average 19.8)
Range: 10m
Cost: 10 mana
Cooldown: 30 seconds
Description: Creates a spray of water that targets a spot within the range of the spell and hits a 1m radius around it, dealing 5–15 water damage (bonus damage for affinity and high intelligence), and soaks the area in water.

Spell Name: Decay
Prerequisites: 90 death affinity, Decay I 1, Area of Effect I 1
Damage: 6.22–10.4 death damage (average 8.36)
Range: 20m
Cost: 10 mana
Duration: 5 seconds

Cooldown: 30 seconds
Description: Creates a 1.5m radius area of death magic that deals 3–5
death damage per second to all creatures in the area of affect (bonus damage
for affinity and high intelligence).

Spell Name: Enrich Soil
Prerequisites: 80 earth affinity, Nurturing I 5, Imbue Magic I 5
Range: 20m
Cost: 100 mana
Cooldown: 22 hours
Duration: 30 days
Description: Blesses a 3x3m segment of land to have all the nutrients
needed to support all common types of plants.

The first two were the reasons Kas had picked his build. They would allow him to farm the land without having to get tools like a plow or watering can. Especially since livestock was at a premium out here, and he didn't relish the idea of breaking the soil by hand. The last two were the additions from the skills Livia had suggested and were quite frankly amazing. An AoE spell that only targeted creatures meant, aside from the obvious combat applications, he could use it on any bug infestations affecting his crops. Although he wasn't sure how big of a problem that would actually be out here; while a few of the beta testers had focused on farming, none of them had been in Gogland.

Enrich Soil was a new spell that he hadn't seen any of the beta testers possess, and its inclusion on his spell list was a clear benefit of asking Livia for help during character creation. At 100 mana per cast, it would completely drain his level 1 character of all mana, but if it meant he didn't have to worry about buying and transporting manure, he would happily cast it on cooldown.

Just the fact that this spell existed would likely cause a ton of speculation on the forums, but Kas didn't think it would be wise to reveal his secrets, not yet at least. He wasn't sure how much competition his products were going to have on the global auction house. Of course, from what he could see, there wasn't a lot of cultivated land around Tallrock, so there should be plenty of local purchasers.

Kas glanced out to see how the disembarking was going. There was still a large number of people milling around near the end of the gangplank. He estimated that he still had a few minutes until it was his section's turn to leave, so he turned his attention back to his skill menu. He only had the seven spells for now, but he hoped he could buy a few more when he got into Tallrock.

He had noticed that the supplies Livia had purchased for him had left a few dozen gold in reserve. It wasn't much, but it might be enough for him to hire someone to move heavy objects for a few days and buy some low-level spells. He didn't really want to be alone in the wild until he had at least some sort of shelter.

There were actually more skills than Kas assumed he would get; his magic heavy build was supplemented by Livia's self-reliance recommendations. He had some with fairly obvious uses like skinning, butchering, herb picking, drying, smelting, stitching, tanning, mixing, crushing, and weeding. The other ones were a little less self-explanatory.

Skill: Sowing
Prerequisites: planting I 1
Cost: 5 stamina
Cooldown: 10 seconds
Description: The process of putting seeds into previously prepared soil.

Skill: Plant Sense
Prerequisites: herb location I 1
Cost: None
Cooldown: 5 seconds
Description: Toggle herb locating. While activated, this skill will mark the

location of any gatherable herbs on your minimap. Only two sense skills can be active at a time.

Skill: Crystallize
Prerequisites: crystallizing I 1
Cost: 50 mana
Cooldown: 1 hour
Description: Condense mana into an inferior mana crystal that can be used to power enchantments, engravings, or magitech.

Skill: Layering
Prerequisites: layering I 1
Cost: 100 mana
Cooldown: 22 hours
Description: Using your own elemental affinities, you implant an elemental affinity onto a mana crystal, giving it the properties of the assigned element. Only personal affinities of 80 or higher can be used.

Skill: Meditation
Prerequisites: meditation I 1
Cost: None
Cooldown: 30 minutes
Description: Enter a meditative trance, which increases mana regen considerably. While in a trance, you will be oblivious to the world around you.

He used Crystallize, since it would eat up a good portion of his mana, and he didn't anticipate having to use any soon. Holding out his hand palm out, he focused on the skill. Immediately, a minigame appeared in front of him. It was a simple matter of connecting blinking dots while avoiding others. It took him about five seconds after he figured out what the game was asking him to do.

The minigame accomplished, he watched as a small rainbow-colored crystal appeared in his hand. The crystal had a dim internal luminosity and cast a slight prismatic beam of light across his palm. He willed the system to analyze the item and pulled up its stats.

Item Name: Inferior Mana Crystal (Untyped)
Item Level: 1
Item Quality: Poor
Item Properties: A crafting material provides 25 mana.
Sell Value: 2 silver.
Created by: Kastigan

Well, he could easily create another one every hour with his current mana regeneration. At two silver apiece, he wasn't going to get rich off of them, but it was nice to have a safety net. Especially since he didn't currently have any use for mana crystals. The 50% efficiency on the mana conversion was a little rough, but he assumed that would get better as his skills increased.

Having looked at all his skills and spells, he took a quick glance at the system inventory. It pulled up a list of items that he possessed as well as the location of the item. The backpack he was carrying was clearly magical because, even as heavy as it was, there was no way he would actually be able to carry all the things it contained.

Inside of it were: two fifty-foot lengths of hemp rope, climbing gear, ten torches, five days' worth of trail rations, a sleeping bag, and twelve packages of seeds split evenly between corn, potatoes, and peas. It also had a leatherworking kit, skinning knife, butcher's blade, smelting kit, drying racks, hammers, nails, an alembic, mortar and pestle, and several glass vials.

If his research was correct, the seeds Livia had bought for him meant it was probably early spring in Gogland. Seasons in Livia were strange; as the landmass was an Alderson disk, there was no season mandated by the rotation of a planet around its sun. Instead, the seasons rotated around the disk in a counterclockwise manner. No one had discovered yet how that worked, or even if there was an in-game reason for it.

Seasons lasted just under ninety days, or a little more than one and a half in-game months, each month being fifty days long and divided up into five ten-day segments called Quints. Each in-game year was 350 days long, as there were seven months a year, each one named after one of the seven gods of Pinnoc.

Kas hadn't looked into the religions of Livia much; he knew that there were several different in-game religions and that the deities were capable of giving their followers power. But he didn't really want to get involved in any religious wars.

He did know that he wanted to stay away from the Ardents, though. They were a fanatical sect that had been the cause of Pinnoc's original schism four hundred years ago, when the King of the time tried to make it the state religion. They tended to burn anyone they considered a heretic, and he had a feeling Livia's recommendation of death magic would qualify him.

Pushing the Ardents from his mind as a problem for another day. He realized that it was just about his turn to leave the windrunner. Waiting for the last few people in front of him to finish getting their stuff together and begin walking off the gangplank to the airship docking area, he got his first real look at Tallrock itself.

It was difficult to say from where he was, near the leading side of the mesa, but there appeared to be a straight drop of several hundred feet on all sides. The top portion was remarkably flat, although it did have a slight downward slant on the coreward side, probably only a couple of degrees at most. The green, black, and white Pinnocian flag was visible everywhere; under all the flags was the pennant of the resident legion: A black griffon wearing a harness and carrying a broken spear on a yellow background.

The game identified it as the banner of the 76th legion and gave a bit of flavor text about them.

Two years ago, High King Tasdel sent two full legions—the 76th and the 137th—over the Spines of Aktrosha to the trailing side of Tallrock. The windrunners carrying the legion never returned, and the more than 12,000 soldiers and crew aboard were assumed dead. However, nine months later, less than 900 bedraggled survivors returned on foot through a high mountain pass. The tale these men told began with powerful artillery destroying all 22 of their windrunners in a single volley.

Those soldiers that survived the ensuing crashes were met with a horror story of survival, as they tried to make their way back to Fort Tallrock. The never seen 'Dwellers of the Mountain' harried them for months. They spoke of mists that came swiftly and suddenly, and when they cleared, the men standing next to you had disappeared without a sound. Frostbite, starvation, and fear ate away at their numbers and sanity until they reached the foothills of the Spine. Free, finally, from the Dwellers' wrath, they returned to the fort, broken.

All of the remaining soldiers were then rolled into a single legion and put under the command of Colonel Holzer, the highest surviving officer. Reinforcements have been slow coming from the mainland; rumor has it that the King has written the 76th off as a lost cause. The pall over the men of the 76th who have seen too much, combined with Holzer's growing resentment, has turned the former quickly expanding frontier town into a dreary place.

"Great," Kas said to himself. One of the reasons he picked the coast was the lack of oversight from the legions. The Spines were a problem, but so long as you didn't travel too deeply into them it wouldn't be a problem, although they did seem to tower menacingly over the mesa on the trailing side.

Moving down the scaffolding, Kas paused, considering what to do next. A large number of people seemed to be gathered around a short stage near the edge of the mesa. He began making his way over to get a look at what was causing the commotion, only to realize that several soldiers were actually herding all of the immigrants in that direction. On the stage, seated at a desk, was a tall blond-haired man wearing a military uniform, colonel's stripes, and the badge of the 76th on his sleeve; Colonel Holzer in the flesh.

Across from the colonel was a man Kas recognized as being one of the first off the ship. To his surprise, it was actually a player, the username appearing over his head as he got closer. The man was bound hand and foot with shackles, and a cloth gag was tied around his mouth, preventing him from speaking. The player was looking about nervously and seemed like he would have run, but his hand irons were held above him and tied to a taut rope that was rigged to a crane.

Holzer appeared to be reading some sort of documentation but would look up every now and again as if to ascertain how many people had gathered around him. After a few minutes, it seemed to have reached an agreeable size and he stood up and turned to the crowd.

"Greetings, and welcome to Fort Tallrock. I am Colonel Holzer, the commanding officer of the 76th Legion, and as such, it is my responsibility to ensure that law and order are maintained throughout this region." Holzer paused for a moment, glancing around. "You have traveled for half a year to get here, the journey is trying, and I understand many of you are eager to begin your new lives. However, as there are a significant number of you that have been sent here in lieu of other punishments in Pinnoc, it seems I must give you an object lesson in frontier justice. For you, this is a new start, a chance at a new life, free of all the entanglements of your former lives. So long as you stay on the right side of the law, it will remain a land of opportunity."

Holzer paused again, looking around at the crowd. "This man, however, thought that he was above the laws of my fort. As soon as he stepped off the windrunner, he returned to his thieving ways. He even had the gall to steal in plain sight of several legionaries." Holzer turned back to the player, whose name was Jared420. "For his crimes, he will soon be taught a lesson. I hope you all will learn from his experience. Here on the frontier we have no prison, no place we can store those who do not abide by the law. It is a harsh and unforgiving place, and our justice is harsh and unforgiving." Holzer signaled to a soldier standing near the crane's controls, and it began to extend. Lifting the now struggling Jared420 off the stage.

It then swung out and over, Kas realizing that it was going to extend over the 100-meter drop to the forest floor below. Jared420 tried to scream but no sound escaped the gag, terror clear in his eyes as he vainly kicked with his legs, his hands grasping the rope in an attempt to climb it back to safety. The crane settled into position with a jolt, sending Jared420 wriggling as he lost his grip on the rope with one hand, his own weight pulling him down, one shoulder visibly dislocating from the sudden pressure on it.

Holzer spoke again, and Kas tore his eyes off of Jared420 to look at the colonel. "Fire as you will."

Turning back, Kas realized that six archers were standing off to one side of the crowd, a number of other legionaries standing near them. There was a fierce exchange of coin between the soldiers. With a sense of horror, Kas realized that they were betting on this man's demise. Then the archers began shooting in order, all the arrows passing harmlessly through the air above Jared420.

Jeers came from the soldiers behind the archers. The objective became clear as more shots were fired; they weren't trying to hit Jared420. The player continued to struggle to climb the rope despite his dislocated shoulder.

One of the immigrants shouted at him, "Stop squirming, you're just making it last longer!"

Kas realized that the archers were trying to shoot the rope holding the condemned man up. And he turned away from the scene, unable to stomach the cruelty any longer, his eyes raking across the stage and stopping on Holzer.

Kas stopped because Holzer was staring at him. His cold blue eyes watching Kas like he was some sort of bug under a magnifying glass. Ducking back into the crowd, he moved to position a drak between Holzer and himself, the drak's large blue form effectively blocking the colonel from his sight.

He shuddered; there had been something in those eyes,

something malign and hungry that was somehow even more terrifying than the execution of the other player. With another soft shudder, Kas navigated through his HUD until he found the logout button, but it was grayed out. The generic excuse the game gave him was that he wasn't in a safe space.

The sound of loud jeering and laughter came from the soldiers and drew Kas' attention back to Jared420. It appeared one of the archers had either missed or gotten frustrated by not hitting the rope and had put an arrow in his previously unin-jured shoulder. With both shoulders injured, the player had stopped squirming, the rise and fall of his chest the only sign that he was still alive.

Kas was the only other player in the crowd that he could see, and he suddenly felt very alone. He felt something heavy land on his shoulder and he looked up. The drak he had been hiding behind had put its hand on his shoulder and was leaning down so that it could speak without roaring. Tears formed in the corners of Kas' eyes, and he looked down, surreptitiously trying to wipe them away.

"It is okay, little one. This thing will make you stronger. My people, they are always treated thus. It lightens my heart to see a human cry for one of us. What is your name?"

"Ma… Kas, Kastigan," he answered, stopping himself from saying his real-life name rather than his in-game one. It was only at this point that he realized that Jared420 was a dragon tribesman, his tusks having been hidden by the gag.

"Well met, Maa'Kas Kastigan. I am called Shura Blueb-lessed," the tall drak said with a slight bow of its head.

"It's… just Kastigan or Kas, not Maa'Kas," Kastigan said automatically.

The drak nodded its head as another cheer went up from the soldiers and some of the immigrants. The rope had finally been severed, leaving Jared420's body to fall to his death below. Death for an unbound wasn't permanent, although he imagined the player would probably recreate after this experience.

Kastigan couldn't imagine respawning in a place where you had already been executed.

With the entertainment over, the soldiers allowed the crowd to disperse; Kastigan assumed that they figured the lesson had been learned. He turned to the drak next to him and smiled. "Thanks for distracting me, Shura."

"It is a pleasure. Come, sit with me, we shall talk." The blue drak led him away from the majority of the buildings to a small green space that had been grown as a park. There were no benches, but Shura's massive form probably wouldn't have fit on them anyway. The tall drak sat down on the grass and then gestured for him to do likewise.

Sitting down as requested, he glanced over at Shura, who seemed oblivious to his presence, staring up at the sky. He took a moment to look the massive drak over as a means of regathering his wits. All drak were big, usually standing about three meters tall, but Shura would tower over even most of its kind. Kas' best guess was that Shura had to be at least four meters from toe-claws to frill. Small dark blue scales covered its back and head, but the neck and inner chest were a lighter sky blue.

After several heartbeats, Shura spoke again. "You are not like most of us on the windrunner. We who were offered no choice but death in a slave pit or forced immigration. You are also unbound. Which means you are special. I wonder, what path do the gods place your feet upon to bring you here to this forsaken country?"

"Uh, I'm not sure about the gods, but I am unbound. I came here to farm," he responded warily, wondering why the large drak would show such an interest in him. From his readings, he knew that the species was relatively rare, they were created during the War of Dragons, special dragon tribesmen were elevated to positions of power over their brethren and blessed by the dragons themselves to take a portion of their form. Since then, their lines had bred true although he had no idea how they reproduced, as there was no way of distinguishing the gender of the unclothed Shura or any of the drak he had seen in the artwork.

His response seemed to amuse the drak, and it laughed. "Truly? Well, mayhap the gods have put us on a path together. Tell me, Kastigan, would you be agreeable to forming a business contract?"

CHAPTER THREE

Arrival 3

Kastigan stared at Shura, confused. He tried to figure out what it was the drak wanted from him. He knew it wasn't his belongings; he had nothing to his name except for the pack on his back and the few gold coins left in his pouch. He was a newly created character, what could he possibly offer the drak?

His confusion must have been evident, and the drak chortled softly. "It is good you are confused. I sense that you do not realize the extent of the treatment that the tribesmen in general, and the drak in particular, received in the Unified Realm. To explain this, I must tell you why I am here. I am a first-generation drakborn of Dragoria."

Drakborn meant that Shura had been born of drak parents and was not elevated to that status based on merit during the dragon war. Dragoria was the land of the dragon tribesmen; High King Tasdel had invaded it thirty years ago during what became known as the War of the Dragons. The tribesmen at the time had been a loose group of mostly localized nomads in a volatile confederation. Tasdel had assumed it would be an easy victory, but the tribesmen had called upon their gods, and their gods had answered.

What followed was a brutal war that only ended when Tasdel's spies stole magitech weapons from Tua'tat and, in conjunction with the Quinthan Windrunners fleet, managed to kill a number of the dragons who guarded Dragoria. In the end, the dragons had retreated rather than suffer further losses to their kind. The remaining tribesmen had no choice but to surrender to Tasdel.

A few of the beta testers had played in Dragoria; it was still a very primal land, the tribesmen having cities that harmonized with nature rather than seeking to tame it.

If it hadn't been for the fact that Tasdel hated non-humans and had imposed harsh taxes on Dragoria, ostensibly as reparations for the war, Kas probably would have started there. The idea of finding some hidden valley where dragons still lived had appealed to him, but the need to make a profit on the game had driven him to Gogland.

"My people are not wealthy. The King's portion leaves few of the tribesmen in a state of plenty, but we have enough to live. For the drak it is worse. My kind were once the leaders of our people, but we were forbidden to follow any path of honor. We are allowed only to fight, and to do the meanest of physical labor." The frill around Shura's head deflated a little, the two curling horns becoming more exposed, like a shipwreck at low tide. "I chose to fight. I entered the ranks of a gladiator arena and fought for the amusement of humans."

Its head tilted down, Kastigan assumed this indicated shame in the drak. However, it was difficult to understand Shura's body language, as it used body parts that humans simply didn't possess. "One day, a weak human man-child desired to fight me to prove he was not a man-child. His father came to me and offered much gold for me to allow his pup to win." Shura turned away. "I was hungry, and this gold would feed my entire village for a year. I sold my honor. After the fight, the pup had me imprisoned and sent here, where his glory would be unspoiled." Shura looked up again, meeting Kastigan's eyes.

"This is my shame. Sis'essikthator." Shura's last words were in Dragorian, but the emotion with which they were spoken made their meaning clearer. Something between asking for forgiveness and accepting judgment for their actions.

Kastigan thought about Shura for a moment. If the story was true, it had selflessly given up its position among its people so that those same people could eat, and he thought there was honor in that, even if Shura no longer thought it possessed any. "I don't see that as shame. You made a hard decision that ultimately benefited your people at great personal cost."

Shura's frill expanded out as it considered Kas and then bowed its head. "It is good that the gods have put us on this path together, Kastigan." Reaching into a pouch attached to the harness the drak was wearing, it pulled out a token and held it out to him. "I was given a token of settlement, but I have listened to the wind, and it tells me that Colonel Holzer will not allow me to redeem this. My business proposal is thus: I intend to be a beast tamer; we shall work the land together. I will try to get something that can be used as a beast of burden for you. We will defend the land together and share the profits equally."

Kastigan considered the land token the drak held out. He reached into a pouch of his own and pulled out both of his tokens. As he did, Shura made a hissing noise, and he looked up, alarmed.

"You have two tokens already?" the drak asked, its tongue flickering in and out. Kastigan immediately was reminded of how much of a killing machine the thing sitting down next to him was. Even seated, Shura was several feet taller than him; they sat a reasonable distance apart just so he didn't have to crane his neck to look up at the drak. He unconsciously leaned backward, a part of him realizing that this was just a fear reaction to an obvious predator looking at him like he was prey.

The reaction was enough to snap Shura out of whatever state of mind it had been in, and it too leaned back. "My most sincere apologies, Kastigan, but having three tokens means that you can accomplish many things. I know you are unbound, so killing you would do me little good. But let me also offer you my vow." Shura paused for a moment as it dug into one of the scales on its arm with a claw until it managed to pry it up just a little. It then dug the claw into the arm, causing a viscous golden liquid to drip from the arm.

"I, Shura Blueblessed, former daughter of Kaktroa, blessed of Assithikeila and Formia, blessed of Sinsensiurtha, do vow never to act against the wishes of Kastigan, to be his scales and talons until the day he breaks faith, or we both join the flight of the dead. This I swear on the blood of the ancestors." Finishing her oath, Shura breathed onto the golden blood on her arm. A small flicker of flame came out and immediately crystallized the blood.

Kastigan blinked, confused by the chain of events. Shura gently picked up the golden crystal and held it and the token out for him to take. Taking them from her hand gingerly, the crystal, now an oblong shape and warm to the touch, was heavier than he would have guessed, while the token had the same heft as the other two in his possession. Looking at the crystal, he could see that the inside was still liquid, small trapped bubbles shifting position within as it changed orientation.

Item Name: Shura's Blood Vow
Item Quality: Unique
Description: The blood of the drak is mixed with the blood of dragons. Any oath said by a drak over its own blood and hardened by its breath will create a crystallized token of that oath that can only be destroyed by breaking the oath.
Created by: Shura Blueblessed, blessed of Assithikeila and Sinsensiurtha

"Uh... thank you?" Kastigan said, not sure of the proper way to accept a blood oath crystal.

Shura nodded her head. She was apparently female, or had been female at some point? Was the former part of her vow because she was disowned? He'd have to look up drak gender information on the wiki at some point.

Kastigan took a moment to consider the risks here. Worst

case scenario: Shura kills him before he can claim the land and steals the tokens. How did the tokens work anyway? Did he use the item near the property? Or did he have to hand them into some sort of official when he knew what land he wanted? He pulled up the information on the tokens.

Item Name: Gogland Land Claim Token
Item Quality: Rare
Description: Can be used in lieu of money at any property assayer to claim land. Each token is worth 5000 gold worth of land.
Cannot be sold.

Alright, so he didn't need to take the tokens with him out into the wilderness, which meant that the worst-case scenario wasn't possible. If he was careful, Shura couldn't double-cross him until after they had purchased the land. The land would then be in his name, so if she killed him later, he would just have to respawn and then have her evicted. If it came to a dispute before the authorities, the reasons she was coming to him instead of just claiming the land herself would work in his favor.

Rolling the situation around in his head for a few minutes, Kas couldn't think of any way for this to go south. Maybe if he had to pay taxes on all three properties? He'd have to ask the assayer if there were any upkeep costs. There hadn't been any in the beta, but they also didn't have background starting pack-ages in the beta either. That could easily have been a feature added to the real game that didn't need to be tested by the public.

"I think I can agree to your proposal. I was going to hire someone to help me move stuff around anyway. I don't know much about beast tamers though, what do we need to get you started with that? Do we need to buy horses?" Kastigan couldn't imagine Shura on a horse; she probably weighed twice as much as one.

Shura's frill rippled in what he assumed was a drak equivalent of a laugh. "No, we will need to find some suitable local creatures. But I think we will need to begin with some smaller creatures, as I have not had much time to practice my skills and will need to level them up before we can hope to tame the most impressive ones. The small ones will hopefully be able to act as either an alarm or as a skirmishing force, but it will all depend on what is available in the surrounding area."

Kastigan's head bobbed up and down as he considered this new information. "Alright, I was going to see if I could purchase some spell scrolls and maybe some skill tomes. I was also hoping to find a map of the region to narrow down the options of where to build. Maybe get some advice from people who have actually been out there."

"Good. There are some things I would like to do as well. Shall we meet back here at midday, or will your tasks take longer than that?"

The shape of Livia meant that there was no sun hanging overhead. Instead, it was suspended in the sky, high to the coreward side. The beta testers had said that it merely bounced up and down, but that made it difficult to determine what time it was, so he switched to his HUD again and brought up the time and had it displayed under his mini-map. It was currently a few hours past dawn. He guessed that made sense. If the days were as long as those on Earth, they would have to change the day and night cycle in the game, or else most people would be playing in perpetual twilight. That would give him about three hours to run his errands. "Okay, that sounds good. We'll meet back here at noon."

Shura bowed her head, her frill fluttering, and they both stood up and headed back into the main section of the town. Kastigan got his first real look at the village that grew up around Fort Tallrock. There were several roughly constructed buildings, mostly stretches of longhouse style barracks and some shops selling weapons, armor, and ingredients for both. Several signs offered to buy various materials gathered from the creatures and land around Tallrock.

Before he went too much further, Kas pulled the mana crystal he had made earlier out of his inventory and used Layering on it since his mana had completely recovered. The crystal began floating above his palm, and he quickly selected earth from the menu that popped up and then completed the simple mini-game to connect the dots. Hoping in passing that the game either went away or got more interesting as his skill leveled up. When it was done, the crystal flared for a moment and then shifted from its current rainbow appearance to a light brown.

Item Name: Inferior Mana Crystal (Earth)
Item Level: 1
Item Quality: Poor
Item Properties: A crafting material provides 25 earth mana.
Sell Value: 1 gold
Created by: Kastigan

Well, that was an improvement! The twenty-two-hour cooldown meant it was going to take a long time to level up, but the crystal was worth five times as much as before. That made sense if it was something you could only do once a day; as he leveled up his condensing that was bound to be worth a good bit of money. He returned the crystal to his inventory.

The commercial district of Tallrock was pretty sparse. A dozen bars, and about the same number of other shops was the full extent of the place. Three of them were blacksmiths, there was a fletcher, two general stores, a carpenter, tailor, alchemist, and a leatherworker.

Stepping into the shop that Kas thought was a leather-working shop, he looked around. The smell of cured leather greeted him as soon he opened the door. Leather armor, sheaths, and saddles surrounded him while the back half of the shop was open to the outside to allow light in.

An older gentleman with a mustache was working on a leather breastplate while a woman that looked like she was probably his wife was tracing a pattern on a thick piece of leather. The woman looked up as he entered and smiled. "Hello, dearie. Look around if you'd like, and I'll be right with you." And then she returned to her work. The man didn't look up but did grunt softly.

With a shrug, Kas began looking over the piles of equipment. He quickly realized that everything was going to be well outside of his price range; he had twenty-two gold pieces and some smaller coins leftover from whatever Livia had spent on his equipment and packs. Most of the newbie equipment was in the five-gold range; the more advanced stuff could cost up to 200 gold apiece. A full set of the lowest quality would clear him out and leave nothing to buy new spells or skill books.

"So, what are you looking for, sir?" The woman came up behind him and surprised Kas, causing him to jump and drop the bracers he was looking at. They both bent to pick them up and Kas barely managed to avoid bumping heads with her, his cheeks reddening in embarrassment. "Oh, it's okay, dearie, sorry for startling you."

"It's okay, sorry for dropping it."

"No harm, it's made to take a bit more of a beating than a three-foot drop onto a flat floor," she said with a soft laugh, obviously trying to put him at ease. The AI was doing a pretty good job, obviously a skilled saleswoman.

"I'm afraid I'm looking for designs rather than finished goods. Do you have any for sale?"

"Of course, they're over here. I'm Agnes, but please call me Aggie." She led him over to a shelf that contained several books.

"Ahh, I'm Kastigan, Kas for short," he said, looking over the books.

"What sort of skill level do you have? We'd be happy to consign anything you do make as long as it meets Jack's standards of at least average quality," she said, gesturing to the man in the back.

"Uh, five, with subskills in stitching and punching at two," Kas said.

Aggie clicked slightly and pulled four books out, and handed them to Kas. "That's a skill book for burnishing and cutting, as well as some basic bracers and lacing patterns. Skill books are a gold each and the patterns are five silver for the pair. I'm afraid we don't have much more you'd be able to use just yet. But if you want to save a trip, I can get you a few more patterns for when you level up a bit."

Kas looked at the four books and then did some mental math. Leather was only one of his trade skills; he'd probably need to get a similar amount for the other two and maybe some for processing. Which meant he'd be spending seven and a half of his twenty-two gold, leaving him fifteen gold and a few silvers. With Shura tagging along, he didn't need to hire someone to come lift heavy things for him, but he should probably figure out how expensive spells were before he spent that much of his money.

"Okay, I need to go find out how expensive spells are to purchase first, but I'll probably come back for these later," Kas said, setting the books back down on the table in front of him.

Aggie quirked an eyebrow. "Well, I can help with that some. What type of magic were you looking to buy?"

"Well, some earth and water utility spells and sub-skills. Then some fire and healing spells and books. Oh, and a mana circulation book. Maybe some imbue spells, if those aren't too expensive." Kas listed off what he needed while ticking his fingers.

Aggie laughed. "Oh, just a few spells then." She paused, considering Kas for a minute. "Well, the legion is the best place for fire and healing. They have a standard of two gold for a sub-skill and ten for major skill books; something tells me that puts healing and fire out of your price range. The Church of the Seven would be the best place for mana circulation. But Jack can teach you some imbuing magic. If you buy all of the stuff you've got out already, I'll only add another half gold for the four basic enchants."

Pulling the mana crystal out of his inventory Kas held it out to Aggie to look at. "Would you be interested in exchanging this for some of that cost?"

Aggie took the crystal out of his hand and turned it around in her hands for a moment, considering it. "Jack's the imbuer. So I can't say for sure, but I imagine we could use these to make some of our enchantments a bit more potent." She pursed her lips and then walked over to Jack, who hadn't looked up from his work since Kastigan had walked into the shop. Aggie placed the crystal down in front of him, and the old man stopped, looking up at Aggie then back down at the crystal.

Picking it up and turning it in his hands, he smiled and then turned to look at Kastigan. "You Kastigan?" When his question was answered with a nod, he stood up and walked over to him. "I'm Jack, pleased to meet you. Can you layer anything but earth?"

Slightly taken aback by the forthright nature of Jack's greeting, Kastigan nodded his head. "Uh, yes sir, water and death."

He could almost see the cogs in Jack's head turning as he processed this, eyeing him up and down. "I'll give you any set of armor and all the books and designs you want under level 15 if you provide me with seven of each type."

Kastigan did the math quickly in his head, a full set of armor came out to at least 40 gold. The designs and books bumped that up to at least 60 gold. Twenty-one crystals would take him three weeks and a good bit of mana, but according to the prompt, they were only worth 21 gold. There was no way the guy was going to be taking that much of a hit unless he planned to make even more money.

"What are you going to do with them?"

"All imbues past the third tier require a mana crystal. If you use an elemental aligned crystal with an enchantment of that same type, it doubles the potency of the enchantment. The stones aren't hard to get, but to layer, a stone requires a high affinity with the element and can only be done once a day. Which makes them hard to find since few crystallizers have the right affinities high enough."

Kastigan nodded his head slowly; that made sense. And since it required a high level of imbuing skill, it wasn't like he was going to be able to use the mana crystals for a while. "Okay, it's a deal."

Quest Offered, "Layered Mana Stones for Jack."
Deliver the following items to Jack within 30 days:

- *7 Inferior Mana Crystal (Earth)*
- *7 Inferior Mana Crystal (Water)*
- *7 Inferior Mana Crystal (Death)*

Quest Acceptance: One complete set of Jack's leather armor, all skill books, and designs under level 15 sold by Jack's shop that you want.
Quest Reward: 1000 experience. 100 reputation with Jack and Aggie. 50 reputation with Tallrock Citizenry.
Quest Failure: Wanted status in Tallrock. -100 reputation with Jack and Aggie. -200 reputation with Tallrock Citizenry. -50 reputation with 76th Legion.

Accept "Layered Mana Stones for Jack"?

The penalty for failure was pretty high, and the addition of a timeframe made him a little nervous. If the stones were stolen from him before he could deliver them, he would be in for a world of hurt. But the rewards were just a little too good to pass up. He glanced back at the armor; he could get a decent set now, but in a month he would have leveled up a few times and be able to wear some much better armor at that point. "Tell you what, I'll give you that stone for the books today. When I deliver the rest of the mana stones, you can give me the rest of the stuff then."

Jack looked at him for a moment and then twirled his mustache. "You drive a hard bargain. I accept."

Quest Accepted "Layered Mana Stones for Jack."
Deliver the following items to jack within 30 days:

- *6 Inferior Mana Crystal (Earth)*
- *7 Inferior Mana Crystal (Water)*
- *7 Inferior Mana Crystal (Death)*

Quest Reward: 750 experience. 100 reputation with Jack and Aggie. 50 reputation with Tallrock Citizenry. One complete set of Jack's leather armor, all skill books, and designs under level 15 sold by Jack's shop that you want.
Quest Failure: -100 reputation with Jack and Aggie. -50 reputation with Tallrock Citizenry.

Kastigan smiled as they both shook hands. The new rewards weren't as good, only three fourths as much experience, but the penalty for failure was also significantly lighter. "Aggie said you could teach me some enchants?"

Jack had already pocketed the crystal, but he nodded his head. "Sure can. It'll take me an hour to make the scrolls, come back then." He abruptly turned and walked away from Aggie and Kastigan.

When he glanced over at Aggie, she just rolled her eyes and gave a slight shrug. "Alright, well, here are your purchases," she said, holding out the books and designs to Kastigan, who accepted them and slipped them into his inventory.

"He always like this?"

"That was actually pretty friendly for him," she said with a wry grin. "Normally, he avoids talking to customers, but he likes you."

"He likes how much money he can make off me, you mean," Kastigan replied with a sardonic chuckle.

"Well, that too. They're both connected in Jack's head,"

Aggie said and she patted Kastigan on the shoulder in a grand-motherly way. "Well, go, do the rest of your shopping. The enchant scrolls will be ready when you come back."

Stopping by an alchemist shop was much the same experience as he had at Jack and Aggie's. The owner, a severe-looking quinthan man named Savas, sold him skill books for steeping, brewing, and cutting, as well as formulas for minor healing, mana, and stamina potions. He was beginning to understand why all the beta testers had hated the quinthans, though, as he had dickered with Kastigan for nearly ten minutes, and he ended up paying five gold, six silver, and eight copper for the books.

The monetary system in the game was pretty simple; everything was a tenth of the next highest denomination. So, ten copper was a silver, ten silver was a gold, ten gold was an electrum. There were other denominations above electrum, but they were mostly only used in large transactions, and gold was considered the base amount that all prices were listed at.

After that, he asked around for where he could find construction skills and was sent to a cianese carpenter named Gurden, who sold him skill books for planing, digging, and support. The first was to make wood flat and was actually a sub-skill of processing, while the other two he was assured were needed to make a proper foundation. He had also picked up a design for a simple, one-room log cabin. All of his purchases from Gurden cost him four gold, leaving him with just under thirteen gold left to buy his spells from the legion and the church.

Asking around, he had discovered that the assayer in town was actually one of the lieutenants in the legion. Her name was Karissa, and she and the other lieutenant were rumored to be the only reason the entire legion hadn't gone AWOL. He hoped she wouldn't need to be bribed to give him a decent idea of where to go to get some good land.

Since the Church of the Seven was near the entrance to the Fort, it was his last stop before seeing how Holzer's men would treat him. It was a more beautiful building than anything else he had seen in town. Two stories tall, with a single bell tower near the front that towered another two stories above the rest of the church, it was made of a single piece of stone that had to have been magically shaped. Colored glass windows appeared every few feet and depicted what he assumed were the seven gods of Pinnoc in various acts.

Stepping through the door of the church, his eyes took a moment to adjust to the difference in light. The windows let in enough light to see, but they changed the color of it enough to darken the entire room. From the inside, they appeared even more beautiful than they had from the outside. Starting on the left side, they changed in general tone from reds and greens to blues and purples on the right side of the door, except for the center panel, which was mostly a cloudy white.

The first set of panels in reds and greens depicted two twin brothers, one planting fields and raising animals while the other was shown harvesting and slaughtering the same. The UI helpfully identified them as Caled and Delac. The next section consisted of greens and yellows and depicted a woman in various states of teaching others, named Talin.

The center section was the cloudy white one and depicted a man standing over a dead dragon who was curled up on itself, named Primus. Underneath him was the altar with black stones set in a mosaic that also showed a picture, but Kastigan couldn't determine what it portrayed from this angle. The next section was in greens and blues and showed a tall man in armor, who stood in various states of judgment, named Arthen. Kas wondered if the worship of Arthen had somehow mutated into the worship of Arden Duden; they seemed like they might have the same root based on what he knew of the Ardents.

The last panel was Yesha, and he was in various states of creating things. He was most often shown in front of a forge, but Kas could see one of him at a loom and another at a pottery wheel. It seemed Yesha was responsible for all the things created. His colors were blue and purple.

"Beautiful, aren't they?" A voice sounded from close behind Kas' shoulder, and he jumped, muttering a curse before slamming his elbow against the door with a loud bang. Turning to look at the source of his surprise, he found the oldest man he had seen in the game yet. Gray hair and wrinkles made him one of the oldest people Kastigan had seen in his entire life. Regeneration treatments made old age a disease of the past.

"I apologize for startling you, child. I did not realize how deeply you were studying the panels." The old man looked Kastigan over, taking in his pack and tools and his general attire. "Tell me, do you favor the twins or the smith?" He gestured to either side of him and raised an old, caterpillar-like eyebrow.

"Uh, all three. I think," Kastigan said, trying not to stare at the old man in front of him. He wore a set of multicolored robes, which were hemmed in greens and blues. Did that mean he was primarily a worshiper of Arthen?

The old man laughed and nodded his head. "Come, sit. My old bones aren't quite up to standing for too long. And I sense this conversation may take some time." He gestured to several of the pews that lined the room, and he took a seat in a spot that would give an excellent view of the glass. Patting the spot next to him, he looked at Kastigan expectantly.

CHAPTER FOUR

Arrival 4

Kas hesitated for a few seconds, looking between the old man and the door. Deciding it wouldn't hurt and might get him what he came for, he sat down next to the old man. He glanced up again at the glass and wondered how it was made; it wasn't stained glass. There wasn't any leading in between the panes, it was almost like they had thinned the stone until it was translucent and colored the stone itself in various sections to portray the images. "How did you make this?"

"Ahh, we did not make it, this is merely a recreation granted by the Seven to their priests. The original was created eons ago during the Age of Blood, and we have simply used it as a pattern to recreate churches on the frontier. The whole thing only took a week to grow once the seed was planted," the old man explained.

Kas could see from the corner of his eye that the old man was staring at him rather than the glass. He didn't really appreciate the stares, but he couldn't think of anything to say so he stared back at the glass. He found his eyes returning to the twins on the left, watching as they gave life and killed.

"Caled and Delac, the sower and the reaper, we worship

them together, for they are inseparable. Caled represents life, the creation and growth of all things, while Delac is death, the end of all things. But together they are the cycle, life growing from death, death reaping life to make room for the cycle to begin anew. It is an understanding of the pattern of life, celebration and mourning but always with a purpose to ensure the cycle is made new again."

Kas had never really heard of a religion that thought of death as 'good.' He remembered some that said you went to a better place, but he didn't believe that, not anymore. "Death isn't a good thing," he finally said, turning to look at the old man.

A slight creasing of his brows was his only reaction. "No, perhaps not. It is, however, a necessary thing. Plants grow, and then die, giving nutrients to other plants and animals. Animals grow and die, and feed other plants and animals. Old kings die, and leave space for new kings. It is the cycle of life; without death, we are not alive."

He let his words sink in, waiting to see if Kas had a response before he turned to look at the glass again. "But I get the feeling you are not here to declare your devotion to one of the Seven." He turned back to look at Kastigan again. "So, how can I help you?"

Kas didn't answer for a moment, his thoughts still lost in death and loss. He stood up and walked around the room; he hadn't been expecting to think about it. This was his escape, so he wouldn't be reminded, just a game. Just a game, it didn't matter. He touched the side of his eye and cleared away the slight moisture there before turning back towards the old man. "I'm sorry, I was looking for some training in mana manipulation. I was told the church sold some skill books for that."

The old man had a sad frown creasing the well-entrenched lines on his forehead further, but when Kastigan switched to business it slipped away, hidden by the public mask he needed to wear. "Of course. We have a number of books for sale." He stood up with a creak of old bones and walked over to an alcove near the side under Yesha the smith. He gestured for Kastigan to come over to look.

There was a small bookshelf there and Kas easily located the book he wanted. "Just mana circulation I for now," he said, picking the book up and showing it to the old man.

The priest pursed his lips. "Perhaps. What are your affinities?"

"I have a minor affinity with mana manipulation, and have meditation and mana projection as subskills."

"Hm, well enjoy your book," the priest said as he turned away from Kas and began to retreat further into the church.

"Wait, how much do I owe you?" Kas asked, reaching into the pouch that contained his money.

"Owe? You owe me nothing; you paid with your devotions to the twins. But I suppose I would also like to know your name."

Kastigan blinked. He hadn't paid devotions to the twins, all he had done was talk to this old man about his belief in the cycle. "Are you sure?" he asked, holding up a gold coin.

The priest just smiled and nodded his head. "Yes, I am sure."

"It's Kastigan."

"A pleasure to meet you, Kastigan. Please come back again when you are able. I am Toris." With that, the old priest turned back and continued to walk further into the church, softly humming a tune that Kas could swear he knew but couldn't place.

With a shrug, Kastigan pocketed the book and coins back into his inventory. Then turned and walked to the door. Before opening it, he paused, looking up at Caled and Delac again. He could feel a distant pang in his chest; the sower and the reaper, the old man had called them. He pushed the door open and the quiet semi darkness of the church was quickly replaced with the bustle of the fort and city the church stood between.

It took him a moment to adjust his frame of mind back to his task at hand. The church had been… soothing? Broody, maybe. It was better than the churches he had spent time in after... He paused, his brain refusing to follow that path and he shook his torso as if trying to dislodge something heavy.

Turning to the left was the fort of Tallrock itself, a roughshod thing of wooden timber palisades and log cabins that contrasted in unflattering ways with the masterpiece of construction he had just left.

There was a gate out of the fort facing the inside of the mesa. The fort itself was built on the tallest part of the mesa, allowing him to see some of the interior. Four large barracks-like structures flanked a parade ground. At either end stood the only other stone buildings that Kas had seen on the plateau. One had a castle-like appearance with the flags of the Unified Realm and the 76th Legion prominently displayed on it, while the other was a single-story structure, and looked to be more business than military. The single flying pennant was tan on brown and featured a chest. The bank and auction house, and his last stop before returning to read his books and learn his new spells.

He made his way to the gate, where there was already a line queued up to get in. He was slightly relieved to see that there were a couple other players here; he had started to think the one who had been hung was the only one on the ship. He had been in the third and largest wave of players to spawn.

The first wave of players was made up of the premium subscriptions. Each premium sub came with a full extended stay pod, a larger starting gold amount and a full 24 hours of play before the second wave was allowed to enter. The second wave was for the plus accounts which came with a dive pod that was only built for single session dives, and they too got a 24-hour period before the next wave. The third wave was for the standard subs, playing with just the neural interface and costing about a hundredth what the premium subs went for.

There had only been a million premium accounts and ten million plus accounts. To buy one of those advantaged accounts, you had to enter a bidding war. The first couple premium accounts only went for a year's salary at Kas' job. The later ones had been sold, and resold, for decades worth of money. The plus accounts had been easier to get, the most expensive only costing as much as a nice luxury car. The benefit of the accounts being the only way to access the new pods from the company. The standard sub had only cost him $500, just under a weeks' worth of salary, plus the $100 monthly cost.

Kas needed to be able to make at least $2100 a month from the game in order to play it full time. He had been watching the auction house during the 48 hours before the third wave and there were already a few items that were being sold that would easily have paid for a few months of his game time. Epic weapons, armor, and bags for the most part, although a few mounts had also been big sellers. You could, of course, buy armor and weapons from the Livia store, but the drops had unique appearances and slightly better stats.

The other players around Kas looked to be from the third wave as well, all dressed in similar starting equipment as what he was wearing. All of them seemed to be focused on combat though, from the tribesman in chain armor and a shield, to the quinthan pair with fire and lightning dancing across their hands. Kas looked out of place with his big pack stuffed with tools. He took a spot at the back of the line and waited for the soldiers to allow the other unbound through.

While he waited, he listened in to their conversations; the two quinthans had decided they were going to try to find a group called the Crows that had apparently set up a town to the southeast. Kas made sure to mark it on his map as another potential location to sell goods at, although from the sounds of it, they were interested in it because it was a lot more lawless than Tallrock. He made a mental note to find out more information on these Crows soon. The line moved along quickly, the guards only pausing long enough to ensure that the unbound didn't have a bounty on their heads before letting them in.

When it was Kastigan's turn to enter, the guard gave him a

once over and asked the same question the others had been presented, "Name and business?"

"Kastigan, visiting the bank, the assayer, and purchasing scrolls."

The guard paused his search through the papers in front of him. "The assayer? What business do you have with her?"

"Looking to purchase some land."

The guard grunted and put his papers down. "Lt. Karissa is on the first floor of the keep, follow the signs for the scout division. Spells you can pick up from any of the magus cadre on the second floor. Bank is that flat building to the trailing side." With a wave, he turned to the next unbound in line and Kastigan was in the fort.

There were a number of legionaries moving around the compound but Kas made for the keep, trying to stay out of the way of any the drilling soldiers and the various unbound that were either training with them or dickering over skill books. The chainmail-covered tribesman that had been at the front of the line was already swinging a sword at a training dummy. Presumably learning how to actually use a sword in the game, Kas wished him luck. The sun was already beginning to turn the mesa towards the warmer side, and inside the fort the wind wasn't there to cool it down.

Having spent the last hour and a half wandering through Tallrock, the contrast between the fort and town was pretty obvious. Where the town looked to have been built of whatever random materials were at hand, the fort used much more homogeneous materials. And everything was still kept in perfect condition. Kas could see the effort put into maintaining it as he watched several soldiers raking the training sands, trimming hedges, or whitewashing walls.

The entrance to the fort was similar, two bored looking guards watched him approach but didn't do anything to stop him. He stepped through the door into the darker interior. The keep had narrow windows, but a number of mage lights illuminated the inside just shy of well enough to be comfortable. He followed the signs to the scout's division, passing two more legionaries on his way.

The office of the 76th legion's scouts was covered in maps and much better lit than the hallways of the keep. A human and a quinthan were busy copying maps, one adding detail to a large map showing the region around Tallrock while the other was copying a smaller, more portable map. A door in the back led to a desk where a woman was pouring over a ledger, a quill in hand as she scratched some notes on a piece of parchment.

Assuming the woman was Lieutenant Karissa, Kas made his way past the two scribes and knocked on the door frame of her office. "Pardon me, ma'am, are you Lieutenant Karissa?"

The woman looked up, blinking at Kastigan. "Yes, how can I help you?"

"Well, my name is Kastigan, I'm looking to redeem a couple land claim tokens, and was hoping you might know some good land near the fort where I could set up a farm." He stepped inside the office and the woman pursed her lips, leaning back in her chair as she considered him.

"You don't look like much, do you?" she asked rhetorically. "Well, most of the land around here is better suited to ranching than farming, a bit too rocky for most crops."

"That shouldn't matter. I'm a cycle mage, and I can ensure the soil is always at its peak efficiency. I was hoping for a defensible location with a ready supply of water." He could always hope that there was a decent view too. After all, what was the point of getting frontier property if you didn't have a nice view to go along with everything else?

"A cycle mage, eh?" Karissa stood up and walked out the door, putting her hands in her pocket and studying the large map on the wall. "Hmm. Well, that does change things a little." The map showed the area in Tallrock with quite a bit of detail, although not nearly as clear as the satellite images he was used to looking at for maps. The scribes of the map had created what he hoped was an easily interpreted version of the world.

Tallrock itself was surrounded on all sides by a thick forest that extended out several miles in every direction. There were a couple of low hills to the west, that gradually grew into much taller mountain foothills as you got closer to the Spine.

A large lake to the northeast was surrounded by more small foothills, before turning into a marsh or swamp twenty or thirty miles to the east. A large section to the south designated a dead forest and a number of skeleton images seemed to indicate some sort of undead plague in that direction.

Probably a dungeon, Kas thought to himself. Four major rivers flowed through the area, although two of them looked like they may have split off of a bigger river somewhere in the mountains.

"Here," Karissa said, following the path of the nearest river to the south of Tallrock until it reached what appeared to be a valley. "The valley is big enough to support a couple of farms, although you'd need to bless all the soil. It's not too far from Tallrock that it would make getting your goods into town hard. The eastern edge is a steep enough cliff that you should be safe from most predators. A couple of really pretty waterfalls there too."

She turned to look at Kastigan. "How many tokens did you say you had?"

"Three," Kastigan said. He was already pulling out his own map and adding the relevant details he thought he would need. The path to the valley was pretty clear, he would mostly just need to follow the river. Although it looked like the cliff face she was talking about was on the south side of the river; he'd have to find a way to cross it. "There any bridges over this river?" he asked, pointing.

"Not really, a few fallen logs that act as bridges. Nothing that would be good enough to get a cart across," Karissa answered. "Three should be enough for you to claim most of the valley. A lot more than you'll ever be able to farm on your own. You want to make the purchase now?"

"I think I'd like to see it first," Kastigan said, after a few seconds consideration. "But I won't be alone, I'll have some help up there with me."

"Good. Even for an unbound like you, that country is dangerous. Not too high up in the foothills for the dwellers to be interested in you, but you should avoid going too much deeper." The lack of scouting into the mountains was obvious; while most of the map was fairly well fleshed out, his valley was just about on the edge of the western explored region. "Also, since you'll be that far west, if you do have any contact with the dwellers, I know there is a standing bounty on information regarding them."

Kas recalled hearing the term dwellers before, but couldn't exactly place it. "Sorry, I know I've heard the term before, but what are dwellers?"

"Something in the mountains. The dwellers are what killed off most of the 137th and 76th legions. If you ever find a legionary that doesn't seem right in their head, they were most likely one of the few survivors of that failed excursion." Karissa shook her head. "Sometimes I think it would have been better if Delac had taken them all, at least Yesha might be able to help them."

Not knowing what to say, he put a hand on Karissa's shoulder. That seemed to be enough for the woman and she gathered herself back together. "Right, well. I should get back to work. We do provide a bounty on any new maps you find or make. Although if you find anything of value in the valley, I suggest you report it after you claim it."

A short laugh at that. "Will do, thank you for your help, Lieutenant. I'll keep that in mind." Taking his leave of the scout's office, he made his way back to the main entryway and up the stairs he had seen there. At the top of the stairs he followed the smell of sulphur until he came to a brightly lit room with four or five people in robes sitting at desks, reading.

He knocked on the doorframe but no one looked up. Next, he tried coughing to get their attention but that didn't work, so he coughed again louder. Finally he stepped into the room and walked towards the woman in blue robes. "Pardon, ma'am?"

She groaned, while the other four mages looked up and laughed. "You owe me two silver! I told you he sounded like water," the mage in red told the one in yellow, who grumbled and handed over the coins.

Looking between the group, Kastigan frowned. "I'm sorry to interrupt, I'm actually looking for earth, water, and death scrolls."

All five of the mages stopped what they were doing and then looked at him in confusion.

"Cycle mage? Huh, wouldn't have guessed we'd get one of your kind out here." The woman in blue he had first addressed stood up, while the brown robed individual came closer. "I've got some water and death, and Dwight can do earth. But nothing too advanced. What are your elemental affinities?"

"Major in all three and then, 80 water and earth, 90 death," Kas answered.

"You're a Delac blessed reaper!" Dwight, the brown robe mage, said with delight. "I've never met a reaper in real life, how many people have you killed?"

"I'm sorry, I don't know that term. And… none," Kastigan said with a slight frown. What had Livia gotten him into?

"Oh right, you're unbound. Reapers are an unofficial designation for cycle mages with high death affinity rather than high life affinity," the woman in blue said. "They have a bit of a reputation, given some of the more famous reapers in history. The King's Reaper cadre, the Green Death, was one of the most decorated units during the Six Crowns war; they were basically responsible for the success of the final thrust into Penthal. I'm Jayden, by the way." She held out a hand for Kastigan to shake.

The other three mages had also come closer when they heard Dwight talk about him being a reaper, and all three of them introduced themselves as well: Russ was in red, Curtis in yellow, and Jino in purple.

"Well, I'm not much of a combatant; I'm going to be a farmer. Was wondering if you had any spells and skill books I could look at."

All five rushed to grab spells they thought he might be able to use. They seemed unconvinced by his desire to be a farmer, as most of the spells they presented him with were combat oriented. He did manage to find a couple that were going to be usable for his life on the farm though. They also gave him skill books for some of the subskills he needed. For earth he got shaking, for water he got filling, and for death he got attrition. Russ gave him the fire magic book and the spark spell for free, saying he would need it out on the frontier. He also purchased three utility spells that would be helpful.

As he looked at the spells, he had the system remove some of the detail on the description; he didn't need to know that it added damage based on his affinity and intelligence every time he looked at a spell.

Spell Name: Poison Spray
Prerequisites: 50 death affinity, 50 water affinity, Death Magic I 10, Water Magic I 10, Single Target I 5, Flowing I 5, Poison I 5, Attraction I 5.
Damage: 10.4–20.9 death and 9.9–19.8 water damage (average 30.5)
Range: 10m
Cost: 5 mana
Cooldown: 2.5 seconds
Description: Shoots a spray of death and water magic that deals 5–10 death and 5–10 water damage.

Spell Name: Poison Bolt
Prerequisites: 50 death affinity, Death magic I 1, Assault Magic I 1, Poison I 1
Damage: 5.9–10.4 death damage (average 8.3) and 1.9–4.18 (average: 3.1) poison damage for the duration.
Range: 10m
Duration: 4 seconds

Cost: 5 mana
Cooldown: 5 seconds
Description: Shoots a bolt of poison energy at the target, dealing 3–5 death damage and applying 1–2 poison damage to the target for the duration.

Spell Name: Spark
Prerequisites: 10 fire affinity, Fire Magic I 1, Assault Magic I 1
Damage: 1.2–2.6 fire damage (average 1.9)
Range: 1m
Cost: 1 mana
Cooldown: 5 seconds
Description: Creates a small spark that deals 1–2 fire damage. Can be used to set things on fire.

Spell Name: Earth Stomp
Prerequisites: 80 earth affinity, Earth Magic I 10, Area of Effect I 5, Shaking I 1
Damage: 6.6–13.2 earth damage (average 9.9) per second
Range: Personal
Duration: 5 seconds
Spread: 3 meters
Cost: 10 mana
Cooldown: 5 seconds
Description: Shakes the earth around the caster, creating a localized earthquake that will do 5–10 damage to all creatures and structures within the range of the spell.

Spell Name: Create Water
Prerequisites: 50 water affinity, Water Magic I 1, Filling I 1
Cost: 5 mana
Cooldown: 5 seconds
Description: Fills up a vessel with drinkable water. Can create up to a gallon of water per casting.

The poison spray spell had just been too tempting to pass up even if it was a bit more expensive than the others. The range wasn't great, but its damage was outstanding, and after talking to Karissa he was somewhat worried about the dwellers and other things out in the wilderness. Also, it looked like it would be an amazing spell to build up multiple skills at the same time. He didn't think it would take too long for him to get his death magic up to level ten to be able to use it.

Poison bolt was actually one of his worst attack spells. It dealt only 17.6 points of damage per cast on average and that was only if the poison was allowed to last its full duration. But he had needed something to get his poison skill up so he could learn poison spray.

After leaving the five mages, he descended the stairs of the keep again, heading for the bank at the other end of the compound. As he entered the front atrium, he was stopped by a large procession of soldiers with the unmistakable form of Colonel Holzer at their head.

Putting his backpack against the wall to allow them to pass, he put his head down, not wanting to make eye contact with the leader of Tallrock again. It was too late, however; Holzer seemed to have seen him and stopped in front of him. "Greetings, unbound," the same voice from before said, a tint of mockery to it.

Looking up, Kastigan swallowed. "Hello, Colonel." Up close, Holzer's features seemed more worn than they had before. His long curly brown hair and mustache and goatee were immaculately trimmed, but the surly look in his eyes made it seem more persnickety than fastidious.

"You are one of the new arrivals, yes?" He said the term new arrivals with barely disguised distaste.

"Yes, sir. I came from Capital."

This caused a frown to appear on Holzer's face. "I wasn't aware we were receiving freedmen from Capital."

"I'm a freeman, not a freedman," Kas said quickly. Freedmen were prisoners that the king granted freedom to in exchange for being sent to the frontier to tame the wilderness. Shura probably fit in the category, although her situation was more complicated than that. The knowledge of his status had appeared in his head as soon as he was asked. The game's way of telling him that his background package had given him a higher social status than most on the frontier.

"Oh? And what brings a freeman out of civilization?" Holzer asked. His voice had lost some of the bite it had earlier, but the sneer on his face hadn't abated.

"Cheap land," Kas answered and Holzer's eyes narrowed slightly.

"An unbound freeman looking to become a..." Holzer paused and looked Kas' equipment up and down. "Farmer?"

"Yes, that is my intention."

Holzer actually laughed, and so did all the soldiers around him. "Next you'll be telling me that you intend to forge an alliance with the dwellers and bring the Kiddeshans into the Realm." He dismissed Kastigan with a wave of his hand and led his followers deeper into the keep.

Kastigan took a moment to breathe—that hadn't gone as badly as he thought it would, based on his first encounter with the colonel, but it was still bad.

CHAPTER FIVE

Arrival 5

Exiting the barracks without really thinking about what he was doing, Kas allowed his legs to walk while he considered the implications of his conversation with Holzer. Why was he so amused that an unbound freeman would be a farmer? What exactly were the bound's opinions on the unbound? He made a mental note to ask Shura about it later.

With a start, he realized he had been wandering the fort aimlessly. Two soldiers stood in front of him and were glaring at him from the entrance to one of the side buildings. Each was dressed in what he was mentally calling the legionaries' uniform. The building itself was labeled Reddy Hall. He stopped and looked around, confused. This was the only building with guards posted at the entrance, although it looked exactly like the other barracks around. "Pardon me, what is in this building?"

The two guards continued to glare at him but neither answered him, so he repeated his question. He took a single step forward and was greeted with a popup.

You do not have the reputation required with the 76th Legion to access this building. You must have at least 5000 reputation points to enter the Spell Forge.

With a frown, he turned away from the building. Was this because he was unbound or because he wasn't in the army? He wished the game had a tutorial; there were too many interactions here that he just didn't understand the social significance of. He turned and began walking towards the bank. He stayed on the path this time.

The bank was like every other bank he had seen in old movies. With the exception of its entrance. It appeared to have been dug straight into the ground; the top floor was reserved for offices and meeting rooms, but all the actual bank business happened a hundred steps down.

There were tellers available to deposit or withdraw. A big magitech board along the top of the main wall gave the current evaluation of Pinnocian gold to USD, the Euro, and the other top ten most often used currencies. There was also a small room you could use to peruse the global auction house.

Kastigan stepped into it quickly to check a few things. All of the auction houses were magically connected to each other, although there were additional fees associated with trying to buy from nations other than Pinnoc. Stopping for a few minutes, he did a few quick searches for the product of the seeds he had acquired as well as mana crystals. No one had listed any of the items he had available to him.

That made sense; the crystals wouldn't be of use to anyone in the near future. Like him, any players making crystals would probably either sell them to NPCs for startup capital or hoard them until they could actually be used.

The plants were in a similar situation, but were probably delayed due to growth time. Player grown plants were a higher quality than you could get from NPC shopkeepers, but they also took up to a week or longer to mature. Even if one of the first players had an agricultural bent, they would still have a couple days before their crops would be ready to sell. He then perused the mounts and animals sections but didn't find anything reasonably priced there either.

Next, he searched if anyone was selling seeds. To his surprise, there were a number of unidentified seed pouches up for sale. Most of them seemed to be by the same couple of sellers, so they must be killing something that was dropping them. Kas put in a few bids totaling three silver but none of the unidentified seeds had a buyout option; he did manage to pick up four pouches of wheat seeds though. His business done, he left the auction house room.

The bank was mostly empty; one other unbound was filling out a form in front of a teller, but there were three more available. All the employees in the bank were quinthans. They all looked a lot like high school cheerleaders, tall, blonde, and slim. He decided to take the booth that was the furthest from the other player. The teller was an attractive elf, she looked to be in her early twenties, but he wasn't entirely sure how long elves lived on Livia. She could be hundreds of years old.

She gave him a polite smile as he approached. "How can I help you today, sir?"

"I'm looking to open an account and deposit some things before I venture out into the wilderness," Kas said, returning her smile.

The woman, who was wearing a name tag identifying her as Lora nodded and took out a few pieces of parchment. "Of course, sir. What sort of account would you like?"

"What are the options?"

Lora glanced over, noting his attire. "The basic account allows you to store up to twenty unique items. Stacked items are allowed, of course, with a deposit fee of two silver per stack. A basic account costs five gold to open and has a ten gold minimum. Standard accounts are good for up to fifty unique items, do not have a deposit or withdrawal fee but cost twenty gold to open with a one-hundred gold minimum. We have additional tiers as well."

"I see, and can I upgrade my account later?" Kastigan asked, pulling up his inventory to check how much gold he had left. After paying for the spells at the legion, he was sitting at just over five gold. Well below the amount needed for even a basic account.

"Of course, you'll just have to pay the difference and, of course, maintain the minimum amount required," Lora answered, shuffling the papers she had retrieved, laying a basic contract on the counter.

"And what is the penalty for not having the minimum amount?" Kastigan asked, picking up the contract and glancing down the sheet.

"You will be unable to retrieve any items from the bank. In addition, if you are below the minimum for longer than a week, your account will be closed and the contents auctioned off."

"I see," Kas said, glancing over the contract. Most of it was the same kind of legalese you would see on a real-world bank, listing the protections offered by the crown for the security of the bank, as well as the company's security policies. The fees involved for bank transfers and the interest rate, a paltry .04% per year on the basic account. He assumed that the higher tier accounts would have better interest rates.

He considered his options. He could open a basic account and deposit the land tokens but that would eliminate all of his liquid assets. He had no idea how long it would take him to get the required ten gold minimum so there was a chance that he wouldn't be able to recover the tokens.

Kas glanced up at the exchange board; Pinnocian gold was valued at just under a ten to one on the US dollar. Which means he could spend $100 to get the required amount. Although with fees that would probably become more like $105. He wasn't sure he had that much liquid currency in real life either, especially given that he was taking two weeks off of work to try to get a new life started in Livia.

He rubbed his chin and frowned. If he couldn't deposit the tokens in the bank then there was a chance that he could get robbed and lose them all. But there was an even more sure risk that he wouldn't be able to retrieve them from the bank if he did deposit them.

It was a matter of risk. Kas' thoughts tumbled around as he tried to consider his options. The fact of the matter was that he just didn't have the capability of spending that kind of currency in the real world. Not without some sort of assurance that he would be able to make that money back in a timely manner. He pulled out the interface calculator and did some quick math.

Assuming he used Crystallize every cooldown he was logged in, and was logged in for eighteen hours a day, that was 18 crystals a day—17 if you didn't count the one that he needed to convert into an elemental one—at two silver a crystal, he was making three gold and four silver a day. Three days would easily get him the gold required to be able to withdraw the tokens easily, faster if he wanted to sell his layered crystals.

He looked up at Lora, who was watching him with the attentive calm that all salesmen eventually developed. Kas reached for a pen and began filling out the appropriate fields on the document. "Alright, I'll open a basic account."

He saw Lora give him a snide smile out of the corner of his eye and blushed a little. Elves in Livia weren't quite like their typical fantasy counterparts. They were still tall and beautiful, but instead of being hippy tree dwellers, they were more avaricious. They ran the banks and created magitech like the windrunners, all in an effort to gain an ever-larger amount of capital. They were a bit like dragons and their hoards of gold. A poor farmer like him would be highly unappealing. Lora had managed to hide her disdain well, only letting it show when she thought he was focused on his application. But his cheeks reddened in response to her sneer.

Quickly finishing the application, he took out the three land tokens and slid them across. "I would also like to deposit these."

Lora's entire demeanor shifted as soon as she caught sight

of the land tokens, from the polite businesswoman persona, she became far more deferential. Even going so far as to bow politely to Kas as she accepted the documents and tokens. He also took out his remaining gold and two silvers, handing them over to finalize the transaction.

"Of course, Mr. Kastigan," Lora said, reading the name of the application. "It's a pleasure doing business with you." She slid the coins into a slot, where they jangled for a moment as they fell. She then took the three tokens and placed them in an envelope and wrote what he assumed was his account number on the side, handing it to a male elf that was behind her. He turned and left with a placid haste.

"The transaction has been recorded in your logs. We assure you that your property will be handled with the utmost of safety and security. Thank you for using Reddy Financial for your banking services. I would like to remind you that you have seven days to meet your minimum balance requirement before the items in your bank are auctioned off."

Kas wondered idly who else he would have used; he somehow doubted there was another bank branch within a hundred miles of Tallrock Fort. "Of course, I'll be back in plenty of time to retrieve them."

He quickly left the bank, slightly confused by the sudden turn of events after she saw the tokens. Were they really that rare? Sure, having three probably was, but most of the players probably received something similar in their starting packages. He probably should check the forums and see what other people were getting, actually. What could they have gotten that was comparable to his land token? Maybe they got extra skill books or something?

He stepped out into the sun again and took a moment to let his eyes adjust; the interior of the bank had been dimly lit by magical lights compared to the morning sun above him. He traveled through the fort and the town, heading back to the location that Shura and he had agreed to meet. He did take a moment as he walked to use Crystallize again. He pocketed that two silver worth of crystal and then sat down on a bench to use his new skill books and scrolls.

The process didn't take long, a few minutes per book or spell. The scary part was how much of his attention it took to really learn the spells. He finished the first one and realized he had a spider crawling up his leg. After a few minutes of madly shaking his pants and then stomping on the spider, he returned to the bench. Getting new spells certainly wasn't something he would want to be doing when he was in any kind of risky situation. He read through all the skill books and then learned as many of the spells as he could, taking only a short break to create another mana crystal midway through.

You have gained the primary skill: Fire I.
You have gained the following secondary skills: Attrition I, Brewing I, Burnishing I, Cutting (Alchemy) I, Cutting (Leather) I, Digging I, Filling I, Mana Circulation I, Planing I, Poison I, Shaking I, Steeping I, and Support I.
You have learned: Create Water, Earth Stomp, Poison Bolt, and Spark.

Kas carefully stowed the Poison Spray scroll away and then looked around for a place where he could practice until Shura returned. He still had about half an hour to burn grinding spells. His first priority was to get his supporting skills up.

Looking through his spells, Water Spray, Shape Earth, and Poison Bolt were the ones he selected. They would allow him to improve his three main elemental magics—earth, water and death—but also give him skill ups in Flowing, Attraction, Area of Effect, Bonding, Poison, and Assault magics. He would have liked to do Earth Stomp as well, but didn't think the top of the mesa was the right place to practice.

The three spells cost a total of 25 mana to cast with thirty-second cooldowns on Water Spray and Shape Earth. With a total of 100 mana, he could cast all three spells four times before he went out of mana or OOM. It would take sixteen minutes at his current mana regen rate of six per minute to regen from zero to full. Meditation and mana circulation doubled his regeneration at the cost of some situational awareness while he focused on the skill. That gave him a total of 640 mana to play with over the course of the half an hour he had until Shura should be back. Which gave him just over sixty castings of all three spells.

There was a bench near the meetup spot that sat on the edge of the mesa overlooking the forest and the mountain range to the spinward side. He sat down on it, folding his legs underneath him, and cast his first spell. Poison Bolt launched over the side of the cliff; by the time it had traveled to the end of its ten-meter range, the bolt just faded away, leaving a green haze in the air where it had disappeared.

He checked his skills to make sure it would improve even though he hadn't been targeting anything. Assault magic had gone up an entire point of XP but it didn't look like death magic or poison had gone up at all. With a frown, he cast the spell again after the five-second cooldown time was over. This time both assault and death magic went up a point.

He had a major affinity in assault magic, but only a minor affinity in death magic, and of course, poison didn't have any affinity at all. He guessed that meant that he was actually earning half a point per cast with a minor affinity and a quarter of a point per cast without an affinity. He cast poison bolt twice more to test his theory and a quick check of his skill sheet proved it correct. Assault magic was now at 4/100, death was at 2/100 and poison was at 1/100.

Satisfied that he understood the basic methodology, he settled into grinding his skills while he waited. A quick glance at his sheet showed that he had gained 90 XP in bonding, 75 in assault, 60 in earth and water, 30 in death, and 15 in area of effect, attraction, flowing and poison. And all three spells were 60% of the way to level two.

Bonding's gains were the big surprise. According to his calculations, it should have been 75 like assault, but it looked like it got the full experience from its explicit call out in Shape

Earth, as well as half experience from its sub school attraction listed in Water Spray. He also got two points of experience in Condensing and three more in Crystallizing.

All in all, Kas was quite pleased with the results of the mid-morning grind. He took a moment to stretch his legs. Getting down to zero mana didn't hurt per se, but the act of draining his mana repeatedly certainly seemed to be associated with a fairly severe mental drain. Like he had just been looking for a bug in his code for the last hour and a half. Stretching his body out, he took a moment to appreciate the view from the top of the mesa.

The nearest Spine of Aktrosha dominated the sky, the snow-capped mountain glistening in the sun. There was nothing visible beyond them to the spinward side, and the forest that surrounded Tallrock continued for miles to the trailing side, a seemingly unbroken stretch of land. He knew that somewhere out there were the grassy plains the Kiddeshans migrated throughout. On the rimward side, a dark smudge surrounded what looked like a massive brown hill; the result of a forest fire? The coreward side featured a large lake a few miles out, but was mostly forest other than that.

Hearing footsteps behind him, he turned to see Shura approaching him. Her battle harness had a few more bags attached to it, evidence of the supplies she had purchased on whatever errands she had been about. He raised a hand in greeting, and the drak returned the gesture. "Get everything?" he asked.

"Indeed, I am prepared. Shall we depart?"

It was only as she mentioned departing that Kas realized he had no idea how to actually get off the mesa. "Sure, is there like… stairs somewhere?" he asked, looking around.

Shura snorted and turned, heading to the rimward side. "No, there is a lift."

They made their way across the mesa, cutting through what Kas could only describe as a shanty town. Semi-permanent structures had been erected in a haphazard manner, the people within would stare at Kas, but would look away as soon as he made eye contact with them. They were all incredibly filthy and wearing tattered rags.

"Who are these people?" Kas asked rhetorically.

"Mostly freedmen, who have no interest in dying by going out into the wild," Shura answered him. "Most of them would have no idea what to do in the forest. The bravest may work the edge for berries or firewood, but most make do with whatever work the legion throws their way."

"That's terrible," Kas said, watching the disconsolate faces around him.

Shura snorted. "They all committed some sort of crime to get thrown in the king's prisons. Murderers, thieves, debtors. The men you see here are not worth your pity. Cowards who are too weak to deal with the hand they have been given. If they were willing to work together, they could go down and be safe enough. They would rather do nothing than break a sweat though."

Kas kept silent; Shura clearly had a fixed opinion of the men. Sure, some of them looked like the scoundrels she claimed them to be, but most just looked like they had been dealt a bad hand.

They moved past the slums and towards a structure that was situated on the rimward side. It was the lowest section of the mesa and set up at the lowest point was a windmill with some very complicated mechanical structures underneath it.

Connected to the windmill was a platform that extended from the side of the mesa a dozen feet. Three massive ropes stretched from the pylons down into the forest below where a similar structure was built but without the windmill. At the top of the mesa were about fifteen guards. Most of them dealing with the line of people waiting to go down into the forest below.

As they got closer, Kas studied the structure. The ropes weren't actually attached to the pylons but rather ended in a loop that was attached to a metallic plate that was affixed to the pylons. At the base of each of the pylons, a legionary guarded a lever. These three men seemed to be far more aware than the other guards, and while he was watching, one of the men was relieved and another guard took his spot. Kas wondered what the lever did, some sort of failsafe device perhaps?

The tram was currently down in the forest, so they were told they would have to wait about ten minutes. While they waited, Kas studied the others queued up waiting to go down. Several of them were unbound; they seemed to know each other previously, as they fit a little too well into the stereotypical party roles.

There was a drak, smaller than Shura, red scaled with curled horns instead of Shura's straight ones, who was wielding a massive spear. The next was a tribesman, short tusks jutting out of his mouth, and he kept poking them as if they were getting in the way. He had a sword at his waist and a shield strapped to his back. Next was a quinthan archer, looking nothing like the rest of the elves he had seen. Kas assumed he hadn't read much about the elves and had assumed they were still the woodland creatures they usually were portrayed as. The fourth member of their group was a guy wearing scale mail adorned with the stylized gavel he had seen in the temple of the Seven and carrying a warhammer. He assumed he was supposed to be a paladin of Arthen.

So they had a tank, a healer, and two damage dealers. Kas and Shura were sitting close enough to them that he could overhear their conversation.

"It's bullcrap we have to wait for the tram, man. I just want to go kill shit." This came from the archer.

"I know, man, I want to go tear some shit up," the drak lamented. He seemed to be enjoying his new body's strength, as he kept picking up barrels and crates in the area. The guards were watching him warily but they clearly didn't want to interfere with an unbound drak unless they had to.

"I dunno if I like these tusks. Feels like I have headgear again," the tribesman spoke up. They didn't seem to be impeding his speech at all, and Kas wondered how the devs had managed that. Or if they had just handwaved the whole thing.

"Yeah, but you'll look sick once you get some good armor. We're all gonna look sweet," the paladin said from off to the side of the group, where he was practicing swinging his warhammer around, obviously trying to get used to the weight.

It was around then that the archer noticed that Kas was also unbound. "Hey, dude," he called out louder, obviously talking to Kas.

"Hi," Kastigan said. He already felt out of place—these four were obviously in their late teens or early twenties. At least a decade younger than him.

"Dude, what are you supposed to be? Some sort of lumberjack?" the drak asked, pointing to the axe that was hanging off one side of Kas' pack. His voice was laced with mockery and his friends chuckled along with him.

"No, I'm an explorer," Kastigan answered, saying the first thing that came to his mind.

"No shit? That's awesome, dude, you should party up with us. We heard about this place called the Dead Hill that is supposed to be crawling with undead," the tribesman interjected.

"I can't, I have a solo quest to explore the mountains," Kastigan said, pointing towards the Spine. Solo quests only awarded their rewards if the player wasn't grouped; he hoped it was enough to distract the group from wanting to come with him.

"Woah, where'd you get a solo quest already?" the paladin asked, narrowing his eyes in clear suspicion.

"I got a special package when I created, quest came with it," Kas lied quickly. He hoped that was believable; he hadn't looked at the other packages, only the ones the dryad had shown him, but considering his package gave him a land token worth 5000 gold, he didn't think it was that unlikely a result.

"Ahh cool, I got this awesome spear with mine, it's a growth type weapon. I call her Skeleton Bane," the drak said, swinging his spear around somewhat clumsily.

Shura snorted at that. All four of the unbound looked at

her, but she towered over their drak by three feet. Kas could tell the archer was still considering taking a potshot at his companion but the paladin put a hand on his shoulder and the archer stood down. So the paladin was the alpha in their teenage wolfpack.

"It's cool, man. If you find anything good out there, let us know. We'll give you a fifth share of the loot if you find a dungeon." The paladin had a smile on his face that didn't quite touch his eyes.

Kastigan had hated these kinds of kids when he had been in high school, and as he grew older their type had only grown more annoying to him. The ones that could smile while stabbing you in the back.

"Of course, you guys let me know if you find anything good down with the undead. After this quest, I'll probably head down there."

"Sure thing. I'm Himmler," the paladin said, pointing to himself. "That's Ssrax, Gurthok, and Slayer," he said, pointing to the drak, the tribesman, and the archer. The text over their heads displayed the drak's name as a much longer string of letters that was unpronounceable. Slayer's name was actually XxXSlayerXxX.

Kastigan had to keep himself from rolling his eyes. There was no way he was going to party with these kids. "I'm Kastigan. A pleasure to meet you all."

They were saved from further comment by activity from the guards. Down below, a guard waved a yellow flag, and one of the topside guards pushed a button. The huge pylons began turning, pulling the trolly up towards the mesa top. Kastigan shifted around, trying to figure out how they worked.

The windmill had been moving the entire time he had sat there, gently creaking in the wind. Perhaps it was powering some kind of battery and they had been waiting for it to charge? It only took about two minutes for the trolly to make its way all the way to the top of the cliff. They then had to wait for the passengers to disembark, which took another few minutes as people were carrying heavy baskets of wood, herbs, and other products from the base of the mesa. Even a group of hunters with several carcasses strapped to a pole.

With Kas, Shura, and the others on the trolley, it began its downward journey.

CHAPTER SIX

The Forest 1

The travel time was only a few minutes, and Kas spent that time watching the forest. There was another platform much like the one at the top of the mesa, but this one didn't have the windmill on it. Still, it allowed for an easy exit when they finally got to the ground. The trees were ancient conifers, towering at least a hundred feet up. The clearing they were in was the only reprieve from the semi-oppressive darkness of the forest floor.

Waving farewell to the four other unbound as they began their trek rimward, Kas looked around. Shura had been shifting the buckles and containers that were attached to her harness, and after several seconds of watching he realized she was putting her armor into place. Her drak body was too large for much actual armor, a fact that was offset by the fact that she was encased in naturally hard scales from head to tail.

She was adding on layers of leather padding in those areas where her natural armor left her moderately vulnerable, namely the joints and around her hands and feet. The last piece she attached were artificial claws, extending her natural claws to be a foot and a half long. They reminded him of an old comic book character.

When Shura was done, she glanced at him, nodding. "We are good to depart, yes?"

Kas nodded his head, glanced at his minimap, and turned to head west. "Yes. Of course."

The clearing where the lift platform had descended was likewise guarded by about two dozen legionaries. They had a small, heavily fortified stone building built around the platform but the clearing was otherwise empty. There were a couple of semi-established paths, mostly leading to the east. But the tall trees meant that there was a relatively clear forest floor, just a few ferns and some scrub oak where one of the forest giants had fallen.

They traveled in silence for a few minutes. Kas found the forest eerily quiet. He hadn't ever been in an old growth pine forest before, there weren't many of them left in the real world. He could hear muted sounds from the canopy above but the area below was mostly quiet. Combined with the semi darkness and the lack of wind, the walk took on a strange calm. Like they were travelling through a dream.

He also took the time as they were traveling to ensure that his mana was never full, and he would cast spells out into thin air, keeping the same rotation he had been using before. However his progress was much slower than before due to not being able to sit and meditate in between castings.

"Why didn't you have your weapons on in camp?" Kas finally asked to break the silence.

"It is against the law for drak to have their weapons out in the fort. Only unbound ones like that runt you were talking to are unaffected by the rules," Shura answered, and for the first time Kas realized that her head was slowly shifting as if searching for something.

"What are you looking for?" he asked.

Shura's frill ruffled in what he was beginning to realize was something between a chuckle and a smile. "Creatures to tame."

"How does taming work exactly?" It hadn't been a section of the game that he was very interested in during his research, so Kas had mostly skipped over it as something to learn more about in the future.

"It varies by the creature. For most, you must knock them unconscious. Not as easy as it sounds, but I have a skill that will help, and someday I may be able to create poisons that will aid me in this," Shura said, and Kas realized he should be looking out for plants to level up his Herbalism skill. Mentally toggling the command to activate his herb sensing skill he surveyed the forest floor as Shura continued. "After they are unconscious, I apply a binding stone near their hearts. This will begin the process of linking our souls, allowing me to control them."

"How do you get a binding stone?" Kas asked, just as a yellow dot appeared on his mini-map, indicating that a harvestable herb was nearby. "Oh, something I can gather, can we stop for a minute?"

Shura turned to look at him, cocking her head to the side slightly. "What do you gather?"

"I have a major affinity in herbalism, and minor affinities in animal and regular processing. So, I can gather herbs, leather, and other animal byproducts." Kas didn't head off the path— there wasn't a path to deviate from—but he did stumble into some of the heavier brush, pushing his way through poking sticks until he found what he was looking for. A small, tri tip plant glowed softly when he saw it, clearly a result of his herb location skills. Focusing on the plant brought up an overlay that told him what it was.

Item Name: Ash Sage
Description: Gathered with the herbalism skill.

Well, that wasn't very helpful. He reached down to touch the plant and another minigame popped up. A three-by-three grid of buttons appeared, and one flashed red, fading as another button flashed; this repeated twice more. Kas assumed they wanted him to repeat the process. So he tapped the buttons in the same order that had been shown to him, and the ash sage disappeared from the ground and appeared in his hand. With a smile, he pocketed the herb and began extricating himself from the bushes.

"That will be very helpful. You don't, by any chance, have an affinity for alchemy?" Shura asked him, having watched the entire encounter with a critical eye.

"Yeah, a minor one actually. I'll let you know if I can make any tranquilizers; probably going to need to get the farm set up first."

Shura bobbed her head. "That is reasonable. To answer your question, binding stones are a conversion you apply to a mana crystal. That is one of the things I was hunting down. I managed to find four crystals while we were in town." The tone of smug satisfaction in her voice made Kas laugh.

"I see, how much did they charge you for them?" Kas figured he could get more than a couple silver off his crystals if Shura needed them.

"I paid a gold and four silvers for the four that I managed to purchase," Shura announced.

Kas almost tripped. "*What?* I was offered two silver pieces for mine."

Shura stopped and looked at him. "You can create mana crystals?"

"Yeah, and align them, but only to three elements."

Shura sat down heavily on her haunches, her triple bent legs allowing for easy sitting without having to touch the ground. "The ancestors truly did bless me when I met you." She bowed her head again. "If you will help me with the mana crystals, we can get significantly more taming done. The spell to create a bond crystal has a four-hour cooldown, so I can only make so many in a day…" She trailed off looking into the forest. "But we will be able to make much more wealth if we can sell the bound creatures than we could with either the bond crystals or the plain mana crystals."

Kas nodded his head. "Of course, we'll have to tame as

many as we can. Is there a limit on how strong a creature you can tame?"

"Yes, the stronger or more intelligent the animal, the harder it is to tame. Some may take multiple bonding stones, or bonding stones that are attuned to the elements they represent." Shura stood back up. "But we can talk as we move; we need to get you many herbs so that you can create the tranquilizers we need."

"Makes sense." Kas continued to move through the brush, now following behind Shura who cleared a path by sheer weight of mass. Kas was happy enough to follow in her wake, although it did mean he got a few bouncing twigs to the face as they shifted back into place behind the drak. "So, you've got the one stone currently? How long does it take for the stone to bond?"

"That also depends, each stone is good for an hour of bonding, and you must keep the creature unconscious for that entire duration. However, there are some creatures that you must tame in a different manner, as I said. Where I am from, there is a species of large lizard that we ride. To bond one, you must get on their back with a bond stone and ride them until they are too tired to run any more. But that is one of the joys of being an animal bonder, I will have to discover how to bond new creatures." Shura's speech had more animation than he had ever seen from the normally stoic drak.

"Alright, so unless we find something that has an unusual bonding sequence, how easy will it be for you to knock something out with your skill?"

"Ahh, well, with only one bonding stone, I think I could easily bond smaller creatures. Maybe something the size of a medium dog? My skills are unpracticed; they were not allowed in the arena. I would need to be much more skilled, or we would need to use some tranquilizers, to get anything much bigger than that."

"What happens after you bond them? Say you were to bond a wild hog. Does it become a pet? Or can I use my ranching skill to breed more and sell them for meat?"

"You could breed them for meat. Think of the bonding as a way to domesticate the creature. Some creatures will make good food stock, and I can bond them relatively easily. That is probably what we should focus on first. After I have gained in skill, we would want to move on to some of the smaller pets with useful secondary abilities. Things like a dog or a hog that can sniff out valuable resources or help fight. After that, we should focus on mounts. I think you would be able to create strains that would sell quite well. Particularly if we can find a new species that is good at both long distance endurance riding and combat. Adventurers will pay many coins for such a thing."

"Alright, so what we're looking for is something like a pig or a chicken that you can bond, then we can breed them with my ranching skill. Hopefully something that has a function beyond just being food, although I don't think I'd object too badly if we found something like a chicken. It'd be nice to get some scrambled eggs every morning," Kas said, scratching his cheek in thought.

They fell into a comfortable silence, the trek through the semi darkness of the forest broken occasionally by Kastigan wandering off to grab herbs. He managed to gather six more ash sage, eight silkweed and a half dozen shadow orchids. He also stopped to use Crystallize on its cooldown. It took two hours for them to reach the edge of the river.

It had looked fairly small on the map, a river of no real consequence. But when they actually got to it, Kas realized that the cartography skills may not have been exactly to scale. About 120 feet across, the river wasn't frothing white, but the current did seem to be quite steady and deep. Neither Kas nor Shura seriously considered trying to cross the river here; they were going to be following the river for some time and there would undoubtedly be a better place to cross.

The path alongside the river was quite enjoyable. The sun was fully visible for the first time since they entered the forest, and there was a breeze. Kas also got his first real look at some of the local fauna. Several otter-like creatures were playing in the river. They decided to take a break and watch them for a while. "What about these things? You could tame one of them, right?"

Shura glanced over at the creatures and considered. "Well, I probably could, however I do not think we should try it. Most herd creatures will attack if you try to bond one of them. So it is best to find one that is isolated, or to separate them somehow. The other alternative is to knock out all of them and mass bond them. That can be difficult though, as it requires many resources and attention. There is also the matter of defending the creatures while they are being bonded. With so many unconscious, predators would be very active. I also do not think they would work well for any of the functions that we need a bonded animal for."

Kas shook his head. "You're thinking about it all wrong. Those things are adorable. The unbound would buy them in a heartbeat. Depending on what it took to bond one, we could make a fortune off them."

Shura's frill fluttered as she considered his words. "If you think we could make coin on them, that would certainly help our other efforts. I must admit that I am not an expert on what the unbound will purchase, but if they will purchase something simply because it is 'adorable,' then we could specialize in making them."

Kas considered that for a moment. Did he want to be known as the otter guy? Not really. "I think I'd rather we get some really awesome mounts and sell those, to be honest. I'd rather be known as the guy who sells griffons than the otter man."

"Griffons would indeed require a good bit of specialization. From both of us, I think." Shura stood up. "Well, we have wasted enough time we should be moving. We still have about three hours of daylight left and I'd like to get as close as we can to this farm location you were suggested."

Kas stood up and, with a last look at the otters, they moved on. They made good time near the river. There were also numerous new herbs to be picked, however it was clear his skill wasn't quite high enough to gather them. Where the ash sage had only required him to memorize four tiles, the water rose had him memorizing fifty. He hoped that as his skill increased, the difficulty of harvesting it would decrease. He did, however, get double experience when he failed, which was a nice perk even if he would rather have the economic boost of actually harvesting the plant.

He was glancing at the herbs in his bag after finding a lower level water plant called river lily when he realized that he had no idea if any of these plants were going to be useful for him. "Shura, do you know anything about alchemy? I have no idea if these are the plants we should be harvesting to get health potions or tranquilizers or what."

Shura shook her head. "I am not much of a crafter. I imagine you will know what you can make after you get to an alchemy station? I do not know of another way to look at your recipes. I am sorry, Kastigan."

"Well, it was worth a chance. What about other uses for mana crystals? I know they're used for imbuing magic into items. I wasn't aware they could be used to make bonding crystals."

"Hmm, I imagine mana crystals can and are used by most professions. I believe alchemists use them, or powdered versions of the crystals, to create some of their potions. Builders use some in advanced structures to empower the magics contained within them. Blacksmiths will use them in their forges to maintain the temperature perfectly. They are almost universally used. Although most often they are found as drops from monsters."

"It is rare to see a person able to create them; few are born with an affinity for condensing," Shura said slowly. "I don't know if that will still be the case when unbound are more common. We shall find out, I suppose." Shura trilled her frill and they continued their trek.

Near sundown, they still hadn't found a way to cross the river or a decent ford. They decided to help the entire process along and found an appropriately sized tree that they thought they might be able to fell in the right direction to create a bridge.

They set up camp in what Kas called a wanderer's pine. The long branches touched the ground, but when you pushed your way past them, there was a surprisingly large clearing at the base of the tree, large enough that Shura only had to hunch over a little to fit her massive body into the space.

Kas took a moment to make a full accounting of his daily activities. He had created 12 mana crystals, one every hour for the last twelve hours of play, minus the one he had sold to Jack. He was left with 11 crystals.

He had managed to successfully gather: 37 ash sage, 2 water rose, 26 river lily, 16 silkweed, and 40 shadow orchid. That gave him two full level gains in Herbalism I and Gathering I, but only 85% of the way to a level in Location I.

He had failed on a lot of the water roses, but finally managed to get a system down where Shura would write down numbers as he called them out. Even then, he had only managed to successfully harvest two out of the dozens of attempts. On the plus side, it had dropped down from 50 buttons to only 48. The others had likewise gotten easier, although ash sage stayed at three. He figured that was the lowest it would ever go.

He had earned another character level a few hours back, giving him three additional stat points to distribute as he desired; he dumped all three into intelligence to up his mana total. The system had also granted him points in strength and constitution from hiking with a heavy pack, while his intelligence, wisdom, and dexterity had all risen from his herb picking and constant mana draining. The stat increases had also increased his HP, mana, and stamina to HP 60, Mana 125, and Stamina 82. Which improved his mana regen rate to one per seven seconds, while stamina stayed at one per ten.

Name: *Kastigan* **Race:** *Human* **Origin:** *Pinnocian-Capital*

HP: *50 -> 60,* **Mana:** *100 -> 125,* **Stamina:** *75 -> 82*

Level: *2,* **XP:** *230,* **XP TNL:** *400*

Attributes:
Intelligence 10 -> 14, Dexterity 10 -> 11, Strength 10 -> 11, Wisdom 10 -> 11, Agility 10, Constitution 10 -> 11.

Regen Rates:
HP Regen: 60s, Stamina Regen: 10s, Mana Regen: 7s, Combat HP Regen: -, Combat S Regen: 20s, Combat M Regen: 14s.

They hadn't seen any creatures that Shura deemed worth their time to tame. Although she did set up some snares that wouldn't kill the target while he was counting his spoils. Hopefully they caught something she liked. If not, they would have some meat in the morning. Shura thankfully could cook. Kas didn't need to eat, not in the game, but food gave great buffs and it felt weird not to have to eat when Shura did. She gave him a plate of something called Traveler's Food which looked and tasted like a BLT.

"Shura, do you know what happens to unbound when we sleep?" he asked the drak, and she looked at him and raised an eye ridge.

"Do you not sleep like the bound?"

"No, I'm going to disappear here and my spirit will go back to where I am from. Are you going to be okay out here by yourself?"

Shura looked around at their secure location in the wanderer's pine, and then nodded her head. "Yes, I should be fine here. When will you return?"

Kas pondered that. "Good question. I'll need to sleep, and do some things out there. Let's say… 7 am?"

Shura agreed and they sat around the small fire she had built, talking for a little while about the things they had seen over the course of the day. Kas logged out a few minutes later.

———

With a groan, Matt sat up from the couch. He was sore from hours of inactivity. Carefully stretching his limbs to work out the kinks, he looked around the room. He was currently living in a small studio apartment. He gingerly walked over to the kitchenette and pulled out a tube of nutrifood.

Ripping off the top allowed the smell to escape, and he grimaced. The smell that wafted out didn't have an analog to any actual food, but did sort of smell like the hovels they had passed in Tallrock. Plugging his nose, he drained the entire tube in one gulp. The trick was to make sure you didn't actually taste it, otherwise you might not get it all the way down. He coughed for a bit, but chased the tube with a glass of water. Shaking his head, he went to relieve himself and then stumbled back to the bed, where he laid down to sleep.

This was the first good day in a long time. Sure, it had started off weird, and he wasn't sure what to think of the colonel, but the walk through the woods had been like nothing he had ever experienced. He wondered if Earth had been like that once, green and full of life. So different from the iron skyscrapers that covered the planet nowadays.

He went to sleep, and in his dreams Lexie and Elam joined him on a hike through the woods next to a river.

DAY 2

Waking up early, as he was accustomed to, Matt quickly handled the rest of his real life requirements. Then he cruised around on the forums for a little while. More information was popping up now that all the waves were in the game. He found a couple of people who claimed to have found 'cheat' builds. None of them seemed to include mana condensing, even the forums that were dedicated to people who wanted to craft. He was super glad the dryad had given him that skill, almost wishing he had put it as a major affinity rather than a minor.

He did find some information on alchemy, but it looked like mats were regional. To counteract this, it looked like you broke down flowers, herbs, and other alchemical components into various typed powders. Once you had the powders, you could combine them in a dozen different ways to get different effects. For example, if you combined a vitality powder with a growth powder you would get a potion called Quick Regeneration, that improved your HP regen rate both in and out of combat.

Making notes of all the information, he then switched over to the regional forums and found the posts focused on Fort Tallrock. He marked this as a favorite so he could come back to it quickly. Most of it was the typical looking for group type stuff. He winced when he saw a cross post by Himmler saying that a guy in the area had received a solo quest as part of their starting package. Luckily, he didn't list the name, so Matt had a little bit of anonymity still. The post listed what everyone had received for their starting packages and Matt wasn't terribly impressed.

Most of them got a piece of equipment that grew more powerful as the user leveled, but capped out at level 20. It would give them a good temporary boost, but nothing like the economic advantage the land claim tokens and their 5000 gold value would give him. Once again, he was glad that Livia had taken a personal interest in him.

Man, he needed to come up with a nickname for her. It was too confusing to have Livia the dryad, Livia the game, and Livia the world. He mentally relabeled the dryad as Liv. The other two were close enough in function that he didn't mind keeping them consistent.

Realizing he had been on the forums longer than anticipated, he activated his link and re-logged into Livia.

———

Waking up in the wanderer's pine was a significantly better experience than waking up in his studio apartment had been. The smell of evergreen needles filling Kas' nose reminded him of the holiday season. Sitting up, he glanced around. He was still wearing his pack, worried that it might not have disappeared when he did had made him a little paranoid. He used Crystallization to create another mana crystal and get that timer started; Layering still had a few hours left.

He looked around. Shura's belongings were still there, but there was no sign of the drak. "Shura?" he called out tentatively, hoping she was within audible range of the pine.

No response. Kas stood up and squirmed through the needles. "Shura?" There was no sign of the drak, not that he had even the slightest idea of how to track something. "Shura?" he called louder.

The forest had been so calm and peaceful yesterday, and Kas was beginning to realize that it was the very reassuring form of the Drak that had made it seem so. Without her protection, he felt small and vulnerable. There was a crack as something heavy snapped a branch deeper into the woods. Turning in the direction of the sound, Kas called out Shura's name again.

No verbal response. But he could hear whatever it was crashing through the forest. He mentally prepared himself to cast his spells, going over them in his head. His palms were suddenly wet with sweat and he crouched down behind a bush near one of the big trees.

Waiting for the creature to show itself.

CHAPTER SEVEN

The Forest 2

With a start, the thing stepped through a massive bush and came into Kas' full view. Three black-tipped horns sat on a massive bony spine that framed its head and the rest of its body. The body itself sat atop six large, thick legs; its body was elongated to fit the extra pair of legs, and covered in dark brown plumage. Aside from the extra pair of legs, it looked very similar to a triceratops.

Its yellow eyes focused on Kas for a few seconds and with a snort it dismissed him. Going back to crashing through the underbrush, its nose to the ground. Thick snorts of breath told him that it was tracking something by smell.

Backing into the wanderer's pine again, Kas didn't want to be anywhere near the creature when it decided that it was more interested in him than whatever it was searching for.

It carefully navigated around a tree, showing surprising agility in navigating around the trunks considering how loud it had been earlier. It finally stopped on a tree several dozen feet away from Kas and sniffed a small yellow leafed plant at the base and began chewing on it happily.

Kas watched in awe as the creature quickly stripped all the leaves from the plant, its long, forked tongue carefully leaving the stem of the plant relatively undamaged. When it was done, the creature curled up into a roll between two large roots and yawned happily. This gave Kas a great view of the flat teeth it possessed.

Clearly, the creature that Kas decided to call a trike had just eaten the dinosaur version of catnip. He grabbed his bag and walked over to Shura's but her pack was considerably heavier than his and he barely managed to pick it up. Carrying it was out of the question; Shura's strength must be off the charts. Or was it some element of the game that wouldn't let him steal things?

Setting his pack down, Kas considered his options; the trike was still curled up under the tree. He assumed that meant he was probably safe; after all, there didn't seem to be much that would be interested in attacking the massive beast. The adrenaline quickly drained from his body and he was left a little tired but otherwise unharmed.

He shrugged slightly, time to work on the plan from yesterday then. He left the protection of the wanderer's pine and walked over to the tall, black fir tree they had seen yesterday. It was situated on a bank with a slight downhill section where the river was narrower, only about sixty feet but deep and quick moving.

With half his attention on the trike, he walked over to the riverside and cast Earth Stomp as he kicked the base of the tree, shaking the dirt away from the roots. The trike didn't seem to mind, so he waited for the cooldown to be over and cast it again, kicking in the same spot. He repeated this process, walking around the base of the tree and kicking to loosen the earth the tree clung to. After three rotations, the roots were clearly visible and he figured he was about ready to start on the next step. The problem was that the next step required Shura. She was going to push against the tree while he used Poison

Spray on the roots, further weakening the tree's hold on the ground.

The theory was that this would allow them to knock the tree over the river and create a bridge to cross. Without the drak's strength, he was going to have to improvise. He cast Shape Earth and slowly shifted the loose dirt from the riverside over to the other side of the tree. It took several castings but, eventually, the tree was leaning out over the river.

"Oh good, you're working on the bridge already," a voice said from behind him and Kas whipped around to see Shura smiling at him, two small rabbit-like creatures slung over one shoulder while a hawk clung to the other shoulder pad.

"Shura! You're alive!" Kas said, his voice a little louder than he intended it to be. The trike snorted and raised its head to lazily consider the two of them.

Shura immediately went into combat mode; she crouched and dropped the two rabbits on the ground, her triple claws extending from their sheaths on her wrist with a flick. "Stay back, Kas. Try to get some spells on it." She spoke quietly, trying not to spook the beast.

"Shura, it's okay. It's high as a kite," Kas said, and indeed the trike considered Shura for a few moments then lowered its head and went back to its nap.

"What… what is that thing?" the drak asked quietly. It out-massed even her large form by three or four times.

"I'm calling it a trike. It came crashing through the woods right after I woke up. Ate some plant with yellow leaves over there, then curled up for a nap," Kas answered.

"Really, yellow leaves? Do you think you would be able to identify them if we found more?"

With a shrug, Kas said, "Yeah, sure, major affinity for herbalism, right? I can probably set it up so that it shows up on my minimap in the future." He pulled up the options on his find herbs skill. He frowned as he scanned through the options. "I think I'll need to go and identify the plant, then I can probably set it up so that they will show up on the minimap. You think you can use it to tame a trike?"

Shura nodded her head, glancing at the curled-up form of the beast. "Yes, I am thinking it will act as an advanced substance. There are many creatures that require a specific type of plant to tame. At the very least, we can use it to lure a creature into a trap where I can then start to try to knock it out or begin the tame."

"Well, we could try now. You've got to have a half dozen stones on you now, right?" Kas asked, considering the big beast. "That thing would be handy to have tamed."

Shura shook her head, pointing to the hawk, "Sadly, the redtail here ate up nearly half of my stones to tame. Although I did get two levels out of him." She stroked the hawk's chest. "He was injured, so it was a much easier tame than normal. I will have to wait until he is hale before we can use him. But I think he will be very helpful in finding smaller creatures for meat and taming. As well as keeping them out of your crops." She trilled her frill at the hawk and Kas shook his head.

"So... should we wait for it to get up, or do you think it's safe for me to go over there and ID the plant?"

Shura glanced over at the trike and then looked around. "I do not think it would appreciate you going towards the plant at this point. It likely still considers it something that it should protect." She shrugged. "We should work on the tree a bit. Maybe that will wake it up."

She dressed the two rabbit corpses she had found while Kas cast a few more Earth Stomps and the tree was well on its way to falling, the top portion of it at least five feet out over the river. "Alright, I'm going to start hitting the roots with Poison Spray," he told Shura, who had started cooking the rabbits while she waited for him to finish loosening the dirt around the tree.

The nice part of the game was that cooking, even using a campfire, was a matter of minutes rather than hours. She offered Kas a plate and he gladly ate it while they waited for Poison Spray to kill the tree's root structure.

Three castings later, Shura and Kas had a long branch propped against the tree, pushing it as the roots struggled to keep the forest giant upright. With a sudden snap, the tree began its descent. Falling almost in slow motion, it landed with a thud that rattled Kas' teeth. The sharp snapping sound of branches breaking before the impact had sent dozens of splinters showering the far bank.

The trike had slept through all of their preparations but didn't take too kindly to the crashing tree. Standing up, it began pawing the ground, angry at being awoken from its nap. Shura and Kas hid behind the roots of the tree.

A few minutes of trumpeting and then the crunch of branches snapping as the trike made its way away from the new bridge. They walked over to where it had curled up and Kas knelt down next to the plant, activating his herbalism skills.

Failed to inspect target, unlock the identification subskill for better odds.

"Can't do it, says I need to learn the identification subskill," Kas said after a few more attempts.

"Well, it is rather distinctive. Although I imagine these trikes will eat up most of it, it didn't do half as much damage leaving as it did coming," she said, gesturing to the warpath the trike had used to arrive vs the one it had just left by. "Looks like they go into a bit of a frenzy trying to get to that... plant. Can we just make up a name for it to use until you get the identify skill?"

Kas laughed. "Yeah, I guess we could. Let's just call it... yellowleaf. It's a crappy name, but that way I'll want to get identify as soon as possible."

Shura shook her head. "That is a silly name, but you are the herbalist."

Traveling up the new 'bridge,' they had to cut away some of the branches in order to progress down the trunk. Drew found that Rock Shard was a great way to do that, the spell's sharp edges allowing him to cut smaller branches that helped Shura's large form get to some of the bigger ones that blocked the path. It also leveled up his magic.

With a start, he realized that he hadn't used Layering yet. He sat down and meditated while Shura cleared the rest of the bridge. He was able to layer the crystal at about the same time Shura managed to clear enough of the branches away from the fallen tree to cross the river.

"You know, I guess I never really considered how much work it would take to clear a tree bridge like that. I kind of always just pictured they would fall mostly cleared, I guess," Kas remarked and Shura snorted. Having done most of the difficult work, the drak was tired for the first time Kas had seen. They rested for a little while, the drak fawning over her hawk.

"So, what are you going to call it?" Kas asked, motioning to the hawk.

"Hmm, I am not sure. It is a male, by the way. The females are bigger," Shura said scratching the beak and around the ears. "I think I shall call him Trouble."

Kas tried to pet the hawk but he didn't seem interested in letting the human near, giving a warning call every time he got close. After several failed attempts at bribery, he gave up for the moment and they began their journey again, traveling along the river bank for several miles before they hit the first waterfall. Kas collected more herbs as they went, but didn't find any more of the yellowleaf or any new types.

The cliff was at least a hundred feet up, although it wasn't quite straight up; more like a 60- or 70-degree angle. Far too steep and tall for either of them to climb up the loose shale of the cliff. The river itself cascaded down in several short increments, limiting the sound of the falls quite a bit, while still creating a beautiful sight.

They followed the base of the cliff for another half a mile until they came to the section the scout commander had told Kas about and began the laborious process of hiking up the hill. It took them almost an hour to follow the small game trail that led up the side of the cliff.

Shura's large mass proved a liability on the narrow trail. Several times they had to wait while Kas shaped the earth into a more agreeable path. The hike up the cliff was broken about midway up by their midday meal. The hot sun and steep incline tired them both out.

"If we do settle up here, we are going to need a better road at some point," Shura said. "But it will be nice to have such a defensible position until we get bigger. We will have to figure out a way to get the bigger animals and wagons for your crops up and down, though."

"Shouldn't be too hard, I guess. Once I get some more levels into Earth magic, I should be able to shape it relatively easily. Without trading away the safety that the slope achieves." They talked for a little while about how to properly defend the location before being rested enough to continue up the path.

When they reached the top of the cliff, they were greeted with a beautiful, alpine, U-shaped valley. The river running down its center must be the remains of a glacier, but it was long since departed. The river was wide and slow moving up in the valley. From what they could see, it stretched out another couple of miles, opening up to at least a mile across before narrowing again near the far side of the valley.

The granite cliffs on either side had a number of smaller waterfalls that probably led into the river. Kas assumed there was a lake or much bigger waterfall at the far end of the valley. Looking out to the trailing side from the top of the cliff, onto a sea of pine trees, Tallrock was visible in the distance, its unusual shape making it stand out among the otherwise unbroken forest.

"Well, this is a beautiful location. The valley looks like it is wide and flat enough that you could grow crops here easily," Shura said, looking it over. "And the valley itself should protect us from most big creatures. I imagine if we can find a good route up, there will be bigger creatures up there that I can tame eventually."

"What makes you think there will be bigger stuff up there?" Kas asked, scratching his chin.

"It's difficult to get to. The harder a place is to get to, the more dangerous the monsters there will be, and with monsters, they almost always get bigger as they become more dangerous," Shura answered. They were making their way down the valley when Trouble began screeing quietly. "He is sensing trouble, I think," Shura whispered as she adopted a combat stance.

Kas backed up a few feet, his eyes darting around. He couldn't see anything. That was, until he looked up. Flying around them was a large form. From here, it was difficult to tell exactly how big, but he could get a general sense of the creature. The two main wings were a black that faded to white near the tips, but the body wasn't feathered at all. Not quite leonine, in the shape of a griffon, or the half horse body of a hippogriff, the creature circling above them looked more lupine than that. A flying wolf? The single large horn on its forehead was the only part that didn't seem to fit.

"Above us, Shura," Kas warned the drak, and when she glanced up, she cursed.

"It's a dire cloud wolf, start walking towards the trees. It likely has a nest near here. But I don't think it will follow us into the trees. If it starts diving towards us, try to run in a zigzag pattern towards cover." The pair was still far from the forest edge, the wind near the cliff keeping it relatively clear. But they made steady progress until the wolf creature realized that they were heading for cover and, with a howl, dove towards them. Shura began running towards the forest and Kas tried to follow. But his shorter legs and overall lower physical fitness quickly left him behind the drak.

Sensing easier prey, the cloud wolf shifted towards Kas. Who tried to zigzag like Shura had told him to. Unfortunately, he was paying more attention to the wolf than he was to the ground he was trying to run over, and he tripped over a rock. A quick roll saved him from a face plant, but he felt the wolf's claw clip his shoulder and his health dropped by a third.

The wolf pushed against the ground with a heavy thud of its wings before pushing back into the air.

The trip saved Kas from an early death, and he cast a Poison Bolt and a Rock Shard at the wolf's departing form. Both spells went wide and he began running toward Shura and the relative safety of the forest.

Flying stones chased after the cloud wolf as well, as Shura tried to distract it from her partner. Luckily, there wasn't enough time for the cloud wolf to get another pass before the pair disappeared into the trees. Kas stopped under a large pine and bent over, his hands on his knees as he tried to regain his breath. Shura's weapons were out and the drak's head was on a swivel as she looked for additional threats.

"That would be one of the bigger beasts," she said a moment later when Kas had collected himself.

"Well, no crap. If that thing is hunting around the area, we're gonna be hard pressed to start a farm. He'll be diving at me every chance he gets."

"She's a female actually; the males don't grow horns. But yes, if this is her territory, we will likely have to either scare her off or kill her. Cloud wolves are highly territorial, so at least we don't need to worry about a pack being nearby." Shura's frill trilled. "She was a magnificent beast, though, wasn't she? Imagine if I could tame her! The cloud wolves back on Middar aren't nearly as big. I bet you could ride that one!"

Kas looked back and tried to imagine being on one of those flying wolves. "I dunno. I like having my feet on the ground. Earth mage and all that jazz." Mostly he just didn't look forward to the idea of trying to tame that beast. The wound in his shoulder was slowly recovering now that they were out of combat.

He took a moment to look around and frowned at what he saw. The forest here wasn't as thick as it was below the valley but it was still far too dense for easy farming. It would take a while to clear the trees from this land.

"You have no sense of adventure," Shura said, shaking her head. The two rested in companionable silence while they waited for Kas to fully heal before starting out again.

The trip through the forest in the valley was uneventful; they stayed in the tree line near the river, and had to hack their way through the underbrush. It was nearly dark before they finally broke through into the base of the valley. They had been hearing the waterfall for the last twenty minutes but when it finally came into view, they both paused in awe.

Falling almost straight down a cliff that was at least a hundred meters tall, the water roared as it collected into a glacier clear lake. The area around the waterfall was more dark rock, covered in moss that liked the cool mist. The ubiquitous evergreen trees also shifted to a strange bright orange-leafed tree that lightened the area considerably.

Around the bend of the mountain, where the sound from the waterfall would be less severe, was an overhanging cliff like the ones he had seen the Anasazi tribe had built their villages into in the Four Corners area of the US.

With one eye towards the sky, the pair walked over to the lake's beach. Kas tested the water and found it to be near freezing. "Glacier runoff," he shouted at Shura. Talking this close to the waterfall was nearly impossible, but the drak nodded her head in agreement and they made their way over to the overhang.

As soon as they passed the sharp outcropping near the waterfall, the sound diminished to a dull hum. Kas paused and looked behind him, amazed at how focused the acoustics of the area were. He wasn't sure if that was just game physics making this little area more pleasant or if there was some sort of real-world phenomenon that would explain the sudden decrease in volume.

"Well, that's convenient," Shura said, her voice starting out loud and then diminishing as she acclimated to the lower ambient noise. "This looks like a good place to set up a settlement. The overhang will protect us from any flying predators, and the area around here is relatively clear. Should be a decent place to start your farm."

Kas glanced around and sure enough, the area was relatively flat; the rocky beach near the waterfall had given way to a clearing of thick grass that looked like it would be a pain to clear out but would otherwise make for very fertile land. "You're right." He scanned the overhang; it wasn't big enough for an entire village like the ones he had seen in the old pictures. But it would easily hold a couple houses and a barn, particularly if they built up rather than wide. "I really like it here, actually. It's gorgeous. Depending on the cost of land, we may be able to buy the entire valley." The location was situated high enough that it commanded a moderate view of the river snaking its way through the valley.

"That's more land than I could ever farm, but we could build a town out here, collect other farmers. It has to be one of the safest places on the entire frontier. If we get hunters who can clear out the wildlife population and if there are some ore veins, we would be almost entirely self-sufficient. I bet we could get a bunch of those people who were too afraid of the wilderness to leave Tallrock. I mean, we'd need to set up some infrastructure first…" He could already see the town growing, the people prosperous and happy. His dreams of being able to play the game for a living realized.

"You may not have a sense of adventure, but you certainly do dream large," Shura said with a slight chuckle. "It will take quite some time before any of that can be realized and of course… we will first need to see how far our land tokens get us."

"Right, yes, of course. I don't expect it to be a city overnight. But there is so much potential here." Kas' smile was plastered to his face as he looked around the valley. "And it will all start here. Don't worry, Shura. I have a great feeling about this place. I'm gonna test the ground."

While they were still near the trees, he slung his pack down, pulling out the pick and shovel that Liv had packed for him and marched over to a spot that had plenty of light. He activated Earth Stomp and kicked the grass. The shaking didn't seem to affect the grass at all. But he kept at it for a full minute. Digging deep into the ground with his shovel, he cut a line through the grass.

When he had a line about five feet long, he switched to the pickax, carefully digging the grass up until he had a five by three piece of sod. "Shura, can you come grab this? I'm thinking we can use it to make a roof." He looked around but saw no sign of the big drak. Thinking back, she had told him she was going to go look around and do some foraging. With a sigh, he tried to lift the sod but soon realized that it weighed far more than he could carry. After several minutes, he managed to drag the sod away a few feet away. Panting and filthy from the effort, he sat down to catch his breath.

Looking at the three by five section of cleared land and then at the meadow around him, he realized just how much hard work this was going to be. "Shit. The next month is going to suck."

With a few hours of daylight still, Kas worked to clear more land, checking every time he cleared another section of sod to see if he had made enough room for a single casting of Enrich Soil. It took him nearly an hour of backbreaking labor to make a three meter square section of land. He had run into more than a few large rocks while he was working but those were easily handled with Earth Stomp to loosen them, and Shape Earth to shift them over to a slowly growing pile near the edge of his 'field.'

When he finished, he stood in the middle of the field and cast Enrich Soil. The mini-game for this spell was far more complex than his previous spells. It required him to connect a few dozen dots with his finger without crossing the lines he had already drawn. He failed the first few times he tried. Happy that it didn't enact the cooldown for a failure, he finally managed it on his fourth attempt. Immediately the soil darkened, becoming a rich black. He pulled out a bag of seeds and used it.

The field immediately took on a tilled appearance. He smiled when he focused on it and managed to pull up a status box.

Field Type: Crop (Wheat)
Field Size: Small
Soil Quality: Excellent
Water Content: Adequate
Condition: Excellent

CHAPTER EIGHT

The Forest 3

Kas spent probably half the time it took to clear the field looking up. Waiting for the cloud wolf to reappear, sure that any minute now he would need to make a break for the tree line again. With Shura absent there wasn't any chance he would be able to fight it off. But he could certainly flee into the forest and hopefully survive another encounter. With the plot almost ready, he retreated to a rock near the tree line and considered his options.

With only an hour or so left before dark, Kas took the time to create a campfire in the shade of a couple of trees. The rocks he had pulled out of the ground earlier lent themselves to the creation of a fire barrier. There were plenty of fallen branches to be gathered in the shade of the forest and he soon had a decently large fire going. He considered eating one of his rations for the regen buff but decided that Shura would likely come back with something to eat. The next task was going to be to create a watering method for his crops.

Create Water required a container to be filled up whereas Water Spray was too much force; it damaged the furrows when Kas tried it. That left him with a couple of different possibilities. He could create a cistern, but that would require him to bake clay or otherwise create a method of condensing the mist in the air into a form that would be controllable. He would have liked the control that allowed him but there wasn't really any good way for him to implement it currently. His next option was to create a trench from the lake with a sluice gate he could open and close when he needed to add water to it.

That was what he figured he would end up doing, for now at least, but he wasn't happy with the solution at all. He promised to go look up on the forums how other farmers were doing it and, in the meantime, began shaping the earth to create a trench.

He took a break at sunset to enjoy the alpenglow as it spread across what he was already mentally calling his valley. What would make a good name for the place? If he was going to create his own town, having a name would be important.

Shura returned with two duck carcasses and another rabbit while he was musing about what to call the valley. "Looks like some good progress," the drak said, looking around the clearing. "Here, come take care of these while I build a fire."

Taking his knife, Kas followed the guiding lines that appeared as he worked to skin and butcher all three carcasses. Too much pressure and he would damage a portion of the byproduct, but it only took a few minutes and he had some badly butchered meat, a poor quality rabbit skin, some feathers, bones, and the creatures' guts which he offered to Trouble. The falcon ate the offal but glared at Kas as he did so.

Kas dug a pit and then lined the top with the flattest stone he and Shura could find, sealing away the unused goods for use later. The two companions shared their evening activities, Shura had little input on the idea of a water source but didn't think they would need much watering; the mist in this portion of the valley was likely to keep everything more or less alive until they could return from Tallrock in a few days. The drak had been looking for the cloud wolf's lair, but after several hours of searching had found no other sign of the beast.

"I think it may have been ranging fairly far afield of its normal hunting ground earlier. If we had been closer, it probably would have pursued us more heavily. I doubt we'll see it often. When we get more established, we could purchase a totem to ward against monsters. With your ability to create mana crystals, we should be able to power it easily enough, although it will be a bit of pain to transport it. Might be better to hire someone to come build it here." She gave the drak equivalent of a shrug, her frill deflating in waves.

"Well, I guess it won't matter once we claim the land. Might be nice to get someone to cut down trees for a bit too. I think I can build the shelter, but getting a plan would make it easier. The one I have requires a bunch of metal stuff I don't have," Kas offered.

"Yes, that will be a priority. Although I'm not sure we will have the coin for that until after your first harvest. You can make something on the morrow that will be serviceable. I think we should stay here for a day or two then head back. Now that we have created the bridge, if we leave early enough in the morning, we should be able to make it back to Tallrock by nightfall."

Kas nodded his head. "Yeah. That should give me enough time to make a few more plots before we head out. What about your plans for tomorrow? Aside from making a shelter, we could use some more animals to trade if nothing else."

Shura stroked Trouble whose wing was still injured, and considered the question. "Well, what are you thinking we should tame? I found a number of tracks in the area. We could start a rabbit farm, although I am not sure how long that would take to be profitable. I would rather get something that lays eggs or can give a warning."

"Could you tame a lady hawk for Trouble? If we could start breeding them, I'm sure we could sell the kids to the unbound at least as hunting companions."

She shook her head. "I doubt I could find another I would be able to tame. As I said before, I was only able to tame

Trouble because he was injured. Normally I would need an alchemical compound to keep him docile while the bonding stone works."

Kas leaned back on his hands, staring up at the stars. "Well, rabbits would take too long and don't produce any usable byproducts unless we want to kill them. They breed quickly, but that's more of a long-term project I think." He bit his lip, thinking. "What about otters? Were there any up here?"

Shura shook her head. "Not that I saw. Although I did not spend much time near the river."

"Goats or sheep?" Again Shura gave the drak equivalent of a shrug. "Well, that leaves what? The ducks for their eggs and feathers? Something new?"

"I will have to range around some tomorrow while you are digging. If I find something that looks promising, I will either tame it or come back and ask your opinion on it."

Kas nodded his head. They had found a wanderer's pine not far from the glade he had begun farming and opted to stay there for the night. Before he logged off, he took the chance to look at his leveling gains for the day.

Strength had gone up two points and constitution had gone up three, while intelligence and wisdom had only gone up a point each. Creating and planting the plot had also pushed him over into level three, and he dumped the three attribute points that gained him into his wisdom, bringing his intelligence and wisdom to 15 each. His Earth Shape, Rock Shard, and Earth Stomp had all gained the most, but he did get some experience in Decay, Spark, and Enrich Soil.

Almost all of his skills had gained experience as well. Herbalism, and both its sub skills gathering and location had gone up a level. Earth magic had actually gained two and was well on its way to a third, the sub skill shaking had gotten to level three. He had also gained another 27 mana crystals, one of which he had converted into an earth crystal. Happy that he had had a productive day, he logged out.

———

Wincing as he came to, his muscles protesting from lack of use, and Matt slowly began stretching out. At least the lack of activity meant that his food consumption was down as well; that would help his wallet. The first stop was to the bathroom. After that he wandered around the small studio.

He eventually popped a food tube and choked down its contents, washing the sticky substance down with a glass of water. It took him a few minutes to really get used to his real body again, and when he was done, he pulled up the forums and began researching all the various types of pets people had managed to acquire. There were some animals that had some clear utility that he made sure to add to his list of things to have Shura watch out for.

Then he switched his attention over to the forums for farmers, looking for how everyone was doing their water delivery. Most of the posts he found were asking how to improve the soil in a plot of land, as they did not have the Enrich Soil spell; Matt gave them a quick once over. There was bound to be a period of time when he had more plots of land than he could cover with his enrich spell. Mostly it involved creating a compost pile and then putting small portions of the enriched compost into the soil when it was tilled.

Matt wasn't real excited about those prospects, especially when he read what people were putting into their compost piles, and he filed the information away as a last resort tactic. Compared to enriching the soil, watering the land seemed to be a far less sought-after option. He wondered if that was because the soil was so much harder to improve or if he was just missing something with the water. He'd check tomorrow and see how far Create Water got him. The three qualities for a crop plot meant that even if water was only adequate, he would get better results than just about everyone else due to his excellent soil and condition.

Condition was the only one anyone else seemed to be

getting anywhere near excellent, although they had to do quite a bit of tilling, weeding, and other random tasks that Enrich Soil did for him. Matt was again thankful for Liv's influence in his character creation.

Stretching again, he felt like he should be physically exhausted, and while he was mentally tired, his body was craving physical exertion. He put on a pair of sweats and some track shoes. As he was clipping his comm to his shirt, he saw that there was a missed call from his lawyer. Staring at the message for a moment, he put it down—deciding to forgo music —and went for a long run. He pushed himself a little harder than he expected, and was back from his two mile loop a minute and a half earlier than normal. He ignored the comm, took a quick cold shower, and went to bed.

Waking up, Matt gulped down another tube and then brushed his teeth. Sitting on his bed, he stared at the comm and the message from his lawyer for about ten minutes before shaking his head and logging into Livia.

DAY 3

The green needles of the wanderer's pine made it difficult to see, especially in the darkness of the predawn morning. A chill was in the air and he rubbed his hands together while he looked around the camp. Shura was still asleep and the big drak had curled into a ball on the other side of the trunk. Trouble was perched on a branch above her, looking like his head was missing. After a few seconds of staring, he realized the bird had tucked it into fluffed up feathers on his back. Shaking his head at the oddness of it, Kas tried to get up and quietly exit the pine.

If there was a quiet way of pushing aside branches and pine needles, Kas apparently didn't know it, and both the other inhabitants were awake by the time he was midway out. Shura growled incomprehensibly at him, while Trouble simply gave him a stink eye.

Outside the pine, the temperature dropped a few more degrees, and Kas put his hands in his pockets while he considered what to do. It was still dark, but the sunup would be in a few minutes, judging by the lightening color of the skies. Stumbling over to his crop plot, he pulled up its info.

Field Type: Crop (Wheat)
Field Size: Small
Soil Quality: Excellent
Water Content: Inadequate
Condition: Great (needs weeding)

Kas frowned; the ambient water was clearly not enough for the field, so he cast Create Water into his mess kit's bowl as he walked down the furrow, only moving on when that section of soil had turned dark from the moisture. Another inspection and the water level hadn't improved at all, so he continued to water the plot until he finished the first two furrows.

Midway through the second furrow, the water content went back up to adequate. By the time he had finished watering all ten furrows, it had improved water content to good. The entire process had taken most of his mana and about two minutes to fully water the plot. He assumed it would take multiple days to get the water quality up past good.

Right, he was going to have to figure out a way to water the plot while he went into town to buy the land. Something that would do a timed release? It was too bad there was no timer or something he could use. He would probably just have to wake up early, water and weed it before they left, and then tend to it the day they got back before he logged off. The game worked in 24-hour cycles, so as long as he tended to the plot at least once a day it would be fine.

Sitting down on a rock overlooking the valley, Kas meditated. When he was nearly back to full, he opened his eyes again. The valley itself was still in a deep shade, the sun not being anywhere near tall enough to get over the mountains yet.

But the sky had filled with reds, pinks, and yellows, and Kas enjoyed the morning chill while he watched the peaks around him turn pink, then lighten to a bright gold that seemed to glow before finally diminishing to its normal snow-capped whiteness.

Returning to the wanderer's pine, Shura was up and about and Kas started a fire to fend off the rest of the morning chill and give the drak a place to cook breakfast. "Sleep well?" he asked.

Shura grunted in response and pulled out some of the meat from the night before, quickly cooking up two portions over the fire and feeding the rest to Trouble. The hawk was looking much better, even going so far as to bat its wings a few times when Shura put him on a roost near the farmland.

"Well, I'm going to take the axe and try to find a couple trees near here that we can use to make a shelter. I imagine you'll be digging most of the morning?" she asked Kas, who nodded his head.

"Yeah, I'd like to get at least two plots of land done today. Then I'll clean up the logs and build us some shelter."

"Sounds good. How many do you think you'll need?" Shura had a lumberjack skill, although she didn't have any affinity. It had been one of the few tasks she was allowed to do back in Gogland.

"I mean, realistically, as many as you can get. But I think we can make do with three or four. Ideally, they'd be small enough the two of us can shift them into position. Maybe twenty feet tall and no more than a foot wide at the base. I'll probably have to split that into large and small segments as it is."

Shura nodded her head, took the axe, and headed into the tree line, while Kas got to the backbreaking work of pulling the sod up. The sound of chopping soon filled the air; Shura must have found a tree not too far away, which was ideal, since it meant they wouldn't have to drag it as far. Well, Shura wouldn't have to drag it as far, because Kas wasn't much help with the whole dragging thing. They really needed a couple of people willing to do some manual labor.

The sun had just begun to peek over the top of the valley's ridge when Kas managed to finish up the second plot. The cooldown on Enrich Soil wasn't up yet, so he took a break while he regenerated his stamina. That compound farm was starting to look mighty tempting. It would take days for him to clear enough of the tough grass to plant all the seeds he currently had in his possession. The mound of rocks on either side of the field already made a low hedge, and earned him skill experience in his Shape Earth and Earth Stomp abilities.

There was bound to be a use for the rocks sooner or later. With a sigh, he got back to work; Shura had already felled three trees and was in the process of chopping down the fourth.

It was just past noon when he managed to clear the third field. This one took longer due to it having a much higher quantity of rocks in it than the other two had. The crude wall had nearly doubled in length and Kas was mentally and physically drained from the magic and muscle he had used to create the plot. Walking over to the waterfall, he took off his boots and dipped his feet in the freezing cold water. As the day had progressed, he had slowly lost his concern over the cloud wolf, and now only occasionally scanned the sky for its silhouette.

A massive shadow passed over him, and he looked up. The creature that was flying across the valley was far larger than a cloud wolf. Judging by the shadow, the wingspan must have been at least forty feet across; the creature was more lizard than bird, a thick sharp beak and featherless wings barely beat as it glided on the hidden wind currents.

Its wings were a spiral of reds, yellows, and browns, and the main body looked to be covered in thin fur in more muted versions of the wing coloration and a golden mane of hair trailed down its spine. Kas had no idea what such a massive creature would even eat, but it seemed utterly content to ride the wind.

The beast disappeared over another ridge after a minute, its aimless-seeming flight carrying it out of sight. Kas shook his head; the creatures on the frontier were certainly different from anything he had dreamed of. That beast could easily handle any transportation to and from Tallrock! They wouldn't even need to build a road. Of course, the fact that it would likely need a large amount of air attuned beast stones and a way to knock that thing unconscious...

Okay, so it was more of a long-term goal. Still, the possibilities of the game were amazing. It would take a team of people to capture a beast like that. How much would something like that sell for? Tens of thousands of gold, maybe hundreds of thousands? What if he could breed them?

Shaking his head, Kas sighed. "Again, long-term goal." He stood up and dried off his feet before heading back to his plot of land. While he waited for Shura to finish her logging, he weeded the wheat plot; it only took a few minutes, the small number of weeds that had grown overnight easily removed from the rich soil.

The farm taken care of, Kas dusted off his hands before beginning the laborious task of debranching the logs that Shura had cut down and dragged towards the clearing. Without the axe, he was forced to rely on Earth Shard to cut the branches off. It took a few casts before the pieces of rock were able to cut most of the branches off, but the experience was good.

"We're going to need more tools if we continue like this," Shura said from behind him.

Kas jumped in alarm, having not heard the drak approaching, which was bad considering she had been dragging a massive tree behind her.

"And I'm clearly going to need to tame some sort of watch dog for you. Anything could have snuck up on you." The drak's frill flattened in disappointment with her partner's lack of awareness.

"Right, sorry, I'll try not to get so caught up in the moment." It was an empty promise and they both knew it.

"Uh huh, well, I'm going to go do some taming. I'll leave Trouble here to warn you if anything comes," Shura said and she left the hawk on one of the bigger branches of the felled tree.

With an eye on his Enrich Soil cooldown, the axe made things easier, allowing him to rotate between using his mana and using his stamina to clear the branches, and it only took him a couple hours to completely clean off one of the logs. He didn't bother debarking it; he was pretty sure that he should, but he didn't really have the right tools for that. Taking a break to cast Enrich Soil on the second plot, he then planted potatoes. He even watered it when an inspection revealed it was low on water as well.

Field Type: Crop (Potatoes)
Field Size: Small
Soil Quality: Excellent
Water Content: Good
Condition: Excellent

Satisfied that he would get at least a few good crops in the next couple of days, Kas headed over to the other trees and began the process of removing all the branches from them. By mid-afternoon, it was clear that he wasn't going to finish debranching even the second tree. Which meant they were going to spend a large portion of the next few weeks in the valley under the protection of the wanderer's pine. Which, honestly, wasn't all that bad, for him at least. Shura would have to spend the entire time hunched over. It wasn't like they were living there, she just had to sleep there. Kas rationalized it in his head, but he still felt guilty about not being able to provide a shelter for his partner.

Working as fast as he could, he only got about three fourths of the way through the second tree by the time Shura returned a few hours before dusk. She came back with three rabbits and another duck, but what was more interesting to Kas were the two small lizards that followed her.

They both hopped about on two feet, with long tails and

small feathered forearms. Miniature theropods? That was the same sub-order as a T-rex and the Utah raptors, but Shura had clearly tamed them. These only came up to about Kas' mid-thigh, but they jumped about and chittered excitedly. One was a dark gray that bordered on black, with a thread of white down its spine, while the other had dark red skin with a crest that was an even darker blue.

They paused as soon as they saw him, running to hide behind Shura's massive form and chirping at the drak.

"Who are these little guys?" Kas asked, kneeling so that he would be closer to eye level with the adorable creatures. As soon as he did, they charged him, their charming chitters turning to angry squeaks. Kas fell backwards in surprise.

"Heel!" Shura shouted and both of the creatures squawked angrily and then slunk back toward Shura, who was glaring at them. Kas sat back up and watched as they butted their heads against Shura's shins in an obvious display of apology.

"Sorry, Kastigan, these are your new pets. They are comp-ies. Mostly scavengers, they eat bugs and other small vermin. I figured we could use them similar to cats. They will keep your crops clean of any bugs that might try to eat them. And we shouldn't need to worry about rodents. Also, they have a toxin in their bite that paralyzes their prey; I think we can use it to create alchemical tranquilizers." She fluttered her spines, in amusement. "That is, if you can control them. This is a mated pair, so we should be able to get little ones from them."

Kas tried to swallow down his fear. They had been so cute and cuddly before they had bared their needle sharp little teeth. Which he now knew were venomous. "Great, they sound like wonderful pets. How exactly do you control them?"

Shura's frill fluttered as she laughed. "Don't worry, the bond will take care of that. First, you should butcher these animals. I will cook some dinner and you will have something to bribe these little ones with!"

Kas cleared a part of the grass since there wasn't anywhere better to do the butchering; he had to keep shooing the compies away as they kept trying to steal snatches of food. He ended up gutting a rabbit and throwing the entrails to them. They happily set to eating together, their happy chirps a strange dissonance to the sound of their eating.

Having never actually seen a live rabbit before, the game was of great assistance in helping him know how to actually go about the process of butchering and skinning the beasts. When he was done, Shura came over to show him how to properly feed the compies.

After a few minutes of feeding them small chunks of meat, a window popped up.

Shura is attempting to trade you two tamed Compsognathus.
Do you wish to accept this trade?

Selecting yes, the two compies suddenly had health bars appear over them. And he was prompted to name them.

"Hmm, what should I name them?" he asked Shura.

CHAPTER NINE

The Forest 4

"That is for you to decide," Shura said and took the meat from where Kas had stored it after butchering the corpses. While she cooked the food, he looked at the two compies and tried to think of a decent name for them.

"How can you tell their genders?" Kas asked. The two miniature dinosaurs were identical save for color to his untrained yes.

"The red and blue one is the male; right at the base of his tail he has a slight bulge. Also, the males are usually more color-ful," Shura answered without looking up from her task.

Glancing between the two compies, Kas thought he could see the bulge, and it was certainly true that the red one was more colorful than the black one. Was that some sort of mate attraction thing? He was pretty sure birds did that too, where the male was much more colorful than the female. "Alright. I'll call you Dino," he said to the male. "And you will be Diane." The system flashed a message asking if he was sure that is what he wanted to name them and with a thought he confirmed the selection.

"Alright, Dino, Diane. Go hunt for bugs." Kas laughed as

the two cocked their heads to the side, considering his orders, then turned and scampered off into the underbrush at the edge of the forest.

Shura had finished cooking the meat and was in the process of feeding Trouble some of the uncooked meat. Kas grabbed his portion of the food; Shura had wrapped it in leaves which he peeled away. The leaves kept the moisture intact and provided a disposable plate to eat from. "Do drak eat anything but meat?" he asked his companion.

Shura chuckled and nodded her head. "Indeed, we can eat most things humans eat. I have been foraging for vegetables to add to meals, but sadly I have been unable to find any. The drak are gifted in the various gathering and crafting skills, but I am afraid it is too early in the season for berries and fruit, and I do not know the local plants well enough to know what mushrooms and tubers would be edible."

As she said that Kas realized that he probably should be the one out searching for other stuff to add to their table. Looking over at the lack of progress he had made on the shelter, he began to feel a little guilty for his contributions to their survival thus far. "Sorry, Shura, I should have gone out looking for something. With my herbalism skill, I might have been able to find something."

Shura shook her head. "No, it is acceptable. We must balance our tasks; I am unable to help you with building the shelter and that will be of greater importance than whatever you might be able to add to our food supply. What are your plans for the shelter, by the way?"

"Well, I am going to make a sort of lean-to. I'll put the logs up against the cliff there, then fill in the area between the logs with smaller sticks and mud. On top of that, I was going to put the sod. That should provide a fairly secure roof and a bit of camouflage. We'll probably have to dig down a bit as well, otherwise you wouldn't be able to stand up in it, but that should be relatively easy, I'll just shape the earth. I'd really like to get some clay instead of mud for the daubing. But I don't have the faintest clue how to look for that."

"What will you do for the sides?" Shura asked, glancing from the trees to the cliff side.

"Well, I was thinking I'd use some of the larger branches to round out the ends. That should give us a little more space without burning too many extra materials. Not quite sure what to do for a door yet, maybe a flap that we can put down?" A thought hit him and he checked his skill list with a frown. "Crap, I forgot to get tanning. I'll have to pick that up when we get back to town."

"It will be very dark in there."

"Oh, good point, I'll probably need to make a hole near the top that the smoke can get out of for a fireplace. We can use mana crystals for light. If you put three or four of them together, they make a fairly good amount of it. Either way, I figure this will probably be a short-term building. Mostly a place for my alchemy stuff, and for sleeping. I imagine we'll both be too busy to spend a lot of time inside," Kas said, looking around.

"We are going to need to get some more people up here though, at least temporarily. I think first priority should be someone who can help process the timber and maybe find minerals and clay. After that I'm not sure, more people who can do some basic manual labor. Clearing the land, dragging the trees back here, maybe a skilled hunter and forager until we can get the crops providing what we need." Running a hand through his hair, he looked over at Shura who, having finished her meal, was lightly scratching Trouble's head. The hawk was leaning into her hand and clicking his beak together happily.

"Hmm, a miner or maybe a dowser first would be a good idea, and I'd welcome a more skilled tracker who could help me find and tame better beasts. Those positions would be better to find someone who would stay here permanently. The pure physical labor we could maybe hire some temporary workers for, clearing the land, building some things. I know that you can build, but it would be easier if we had someone doing it full time, so that you could focus on your other skills that will ultimately be more profitable."

Kas nodded his head along to Shura's words; the drak certainly knew what was possible in the world better than he did. "Why would we need a dowser rather than a miner? Don't they just find water?" Dowsing was another one of those affinities he had considered taking.

Shura trilled her frill in laughter. "No, dowsers can find anything. A competent dowser would be able to tell you where all the mineral nodes in the area are. They could also tell you the direction of any herbs we're looking for; yellowleaf, for example. Or a particular monster. Most trackers will have at least some skill in dowsing, the problem is that you need to know what you're looking for. A dowser can only find similar objects, so we would need a sample of a yellowleaf plant in order for them to be able to find more."

Kas nodded his head thoughtfully. "So, we could be sitting on a bunch of really rare, unheard of ore, and a dowser wouldn't be able to tell us because they don't have anything to compare it to?"

"That is correct. Similar things happen with creatures. A dowser would not be able to find that cloud wolf unless we had some fur from it, or another cloud wolf, to base it off of. Trackers use dowsing after they find a bit of hair to more accurately track their prey."

"How does that work with creatures? Like, can you find all cloud wolves with a single cloud wolf's fur?"

"Not exactly. To be honest, I'm not entirely sure how it works, I just know that if you have something of the specific animal you are trying to find, it is easier. Also, what you have of the creature can determine how easy it is to find. Blood is best, fur or scales are okay, spore is less than ideal."

Kas wrinkled his nose in disgust at the idea of carrying around a monster's poop just to try to find it. He got up and called out to the two compies, who quickly scampered back into camp. Dino had a fat beetle in his claws that he had a bite taken out of, while Diane was carrying a similarly half-eaten rodent.

"Wonderful, you can finish those," Kas said while trying not to look too closely.

The two compies chirped happily and quickly ate the rest of their meals. Dino's beetle was finished much quicker than Diane's rodent and he tried to sneak a bite of her catch. The black female snapped at him when he tried, and he chirped in indignation. He ran behind Kas' leg and then chirped angrily at her.

Kas couldn't help but laugh at their antics. He reached down and scratched Dino's head, the little turkey-sized creature leaning into the scratch. Diane came over to his other side, chirping piteously until he began scratching her head as well.

Playing with the two compies for a while was fun. But as the sun set, he headed back to the wanderer's pine. Shura and Trouble had already retired for the night and they both looked up as he made his way into the temporary shelter. "I meant to ask you, Shura. Will the compies be alright if we leave them here? I don't really want to take them with us."

"Of course they will; they are wild creatures, after all. You might want to build them a burrow near the farm though." With that the drak closed her eyes and presumably went back to trying to sleep. Kas sat down and the two compies snuggled next to him, Diane between his legs and Dino under one of his arms. He laughed; the two creatures were adorable in a vicious scavenger kind of way.

He focused his magic on Earth Shape and created a deep burrow for them to sleep in when he logged off. It took a few castings and he was nearly drained of mana by the time he finished, but he felt better knowing they would have a safe home here in the pine.

The last thing he did before bed was check his gains for the day. He had earned two points of strength, intelligence, and agility, and another point in constitution and wisdom. He had also leveled up again, which gave him three more stat points to distribute. He decided to bump his intelligence up to 20, to see if there was any benefit gained from getting it up to a second tier.

Kas didn't discover anything spectacular. He also gained ranks in: assault magic, area of effect, bonding magic, attraction, two in earth magic, shaking, water magic, filling, flowing, mana manipulation, meditation, mana projection, mana circulation, construction, animal processing, butcher, skinning, condensing, crystallizing, farming, and tending.

––––––––

Logging out, he went straight to bed, ignoring his comm that buzzed to tell him that he had missed calls. In the morning, he checked the forums but didn't find much useful. The farming forums were still abuzz about the best way to improve your soil, the Tallrock forums talked about getting a massive gang of players together to go raid an undead fortress somewhere to the south called the Dead Woods.

He did finally look at his comm; his lawyer had called a few more times. He also discovered that most players were at least level five or six at this point. His slow leveling speed was due to not having killed anything, although his steady increases from crafting weren't keeping him that far behind everyone.

With a shrug, he logged back in.

DAY 4

The cold mountain air made him shiver. The compies weren't anywhere to be seen, but by creating a mana crystal, he could see their dark forms in the bottom of the burrow he had dug the night before. They didn't seem eager to rouse yet, although one of them looked at him and gave a soft chirp before going back to sleep. Satisfied that they were safe, Kas managed to escape the tree without waking Shura up. The predawn chill felt good on his exposed skin.

Breathing in the crisp air, he closed his eyes and smiled. This world was so different from everything he had ever encountered in the real one. Aside from Shura, he was one alone out here in the wilderness. It was a strange kind of solitude. He felt like he should be lonely, but he wasn't, he just felt... free. Unshackled by the expectations of the people around him, he still had responsibilities, sure, but they weren't so pressing. They were goals that he had set for himself rather than requirements put on him by a boss or family.

A yellow dot appearing on his minimap as he walked through the trees diverted his attention from his musing and he walked towards it. There glowing a pale yellow in darkness was a six-petaled flower the color of the moon. Kneeling next to it he pulled up its information.

Plant Name: Dawn Lily
Description: Gathered with the herbalism skill.

Hoping that the thing didn't have too hard of a minigame, he tried to gather it. To his surprise, the minigame that appeared wasn't the same as the others. Whereas those had been more of a memory game, this one had two rows of lines with an empty space in the middle with twice as many lines.

There was also a timer up at the top that gave him two minutes to complete the task. Each line was a block of color; they were all a shade of yellow, and the text above them said that he had to order the lines from darkest to lightest. With a shrug, he organized them as proscribed. It took him almost the entire two minutes and he made a last-minute switch before hitting the accept button at the bottom.

The dawn lily appeared in his hand, as all the other successful gathers had, but that wasn't the only thing he had gathered. A slim book, its heft and weight similar to the skill books he purchased back in Tallrock, sat underneath the flower. It was too dark to read the cover of the book, but he did a little dance. This was going to either make him a few gold, or save him a few gold if he didn't know the skill already! He juggled items, putting the lily away in his inventory while pulling out a few crystals. Then he shook his head; he didn't need to be able to read the title—he put the crystals away and pulled up the stat screen for the book.

Item Name: Herbalism - Nocturnal Gathering I
Item Rarity: Uncommon
Item Description: Teaches the user how to gather nocturnal blooming plants.

"Of course there are plants that only bloom at night!" Kas whispered to himself. If the dawn lily was any indication, there were probably a number of plants that only spawned at certain times of the day. Meaning he would have to try staying logged in at various times if he wanted to find all the rare materials. He also probably needed to start drying all the herbs that he had found. Or at least grind some of them up into dust? He wasn't entirely sure how long herbs were good for.

When he got to the clearing, he pulled out the mortar and pestle from the pack and took out some ash sage. Placing the herb in the mortar, he pushed the pestle in and another minigame popped up. This one was a circle and inside the circle was a dot, the end of the mortar was another dot, he had to follow the dot to grind the flower.

After about ten seconds, he completed the game, which gave him a 73% result. Looking in the mortar, he had created a paste rather than the powder he had been expecting. Probably because he hadn't dried the ash sage first. Draining the paste into a vial, he examined it.

Item Name: Vial of Healing Paste
Item Rarity: Common
Item Description: Created by grinding an herb with healing qualities.
Healing paste can be applied to bandages to improve the amount of healing they do, or directly to wounds to speed up recovery.
Duration: 11 hours, 59 minutes.

Alright, so that was useful, but he was going to need to dry all his herbs before he used them; the decay timer would severely limit his profits. Or maybe he would just sell this batch to the herbalist in Tallrock and work on the next group. He wasn't sure how long something took to dry and he would probably lose some money in the process but he needed to generate enough wealth to get the land claim tokens out of the bank anyway. That needed to be his first priority.

It was still an hour or so before sunup he guessed, so taking a few of the mana crystals out, he read the nocturnal gathering skill book, and then went for a careful walk through the forest. He didn't travel far, not wanting to be too far from Shura. Finding a few more dawn lilies and another flower called night-bloom, he also discovered his first mushroom: an ugly looking polypore growing near the base of a tree called sheep's head, which he was pretty sure was edible. The sheep's head used the normal minigame, while nightbloom used the nocturnal one.

The lightening sky saw him heading back towards the farm, wanting to get the fields tended before they left. The real deadline for leaving was when he cast Enrich Soil; the timer on that was a few hours after sunrise, plenty of time to get to Tallrock before dark.

Dino found him before he got back to the clearing, the little compie chirping happily as he trailed along behind Kas, snatching up insects as they traveled.

When they got back, the sun had just begun shining on the far side of the valley. He inspected his fields and was happy to see that one of them needed to have the bugs removed. He told Dino and Diane, who had joined them in the clearing, to clean it out. The two dinosaurs happily went to work catching and eating the bugs while he weeded and then watered the two planted plots. Shura woke up while he was working on that and warmed up their breakfast, cooking the sheep's head mushrooms at the same time.

After breakfast, he worked on hanging small bundles of all the herbs that he had collected from the branches inside the wanderer's pine. It wasn't an ideal location, but it would have to do for now. When they returned in a few days, hopefully the herbs would be ready to grind and he could start leveling up his alchemy skills.

Doing some quick math, he decided to hold off for now on selling the herbs. He would be able to get his land claim tokens out just by selling his mana crystals, and he was hoping to grind up some alchemy skill.

Kas picked up where he had left off with the log. "I would love to have a chainsaw, that'd be grand. But no, I'm just sitting here chopping away at branches with an axe and magic." He smiled to himself as he realized he was using magic for such a simple task.

Shura had disappeared into the forest, having left Trouble behind to watch the two compies. The two diminutive dinosaurs soon finished their bug chasing and were now happily playing among the branches Kas had chopped up.

Kas was able to finish the second log and start on the third. "I really need to get a skill book for this." He was almost positive the reason it was taking so long was because he didn't have one.

The cooldown on Enrich Soil ended just after nine in the morning and he cast it on the third field, deciding to plant corn in this one. Shura hadn't yet returned, although she should be back in the near future, so Kas went to explore the fiery orange trees near the lake. After a couple of tries and switching to new trees, he managed to identify them.

Plant Name: Chissock Tree
Description: The Chissock is a fruiting tree whose fruit ripens during the late summer and early fall.
Condition: Healthy

Looking at the dozens of Chissock trees, Kas wondered how much fruit they could get from the grove. It would be another nice source of income; he'd have to get the compies to patrol around here for bugs. They shouldn't need to cut down most of them. Since they grew near the waterfall, the area could make a great park. He doubted anyone would want to live there due to the noise around the falls. He inspected a few others but didn't see the need to interfere with the trees much.

Enjoying the stroll through the beautiful trees, he made his way back to the farm. Shura was waiting for him.

"Find anything?" Kas called out.

"Nothing extraordinary. I did find a game trail that I'd like to follow when we get back. You?"

"Nothing really vital to the short term, but those orange leafed trees out by the lake are fruit bearing. So I'll probably see if I can find some orchard tending skills, see if we can't get additional income out of them."

"This is good, shouldn't take too much extra work. And since they are already mature, we should be able to get produce from them this year."

"Yeah, won't fruit until the end of summer though, so we've got a while before they contribute anything." Kas then turned to look at the two compies that were happily chirping around the farm. "Okay, you two, I want you to stay here and guard the farm from the bugs, okay? Stay safe and hide in the burrow if something big comes along, alright?"

Dino and Diane both looked at him confused, but after a few repetitions they seemed to understand what he wanted them to do. Diane took off towards the edge of the clearing, and appeared to be patrolling it. Dino caught up and followed along with her.

"Well, hopefully that works." Watching them run off he shrugged and turned to Shura. "You ready to go? I just need to grab those skins; I figure if we sell them and hire some more people, that will be worth more than what I could make from them."

"Yes, Trouble should be healed by midday, so I'm going to bring him with us. When he is recovered, he can scout ahead for us," Shura said, helping him move the heavy rock they placed over the various crafting materials they had gathered.

"Alright, let's go then." Kas looked back on his three fields and then shrugged, nothing he could really do for them currently. They followed the river out of the valley until they got to the valley's edge, and they followed the ridge until they came to the path down.

"This looked wider on the way up," Shura said nervously. The two-foot-wide trail certainly did seem daunting when they looked down. Kas searched the sky, worried about the cloud wolf attacking them as they descended, and then headed down, Shura following him.

The descent was much quicker than the trip up, and Kas had to stop himself from running down the mountain a few times, sure that Shura wouldn't be able or willing to follow a quicker pace. They were in the trees again after half an hour, and making their way back to the river.

"So, have you thought about the name for the farm yet?" Shura asked.

"I have. I'm not very good at naming things, though. I was thinking something like Red Lake, or Wolf Falls? Mountain Gorge?"

Shura pondered those names for a few minutes. "I do not think we should call it Wolf Falls; that might scare people away. The others are perhaps a bit too generic for normal use."

"Yeah, I guess it's a bit generic to use something like Pine Valley." Kas frowned, thinking about it. "What about Miranda Lake?"

"What is a Miranda?"

"Not a what, it is a name. It means worthy of admiration or wonderful. I think it fits the lake and what we're trying to do there."

"I am okay calling it Miranda Lake," Shura said after a few minutes of thinking about it as they hiked through the forest.

"Alright, that's settled then, we'll call it Miranda Lake," Kas announced.

"And what shall we call the valley and the farm?"

"Uh, Miranda Farm? And Miranda Valley? Do we need to come up with something more active than that? I remember they used to call ranches the Triple K Ranch or something like that."

Shura laughed, and shook her head. "No, I don't think we need to go that far. I think Miranda Valley is fine, but would you not rather have your family name on the farm?"

"Huh? Oh, well, I guess I could. But what about you? You're contributing to it, so it shouldn't just be my name. We could call it the K&S Farm? For both our names."

Shura stopped and looked at Kas for a moment, her expression unreadable. "I would be honored to have it be called the K&S Farm," she finally said, and then began moving again.

Kas blinked, unsure of how exactly to take his partner's reaction.

CHAPTER TEN

The Forest 5

They walked in silence for another thirty minutes, Kas stopping every few minutes to gather more herbs and use Crystallize on cooldown.

As Tallrock came closer, his thoughts turned to his two meetings with the commander of the fort. Colonel Holzer's strange antagonism towards him in both meetings seemed entirely unprovoked. During the first meeting, he seemed to single him out because he was unbound. Was that him just reinforcing the lesson for those who were effectively immortal?

It was the second meeting that was even more peculiar. Holzer seemed almost offended that he was an unbound freeman and going to spend his time farming. Did the colonel hate unbound for some reason? That seemed like a strange design choice.

"Shura, what do the bound think of the unbound?"

"Hmm, that is a difficult question to answer," Shura said, turning to look at him. "Perhaps it will help me to answer if you tell me why you are asking this question?"

"Well, I was thinking about Holzer. He seems to dislike unbound and I'm trying to figure out why."

"Ahh, this is not so hard a question. I asked this question myself when we were in Tallrock." Shura paused for a moment glancing up at the sun. "Colonel Holzer was a member of the legions that were sent into the mountains; he is the highest-ranking officer who survived. Do you know how many legions King Tasdel has lost so completely?"

"I don't. I only know a little bit about the Unification War and the War of the Dragons. I don't know much about the specific battles of either."

"There have been four lost legions. The first two were at the beginning of the War of the Dragons. The great ancestors had just been summoned by the Redaxes, and six of them together blitzed through several regions, eliminating the 5th and 63rd legions. The 76th and 137th were lost here to the dwellers. The problem is that while the 5th and 63rd legions were destroyed, they at least injured the ancestors.

"None of the survivors of the dwellers can even agree on what the dwellers look like. They were just boogiemen who attacked in the night and left nothing of their victims. The fact that they were so completely defeated..." Shura trailed off, shaking her head. "It was a blow to the Unified Realm that Tasdel will not soon shake. Many believe that Tasdel is too old, and he should abdicate his throne in favor of one of his heirs.

"Tasdel needed a scapegoat for the bad reputation he received as a result, and Colonel Holzer was the man."

Kas frowned. It was logical that Holzer being made a pariah for something that wasn't really his fault in the first place was bound to make the man at least mildly antagonistic towards just about everyone. "That makes sense, but why would he hate the unbound specifically?"

Shura laughed. "I was getting to that part. After Holzer had been exiled here, never to return to the homeland, the king promised that your kind would lead the charge into the mountains. And where the legions—Holzer specifically—had failed, the unbound would succeed."

Kas considered that his fellow players would like nothing

more than to wage war on an unknown and unassailable force in the mountains, and of course all the loot, titles, and world firsts that would entitle them to. From a game perspective, it made perfect sense. The people who started on Gogland would be able to develop the infrastructure and maybe open up a portal that would allow fast travel between the continents.

They would then be able to charge the other unbound for the use of the portal, both to and from. While the guilds that were established in other countries did the first round of end game content, Gogland would be slowly building up to be a new 'expansion' they could announce. The players would then flock to the mountains to wage war against the dwellers. The genius part of it all was that it was all dependent on the players themselves building the portal, and exploring enough to find the first dungeons.

Kas shook his head; the depth of the game world was amazing. How many similar plots were being developed? Would this happen at the same time as King Tasdel died and his Unified Realms went into a war of succession, or after? Either way, there was always new content for the players to battle through. All they would need to do is tweak the power levels of all the monsters a little bit so that it would match the high-end players to be the end game content at the time.

What that meant for Kas, though, was that he needed to get his town ready. If he could set it up to be that focal area when all the traffic started happening and the war went into full swing, he would be able to retire on the profits of owning the forward operating base for the entire conflict. Making it a race against time. He had to make Miranda Valley the hub, and that would take a lot of work and effort.

Lost in his thoughts of the future, he bumped into Shura who had stopped in the middle of the path. Trouble was chirping quietly on her shoulder, the drak scanning the trees carefully.

"What is it?" Kas whispered.

"Not sure, Trouble senses... trouble," Shura said softly and Kas had to stop himself from laughing at the wordplay.

Kas mentally reviewed his spells as he joined Shura in searching the trees for the cause of Trouble's concern. The source became evident as five dirty-looking men left the cover of the bushes a few dozen feet ahead of them. Two of them were holding bows with arrows knocked but not drawn back, one more had a sword and shield, a fourth carried a staff and was clothed in robes, while the last had a massive greatsword strapped across his back. The nametags over their heads told him they were all players.

"Well, well, look what we have here." The man who spoke was the one with the greatsword, whose name was Rob'n Locksley.

"Looks like a crafter and his bonded companion," the staff wielder said with a wicked grin.

"It does indeed. Well—" He paused and glanced at Kas' nametag. "—Kastigan, looks like you owe us a toll."

Shura snorted, glancing at Kas to see what he was going to say to the man. As the only bound here, the stakes were highest for her. She was the only one of them that wouldn't be able to come back to life.

"A toll?" Kas asked, playing for time while he considered his options. He knew Shura had spent years in the arena, but he had no idea what that meant as far as her ability to fight. Could she take all five of these brigands? Even if they did win, they would just hold a grudge against them, and if they ever found out the location of Miranda...

Kas didn't see a situation where he came out ahead of this. "A toll for what?"

"For passing through our part of the forest," Rob'n said. They had already crossed over the tree they had made into a bridge, so they were on the Tallrock side of the river.

"I wasn't aware that anyone had claimed this section of land. If you'll just show us the deed, I'd be happy to pay your toll," Kas answered. He glanced over at Shura who seemed to be very carefully breathing in and out, trying to control her anger.

The mage in their party seemed to have noticed the same thing and, considering the massive drak, was slowly backing away from the front lines. Unfortunately for him, it was too late. Shura took one last deep breath in and then exhaled.

Crackling lightning swept out in an arc in front of her, connecting first to the greatsword held by their 'leader,' and then arcing from that into the sword and shield and armor of the other three combatants. The mage, having backed away and not carrying any metal, was hit last, the lightning shredding through his thin robe.

Kas stared in awe as the men's bodies convulsed for a few seconds and then collapsed. Shura waited until the lightning's aftereffects were over, and then went about slicing their throats. The methodical way the drak went about killing the bandits was only overshadowed by the popup that appeared once they were dead.

Your party has slain five wanted bandits. Please visit your local bounty board for the reward posted for their death or capture.

Blinking away the notification, Kas considered his position. The bounty on their heads was proof positive that these were 'bad guys,' but he still wasn't sure how he felt about Shura's summary execution of the men. Although, given Holzer's demonstration that first day, the punishment they would have received was probably the same result if they had just captured them.

While Kas had been considering the implications of frontier justice, Shura had been looting the bodies of the bandits. She tossed a number of coin purses his way while she began the task of stripping armor off the bodies. Kastigan didn't even realize she had thrown them until they hit the forest floor.

"Are you alright, Kastigan?" she asked as he searched around in the undergrowth for the pouches.

"I, what?" Kas tried to shake the shock from his system, but he was watching the large drak with obvious confusion in his eyes.

"These men were bandits. They were going to kill us and take everything we had. I applaud your efforts at distracting them while I built up enough breath to take them out. That was very clever."

Red spots appeared on his cheeks when Shura complimented him for something he had been doing unintentionally. "I didn't mean to. I didn't know you could do that."

"Use my breath weapon?" the drak asked while she organized the rest of the loot.

Death in Livia, for players anyway, didn't mean you lost all your gear. Every non-soulbound item had a chance to be dropped when you died. Unlike the older games, you could actually trade soulbound items, but they could only change owners by intentionally giving them away. You also dropped any treasure type item you were carrying when you died, including all the coin you carried on you.

Anything that was flagged stolen was also dropped upon death, and the system took a pretty liberal interpretation of stolen. If you coerced someone into giving you something by force, the game considered that theft. It was also impossible to deposit stolen items into the bank, preventing them from being dropped on death. There were ways to launder an item to get rid of the stolen marker, but Kas doubted these newbie bandits used them as they cost more than most of what they would have looted.

"Well, sure, but also you just killed five guys so easily," Kas answered Shura's question. He had recovered all five coin purses and was in the process of counting the loot obtained. There were a number of rings and semi-precious stones among the coins, as well as a number of mana crystals.

Sadly, none of the crystals were attuned, but even then, Kas guessed that he was looking at close to 50 gold worth of various coins and treasures. It felt like a weight was lifted off his shoulders completely. They wouldn't even have to sell any of his own crystals to be able to pull the land claim tokens out of the bank. Wanting to laugh out loud, he looked up and saw Shura stripping the dead men's gear off of them.

The sight dampened Kas' mood considerably. His personal ventures were safe, but the cost in human life had been excessive. Walking over toward Shura, he helped strip the last of the dropped gear off the bandits and started organizing it into types. The one-handed sword used by the one guy with a shield dropped, as did one of the bows. Sadly, the staff the caster had been using was not among the loot. They did collect a couple of mismatched leather armor pieces and a large amount of stolen crafting goods.

"Do you want the bow?" Kas asked the drak.

Shura looked at the bow and shook her head. "Bah, flimsy human weapons. I would break it almost immediately." The short bow did seem tiny compared to the large drak. Kas had no use for either of the weapons so they joined the piles of stuff to be sold.

"Is there somewhere we can post all these stolen items? So that their owners can come claim them?" For the most part, it was low-level unprocessed crafting materials; pelts, herbs, ore, and the like.

Shura trilled her frill in laughter. "These men did not leave anyone alive. Still, I suppose we could declare it at the bounty office. Most of it probably isn't worth it to the few unbound they might have killed, and I doubt any of the bound have families that will be able to come claim it." She handed Kas the five bounty tokens that the bandits had dropped.

Pulling up the info on the first, he read through it.

Item Name: Bounty Token (Rob'n Locksley)
Description: Proof of completing a dead or alive bounty. Return to any bounty office to collect the posted reward.

The other four were similar, only the names on the bounty

tokens were different. Placing all five in his pockets with the coin, he then surveyed the rest of their gains.

They ended up with a large selection of hides from a wide variety of animals, all of them bigger than the ones that Kas had gathered from the rabbits Shura had hunted. They decided to bury them in a cache near the river, which he marked on his minimap. They would pick them up on the way back to Miranda. The rest of the trade goods loot, save the herbs which Kas kept with him, was put into Shura's packs. None of the gear would fit Shura, and Kas didn't find anything that was better than the armor he had gotten at creation.

"Shouldn't we bury the bodies?" he asked, looking between the five corpses with a frown.

"No, it would take you too long to dig a pit deep enough to prevent the scavengers from getting into it. We are losing light and we have much we need to accomplish back in town."

Glancing up at the sky, Kas couldn't help but agree. They had a few hours of light left, but they needed to sell everything, buy the land, find a place to sleep, find more skill books, and find people willing to do some work out on the farm.

With the bandit's looted coin, they no longer needed any extra money, so to make better time Kas didn't stop and gather any of the herbs along the way, although he did continue to cast his spells at the trees and small wildlife they saw.

They reached the base of Tallrock with a few hours of daylight to spare. The guards at the base took one look at the bloodstained drak next to him and kept their distance. While they waited, other groups approached and Kas watched them collect a tax.

Studying Shura for a moment, he could understand why they didn't want a confrontation with the big drak. Standing over thirteen feet tall, with a blue sinewy form built for violence. Most drak were 'only' big, standing somewhere in the ten-foot tall range. With Shura's height and muscled form, it was no wonder she had been such a successful gladiator. Still mostly clean, the real intimidating factor for the drak were the bloodstains on her armor. Kas' own armor had gotten dirty, but had cleaned itself after a few hours, leaving him with still new looking gear. Did the NPCs just not get the equipment cleaning magic?

After about twenty minutes of waiting, they took the lift back up to the top of the mesa. Tallrock sprawled around them.

"Alright, let's head to the bounty office first," Shura said and they picked their way through what Kas had mentally labeled Midtown. Tallrock was split into three distinct districts: the fort, Midtown with its shops, vendors, and upper-class citizens, and Shantytown, where all the people without trade skills or willingness to venture far into the forest lived.

The bounty office was the building in Midtown closest to the fort. It was a single-story structure, built in the same log cabin style that most of the area was constructed in. A large sign above the entrance held the bounty emblem, a six-pointed star surrounded by a wreath of laurels. It reminded Kas of old-school sheriff badges back before dermal badges became a thing.

Since the door was too small for Shura, Kas went in alone. He was greeted by a tall cianese man—well, tall for a cianese man, which put him at just under five feet with a broad, muscular frame, and a long beard.

Taking one glance at Kas, the cian clearly dismissed him. "It costs two silver to post a bounty of a gold, that's the minimum amount, and you'll need to provide proof that a crime was committed."

"I'm actually here to turn in a bounty," Kas said, looking around. "Also, we found a bunch of stolen items on the bandits, I was told you could hold them here if anyone can claim them?"

As soon as Kas said that he was turning in a bounty, the dwarf turned and gave him his full attention. "Aye, you can put it down here, or bring it 'round back if it's too large to get through the door."

"I'll have Shura drop them off there." Stepping out, he told

Shura about the back entrance and then headed back into the building.

"Alright, she's bringing them around back. What do you need from me to turn these in?" Kas asked the dwarf, placing the five tokens on the counter between them.

"Non-guild rate is 80% of the listed bounty." The cian picked up the tokens and scanned through them. "Give me a minute to find out how much that is," he said, walking back into another room.

While he was waiting, Kas looked around the room. Hand-drawn images of bandits were beginning to populate the room's walls. Most of them had bounties in the 50 gold or more range, but they all looked far too dangerous for him to take on. Shura might have been able to capture some of them, but he doubted it.

The most expensive was for a man by the name of Corvus; he led a treasonous organization called the Ravens. They had apparently set up their own city-state somewhere in the forest southeast of Tallrock and were interfering with some of the operations of the legion. Reading through the posting, it sounded more like Holzer was trying to get rid of competition than this Corvus was actually doing anything menacing. The bounty for Corvus was set at 200 gold, and a number of his lieutenants were also listed for lesser amounts.

The dwarf came back in with a pouch of gold, and Kas turned away from the notices. "Well, you're in luck. Most of them only had minimal bounties on their heads, but Rob'n Locksley was worth an entire 10 gold. Total comes to 14 gold. At the 80% you get for not being in the guild, that'll be 11 gold and 2 silver."

"How much is it to join the guild?"

"It's twenty gold for a year. But we waive the fee on your second year if you bring in more than a hundred bounties."

Kas shook his head. It might have been nice, but he wasn't going to give up all his gold. There wasn't a chance he was going to be spending most of his time hunting down bandits and turning them in for bounties.

"Alright, I'll take the gold now, thank you," Kas said and the dwarf slid the pouch to him. "How long do you hold the stolen goods for? Before I can claim it as my own?"

"A full month," the dwarf said with a smile.

"Alright, I'll be back in fifty days. Do I need to sign anything saying that I dropped it off?"

"Yeah, follow me; we'll get it all tagged up for you." The dwarf led him through a room where a large filing cabinet and a few offices were to a back room with a much larger door that Shura was busy unloading goods into. A second dwarf was going through the process of sorting everything into different piles. Probably organized by who it was stolen from, based on what each pile contained.

"You'll get 20% of anything that is claimed, and 80% of anything that is unclaimed," the dwarf told Kas as he began helping his partner sort through the belongings.

It only took a few more minutes and they were done. They received a token to claim the items and went on their way. "Alright, I need to go to the bank and sort out the land. Can you look around for the people we need to hire and find a place for us to sleep?" Kas said after they had walked a few feet.

"I can do this, yes. We are looking for a dowser and a logger or carpenter, yes?"

Kas nodded his head. "Preferably a miner too, and preference goes to people who will stick around for a while over temp workers."

Shura's face contorted in an approximation of an eyebrow raise. "Temp workers?"

"Temporary workers, people who are just there for a few days or weeks. I'd like to only hire those on for something like harvest season," Kas answered and Shura nodded her head in understanding.

"Very well, should we meet at dusk at the park we first talked at?"

"That'll work, I'll see you in a few hours."

The two split up, Shura heading deeper into Midtown while Kas made his way to the entrance of the fort. This late in the day, there wasn't a line, and he was let in after a cursory check by one of the guards. He made his way to the bank across the mostly empty training grounds, and went down the steps into the depths of the building. The same clerk he had talked to before was standing behind an empty desk so he made his way over to her.

"Hello, Lora," Kas said as he pulled out the coins from his pouch. "I'd like to make a deposit and withdraw items."

The blonde elf smiled politely as she bowed, "Of course, Mr. Kastigan. I'd be happy to help you."

First, Kas took out five gold from his pouch and then slid the rest over the counter to the elfess who counted the coins. "Depositing fifty-four gold and seven silver then?" She slid the coins over to the side where they slid down a metal shoot, making clanging noises as they made their way to whatever storage area the bank used for its coins. "What were you looking to withdraw?"

"All three of the tokens I have stored, please."

Lora nodded her head and motioned to one of the elves standing behind her to go and fetch the items. "Kena will bring you the items in just a few minutes. Unless you have any other business with us, I can provide a lounge for you to sit in while you wait?"

Considering the cost of the other account types, he didn't have anywhere near the required currency to open up a standard account yet. There was also the fact that he was going to have to withdraw some money in the near future to pay his rent, so it was better to keep his account at the lowest required minimum. "No, I'll just wait for Kena."

"Very well, and thank you for using Reddy Financial," Lora said with another slight bow. She stepped away from her desk and led him to a small lounge just off the main floor. There wasn't anyone else in the room, but the chairs did seem comfortable. With a bow, Lora bid him a good day and left, presumably returning to her desk.

The seats here were very nice; he'd forgotten how much he missed having something like a padded chair while he was out camping. He had been using rocks and logs for the past few days and his legs and rear-end made known their displeasure at not having a proper chair until now.

Kena didn't keep him waiting long. The elf was almost an exact replica of Lora; her long blonde hair and slender body would easily have earned her a modeling gig in the real world. She verified his name and then handed him an envelope similar to the one Lora had placed his tokens in when he deposited them.

Thanking the quinthan who promptly left the room, Kas opened the envelope and sighed with relief that the tokens were still there. Slipping them into his inventory, he took his leave of the bank, heading for Lt. Karissa's office and the last step before he owned Miranda Valley.

CHAPTER ELEVEN

Miranda Valley 1

The main building was likewise mostly deserted, the few guards posted at the entrance notwithstanding. He made his way to the map room where he had seen Lt. Karissa on his previous visit to the fort with a spring in his step. The door was open, but the scribes that had been marking the map last time were gone. Lt. Karissa sat at her desk working on some paperwork when Kas knocked on the door frame.

"Pardon me, lieutenant."

Karissa looked up and gestured for him to come in, a finger held up telling him to wait while she finished the line she had been writing. When that was done, she sprinkled some sand on the ink and looked up at him. "Ahh, the reaper has returned."

Kas blushed a little. "Ahh, the mages have been talking to you, I take it."

Karissa laughed. "They couldn't stop talking about the infamous reaper that had arrived looking for spells. Although, it did take me a few minutes to match you up. I thought for a bit we'd gotten two cycle mages here; they were convinced you were going to storm the mountain with an armada of bramblewights."

Kas shook his head. "People don't seem to understand I'm not interested in the combat side of things. I'm just here to make a living farming. Speaking of, I went to the valley you told me about and I'd like to buy it."

Karissa smiled. "Excellent, I've been told it's a charming little hanging valley. How much of it were you hoping to buy?" As she said this, she pulled out a map. A three-dimensional display appeared over it, with controls that would allow Kas to select sections of it for purchase, as well as how much it would cost him to complete the transaction.

Selecting the entire valley only cost him 10,736 gold. An astronomical amount for most people, but more than 4000 less than his three land tokens allowed him to purchase. Selecting a larger range to either side quickly increased the cost of the land. He sat and fiddled with the controls for a few minutes, eventually selecting a large section of the undiscovered mountain range beyond Miranda Valley. Because it was unexplored, the land was excessively cheap and the last 4264 gold almost tripled the amount of land he could purchase.

Granted, most of that was probably worthless mountain slopes, but it also gave him the mineral and hunting rights to anything found on it. Kas figured that the odds of there being something worth the cost were pretty good, and he felt a little like he was getting the better end of Seward's Folly. The Secretary of State William H. Seward purchased all of Alaska for just over seven million dollars from Russia, the rich natural resources of the land more than making up for what most of his contemporaries thought to be a bad deal.

There was the small problem that most of that land was also probably contested by the mysterious dweller tribes of the mountains. Kas figured they would eventually be driven out, even if it was more of a long-term investment. Selecting the land and clicking the finished button caused the projected map to disappear and Karissa slid it back towards her so that she could get a better look at it.

She whistled softly to herself as she looked over the claim. "Well, you don't dream small. That will be 14,997 gold."

Pulling the three land claim tokens out of his inventory, he handed them over to the lieutenant. Karissa gave each token several moments of intense scrutiny before casting a spell. In a flash of light, the tokens disappeared and the ding of system notifications filled his ears.

Congratulations on your land purchase! Would you like to name any of the explored regions?

Selecting yes, and highlighting the valley, he labeled it Miranda Valley and then confirmed his decision. The rest of his land was unexplored so he couldn't name any of it, not that he knew what he would call it anyway.

"Congratulations, Kastigan, you are now the sole landowner of Miranda Valley. I'll have the scribes update the public maps tomorrow, but your claim is good, effective immediately. Glad it went to someone who is going to appreciate it. Also, I like the name, Miranda suits the place."

Kastigan basked in the lieutenant's approval for a few minutes, only stopping when he realized that it was a piece of computer code that was complimenting him. Karissa was probably programmed to compliment any name choice the player made.

Glancing at the big map taking up most of the wall, he saw a blinking red icon. "Oh, we also made a bridge across the river here. It's not much, just a felled tree with most of the branches cut off. But it's a lot safer than any other crossing we could find."

Karissa nodded her head and made a note of it in her ledger then fished out a few silver coins from her belt pouch. "Here is your reward. We have a standing bounty on passes, bridges, and fords. And, of course, any dungeons you might find."

"Oh, excellent," Kas said, glancing over the map, looking

for any icons that would indicate a dungeon. "I take it no one has found any dungeons yet?"

"No, I expect someone will be returning shortly once the next few groups come back from their excursions towards the rim. There is a large collection of undead, and I expect there will be a dungeon at the heart of it. No one has told me if they've found the entrance though."

Kas was reminded that Himmler's group was going in that direction looking for a lot of undead, however looking at the map it looked like the area was in the upper level 30 range. "Looks like a dangerous place. I'll have to avoid it."

Karissa laughed. "Well, at least you have some sense in you. Unlike most of the unbound that come in here. They're all looking for the most dangerous place they can find. Going on about getting first titles and badges." Shaking her head in reproach, she added, "Well, I should get back to my work. Congratulations again." With that, the lieutenant headed back into her office and the paperwork he had interrupted.

Taking his leave of the assayer, Kas headed out of the main building, wanting to get out of the fort before he had another uncomfortable encounter with Holster. His luck held and he was soon exiting the gates.

Glancing around, he saw that the door to the Church of the Seven was open and he figured he would go see if the old man he had talked to before was there. He was curious if he could acquire any more free spells from the man, but also interested in hearing more of his conversation about the gods of Livia.

Peeking in through the door, he saw that a dozen people were seated around the chapel, almost all of them unbound players. It looked like they were undergoing some sort of initiation rite to join the priesthood.

Not wanting to interrupt them, Kas turned and headed into Midtown. His first task was to find Jack and Aggie's shop and see if he could pick up a skill book for tanning and drop off several of the crystals he owed for the quest he had gotten from the eccentric old leatherworker.

Ten minutes of wandering through the shops revealed nothing familiar, so he had to stop and ask for directions. The first person he asked gave such an incoherent response that he had to ask three more people, each giving him slightly more accurate information until just before sunset he found the shop. He made a mental note to navigate from the windrunner landing platform which was the tallest structure in the area. The back section of Jack's shop was already closed up and the door was locked when he tried it.

Knocking a few times brought Aggie's face to the small window. When she saw who it was, she happily opened the door. "Kastigan, welcome, welcome. Come on in, dear." She pulled him in, then looked around suspiciously. "Sorry, dear, it's not safe around the town so close to dark." She had a wicked-looking dagger in one hand but sheathed it as she ushered him deeper into the shop.

The smell of leather was still thick in the air, but that was the extent of the familiar items for him. The main section of the shop, all the displayed pieces, had been rolled up and their living accommodations had been put out. Several of the boxes and counters were cleverly designed to fold out and hid a bed, washing basin, and other household devices. There was a pot cooking over the fire Jack had used to heat his leather; the leather-working supplies moved aside to make room. Jack himself still sat near it, a lantern illuminating a pair of leather greaves he was stitching up.

"What brings you by so late?" Aggie asked in what Kas assumed was the same tone of voice that every grandmother used to scold her grandchildren for doing something foolish.

"Sorry, we just got back into town, and are leaving at first light tomorrow," Kas said, pulling out the crystals he owed Jack. "I was hoping I could deliver some of the crystals I owe you, as well as pick up a few skill books that I am beginning to realize I am lacking."

"Well, I'd be happy to take those off your hands. Jack will probably be using them in the near future, anyway." Pulling out a leather satchel, Aggie carefully took the crystals from Kas, and then put each crystal into a specially crafted pocket, securing them individually with a clasp. When the four crystals had been put away, Kas got a notification with an updated quest text, but it had no new information other than updated amounts owed. "As for the books, what were you looking for?"

"Well, specifically, I was looking for a tanning skill. We have found a good number of pelts, but I don't know how to turn them into usable leather," Kas answered while Aggie walked over to a portion of the room and began pulling out a few books.

"Well, tanning itself is actually spread out among a number of different subskills in the animal processing category. There is the base sub-skill tanning, and then of course under that is soaking, scudding, treating, stretching, and smoking," Aggie answered with a matronly smile. "Most people find it's easier to just bring their goods to a tanner, not to mention easier on the nose. A lot of the substances you'll be needing do not smell pleasant."

Kas considered Aggie's words while looking at his skills sheet. With a minor affinity in animal processing, he would get a relatively large return for the effort. More importantly, it was something that he could do to add value to their efforts. Anything that added to the bottom line meant he was that much closer to being able to play Livia full time rather than scraping together a few hours after work when he was already dead tired. Judging by how long everything had taken him to do in the game, that meant he'd have to be even more self-sufficient. Twelve hours of traveling to Tallrock and back from Miranda would be several days' worth of effort.

That was probably one of the reasons that Miranda hadn't been claimed already, now that he thought about it. The travel time would become insignificant once more players got mounts and the infrastructure was developed, but right now? Who would want to spend a day traveling somewhere when there were plenty of quests and opportunities to level near the fort?

That also meant that if he wanted to attract players to Miranda, he was going to have to figure out things for them to do near the valley and create some decent infrastructure around the area, roads or some sort of flying animal service.

That was all for later, though. For now, he needed to decide if he wanted to tan his own hides or pay someone to do it on those few trips back to town he made. "Well, I plan to settle a good distance from Tallrock. I just purchased some land a few miles on the spinward side. So I'll need at least tanning."

Aggie had already set aside three books for him. "Congratulations on purchasing some land. That's the first step towards starting up a farm of your own. Sadly, we only have tanning, scudding, and treating, as far as skill books are concerned. The others you'll have to go find a tanner to learn." Aggie handed the books over to Kas and then looked him up and down. "That armor hasn't seen much use yet, were the forests not dangerous?"

Kas blinked. Now that he thought about it, the lack of animals and monsters to fight in the wilderness was somewhat strange. In most games, there would have been huge collections of low-level wolves or rabbits or something to kill. Something for everyone to use to grind up levels, but he hadn't seen anything like that. Not that he imagined wolves in Livia to be 'easy' monsters. Actually, come to think of it, he couldn't imagine what was an appropriately difficult encounter in Livia.

Shura's breath had been enough to kill five low-level players. The smart players would be spending their time with trainers, getting as many skills as they could before they went out into the wilderness. Players in groups like Himmler's Posse could probably easily take down smaller predators, but anything more dangerous than a single bear would probably kill them. No wonder he had been asking for help on the forums; if he had actually run into a level 30 field dungeon, the players were woefully underprepared to conquer it.

"We've either been very lucky or my companion is much better at deterring difficult fights than I realized." Shura had been guiding them although they had been following the river. The massive drak was probably considered an apex predator in the area. Remembering the trike, he couldn't help but think that there must be something that fed on the massive beasts. Still, the drak would probably deter all but the super predators of the forest.

"Companion?" Aggie looked towards the door and frowned, clearly thinking she had left Kas' friend out in the gloaming air.

"Yes, I was supposed to meet her soon at the park near the airship."

"You left a woman out alone in the town near dark?" Aggie's frown showed her dislike of that.

"Well, she's a drak gladiator, I assumed she would be fine."

Aggie frowned even more. "A drak? What are you doing dealing with the dragonscum?"

The vitriol in the kindly old woman's voice reminded Kas that drak were not well-liked in the Kingdom. "She's been helping me out. She's much better suited to the wilderness than I am. I'd be afraid to travel without her."

A snort answered his response, the old woman clearly not thinking much of the company of a drak. "Their kind killed a lot of good men," she said before turning back to Jack. "Jack, do you need anything from Kastigan before I send him on his way?"

Jack looked up for a moment, taking in the scene with his irritated wife and Kas, and then shook his head. "No, dear." He turned back to his work.

Ushering Kas out shortly with his books, he heard the multiple locks on the door as it was closed behind him. Shaking his head, he wondered why Aggie would have such an intense dislike for the drak. She was old enough that he supposed she might have had some loved ones killed during the War of Dragons. Maybe that was why she still remembered it when the drak were the embodiment of their enemy. It had been so long since there had been an outright war on Earth that he had no real reference point to what going through one did to a person.

Leaving the intricacies of post-war xenophobia behind him, Kas made his way quickly through the darkened streets. As he walked, he got the unnerving sensation that he was being followed. Making his way to the park he looked around, but Shura's large form was nowhere to be seen.

Already the sun had passed beyond the core of the world, disappearing in a brilliant flash of light that illuminated the clouds in poignant displays of cerulean and crimson. The last vestiges of light lingering blood red on the mountains as the alpenglow flared to life, a stark demarcation between the gray and red. It seemed an ominous sign, the color of the mountains portending violence.

With a suddenness that startled him, the alpenglow faded and the entire world was shrouded in darkness. Looking around, he saw the large form of a drak approaching through the park. Glad to have the comforting safety of Shura after the strange chill the sunset had placed upon him, he called out to her, "Shura, over here."

The form turned, making its way towards his voice. He considered pulling out a mana crystal to light the path a little but didn't want to flash so much wealth in Midtown's now-ominous night. When the form got close enough, Kas realized his mistake. While large, the drak before him was not big enough to be Shura. Turning to flee, a taloned hand snagged his back and lifted him up. With a shout of alarm, he twisted so that he could see the unfamiliar drak.

In the darkness, all he could see were straight horns, denoting a male drak. The scales were lighter than Shura's, white maybe? It was difficult to tell.

The head cocked to the side, the frill shifting in a way that Kas had begun to recognize as curiosity when Shura did it. "Hmm, strange you almost seemed to trust me." The voice was deep, masculine and rumbling. The hand easily shifted, pulling Kas closer to the drak's face.

Briefly considering if he should try to kick the man and escape, he decided against it. The man was clearly far more advanced in his physical statistics than Kas, and he could probably easily catch up to him. "I thought you were a friend." The white scales of the drak made it easier than it should have been to see in the gloom. The grip was uncomfortable, his armor digging into his legs and shoulders, especially where he could feel the sharp talons of the drak pushing into the meat of his back.

"So I gathered. This Shura of yours, is she blue?"

Kas' mind spun. Was this some sort of drak turf war? Did Shura have enemies that she hadn't told him about? What did it mean that this one was so much lighter in coloration than Shura? Knowing how much most humans hated the drak, he decided to bank on the fact that he was friends with one to keep himself out of danger. "Yes, she's blue."

The drak snorted, and then set him down, waiting a few seconds after his feet touched the ground to ensure that Kas had regained his feet. "Well, in that case, you will take me to her."

"There is no need to scare the human, Forthan, I'm right here." Shura's voice came from behind them, but the drak's form blocked his sight of his blue-scaled friend.

The white drak let loose a noise that was half growl and half speech. Kas could tell that it meant something to Shura because she responded in kind. Kas slowly backed away from the two, unsure what exactly was going on here. They continued to growl back and forth and Kas circled around until he could clearly see Shura's form against the darkened backdrop of the mountains.

Behind them, Kas heard the sound of voices and turning he saw two legionaries with torches approaching. Expecting them to act to defend the peace, he was instead confused when the two heard the growling, stopped, and then turned around, walking with haste away from the park.

The heavy sound of flesh thumping against flesh drew Kas' attention back to the drak behind him. The growls had apparently escalated to open violence; he heard them crash against the ground, the growling having turned more visceral, losing whatever semblance to speech it once held. It was nearly impossible to tell what was going on as the two fought. Kas was reasonably confident in Shura's ability to win; she was much larger and had shown nothing but competence in combat thus far, but the unknown drak had been every bit as imposing as Shura was.

For long seconds, he heard the two growl and rip at each other, the occasional scrape of claws on wood or snaps as they broke limbs off the bushes. The longer it went on the surer Kas was that this wasn't a malicious attack. It sounded terrifying, but if they were using their full strength one of the two would have been killed by now. So what exactly was going on?

With a final thump, the growling cut off. He heard the sound of flesh on flesh again as the winner ensured their victory. It was impossible to tell in the tenebrous light of Midtown. But the remaining drak stood tall then turned towards Kas, a growl emanating from deep within their chest.

"Kastigan, I will need your help getting this fool somewhere safe." Shura's voice released the tension that had been building up within Kas since the fight had started.

"What was that?" Kas moved closer to Shura, taking careful steps to avoid tripping.

"I will explain later. We need to relocate before the guards return and imprison both of us for disturbing the peace." Kas was amazed that Shura had been able to notice the guard's swift retreat despite her imminent fight. When he finally got to the still form of Forthan, he wondered idly what exactly Shura was hoping he would be able to do. There was no way he would be able to lift more than an arm of the much larger drak. With a grunt, she picked him up in a fireman carry.

Shura gestured him forward. "Come, we must leave. Use some of the mana crystals to light the way."

Fishing several from his inventory, he held them out to light the ground; the visible signs of the fight were obvious. Broken branches, torn grass, and a dark liquid that Kas assumed was blood marking a fifteen-foot radius around where they had scuffled. "Where are we going?" he asked; there weren't exactly a lot of places to hide on the mesa.

"The chapel. I don't think the church will turn away the injured, we just need to ensure that we bypass the legion."

With a nod, Kas speed walked forward, his light crystals doing little to illuminate the path, but the large drak seemed to scare away anyone attracted to the light. Midtown itself was completely dark, every window shuttered tight.

Ten minutes later, they had circumnavigated the shops and arrived at the back of the chapel. A side door was barely visible in the darkness and Kas knocked on it urgently. The cast stone building echoed his knocking ominously, and he could see light from the front of the chapel; the stained-glass windows were illuminated from within.

The fort had numerous guards patrolling, their torches creating small bubbles of light. With a creak the door opened. The old man Kas had talked to before poked his head out.

CHAPTER TWELVE

Miranda Valley 2

The priest peered at the group, taking note of Kas, then Shura and her burden. "The worship of Delac does not usually require a midnight sacrifice, young sir," he said, turning to look at Kastigan. "That said, you should probably come in and explain before the gendarmes arrive." Kas blinked at the use of the French term. Was there a place in Middar where French was the native language?

For the most part, Earth no longer had regional languages; everyone pretty much spoke English, at least in public. Although the French had managed to hold onto their old habits longer than most. The only reason Kas even knew any French words was because of an ancient play called Les Misérables that was still popular.

The priest led them through some of the inner rooms of the chapel, all of them adorned in what would only be considered excess comfort here on the frontier. They finally stopped at a moderately-sized room with two beds in it. The addition of Shura and the white drak made the room seem much smaller.

Not trusting the bed to be able to hold the drak's weight, Shura set him down on the floor in the middle of the room.

Kas sat on one of the beds while the priest attended to the injured drak. Shura took a spot on the floor between them, lifting the sense of unease that her imposing bulk cast upon the room.

Finishing his examinations, the priest sat on the bed opposite Kastigan, then looked at the two still conscious intruders. "So, who wants to tell me what exactly happened here?"

Not knowing what exactly had caused the white drak to attack, Kas turned to Shura and raised an eyebrow. "I'm curious to know that as well."

Shura's body language seemed to indicate embarrassment, but she looked at the priest. "I am Shura Blueblessed. This one is Forthan Whitekin," she said, poking Forthan's leg with a talon. "He challenged me to a sh'kar and lost."

The priest laughed at that. "I see that he did indeed." The tension left the man's body and he relaxed at this revelation. "You showed admirable restraint in his injuries. He'll have nothing more serious than he would have received from a heavy night of drinking." The emphasis was clearly on heavy in this instance.

"I'm sorry, what is sh'kar?" Kas tried to say the Dragorian word but he could tell he had botched the pronunciation heavily.

Both his companions turned to look at Kas and the priest actually started to laugh. "Of course, I forget that you are unbound, Kastigan. Shura, perhaps you should tell your friend about the sh'kar."

The tips of Shura's frill were pressed close to her head, a sure sign of embarrassment. "Kastigan, you know that the drak come from the Dragon Tribesmen. The sh'kar is how the tribesmen acquire a mate. The weaker of the two will challenge the stronger. If they fight well, the stronger will accept the lesser as their mate."

Kas blinked, looking at Shura. "You're telling me that was all some sort of mating ritual?" Shura nodded her head meekly, the frill on her head still pressed tight against her skull.

"Well, you won, right? What happens to Whitekin here?" Kas asked, gesturing towards the unconscious drak.

"By convention, he becomes my sukar for ten months and a day." Shura kept her head down as she explained this.

"And what exactly is a sukar?" Kas couldn't help thinking the name sounded suspiciously like sucker.

"In Pinnoc's tongue the closest translation would be, he is my slave or servant. The problem is that to act as such you will have to accept him, as I will be on your land."

"I don't really like the idea of a slave," Kas said. The idea that this drak could insert himself into his life with so little warning simply because he wanted to mate with Shura was incredibly disturbing to him. Not to mention the idea of keeping a slave was anathema to everything he had grown up believing. Turning to the priest, Kas lifted his hands in frustration. "There has to be some sort of religious law against owning a slave."

"Arthen does not look kindly upon those who force others into slavery of their own will. But Forthan knew the price of failure when he challenged Shura. As such, the morality of sh'kar has been upheld by the Lord Justicar himself," the old man responded.

Well, there went his divine get out of jail free. Glancing at Shura, Kas realized that maybe she was looking for an out as well. "Do you want him as a sukar?" he asked the blue-scaled drak.

"I…" Shura paused, considering her response. "Do not know. It would be nice to have another drak around; there are few of us, even back in Dragoria. We could certainly use the assistance he would provide us. We would not need to pay him, only provide his food and shelter."

From a purely financial aspect, they couldn't get much better than a free drak servant. While smaller than Shura, he was still huge, and having two combatants around would certainly deter any bandits like the five they met in the forest earlier that day.

Kas nodded his head. "Whatever you want, Shura. If you'd like him to join us, I'll happily provide him the shelter. You'll probably have to do the food, though."

Shura's frill trilled in the drak approximation of laughter. "Yes, we shall take him in then."

"Excellent. Now that is all settled, I have a few questions," the old man spoke up. "First of all, I'm going to introduce myself. I'm Toris, the senior cleric of the Seven in the Tallrock chapel, and devotee of Arthen. You are both sitting in one of the cells we prepared for traveling clergy." Taking the cue, Shura introduced herself as well.

"Well, now that we are all friends, let's discuss how much my assistance is going to cost you," Toris said, looking very stern. Kas' heart sunk a little—in most games healing cost money, and he was pretty sure so did an overnight room. After his previous encounter with the priest, he was hoping he would just give it to them for free.

"Today's price will be a truth. Kastigan, last time we spoke we talked of the twins, Caled and Delac, and their domains of life and death. There was something you thought of, some death in your life that you did not want to speak of. The cost of my assistance is the story of that memory."

Blinking in surprise, Kas would rather pay in coin, but he got the sense that Toris would not accept anything shy of his stated price.

"Are you sure that's what you want?"

"I am," Toris said with a quick nod.

"I can leave…" Shura said, picking up on the Kas' mood.

"No, this is not for me to hear, but for her. Stay here tonight, your sukar will be fine in the morning," Toris said, and Kas could swear the old man chuckled as he pronounced the word. As Kas silently vowed never to call Forthan anything but his name, Toris quietly left the cell and closed the door behind him.

Taking the time to steady his thoughts, he studied the white-scaled drak. He was attired similarly to Shura, in more of a harness than any actual clothing. The white scales almost had an opalescent appearance and were quite beautiful as they captured the flickering flame of the candle. There was some marring on the scales near the hands and along the arms, evidence of past injuries. Continuing to scan the drak until he had gathered his thoughts, he turned back to Shura.

He realized that there was a part of him that wanted to talk about it, maybe that needed to talk about it. The therapist had said he would get to that point eventually.

"If you would rather keep your secret, we can find somewhere else for the night."

"No, it's fine, Shura. It's not... a secret. Just something that I don't talk about. Where I'm from, that is, where I go to when I disappear from here, I have... had a family," Kas said. Not wanting to look at Shura, he instead looked over at the candle, watching the flame flickering.

"Healing is very different there, in some ways better, in some ways worse than here on Livia. It was difficult for my wife and me to get pregnant. We went to a lot of specialists, spent a lot of money and time trying to have a baby. And then, finally, it worked." A bitter smile played across Kas' face.

"She was pregnant and everything was right in the world." The smile slowly faded. "Until it wasn't. We went in for a checkup and they found out that something was wrong. She didn't have enough amniotic fluid in the womb. They ran more tests, and we were told he had Potter's Syndrome; his liver hadn't developed properly. It is one of the few things they can't fix, and they deemed that he would be born unsuitable for life. My wife decided to carry him to term."

"He was so perfect. I mean, he was squishy and red. And so, so tiny, but perfect." Kas rubbed his eyes, staring into the flickering flame. "He never opened his eyes. I'll never know what color they would have been." His voice cracked as he remembered. He stopped talking then, letting the tears stream down his face.

"What was his name?" Shura asked, her voice so soft he could barely hear it.

"Elam, we named him Elam. It means eternity in an old language back home."

Shura nodded her head, whispering the name. "It is a good name, a strong name. I am not sure what the Seven believe, but among my people when a child is taken, we say it is because he was taken by the Dragons back to their home. That he had too much of fire and lightning in him, and could only be raised there among the ancestors. It is these children who become the new ancestors, there to protect our people when we are in our darkest hours."

Kas nodded his head but internally he wanted to scream. He didn't want his son to fight, he didn't want Elam to have to suffer like that. He just wanted him here, with him. Picking up the pillow, he clutched it tight to his chest. He felt Shura put a hand on his back, with a thought he told the system to log him out.

———

Matt came to on the couch, his eyes felt tired, and when he touched them he could feel the salt deposits that had built up while he played. Rubbing them away, he sat up then leaned into his knees. He hadn't said Elam's name in months; it was one of the things Lexie hated the most. That he refused to talk about him, when that was all she had wanted to talk about. Feeling his ragged breathing start to settle down he stood up, taking a few minutes to take care of his physical form.

The movements were mechanical, he was going through the motions. There was a portion of him that wanted nothing more than to never think or talk about Elam ever again, and another that wanted to hold onto that memory, afraid that someday he wouldn't be able to remember him anymore. When he was done, he sat back down, staring into nothing. The comm buzzed and he looked down at it; his lawyer was calling. Had been calling regularly judging by the number of missed calls.

With a sigh, he accepted it in voice-only mode. "Hey, Jerry."

"Matt! You actually answered. It's a miracle." Jerry had been his lawyer for a long time, he probably wasn't super qualified to be a divorce attorney but Matt didn't care.

"I'm really tired, Jerry, been putting in a lot of hours on a new project."

"A new project? You need me to start getting a run-up for it?"

"Not yet," Matt lied; he hadn't done any work at his old job since Elam.

"Sure, look, I just wanted to tell you that Lex… your wife's lawyer and I have hammered everything out. It's a pretty good deal, everything you wanted."

Matt couldn't help but let out an ugly snort. He hadn't wanted anything. Which meant Lexie was keeping everything— he had no idea how she could live in that house still, not with Elam's room sitting ready.

"There is one small problem though." Matt winced, wondering what condition Lexie had attached to the divorce. "She said she would only do it if you had one final dinner at the house."

Matt didn't say anything. How could he? He couldn't go back into that house, not with all the memories there.

"Matt, you still there?"

"Yeah, I'm here. I can't do it for a few weeks, I can't get away from this project for that long."

"When are you going to tell me what this new project is? You know I'd be happy to handle all the paperwork. I haven't seen you do real work since…" The voice trailed off; he had learned to avoid talking about the incident.

"Look, I'll tell her, she'll be happy that you're working again. I'm sure it'll be fine. Just let me know when you're free and I'll get everything set up."

"Thanks, Jerry."

"Hey, is this going to be the best time to get a hold of you? You know I called about a thousand times the last few days."

"Just, send me an email, I'll get back to you as soon as I can."

"Hah, no chance of that happening. We've been friends for long enough for me to know how terrible you are at that stuff."

"Right. Uhm, yeah, I'll try to surface around this time, maybe a bit later usually."

"Alright. Hey look, we should go out, get some drinks."

"Can't, sorry, Jerry. I'm beat, I'll talk to you later. Thanks for calling."

"Anytime, buddy. Get some sleep."

"Will do. Night, Jerry."

"Night, Matt."

Ending the conversation with an unnecessary hand gesture, Matt sighed, his thoughts in too much turmoil to sleep now. He opened the Livia forums. The general forum had a few dozen threads talking about bonded companions. Remembering that the bandits had called Shura his bonded companion, he pulled up the highest ranked one.

Apparently crafting professions had a chance to get a bonded companion. This was someone that was there to help you level up, most of the time they would help teach you your craft and became a mentor in your skills. Realizing this was exactly what he would have gotten if he had picked the mentor starting package, he shook his head, wondering if the game considered him a crafter or not. His skills were technically capable of making him very combat capable. Sure, he had a couple of support skills, but for the most part, it was pretty well set if he ever wanted to actually get into combat.

Shura also seemed significantly more powerful than most of the bonded companions that he was seeing people post. Maybe that was due to his talking to Livia and selecting to live on the frontier? He wouldn't have needed a very powerful companion if he had started up a farm in the middle of Pinnoc. It was good to know that Shura was designed to supplement his weaknesses. He thought back to how they had met, how she had seen him taking compassion on a dragon tribesman and then wanted to help him deal with the unexpected death.

There were probably a lot of potential companions around the starting zone, and he just managed to connect with Shura first. Just luck then; for the first time in over a year luck had been on his side.

Needing something to calm down his troubled mind, he sorted through the forums, hitting up the agricultural and Tallrock ones as well as some of the more general ones. After almost an hour, he was tired enough that he could sleep and he closed his eyes, clutching the spare pillow tightly.

Tonight he didn't want to feel alone anymore.

When he woke up the next morning he didn't even bother to get up, just gave the mental command to log back into Livia, ready to apologize to Shura.

DAY 5

Appearing in the dark, he created a mana crystal and by its meager light, he managed to make out the cell that Toris had left them in. Shura was asleep on the floor near the door, her pack acting as a pillow and Forthan still lay where he had been deposited the night before. There honestly wasn't a lot of space left in the room with two unconscious drak on the floor. He would have to wake Shura up in order to leave the room, but he took a moment to review his skills and layer a crystal.

There had been good progress in everything that he had been working on, gaining points in every stat from the forced march yesterday and the continuous casting of spells. The associated skills had also gone up; he was still shy of where he needed to be in order to learn the new spell, but he was getting there slowly. He figured it would only take a day or two more at the current rate. He hadn't passed any major milestones yet; he wasn't even sure if there were major milestones aside from getting the next tier up.

Having delayed as long as he could, he began the process of

extracting himself from the bed and stepping over the sleeping drak. There was just enough room for him to slip past Shura and open the door. The hallway was much better lit, and he easily found his way to the sanctuary where he had met Toris on his first day. A number of lights set up around the room caused the glass windows to be appropriately lit despite the early hour.

Taking the time to really examine the room, he looked again at the images of the gods. With a frown, he realized that while it was called the Seven, he only saw five panels with six gods. Caled and Delac shared a panel, then Talin the teacher on the spinward side, Primus towards the core, Arthen the judge and Yesha the smith on the trailing side. He realized where the seventh one was as soon as he approached the central area near Primus. On the floor, in brilliant mosaic rather than stained glass, was a seventh god.

The UI informed him that this one was called Tempis, and while all the others had been created in different colors of illuminated glass, the stones that made up Tempis' section of the chapel seemed to absorb light. Amazed at the artistry that portrayed a god in nothing but shades of gray and black, he stared at the stones seeing the scenes of destruction and darkness. There seemed to be a fitting symmetry to the building, each god opposite another.

Across from Talin the teacher was the Arthen the judge. A designation that only by obtaining knowledge can we be held accountable for our actions. Across from Caled and Delac, the twins of death and life, was Yesha the shaper. Living beings were required to create; they needed to shape the world around them to live. Primus and Tempis were no different. Primus the creator, and Tempis the destroyer, just a different version of Caled and Delac, more concerned with the world and all things that were in it.

Marveling at the depth of meaning behind something so simple, Kas wondered about how Livia was actually created. It had been too large for a human to handcraft every area. Even if they only stuck to those sections of the map they were allowing new characters to create in, there was just too much space. They had instead created concepts and generated the world. They had probably modified individual portions of the world, but the sheer mass of Livia meant that it was entirely likely that there would be players who were literally the first human to see something.

It was almost enough to make him want to be an explorer. There wasn't much chance to see something for the first time in the world. Humans had long since tamed Earth, turning it into an industrial megacity, and every other planet in the solar system had long since been fully mapped. The generation ships were too slow for him to see anything new in his lifetime even with longevity treatments. That was assuming he could even secure a spot on one. In short, there wasn't anywhere that he would be first.

Was that what had motivated Magellan, Armstrong, and Cortez? The thrill of being the first person to ever see something? It was an intoxicating thought, something he would need to try to do later after Miranda was self-sustaining.

Shaking his head, he turned away from the mosaic of Tempis only to discover that sometime during his introspection Toris had appeared behind him. The old man stood far enough behind him that when he turned and saw him, his presence didn't startle Kas.

"Good morning, Kastigan," the old priest said with a smile. "If you keep showing up in the sanctuary like this, I'm going to start to think you're dedicating yourself as a priest."

"Morning, Toris." Kas said with a polite smile. "Sorry, I just came to admire the artistry."

"Ahh yes, that's what you said last time too, if I recall." Toris smiled again and gestured for Kas to sit. "Please, take a seat while we wait for your companions to rise."

Kas nodded his head and took the seat indicated.

"I would like to hear your thoughts on the gods. It is always very enlightening to hear what others discover."

Kas took a moment to consider the priest. He had already

gotten him talking about Elam, something he would never have imagined he would do when he first logged into Livia. Not that he was surprised. The first AI to pass the Turing test had been created long before he was born. In the current day and age, mature AIs ran most of the world. The AI behind Toris was probably a better therapist than any human could hope to be. It made sense to have the clerical AIs be able to take that role, as there were bound to be people who needed the assistance when you had such a realistic world.

"I was considering the duality of the Seven. The way you have them displayed here, it's like they are each just natural responses to each other. Knowledge and judgment, life and death paired with creating things, creation and destruction."

"Ahh, yes, there are some that believe that the Seven are merely representations of a single unifying theory. You see in all three of the opposites, there is a recurring theme. I like to call it the wheel. Death, destruction, and judgment become life, creation, and learning. It is the wheel that pushes progress forward. It is a simple abstract, but without it where would any of us be? There isn't a civilization on Livia that would exist without the wheel.

"It is the basis of every culture and people. To progress past a certain point, you must develop the wheel. The gods are a representation of that requirement, even they play their part in the wheel that turns all of creation forward. It is the duality of life and death, darkness and light, good and evil. One cannot exist without the other, and without that duality, there is no progress. It is not surprising that a cycle mage like yourself would focus on that aspect of the gods." Toris gave Kas a grandfatherly smile.

"You're more priest than you realize." When Kas opened his mouth to refute that statement, Toris raised a hand, "No, I understand that you don't want to be a priest. I think it is partly because you do not understand what a priest really does. Tell me, what do you think I do?"

Kas blinked, what did Toris do? "I guess… you tend to the chapel and talk to people that come in?"

With a soft chuckle, Toris nodded his head. "I do indeed do those things now. But I am an old man, and this is a task which suits my old bones. What do you think I did in my youth?"

Kas had never really thought about what Toris did when he was young. "I guess, just more of this?"

Toris shook his head. "No, in my youth I was a traveling Justicar. I used to ride a circuit in Penthal, dispensing justice. The life of a Justicar is a difficult one; you are judge, jury, and executioner, and while some people welcome the justice I dispensed, others reviled me for it. I spent most of my youth hunting down bandits and murderers, and burning their operations root and branch."

Kas blinked again, considering the old man in front of him as a one-man army riding through the mountains of Penthal. It was difficult to imagine, to say the least.

"Okay, so what do the priests of the twins do?"

"They reap and sow. They cull the weak and wicked and provide sustenance to the rest. They farm," Toris said with a grin. "One of my parishioners tells me you have purchased a plot of land and intend to farm it. You are a cycle mage. Everything you do will further the work of the twins; it is a part of you as much as their breath is a part of the drak, and coin is a part of every quinthan."

If Toris was going to say more, they were interrupted as Shura and Forthan arrived in the sanctuary. Forthan looked a little groggy still, but otherwise none the worse for wear after the fight the day before.

CHAPTER THIRTEEN

Miranda Valley 3

Forthan stood behind Shura, having already adopted a very subservient posture, which Kas thought looked very unnatural for a drak. Kas stood as the other two came into the sanctuary.

Toris waved them over but he didn't bother to stand up. "Sorry, my old bones aren't quite up to all the standing up and sitting down as courtesy demands."

Shura seemed to understand and she gave the priest a bow when she approached. "I would like to thank you for your assistance last night. Most humans do not... tolerate our culture as readily as you did."

"Of course, I spent most of my youth in Penthal. You learn a little bit about Dragorian customs there." Toris again gestured for the two to sit. "Please sit, we have some small matters to discuss before you set off for the morning."

Kas wasn't sure if Toris had planned it this way, but the thick stone benches of the sanctuary were the first furniture he had seen since he started playing that a drak could sit on without fear of breaking it. Once they were both seated, Toris turned to Forthan. "We have not been properly introduced. I am Father Toris. Shura told me that your name is Forthan?"

The white drak simply nodded his head in response to the query.

"Well, Forthan, could you please tell me the circumstances under which you came to Tallrock?"

Forthan had little of the confident air Kas had seen in the drak the night before. In the darkness, he had seemed to be some sort of ubermensch, now he reminded Kas of a kicked dog. Without looking up he responded to Toris' question. "I purchased a ticket."

Kas blinked. There weren't a lot of freemen in Tallrock, and from what he understood of the drak, there was little chance that a drak would have the resources to be able to immigrate without becoming a bondsman. Bondsmen were sort of like indentured servants from colonial America. They promised to work for someone for several years in exchange for passage to Gogland. Toris seemed to be as surprised Kas was, the old man raising an eyebrow at the unexpected revelation.

Shura took pity on the two humans and explained, "Forthan comes from one of the farthest rimward tribes. His family did not directly participate in the war, and their lands were largely unscathed by the conflict."

Kas could only imagine what sort of damage a dragon, or weapons designed to kill a dragon, would do to the land. Dragoria must have large swaths of desolate wasteland. If they did not join the war, that would have made him a Dragorian noble with all the lands and assets still at their disposal.

"I see, and what would induce a wealthy drak like yourself to immigrate to Gogland?" Toris asked.

Kas watched Forthan as he shot a furtive glance at Shura. He mumbled something under his breath.

"Sorry, my ears aren't quite what they used to be," Toris said, leaning forward.

"I came for Shura."

Glancing over at Shura who was looking away, he guessed that Shura already knew about his reasons. She had said she would be willing to accept him as a sukar, so she must not have hated the idea of spending time with him. But Kas couldn't help make a comparison to guys he knew that moved across the country to date women they met on the internet.

"My family owns the arena that she fought in. However, it would be improper to issue a call to sh'kar while she is an employee of the estate. I had intended to do so as soon as she ceased to compete. Those plans were derailed when she was exiled. I followed her here." Forthan shrugged.

Kas shook his head, the man obviously knew he was going to lose if he had seen Shura in a fight, but he had challenged her anyway; was he hoping to impress her? Or was there some aspect of 'letting her win' when it happened? He didn't know enough about drak society to understand the intricacies of the situation, he was sure there was some subtext that he was missing in all this.

Toris had nodded along with Forthan's words like he was expecting them. "Well, in that case, I will leave the three of you to your journey. Good luck, Kastigan, Shura. A pleasure to meet you Forthan," Toris stood up with some effort and began walking to the back of the chapel.

Kas looked between his two drak companions and then at the retreating back of the priest, standing up and shaking his head. "Alright, we should get going soon, I want to be out of town by ten." He glanced at Forthan. "I'm not sure we were ever properly introduced. I'm Kastigan, I'm a cycle mage, Shura and I bought a large tract of land about a day's journey from here in the foothills of the Spine."

Forthan looked from Shura to Kas, and then back again, "I am Forthan Whitekin. I am a weapons specialist, although not as skilled as Shura Blueblessed."

Kas nodded his head. "Always good to have more muscle; we live in a dangerous area." He turned to Shura. "We still need to go recruit a dowser and buy a skill book for de-branching, as well as a tracker." He paused, considering. "Unless you found some people last night?"

Shura shook her head. "I was unsuccessful in attempting to

recruit a dowser or a miner. I did find a woodsman with some experience with building, but he did not seem interested in relocating permanently. He agreed to meet us at the lift during the ninth hour."

"Well, that's not ideal, but I guess beggars can't be choosers," Kas said. Exiting the main entrance of the chapel, he held the door for Shura and Forthan who both looked at him confused for a moment before following him out.

"Thank you," Forthan said, bowing slightly to Kastigan.

Not entirely sure what he had done to deserve such profound thanks, and not really wanting to dig any deeper than he already had into drak culture, he let it drop. He considered where to go. Midtown was bound to have a number of people looking for work, but they weren't likely to want to resettle. With a glance at Forthan, he asked, "Do you have belongings you need to gather?"

"I do. I also have a dowser in my employ."

Shura and Kas both turned to Forthan. "Right, do you have a lot of people in your employ?" Kas asked curiously.

"No, not a lot. I have the aforementioned dowser, my squire, five bonded footmen, and two skilled bondspeople, one who is a chef and the second who is a weaponsmith." Forthan's manner of fact tone led Kas to believe that he didn't consider a retinue of ten to be very large at all.

Shura and Kas just looked at him in amazement. "How rich are you exactly?"

Forthan had the grace to look embarrassed by the question. "I'm afraid most of my wealth is tied up back in Dragoria. I had intended to purchase land on the mesa and set up another arena."

"I see." Kas looked over at Shura who just returned the glance with a shrug.

"Well, your people can come with us if you'd like? We could always use more hands out there, but it's mostly empty land at this point."

"I think it is best if they accompany us. I have no doubt that between Shura and a cycle mage, you could handle most things in the wilderness, but many hands make light work as they say. Besides, Colonel Holzer does not seem interested in allowing an arena to be built. If your valley is acceptable, perhaps I will build it there."

"Well, I guess I could sell you some land, we got a pretty good deal."

Shura spoke up now. "Excellent, how much of the valley were you able to purchase?" She seemed excited about the prospect.

"All of the valley, and about eighty square miles of the mountain above it. It was unexplored so it was cheap, and I figured there were bound to be some natural resources we could leverage."

Shura blinked at him. "You got all that for three land claim tokens?"

Forthan did not seem entirely pleased. "Is the land so poor that they were willing to sell it for so little?"

"No, I wouldn't say it's poor. Plus with my magic, the soil quality is sort of irrelevant; I'll be able to grow excellent crops there. And Shura should have plenty of land for her animals— we can use it to graze some of the herbivores, if nothing else. Plus the view is amazing."

Forthan did not seem convinced, but without the ability to change their minds he accepted it with a shrug.

"Any ideas on where we could find a miner?" Kas asked the white drak.

"I do not, but perhaps Costache, my weaponsmith, may have met some. We can always ask him." Forthan turned and began walking off towards the other end of Midtown.

With a glance at Shura, who only shrugged in response, the two followed the white drak.

"So, you had a rich guy in love with you, eh?" Kas teased Shura as they walked.

"He was always a little too sure of himself for my taste, but he means well, mostly."

"I guess what I don't get is why you didn't just marry him and use his money to help your people."

Shura glanced over at Kas for a moment and then sighed. "In Dragoria, I could not marry Forthan. My family's station was too high above his. Perhaps it is an old way of measuring things, but my parents would never consent to a marriage of convenience into such a dishonorable family."

Kas shook his head. "So wait, where do you and he fall in the drak social strata?"

"My parents have a rank equivalent to the human rank of a count. And he would be... a baronet," Shura answered after a few moments of thought.

Kas blinked and looked back at her. "Sorry, you're a countess?"

"No, it is not so simple. My mother is a High Speaker, and my father was a War Chief. These would be ranks similar to a cardinal and a general in human society. However, among most of the dragon tribes, there is no such thing as an inherited rank. I do not have my mother's gift to speak to the ancestors, and the king will not allow another war chief to rise among the clans. Perhaps if we had won the war, I might have been groomed to take my father's mantle. But when we lost the war..." Shura trailed off and then gave the drak equivalent of a shrug.

"So if you can't inherit, and your father wasn't allowed to teach you his skills, what does that make you exactly?"

"Nothing," Shura answered. "A failed gladiator."

"Then why couldn't you marry Forthan?"

"My people have lost much since the war, but there is one thing the king cannot take from us. He cannot take our honor. So while I am nothing, someday the king will fall, and then my family will regain our place. Honor forbids me from taking the hand of an unworthy mate. Until Forthan can make a better showing than he did last night, my honor will not allow it." Shura's voice had a fatalistic melancholy to it.

Kas tried to process the stubbornness that forced her to hold onto a familial honor that no longer actually meant anything. It was so foreign a concept compared to how he viewed the world; his family hadn't even met Lexie until just a few days before the wedding. He would never have even considered asking their opinion, let alone refused to marry her based on it.

Trying to picture that kind of familial connection was hard for him; he didn't feel that way towards anyone anymore. He shook his head, because it didn't matter. Soon King Tasdel would die, and the drak would hopefully be able to free their people from the dire straits they were currently in.

They didn't talk for the rest of the relatively short trip through Midtown to the building Forthan's people occupied. It was a small building, a little bigger than Jack and Aggie's shop, with two dragon tribesmen standing near the entrance in matching armor. They both saluted Forthan when the group got close enough.

"Wyces, Wropaios." Forthan nodded to both men. "This is Shura Blueblessed and Kastigan. Please gather everyone, I have things that must be said."

The looks on both the tribesmen's faces as Shura was introduced showed clear disappointment. Kas realized they must have known her name, and known Forthan's designs in courting her.

"It is all right, Shura and her landlord have accepted me as their sukar. Gather the others and we will discuss how this changes our plans."

The one Forthan had called Wyces saluted and then disappeared into the house; Forthan and Wropaios stayed outside. The house didn't seem large enough for all of the white drak's underlings to gather, so Kas assumed they would be holding this meeting outside. It didn't take long for several additional tribesmen to arrive. Each saluted Forthan when they saw him before standing in a loose formation near the entrance to the building.

There was a kind of small courtyard created by several homes being built in different shapes without any real forethought. It worked for their purposes, but Kas wanted to make sure that nothing like that happened in Miranda as it ended up looking very sloppy. The next to arrive was Forthan's squire, a black scaled drak without any horns, which Kas remembered indicated they were still adolescents. The black drak saluted Forthan and then took a place at the head of the footmen's formation. To his surprise, the next person out was an unbound.

The name above her head was Shannon. She had sharp Asian features, her hair was tied back in a high tail. A quiver and bow settled comfortably across her back, and leather armor similar to Kas' own about her frame. Her exposed ears had a slight point to them, indicating she was probably half-quinthan, and around her waist were a number of strange devices whose functions Kas couldn't fathom.

"Ahh, Shannon, I'm glad you're here," Forthan said, turning to Kas and Shura. "This is my dowser."

The player looked Shura over and smiled. "Good, you find blue drak. That mean our contract over?" She spoke in clipped English. The translation software of the game was fantastic, which meant she actually spoke like that on purpose. Kas wondered where on Earth she came from that she was learning such horrible English. While English was taught everywhere, there were still a few places that taught their children multiple languages. Was it a roleplay decision?

"No, I was actually hoping to hire you for a longer-term contract. Shura and Kastigan have purchased some land, and are hoping to fully explore and exploit their resources," Forthan responded.

Shannon looked at Shura and then at Kas, frowning slightly. "Same price per day," she finally responded after a few moments of consideration.

"Acceptable. Have Winnog draw up a new contract. Please take a seat and I'll explain where we're going." Forthan nodded toward the black drak, whom Kas assumed must be Winnog.

Shannon sat down on some grass while they waited for the rest of the group to arrive. The next appearance was the second cianese person Kas had seen in the game, looking very much like your typical fantasy dwarf. He looked to be in his late forties, a thick beard covering a stout frame. What did surprise Kas were the three short horns growing out of his jaw, the beard flowing around them in three orderly plaits. Not quite typical fantasy then. The man was clearly the smith, wearing a thick leather apron and sporting massive forearms.

"Welcome, Costache," Forthan greeted the cian, who just nodded his head before squatting next to Shannon.

The last to arrive was a full-blooded quinthan. He was decked out in full chef's attire, big puffy white hat and all. As he walked out, he muttered about being interrupted. Several sharp-looking knives were positioned in pockets around his person, and Kas got the sense that he knew how to use them for more than just cooking. Following behind him was Wyces, the tribesman Forthan had sent to gather everyone together.

"Thank you, everyone. As you know, last night I issued sh'kar to Shura Blueblessed. I lost. As such, I have become her sukar. Kastigan here is her landlord, and a cycle mage. We will be relocating to their land. I must warn you that it will be a rough living situation for some time, as the land is still raw. We'll be leaving at ten o'clock.

"Wropaios, and Winnog, I'm going to leave the two of you here to close up shop; I'll send Blinall to get you in a few days. Any questions?" Forthan glanced between the group. "Adel, Costache, will you two be able to join us now or would you like to wait to join the second group?"

"I do not have the pots to cook over a campfire. I will need to go purchase them," Adel said with a sniff, the haughty quinthan clearly displeased with the prospect of roughing it.

"Might as well get out there. I doubt anyone else would know how to build a proper forge," Costache muttered into his beard.

"Alright everyone, we leave in two hours. Adel, get the men enough food for a few days if you can. We'll set everything up as soon as we can. Winnog, I need Shannon's new contract as soon as possible. Let's move everyone, time is burning."

Forthan's people dispersed quickly. It was clear that they were well-trained and disciplined. With the notable exception of the quinthan, they all did their tasks without complaint.

Kas looked at Shura and then shook his head; the two of them were far enough apart from the group that they could talk without being overheard as Forthan went about the process of getting everything ready for departure. "Well, that's not exactly what I was expecting when we headed here."

Shura laughed. "No, not really what I was expecting either. I was wondering if you could share the map of what we own. I would like to see it."

"Oh, of course." Kas opened up his interface and after a few moments found the UI option to share his map. "The unexplored stuff was so cheap, I got as much of it as I could."

Shura whistled softly as she looked it over. "This is a pleasant surprise. I was not expecting to be able to purchase the entire valley, let alone all this. I am sure we will find something of value in all this land. At the very least, you'll probably be right about using it as grazing."

"Right, we've got time. I'm going to read my skill books. Anything else that we need?"

"Hmm, I think you'll find that Forthan will be bringing everything that we need. He is a poor fighter—by drak standards, at least—but his family is well known for their administration skills, and he is a worthy successor in that regard."

"Well, that will probably help." Kas didn't particularly want to give someone else control over his land, but it would be nice to have someone to bounce ideas off of at least. Depending on how willing the drak was to concede him ultimate say.

Shura and Kas made arrangements to meet with Forthan's group at the lift at ten, while they went to go talk to the woodsman Shura had talked to the night before. "So, what do you know about this guy?"

"Not much. He's human, said he could chop and clean trees in a timely manner. I did not ask him much more than that."

Kas shook his head at Shura's disinterest in the man's life. "What was his name?"

"He said it was Max."

"Just Max? Was he unbound?" Kas had noticed that most of the bound had much more exotic names than the ones he was used to in gaming. A simple name like Max shouted player at him.

"No. He wasn't unbound; he's a man of few words though. He signed up when I told him it was a day's travel away from the fort, said he was sick of all the people."

Kas looked around. The city wasn't exactly empty, but it certainly had a sparseness to it that made him feel like they were mostly alone. Then again, the real world had been made into concrete jungles. Modern day Earth made it difficult to be more than a few dozen paces away from another person. The idea that there were 'too many' people in the area seemed strange to him. If anything, he was a little worried about how few people there were.

After winding through Midtown, they finally arrived at the lift; the last member of their party was waiting off to one side. He stood up and walked their way when he saw Shura, an easily identifiable figure given that she stood twice as tall as most people. Slung across his back over a backpack was a massive axe, while two smaller hatchets were fixed to either hip. The backpack itself was full nearly to bursting, and Kas assumed he was bringing everything that he owned with him.

Shura lifted her hand in greeting. "Hello, Max."

"Hey, glad you made it. This your partner?" Max asked. He had an easy-going nature, his movements seemed to sort of slink along. Not in a mischievous manner, but rather more like he just couldn't be bothered to put more than the very minimum amount of effort into any particular action.

"Yes, this is Kastigan." Shura inclined her head.

"Pleasure, you're Max?"

"Yes sir, Max Martin, logger and woodsman."

"Nice to meet you. We ran into some unexpected delays and there will be several others joining us in an hour. Did you two sort out a price yet?"

"We didn't, but I'm more interested in cooked food and a place to stay. You provide those, and I'll bring in the logs and help you build."

"Well, we don't have any buildings yet, but with your help I'm sure we can get some up soon, and we have a chef coming with us, but he'll be a few days behind us."

Max shook his head. "Can't do it. Come back and find me when you've got some buildings."

"Fair. How about I pay you three mana crystals a day until we can meet your standards?"

"What quality?" Max asked, scratching his beard thoughtfully.

"Poor for now, although if I rank up, I'll give you whatever I make that day."

"Alright, that's fair, I can work with that. How many people were you intending to bring out there?"

"Ten, I think?" Kas did some quick math. "Eleven with you, but hopefully, we'll get more."

"Well, sure beats having to watch out for my stuff with all these vultures." Max gestured towards the shantytown, and the group of dirty and wretched-looking men milling about between the town and the lift. "It's almost to the point that I feel safer out in the woods at night. Half these men can't find a way to put coin in their purse or food in their mouths. And two new shipments in the last couple days haven't helped anything."

"Yeah, I've only spent one night here, and it certainly was more dangerous than the nights I've spent out in the woods."

Max didn't seem convinced by that but after a glance at Shura, he shrugged.

Kas looked around. "Well, now all we need is to find a miner."

Two of the rough-looking men that had been milling about

near the lift approached, they were both shorter than normal with a stocky build that reminded him of Costache. The two men looked similar enough that they were probably siblings, although it was hard to tell under all the dirt they were covered by.

"We're miners," the taller of the two men answered.

"I don't suppose you can prove that?" Kas asked with a frown.

"Well, not rightly, no," the taller one stated. "But you sound like you're going pretty far out into the wild. Wouldn't agree to go without believing I could do the work. More risk of you leaving me out there alone. See?"

Glancing over at Shura to see her opinion, the drak leaned down and looked at the two men. "They have a point. They will need to be properly washed before we leave though."

"I suppose you don't have any equipment either?" Both men responded to Kas' question with a slight shake of their heads. "Well, I guess we'll have you helping Costache with the forge until he can make you some.

"You heard the drak, get yourself cleaned up in the next..." Kas checked the time on his interface. "Twenty minutes and you can come with us."

Both men nodded their heads, the shorter one remaining silent. "Oh bless you, Lord, you won't regret it, we're good miners, you'll see."

Kas had a feeling he wouldn't see, but with three drak and several armed tribesmen, he didn't think these two would be able to cause much trouble.

CHAPTER FOURTEEN
Miranda Valley 4

The two miners did manage to get cleanish and return in time for them to depart, although it was a close thing. Kas asked what their names were, and as before the tall one was the only one that talked. "I'm Simeon, and this is Gus." The two were still in worn down rags and carried little beyond the clothes on their back, each having a stick with a bundle of belongings wrapped up in a blanket around one end over their shoulders.

"Costache, these are the two miners we found. I'm going to put them under you until we can secure a mine," Kas said after introducing the two to the cianese man.

For his part, the smith looked them over and then snorted, before grilling them on their skills and knowledge. When he started going into different types of coal, Kas figured it was time for him to make a break for it.

Since they had such a large group, the guards did an off-schedule use of the lift. Reducing the time they had to wait for the lift by quite a bit, the people who had been waiting longer grumbled but didn't seem interested in angering a group of two drak and their guards. Forthan allowing the two groups who had waited for the longest on the trip helped reduce the grumbling.

Forthan's retinue maintained the disciplined air that had epitomized their first interaction. The tribesmen did their jobs with a quiet efficiency that Kas envied. Each of the three that was accompanying them carried a backpack that looked to be stuffed so full that Kas doubted he would even be able to carry it, despite the stat gains he had acquired in the past few days' worth of work. The cian's was almost double the size of the tribesmen, and from the clanking it made as he shifted, filled with heavy metal tools.

Shannon's pack was about the same size as Kastigan's, although she had acquired a thick, metal-shod walking staff with some sort of yellow crystal on one end. The other unbound seemed to make a point to ignore him, instead spending the trek down double-checking the latches on the dozen or so devices she had hanging from her belt. Now that he had a few minutes, most of them looked like variants on a wand, although two or three of them appeared to be some sort of metallic balls.

Shannon looked up as Kas was studying her belt and quirked an eyebrow at him, taking it as an opportunity to talk to the other unbound. "Hey. So how does all that stuff work?" he asked, pointing to the belts.

"Most of it just requires I circulate mana through it, and then activate a skill. They all give me a slightly different response, and accuracy is based on how high my skills are." Unbuckling one of the metal balls, she showed it to him. It consisted of a dozen metal bands in groups of three. "This one called hona. Each band move separately, they end up all pointing at item I pick. Used for find depth of thing, use three points, make calculation."

The strange clipped accent Shannon used annoyed Kas. Sure, if she was an NPC it would be one thing, the AI having been programmed to speak in a certain way to increase immersion. From a player, it just sounded like she was trying to be confusing.

"Is that your real accent?" Kas asked, considering the half-quinthan with a slight frown.

Shannon had the presence to blush. "No, I just figured it would be fun to roleplay it. Pretend I was raised somewhere in Thel'khan and got stuck here when the veil went up."

Kas reached out a hand to touch the ball and Shannon snatched it away, putting it back in the pouch at her belt. "Almost all of my tools are very delicate, they can easily be contaminated by external sources of mana. Such as the kind a cycle mage exudes."

"Oh, sorry. I didn't know."

Shannon nodded her head. "Yeah, not many people know much about how dowsing works. One of the reasons I picked it, wanted to do something few people do, plus I wanted to explore stuff. This gives me a way to finance explorations. What about you? What do you plan to do with this land you purchased?"

"Farm. I picked cycle mage because it would let me farm with magic. I figured that was a way to make money without having to go dungeon diving."

"Wait, you mean farm like agriculture?"

"Yeah, I have a couple fields growing already. We came out here the first day and scouted it out. Just had to go back and actually buy the land and... you know, get some more people."

Shannon actually laughed. "Yeah, this is a few more people than just you and the drak. She your bonded companion?"

Kas nodded his head. "Yeah. Wait, is Forthan yours?"

"No, either I missed mine or I have enough combat skills that they didn't think I qualified for it."

"Wait, you can miss your companion?"

"Yeah, if you choose not to talk to them, or you tell them no. There were a couple of people on the forums talking about not wanting someone following them around, so they declined it. They were whining for CS to give them a new one, but the community manager told them it was a one-time deal. A bunch of people recreated so they could acquire one."

Kas nodded his head thoughtfully glancing over at Shura.

"You got super lucky. I don't think I've heard of anyone with an arena champion for a bonded companion."

"Shura is pretty great," Kas said, starting to feel a bit uncomfortable.

"Aren't cycle mages supposed to be pretty good at combat? How did you even get one?"

Kas breathed out and then shrugged. "I dunno, I think the dryad that helped me create my character liked me."

"Dryad? I had some sort of weird mechanical dwarf thing help me through character creation. And there was no way that guy would even be able to like someone, let alone give them special treatment because of it."

"Huh? Weird. Yeah, I got a dryad who called herself Livia, she helped me sort my build out to fit what I actually wanted to do."

"Lucky wanker." Shannon tossed her hair in irritation. "You must have been a nun in your past life, too much karma built up in your favor."

Kas didn't want to get into it with Shannon, but if he was actually getting a lot of luck in the game, then it was all recompense for how crappy his life had been going in the last year and a half.

"Yeah, I guess. I guess Forthan hired you to find Shura?"

"Yeah, I told him she was near the park and he went and did his challenge thing."

Kas nodded his head, but any further conversation was interrupted as the lift landed. The disembarkation process was quick, but he got separated from the unbound in the mill. He ended up between Shura and Forthan, the much larger drak easily clearing a path he could walk behind.

The size difference between the two became very evident. Forthan was large, Kas guessed he danced around the ten foot mark and was on the tall side, compared to most of the drak he had seen. Shura was on an entirely different level, with an extra three feet in height and nearly double the bulk of Forthan.

He wondered if his good luck from Livia's blessing really was that influential on his life up to this point. When he thought back on the events of the past week, there certainly had been some lucky moments—meeting Shura, escaping the cloud wolf, and even the confrontation with the bandits in the woods. They had dropped enough gold that he hadn't even needed to sell any of his mana crystals yet, which was a good thing, because not everyone was going to fit in the wanderer's pine that Shura and he had bedded down in.

With Max there, he would hopefully be able to get some more permanent structures built in the next couple of days. But either way, that meant that he wasn't likely to be able to get a spot to set up his alchemy set in the near future unless he could find a way to make housing and a workspace at the same time. Since he was near Forthan, he decided to broach the subject of labor distribution with the white drak.

"Forthan, I was just considering logistics in my head and was wondering if you could shed some light on what abilities all of your people have."

With a frill of his head that spoke to surprise in the drak, he paused for a moment to consider his words before answering. "Damaemon is the most senior of my footmen, he is skilled with most one-handed bladed weapons and shields. Wyces is our polearm specialist. Tryrynall and Blinall are both archers. Wropaios is also a polearm specialist, but he and Winnog are both back at Tallrock."

"I assume they're all skilled in their respective weapons. I was more asking about auxiliary skills. For example: do either of the archers know how to make arrows, and can they hunt for food?" Kas tried to direct the conversation towards the path that would help him determine how to run the settlement.

"Ahh, I see. You are trying to determine how best to use everyone to get the farm up and running quickly. Well, in that case, Damaemon is somewhat skilled in construction, as well as equipment maintenance. Wyces is a trap specialist, but also a passable tailor. Tryrynall is still very young, but I think he could become an excellent ranger or hunter. Blinall is our bowyer and fletcher. Wropaios fancies himself a magitech engineer, although I'm not sure he's built anything that didn't blow up on him.

"Costache is a weaponsmith first and foremost, but he is apt enough at smelting and regular smithing, although he'll not be happy if you set him to making nails. Adel is an accomplished alchemist, although most of his interest lies in making good tasting potions, rather than potent ones. Shannon, well, she is unbound like you. I'm unsure what exactly her entire skill set is."

"Excellent, that leaves us with a few options. I think the first thing we're going to need is to have Wy... Wykees... Okay, first off, I need to give them all nicknames, I don't think I'm built to pronounce tribe names." He spoke louder so that all the tribesmen could hear him. "I'm going to call you: Damae, Wyk, Tryry, and Bliny." Kas pointed to Damaemon, Wyces, Tryrynall, and Blinall in turn. "The other guy is going to be called Rope. Anyone got a problem with those nicknames?"

The tribesmen just looked at him for a moment then turned back to the trek, following Shura's blue form through the forest.

"Alright, so, we will need to get Wyk and Tryry out hunting for food. That's probably the highest priority. Bliny and Shura will probably join them, at least for the first few days. Shura will be looking for new creatures to tame either way. We'll have Max working on getting us wood while Damae and I do the actual construction. Might need some help from Costache and the two miners, but we'll see how busy Shannon can keep them when we get there."

"Costache will want to put up a forge and smelting furnace pretty quickly. That will have them searching for rocks for quite some time."

"Well, I have plenty of rocks from the fields; we'll need to figure something out for the mortar though. Not sure what will hold up under the kind of heat he's likely to be using."

"Hmm, I'm not sure. Costache would know best, I suppose."

Kas nodded his head; he was already thinking about how he was going to position all the buildings.

They made good time, Kas not wanting to slow everyone down by stopping to pick up all the herbs he saw on his minimap. It was a tempting prospect, and he almost turned it off, but figured that getting his herb location skill up was worth the temptation.

He continued to use Crystallize on cooldown and also managed to keep Layering on cooldown despite its 22-hour timer. Tonight was the night he was going to lose some sleep to make sure he didn't waste any of the cooldown.

There was a minor issue with the bridge—the silent miner, Gus, almost fell in. Some quick thinking on Max's part kept one of their weakest members from being separated from the rest of the group.

The trip from the bridge to the cliff was likewise without incident. Kas did have to expand the path a little, Costache's pack and the cianese man's wide stance made some of the narrower spots that the draks climbed over impossible, and no one that could fit in the gap could actually lift the pack.

Everyone paused after they rejoined the river at the top of the cliff and admired the view the valley provided, resting for a few minutes now that they were almost there.

Shannon approached Kas while he was refilling his water-skin. "Hey, so what exactly are you looking for first?" Kas was glad she had dropped the weird roleplaying accent she had previously adopted.

"Hmmm, iron, I think. If there isn't any of that, then copper and tin to make some bronze. Although I'd really rather skip that stage altogether."

Shannon nodded her head thoughtfully and pulled out a Y-shaped metal rod. "This is a divining rod. It works best if you have some of the material, called a primer, you want to find, but I can look for major deposits without one. The downside to this method is, of course, they have to be pretty close by and large, especially at my skill level."

Kas nodded his head thoughtfully before calling out, "Hey, Costache! You have any iron you can lend Shannon?"

The cianese man was a dozen paces away, and fished out a small scrap out of his backpack. "Aye, I stocked up on a couple of things before we left." He handed the scrap to Shannon. "You skilled enough to detect different qualities of iron?"

Shannon shook her head. "I don't think it'll matter much at this point. We can try though." She was already putting the scrap of iron near the base of the Y on the divining rod. She held the two arms in either hand and, closing her eyes, began to channel mana into the rod. At least, that was what Kas assumed she was doing; there was no obvious effect of her dowsing. After nearly a minute of having her eyes closed, she opened them again and shook her head.

"That was the hardest skill use I've ever done. I'm not sure if it's because of interference or distance or what, but I ended up failing. Maybe I'll have better luck as I walk around." She seemed a little upset by how difficult the mini-game had evidently been.

"It's alright, we're not in a huge rush. We'll give you plenty of time."

Shannon's hand hovered over a pouch at her side. "I can try to augment it with a mana crystal, but that's not part of the original contract."

Considering the options, while the two silver each crystal was worth wasn't a lot, they could easily add up. Although, if he could find some iron and start collecting income based on finding minerals on the property, then he would be in an even better spot. "Tell you what, we'll have you try it a few more times, and if you still haven't found anything, we'll start augmenting it."

They started up the river again shortly afterward, stopping

long enough for Shannon to dowse every ten minutes or so. Each of her attempts was as difficult as the first and all of them resulted in a failure. "It's almost like..." The half-quinthan trailed off, her gaze directed towards the cliff above the waterfall where the fields had been.

"Like what?" Shura's frill was raised in an approximation of worry, her gaze following Shannon's to the top of the cliff.

"Like there's something blocking all my attempts. I'll have to try a few of my other tools to be sure, but I'm almost positive there is something up there blocking the magic."

"Strange, I haven't had any issues with any of my magic."

Shannon tried a few other spells. "It looks like it's only divination spells that are affected." Scratching her ears thoughtfully, she asked, "That's weird, right?"

Not entirely happy to hear that his valley may be the source of some sort of anti-divination, Kas just shrugged. "We'll figure it out later. We're almost to the camp."

The game trail along the river was much harder to follow than the one Kas and Shura had taken through the thicker woods on either side of the river. The thick groves of cottonwoods and brush near the riverbank made it nearly impossible to navigate. The difficulty of the terrain nearly doubled the time it took to travel from the mouth of the valley to the base, but it had also given Shannon as equal a distance between the two sides of the valley as they could get. They moved away from the river as soon as she decided there was a blockage, making better time.

Entering the small glade they had put the farms up in, Dino and Diane scurried over to see Kas, the two little lizards jumping up and down excitedly around him. Taking off his pack and putting it down, he picked up both the little compies. Dino immediately scrambled up to curl his tail lightly around Kas' neck, his head perched atop Kas', and began chirping happily. Diane was content to curl up in his arms, snuggling her head into his chest.

The rest of the group put down their weapons when it

appeared as though Kas was familiar with the two beasts. Costache was the first to ask, "Friends of yours, I take it?"

"Yes, this is Diane, and the one on my shoulder is Dino. We left them here to watch the place." Both lizards chirped happily, but it didn't take long for them to grow bored. Diane hopped down first, running over to Damae and sniffing at his booted foot. When the tribesman attempted to scratch her head, she chirped angrily at him and snapped at his finger. Luckily Damae was quicker and he pulled it back. Diane had already run away, hiding behind Kas' boot and chirping angrily at Damae.

Dino took the opportunity to jump off Kas' shoulder, leaving behind a flash of pain telling him that the compie's sharp claws had scratched his neck in his haste. Both of them on the ground, they began circling Damae, chirping at him angrily.

"Dino, Diane, calm down, Damae is a friend." The command gave them pause and the two compies turned to look at Kas, chirping softly in obvious confusion. "Go find bugs." Kas pointed into the forest and the two diminutive monsters took off to complete his command.

"Sorry about that, we'll get them trained better soon."

"It's okay, I'm sure they'll be good guard animals. We'll just have to get used to what all their chirping means," Damae said with a shrug, glancing around the clearing. "Alright, let's get the tents set up before dark." Pausing for a moment of thought, he turned to look at Kas. "Where did you want us to start?"

"Well, Shura and I set up over there." Kas pointed towards the wanderer's pine. "But the permanent structures are all going to be over there under the overhang."

"We'll set up by the tree line for now then, that way we won't have to worry about moving them as we build."

Immediately the other three tribesmen got to work. Costache and the two miners had already wandered over towards the valley wall, where the cian was tapping on the wall in an interesting way, giving barked instructions to the miners.

Shura and Forthan had dropped their bags next to Kas' pile of rocks and were heading towards the waterfall. With a shrug, Kas headed over to his fields, checking each one for anything that needed to be done.

It was immediately apparent that something had gotten into the cornfield; almost half of it had been smashed flat. Several of the small shoots had been uprooted, and it looked like something had created a nest.

"Shura!" Kas shouted. There was no clear evidence that whatever had destroyed the field was still around but he suddenly felt less safe in the area. The big drak arrived a few minutes later, her claw like weapons equipped and held in a ready stance.

"What is it?" Shura asked, looking around wildly.

"The field," Kas said, pointing and the drak looked around and then snorted, putting her claws away and then dropping to all fours as she inspected the ground around the destroyed field.

"Cloven hoof, fairly big," Shura said, pointing out some tracks. "Looks like some sort of boar or pig." She sniffed at the ground and then turned to Kas. "I'll set some traps up on the runs, but if we don't catch it tonight, I'll go look for it in the morning."

Doing what he could for the damaged field, he straightened as many of the stalks as he could, but still only about a fourth of the field was undamaged. Pulling up the interface on the corn field he frowned.

Field Type: Crop (Corn)
Field Size: Small
Soil Quality: Excellent
Water Content: Adequate
Condition: Heavily Damaged

Unlike previous conditions, there was nothing Kas could do to fix this one, as he didn't want to waste more seeds. He would just have to see what happened with the harvest. The corn field handled, he cast Enrich Soil on the spare plot he had prepared the day before, quickly planting a field of corn. He then took the time to water all three fields; the wheat plot didn't have any special conditions on it.

That probably meant it had likely needed bugs removed again, and the compies had already cleared it. The potatoes needed to be weeded, and he cleared enough of the strange purple sprouts to clear the condition, putting all three of his plots at excellent in all three categories.

The wheat had also increased its growth stage and was now considered sprouts, thick blades of what looked like green grass peeking out of the dirt. With a smile, he turned back to the rest of his work.

Max had already gotten to work on the two remaining trees that Shura had felled before they left, easily stripping them of their branches with quick and clean movements.

Seeing his progress, Kas was convinced that there was an element to the world that didn't require you to have the skill to do something but certainly made it much faster and easier if you did.

Since the logs were looking to come much faster, Kas spent the next twenty minutes shaping the earth near where he planned to make the first shelter, creating pits and then directing the tribesmen to place the clean logs into them, leaning them back against the wall and then filling the earth back in around them to keep them from shifting. He then compressed the earth around the logs until it was as hard as he could make it. The result was that each log still had a fairly good pit around it, but Kas would fill that in when he lowered the internal floor of the shelter.

To do that though, he first needed to clear the area. With a few judicious Earth Stomps, he managed to loosen the soil enough that it would be easy to move. He was pleased that the hardened earth he had created around the poles didn't seem to have moved at all, other than to settle a little with all the shaking. He was so caught up in his work that he didn't even realize that all the workmen in the clearing had stopped what they were doing to stare at him.

"Sorry? I was just clearing the ground here a little," Kas said, and everyone went back to their tasks. Was magic really that rare? He knew that draks were unable to learn anything except the elemental magic of their breath weapons, but he was pretty sure there were mages among the other tribesmen. He wasn't sure about the cianese, but quinthans had plenty of magic. Perhaps it was not him doing magic but rather what spells he was using? Localized earthquakes, as a concept, he realized did sound a bit scary as he considered their response.

With a shrug, he went back to moving the rocks out of the shelter. Actually, he pushed them to the wall of the lowered section he was making, creating a more solid barrier around the outer edge. He also dug additional holes for more logs to be placed. Pushing the spare dirt out of the structure, he created a massive pile of loose dirt, unable to move the roots and other plant debris, the internal area was filled with a bunch of knotted matter. He'd have to scrape all that stuff out later, but for now, he left it there.

All this had eaten away at the rest of the daylight, and his stomach rumbling reminded him that he hadn't eaten anything in the real world. Luckily Shura had already started dinner, and he sat down with the group to eat his meal. Everyone was pretty quiet, the group of tribesmen the most comfortable, all joking among themselves. Costache and Shannon likewise seemed pretty at ease, while the two miners stayed off to one side, happily eating their portions and then staring hungrily at the leftovers.

Shura took some pity on them and gave them both an extra-large second helping. No one else seemed interested in more, and the group went about cleaning up camp as darkness fell. The guards set up a rotation among themselves. Kas decided it was time for him to head back to bed himself and, traveling towards the wanderer's pine, he was surprised to discover that Dino was curled up outside the den while Diane's head peaked out just a little bit, resting her head on his thigh. Both of them raised their heads long enough to see that it was him before settling back down.

"Hey, guys, what are you doing in here?" he asked, pulling out his bedding and rolling it out close enough to scratch the two lizard's heads for a few minutes. As he was scratching them, he glanced into the pit. He couldn't be sure, since Diane blocked most of the tunnel down, but he didn't see any eggs. Kas had been hoping the two would be up for mating already. He wanted to give all his people a little compie of their own, and the eggs might have helped him win some friends among Forthan's followers.

"Well, I'll see you two later," Kas said, stroking Diane's neck before logging out.

CHAPTER FIFTEEN

Miranda Valley 5

The real world had not changed much since the last time he had checked to make sure Earth was still turning. He did find two pieces of relevant information on the Tallrock section of the forums. The raid group to take out the undead in the Dead Forest had been wiped out to the last man. The accounts and streams of the fight showed waves of undead beasts, topped off with several 'small' undead dragons or wyverns. Small in this instance was, of course, a relative term as they had a wingspan of a dozen feet.

The respawning players were then fined for indecent exposure upon their reentry to Tallrock. The outrage over Holzer's choice incited several angry diatribes, and even a couple attempts at raising a raiding party to kill the colonel. Thankfully cooler heads prevailed, and only a couple of people had been incarcerated, while the full-scale riot had been averted.

The second piece of information was mostly in response to the first. A lot of people were talking about moving away from Tallrock itself to a town called The Roost. Most people seemed skeptical of the location, since it had a reputation as being a haven for the unscrupulous. The bandits that had attacked Matt and Shura had been carrying crow medallions, which was supposed to be the mark of those who could travel freely through the lands controlled by Corvus—The Roost's leader.

All the activity in Tallrock seemed to be focused to the rim and trailing side. Which was fine with Matt, as Miranda was in the opposite direction. He did weigh the idea of turning Miranda into a player town already but discarded it as there wasn't enough infrastructure to keep the players happy. Maybe in a few months, he could start inviting people to base out of the valley.

With nothing else of note as far as news, Matt spent his time researching early settlement types. He was pretty sure he didn't need to build a full on keep just yet, and ideally, he would build that in the overhang, but that was a long-term goal and he would need to complete some intermediate steps. The easiest thing for defenses would be to build a watchtower. They would probably need one at the farm as well as at the valley's mouth, but they wouldn't do any good until he had the people to man them. Which he currently didn't.

A small picket fence would have to be built soon; digging a ditch and using the excess earth to raise the area he built the fence on would add an extra layer of defense. That would mean taking precious time and resources away from building the sleeping quarters. He was pretty sure that morale would take a dive quick if people had to bunk down together in the wilderness for too long.

The lean-tos that he had started working on when it was just the two of them weren't quite what he needed for a relatively large population boom. Building a longhouse would give everyone shelter, and could later be converted into either a barracks or an inn when people started building their own personal dwellings. The problem was that he didn't have a plan for a longhouse, he only had one room cabin plans.

Pulling up an art program, he recreated the clearing, placing his farm plots and a few dozen extras near the overhang. He wanted the main section of the settlement to be in the overhang. Like a keep that could be retreated into if they were attacked. After that he placed a smithy near the waterfall, hopefully whatever kept the sound out of the main camp would work for the hammering they were bound to be doing there as well. Then he put up two longhouses near the forest edge, leaving plenty of open room for other development.

Next, he placed the picket fence around the area. It would mean pushing back the forest quite a bit in a few spots, but that would also give them the lumber they needed for the rest of the construction. He left a section of the trees up, wanting to keep a park-like area for later. With all that done, he examined his work with a critical eye. He was sure there was room for improvement but for now he had a rough idea of what he wanted the village to look like.

At least the rough design was done, so he had an idea of what he wanted to do next, even as much as he had planned would still take a few weeks to develop and that was assuming that there were no setbacks in the development.

Taking care of the rest of his needs as he did his research, Matt stayed up a little longer than he had anticipated and went to bed with the beginnings of a headache. He overslept his alarm and logged back in just after dawn.

DAY 6

Stretching into a yawn, he glanced around the wanderer's pine, there was no sign of Diane or Dino and, glancing in the pit he had made for them, there was still no sign of eggs. With a shrug, he shifted his belongings around a bit while he cataloged all the things he hoped to accomplish for the day.

The first task was going to be the fields; he needed to cut another plot out of the thick sod and tend to the previous four. After that, he was determined to figure out a better water delivery system. He mentally kicked himself for having researched building types rather than looking for a better solution to his water troubles.

After the fields, he needed to get as many buildings constructed as he could. Finding something to put in as daubing between the main beams was going to take some work; hopefully Shannon would have better luck finding clay than she did with the iron earlier. Speaking of Shannon, he'd have to ask the dowser to make a round of the valley looking for various materials. The sooner they could figure out what natural resources the valley had, the sooner he could start figuring out the next few stages of the plan.

Trying to think of something else he needed to do today, he realized that all his other plans resolved around buildings being complete or finding natural resources. Since he couldn't realistically plan those out, he made his way out of the pine's enclosure. As soon as he got into the clearing, he found Shura and Wyk already at work cleaning the night's trapped animals. Which, in this case were more of the duck-like creatures and several large rodents.

Wordlessly taking a couple of the ducks off to one side, Kas began de-feathering and butchering the carcasses. His skills in animal processing made his work much faster and allowed him to waste less raw materials than either of the other two, and they happily let him take over the chore. Dino and Diane decided that it would be an opportune moment to make their presence known and they chirped sadly at him until he relented and tossed them some of the entrails.

Having cleaned and quartered all the game, Shura set about cooking it. Kas meanwhile tended to his farm. All four plots needed to be weeded; this was fast becoming his least favorite daily debuff on the fields, since it was the only one that he had to attend to with physical labor.

Breakfast was served midway through the first field, and he welcomed the break from being bent over the field picking weeds. As he ate, he watched the crew. Forthan's men all shared an easy camaraderie, built up over the six months that the ship took to get here, no doubt. Shannon was likewise at ease, although she had a few implements out and seemed to be tweaking them to an esoteric standard Kas couldn't begin to fathom.

The two draks sat apart from the rest, their duo quiet. Kas could sense the tension made visible by the frills on each drak's head that stood nearly straight up. He wasn't sure if it was because of Forthan's sukar status or if there was some other aspect at play, but the drak's breakfast was devoid of the chatting that epitomized the rest of the retinue's conversation.

The two miners sat apart from everyone. They were much cleaner than they had been originally, but trail dirt covered their entire bodies while their hair remained a greasy mess. Both appeared sullen compared to the rest of the crew, but they ate with gusto and then eyed the pot looking for more. Food wasn't abundant, but there was enough. He mentally added foraging for herbs to the list of things he should do before dinner.

Forthan approached him as he was eyeing the forest, trying to decide what path would provide the best return.

"Kastigan, have you created assignments for the day?"

Looking up at the white drak, he blinked. "Uh, was I supposed to?"

Forthan's frill fluttered in amusement. "Not necessarily. Although it might help things along. If I may make some suggestions?"

Kas nodded, gesturing for the other man to sit. "Sure, what have you got?"

"Well, if you sent Shura, Tryrynall, and Blinall out hunting, they could possibly also search for potential bond marks and whatever destroyed your field. Costache and the two miners can head along the cliff face in the opposite direction as Shura's group. That covers the two most likely locations of ore in the valley. I suggest you send Shannon with one of those two groups. Max and Damaemon can focus on getting more buildings ready. I know my men would appreciate a solid roof over their heads before a storm hits.

"I'll stay here with Wyces and help Max. We can at least drag logs back to the clearing if nothing else. Although I'd suggest Wyces set up more traps at some point. While you tend the farm, and then help Damaemon with the construction."

Kas nodded his head as Forthan spoke, the drak's division of labor sounding good to him. "I like it. I'll probably also go out and try to find some herbs to add some more greens to our otherwise protein rich diet."

"A good suggestion. I'd be happy to accompany you while you forage; we cannot have our fearless leader dying to a cloud wolf."

Right, the wolf was still around. They hadn't seen her since that first day, Shura's assumption that they must be at the edge of her territory seeming to be correct. "Well let's hope whatever destroyed the field would be a good bond—we should keep an eye out for other large creatures—eventually Shura is going to want to tame something bigger than compies. Oh! And clay. A supply of clay would help a lot."

"I'll be sure to tell the groups to keep their eyes open for those."

With the thought of the cloud wolf, and the unknown nature of the valley, Kas considered the teams. "I feel like we should put some more combat capability in Costache's team. What if we split the miners, and put Bliny in the group with them? I imagine Costache can handle himself pretty well, and that gives each team a ranged combatant."

Forthan glanced over at the miners and then nodded his head. "Probably a wise choice. I'm not sure the miners will be willing to separate though. I have not heard the shorter one talk since they joined the party."

Kas realized that Gus hadn't talked at all yesterday, and the two miners staying away from the rest of the group meant that even Simeon hadn't talked much. "I'll go talk to them, see how they feel about splitting up."

Forthan nodded his head. "Very well."

"Before you go, I was thinking over the plans for the village and made up a diagram and was wondering what you thought of it." Kas had drawn up his plans on the in-game map and shared them with Forthan.

The drak examined them for a few minutes. "It is a good start, but we should plan out the development a bit more before we start building any foundations for the buildings. I'll think about it today, and get you something back before you disappear for the night."

"No rush, that's several ten-days' worth of work as it is. We have plenty of time to get it right." Bidding Forthan farewell, Kas walked over to the pot. Grabbing two more bowls of stew, Kas headed to the two rocks that the miners had staked out as their own. "Hey guys, I brought you some extra. Looks like you could use it." He held out the bowls. Gus half reached out to grab it, but then glanced at Simeon. The taller of the two miners gave a slight nod before reaching out to grab his own extra bowl.

"Thank you, sir," Simeon said, refraining from shoveling the food into his mouth so that he could talk. Gus didn't seem to have a similar compunction and was slurping his second helping of breakfast with gusto.

"So, we're going to send out two groups to scout the valley, looking for any ore we can find. I assume you have an ore detection skill?"

Simeon had taken a bite while Kas spoke, but they both nodded their heads in response to the question. "Well, I was hoping you two wouldn't mind being split up so that we can hopefully cover the entire valley today. Shouldn't take more than about half the day, and we'll be splitting most of the combatants between the two groups. You should be safe either way."

Gus stopped eating when Kas mentioned splitting the two, glancing at Simeon. The two appeared to be having some sort of mental debate then Simeon nodded his head. "We can do that, sir."

"Alright, good. Forthan will tell you which group you should be in." Kas thought about asking them if either of them had any other skills but didn't want to spook the two any more than they already appeared to be.

The two hunting parties took a few more minutes to organize themselves, but then headed off. Shura, Gus, and Try headed to the left of the waterfall, while Costache, Shannon, Bliny, Simeon, and Wyk went to the right. Meanwhile, Max, Damae and Forthan were busy dragging logs out of the forest, cleaning them up, and setting them in the holes Kas had dug the day before.

Kas himself got to work on weeding and watering his plots and preparing the fifth plot of land for planting. It was mostly busy work. Keeping his hands busy while his mind was free to consider the various issues that he was dealing with.

The first, and most pressing, issue was money. He needed to make enough money off the game that he wouldn't have to go back to his old job. The key to that was exploiting Miranda Valley's wealth. Hopefully they would find some good mineral caches, and he would find some valuable herbs. The question became what he should do with the herbs that he found. He could sell the dried herbs themselves, which would probably make a decent amount, especially since there were likely more people trying to be alchemists than herbalists.

Basic economics said that the further down the supply chain you got, the more value each item would have. Unless there was a resource scarcity. He couldn't be positive yet, but he was pretty sure that right now all basic materials were in limited supply. Which meant that it was entirely possible he could make more money on the raw herbs, or at least the ground up powders, than he could make with the finished ingredients. People paying to level up in the hopes that alchemy would pay off later.

The downside to that was, of course, that he wouldn't be getting any skill experience himself, and his own alchemy would fall behind. Considering he had a major affinity in it, he had to assume that Liv thought he would be better off turning them into potions. However, the AI just knew he wanted to be a farmer; she didn't know about his need to make money immediately. Especially since the more he made, the more he could reinvest back into the game.

Already at a disadvantage since he planned to use his in-game wealth to support his real-world lifestyle, he would fall behind those with disposable income that could play full-time and invest everything back into the game. Either way, playing full-time should hopefully give him an advantage over those who simply played part of the time because they were supporting themselves in the real world.

Internal musings kept him occupied until he had finished weeding all the current plots. Moving over to the next location, he went through the familiar routines of cutting and removing the sod, then using Earth Stomp to remove the rocks, creating another pile of them. He considered spending the effort to move them over to the first house, but decided against it since Costache was probably going to need a good amount for the smeltery and forge.

Glancing at the time, he still had an hour before noon and he managed to cut out about half of the next field before deciding it was time to take a break. Lunch took the form of left-over sandwiches prepared by Forthan's chef before they left Tallrock. Damae, Forthan, and Max joined him, although the conversation with the group was quiet, everyone seeming lost in their own thoughts and unwilling to intrude on each other.

Finishing his sandwich, he stood up. "Well, I'm going to go hunt for herbs, I should be back in a couple hours. Damae and Max, you guys have anything you need from me before I go? I'm hoping we'll have enough logs to finish the first structure tonight."

Both men shook their heads in response and brushing his hands off, he walked toward the woods. Dino and Diane chirped excitedly as he walked out of the clearing, the two compies running around in circles around him and chittering to each other. Forthan's large white form acted as a reverse shadow as the drak trailed him through the forest.

The next two hours mostly involved Kas laughing at the

antics of the two compies while picking up every herb he could find. There were a couple new ones that showed up on his herb location skill. Nymph's Blood was a crimson moss that grew on the coreward side of trees, which Kas thought was odd. Silki grass was a strange spiked grass that grew in the darkest shadows of the forest floor. The last came from a blue bell type plant called a blue trumpet, but he harvested a strange L-shaped seed pod that hung heavily below the flowers.

Forthan was more hindrance than help, his horns getting stuck multiple times while trying to traverse the low hanging tree boughs. The white drak's grumbling a few dozen steps behind him drawing a wicked grin from Kas as he moved easily through the undergrowth. More than once the compies brought him something they found of interest: a rock, some twigs, or a half-eaten rodent. Kas lauded them each time, mostly because they were so excited to be giving him something that he felt bad not praising them for their accomplishments.

In addition to the three new types of herbs, Kas also encountered a thick bush with long thorns protecting some beautiful purple berries. After stabbing himself on the thorns for the third time, Kas opted not to collect any more berries. Forthan's thick scales made collecting the berries much easier and he collected about a pound of the berries with relative ease. To his surprise after he inspected the berries, he was prompted to name the plant.

Did that mean he was the first player to encounter it? With no real way to determine if they were truly the first to discover them, Kas called them Fangberries and confirmed his selection.

Congratulations, you have discovered a new botanical species. You have been granted bonus experience to your herbalism skill and granted the subskill: Plant Identification.
1/10 conditions met to earn title: "Gogland Explorer"

Kas had heard about titles; there had been a couple of people that managed to unlock some of them, and they had all given fantastic boosts to the people who had managed it. The problem was that the qualifications seemed to differ from person to person and rarely were they repeatable. The Gogland Explorer was a good example. How easy was it to discover a new species? It wasn't like you could show someone where the new species was. Although explorer groups could probably all find at least one.

Spending the time to identify every plant they passed slowed down their travel speed considerably, and Forthan was clearly bored out of his mind. The drak began throwing rocks for the two compies to chase after, while Kas did the new minigame to identify plants. This one was pretty fun. A flower would appear in the middle of a field and you had to target incoming bugs with seeds before the bugs could eat the plant.

Kas got pretty good at the game. The penalties for failing were also innocuous. He couldn't identify the same plant as the one he had failed on. Since most plants grew in clusters, it usually meant he just had to shift to a different one in the group. Using identify did allow him to find several edible tubers that he otherwise would have walked right past. Kas was excited to get back to camp and break open the strange melon-like roots to see what they looked like inside.

The identification minigame was so fun that Kas stayed out longer than he had anticipated. And they arrived back at the farm just four hours later. Both groups of explorers had also returned; the tribesmen and Shura were dragging several logs over to where Max was busy debranching them. The woodsman had managed to clean another dozen logs while Kas was out foraging. The miners and Costache were busy dragging rocks over to a spot near the base of the waterfall.

Shannon was the only one not actively moving heavy things, the dowser looking like she was making annotations on her UI as she was staring off into nothing and making weird hand gestures.

"Hey everyone, how did it go?" The compies chirped

happily as they ran over to Shura, clawing at the drak's legs as she hefted a massive log over one shoulder.

"Good enough. We didn't find anything, although Costache's group did." The blue drak half dropped, half tossed the log onto the pile. "We can talk about it over dinner. You should go plant your field." She pulled out several small tidbits of meat to feed Dino and Diane.

Kas realized that he still hadn't cast Enrich Soil on the plot he had cleared earlier that day. The timer had expired about twenty minutes previously, and he hurried over to cast it without answering Shura. He only failed to cast the spell two times tonight, an improvement over his previous attempts.

With that done, he pulled all his seed pouches out of his inventory, glancing at their labels. He had one pouch each of potatoes and corn, two more pouches of wheat, and three more pouches of peas. He decided to plant another potato field, tucking the other seeds back into his inventory. He had also managed to get ahead of task and had two empty fields ready.

Hopefully he would find some of these more valuable seeds that Liv had said he would acquire. Or he won some of those auctions that he had put in low bid for; they still had a few days left on their week-long auction. He then began casting Create Water into his bowl and then pouring it on the field to raise its water stat. He reminded himself that he really needed to get a better irrigation system in place. Watering the way he was would only keep taking more and more time.

Finished with the crop, he headed back over to where Shura and the others were already gathering for dinner. He pulled out several of the roots and used his dagger to split them down the center. The melon's flesh was white like a potato, while the skin was bitter. He decided they would need to be peeled and stewed to be edible. But hopefully he had a potato-like equivalent that was more valuable than a potato. All depending on how they germinated.

Making a mental note to search similar plants, he put them aside for later consumption. Shura had already prepared the game they had caught earlier. Dinner was roasted rabbit and some sort of rice ball that Adel must have prepared.

"So, what exactly did you find?" Kas asked Costache when the cian sat down next to him.

"Started off normal enough. We found a few veins of copper, iron, and tin, nothing too amazing but easy enough to gather on our way to the real prize. About a mile and a half along the valley edge, Shannon was doing her dowsing and she got a massive reading that led us to a narrow cave entrance. We didn't travel too deep into it, but I found several rich deposits of the three metals we'd discovered already as well as a few regular nodes of higher-grade metals."

Kas blinked, trying to process what the dwarf had said. "So... we have a mine?"

"Oh, we do indeed, just one wee problem."

"What's that?"

"We got about three or four hundred feet into the cave, and I noticed tracks. A few dozen more paces and I saw more. You've got a mine already, but it's infested with kobolds. We'll have to clear them out before we can mount any kind of serious mining operation."

"What kind of kobolds are we talking about? The lizard ones, the dog ones, or the house sprite one?"

Costache looked at him a bit strangely. "Kobolds are like, tiny, evil draks mixed with a goblin."

"So, the lizard ones."

CHAPTER SIXTEEN

Miranda Valley 6

The problem with kobolds, Kas was told, was that they really, really liked to set up traps. Not only did they enjoy setting up traps, but they were really good at doing so. The other problem was that neither Shura's thirteen-foot frame, nor Forthan's ten feet of height were short enough to enter the mine. Which meant that they were down their two most powerful fighters. That meant that any attempt to clear the mines would be limited to the tribesmen, Shannon, Costache, the miners, and himself.

Max point blank refused, saying he had no interest in going underground. The miners were originally uninterested in coming but were talked into it. Damae's sword and shield were short enough that they wouldn't be too much of a hindrance in the narrow caves. But the other three tribesmen's primary weapons weren't entirely suitable to the environment. Wyk's spear was traded out for a long knife, while Tryry and Bliny both had short swords. None of the three were entirely adept at using these alternate weapons.

Shannon had two knives she produced that looked a little worse for wear but otherwise serviceable. The dowser didn't have a lot of skill using them, but she wasn't anywhere near as afraid of death as Kas' bound companions. And, of course, they had what little help Kas' magic might end up being, but he had most of the same limitations the archers did. In total, that brought their delving team to seven strong.

All of this was discussed over dinner since no one felt like trying to roust the kobolds from their den before bed. There were other preparations made; Gus and Simeon were actually able to enchant light on stones—necessary magic for every miner, they said, as one could never be quite sure if there might be flammable gases in the cave.

Kas finished up his meal and then went to work on trying to finish the buildings. Max and the rest had set up eight more logs, completing the infrastructure for the first building. It ended up being about fifteen feet wide and just over twice that long. Taking the time to move more dirt, he managed to lower the depth almost three feet. With the sloped ceiling, the exterior side of the building's roof was much lower than the side abutting the cliff, creating a space that was tall enough for Shura to stand up straight without knocking her horns against the ceiling.

Both of the draks would find the entrance difficult to use though; he kept the opening small, knowing that it was unlikely they would need to use the building. About five feet across and eight feet tall, it was still larger than he would have liked, and depending on how harsh the winters were, he would need to figure out a way to keep the draft out during the colder weather. That was a problem for another time though; it was just barely spring now, so he had half a year or more to worry about winter.

Now that the infrastructure was in place, Kas began the slow process of moving the spare earth to fill a mesh made of branches that had been removed from the logs. Once the dirt was in place, he would cast Create Water, turning it into mud that he could more easily shape around the branches. At some point, he would need to get more earth, but he had plenty of material at hand for the lower sections of the building. Once he had a six by six part of the wall covered with the lattice, he walked over to the piles of sod he had set aside.

Placing the sod against the wall in two by six sections, he realized the grave mistake he had made. The mesh that supported the turf was just that, a mesh. Meaning that there was loose dirt on the underside of the grass that would inevitably fall in small amounts on anyone under them. He would need to find something to prevent the dirt from falling through. More mud, perhaps? But wouldn't the grass eventually send roots down and solidify the entire ceiling? Would it even matter if they didn't have people walking all over the sod?

Putting that all aside, since there was no real way for him to know if this was even going to be an issue, he began the process of creating the lattice on the next section of the building. There was only a half an hour of light left at the most, so he worked quickly. He began the process of weaving the next lattice of sticks together but gave up midway through due to being unable to see what he was doing. Standing up and stretching, he examined the wall.

"Why isn't this giving me a minigame to play?" Kas tugged on his ear as he considered the problem. Every other trade skill he had done, except for clearing the land, had used a minigame to accomplish things. That prevented him from actually having to know how to do the activity. It allowed him to harvest complex plants or cast spells without knowing how to actually clear the dirt away and cut the proper portions off the plant. So what was different about those things?

Was it because he actually knew how to do those things? Or was it because he was trying to do something that the system didn't allow for? Did he need a recipe or an unlock before the system would take over? What about clearing the land? Frowning, he walked over to an empty spot near the fields he had already cleared. He began digging through his interface.

Livia's interface was simple, streamlined in a lot of ways, but that simplicity hid a lot of the more advanced features that were buried in the sub-menus. As he dug through them, he eventually found what he was looking for. Under non-standard crafting, there was a tool called world crafting. Clicking on it brought up an overlay on his vision, he then clicked the copy action, selected one of his preexisting fields, and then duplicated it on the new section of land.

Immediately, a minigame popped up. There was a timer in the bottom right as well as a move counter. The objective was to shift blocks so that the blue block could slide through a hole on the opposite side of its origin. There were half a dozen blocks already in the square that had to be maneuvered around, and it took Kas a lot longer than he anticipated to get the block across, he finally managed it as the timer hit the ten-minute mark.

To his relief, the thick grass that he had spent hours clearing for the other plots rolled itself up and then appeared at his feet. The dirt underneath was exposed, along with a number of the rocks still in the field. He would still need to clean out the stones, but this had already saved him a bunch of time. Glancing back at the completed section of the structure, he was tempted to try the tool to copy the completed part onto the others but decided it was late enough as it was.

Returning to the campfire where everyone else had mostly settled down, Kas watched as his little town went about the random tasks they had left for the day. The two miners again sat off to the side, alone and not talking. Forthan's men were practicing slightly off to one side of the camp by the light of strange glowing rocks, Forthan and Shura giving them instructions. Shannon was nowhere to be seen, and he assumed she had logged off for the day. Leaving Max and Costache unaccounted for, Kas looked for the two craftsmen but didn't find them until he saw the light behind the impromptu practice yard.

Heading over to the two craftsmen, he heard them arguing, but before he could figure out what they were talking about, they noticed him, and the argument was cut short. "'Ello, Kas, what can we do you for?" the cian smith asked, even as Max harrumphed and grabbed his axe before heading into the woods.

"Oh, I was just checking to see how everyone was doing. Wanted to make sure everything was taken care of before I went to sleep," Kas said, eyeing the two, and with a nod of his head towards Max, he raised an eyebrow to the dwarf.

"Hmm? Oh, nothing to be worried 'bout none. The Veiler had some work he wanted done, but did'na like the price I quoted him," Costache said, dismissing Max with a wave of his hand.

"What sort of work? If he needs something, he should have come to me. What's a Veiler?" Kas asked curiously.

"Ahh, forgive me. I forget sometimes, how little the unbound remember about the world." Costache sat down on a log and gestured for Kas to join him. "It just means he's from Tua'tat." When Kas didn't seem to understand the significance of that, he explained more. "Right before the end of the War, as the legions started to take out more and more of the dragons, the Empire of Tua'tat erected a magitech barrier around their entire country. It's called the veil, and it did a right good job of stopping Tasdel from trying to expand to the east. Prevents everything from going in and out of Tua'tat.

"Only problem is that they couldn't exactly tell all their people that they were doing it, right? On account of being afraid the King would get his people in, they just turned it on one day. All their people what was out trading or traveling got stuck out just as solid as Tasdel. So, we started calling them Veilers on account of them being on the wrong side of the veil. I imagine it's a rough life for them. Tasdel didn't take too kindly to the whole thing.

"A bit of a double meaning actually. After he won the Dragon War, he even started marching folk to the Veil and killing them to make Tua'tat open up. Didn't work no more than you'd figure it did. Those that lived through those times had passed through a 'veil of darkness' and were doubly called as such."

"That's horrible," Kas said, frowning, his eyes searching for Max's form in the darkness.

"Aye, Tasdel isn't much loved outside of the Capital. Just 'bout everyone who isn't fully blooded Pinnocian or a quinthan has come on tough times under his rule."

"What about your people?"

"Oh, Cian's been broken since the original formation of Pinnoc. Back before even the succession wars, Ald Pinnoc incorporated us into the empire. We had a bit of a breather during the succession wars, but truth be told, the Republic was on its last legs when he came in. Ald didn't so much conquer us as just walk in and offer us food." The smith sighed heavily, glancing at the Tribesmen practicing. "Most of the Realm don't think highly of us. We mostly stick with the rest of the non-humans, we're a poor people, and that always makes for unsavory sorts."

"I had no idea." Kas scratched his ear as he tried to think of something to say. "Seems like most of the people here are refugees of some sort."

Costache actually laughed at that. "Aye, aye, that we are. Only those what ain't have much or are forced to make the passage. Sure, you get some idealists like yerself, but for the most part, Gogland ain't much more than a distant place ta die."

"You'd think they would want to come out here. It's not like the King is going to be able to continue to persecute your people here."

"Sure, sure, if'n we live. But it's a hard life out here too, and the King's getting old. Most people suspect there be another succession war, and things will get better back in the mainland."

Kas nodded his head. "True, it's going to be hard work to get everything going here, but I think it will be worth it. This is going to be someplace special, Costache, just you wait."

A dark shadow passed over Costache's face as he said that then he smiled. "Oh, I don't doubt that it will, lad." He thumped Kas on the back hard enough to send him into a coughing fit. "Well, I'm not gonna sit here and natter your ear off all night. You should get some sleep, big day tomorrow."

When he could breathe again, Kas nodded, but Costache had already set off to rejoin the rest of the group. It was only as he left that he realized that the smith hadn't told him what Max had needed to be done. He narrowed his eyes, sure that he had purposefully changed the subject on him. "I'll have to remember to ask Max what that was all about."

Opting to head back to the pine and his bed instead, he heard chirping as soon as he entered. Diane and Dino happily hopped along as he walked over towards the nest and his bed, sitting down. Diane butted her head against his chest until he started scratching her.

Not to be outdone, Dino chirped at him until he began scratching him as well. Sitting there and enjoying the attention, the two did eventually get bored. Dino first tugging on Diane's tail, she then twisted around to snap at him. With another chirp, Dino pulled again, causing Diane to chase him, the two compies using Kas' legs as barriers. Either hiding under them or running around them. Eventually, Diane jumped from his knee to his shoulder, curling her tail around his neck as she balanced, one claw against his ear.

Dino tried to follow but mistimed his jump, headbutting Kas and then falling into his arms. Kas couldn't help but laugh as he scratched the failed jumper, Diane bumping her head against his cheek and emitting a trilling sound that Kas assumed meant she wanted to be petted too. Pulling her off his neck, he placed both dinos in his lap, where they curled around each other as they tried to adjust so that he would scratch the part of them they wanted him to.

After a few minutes of that, they settled down, laying their heads side by side on his knee. Using one hand, he stroked their spines. He had never had an organic pet before. They had fallen out of favor years ago with the modernization of Earth, leaving too few areas for them to be exercised. He had read about them, but never really understood the appeal until now. The two little dinosaurs were fun. It had been a long time since he'd been in the mood for fun.

Even joining Livia hadn't been because he wanted to enjoy the game, but because he wanted something so drastically different from reality. Here he was, in a world so different from the one he had been born into, a world where you could have pets, and be miles from another human. He wondered if his goal of making a farm was too small. Watching those two lizards had rekindled something inside of him that had died with Elam.

Shifting the two lizards, he picked them up despite a few tired protesting chirps, and deposited them in their den so that he could log out. Just shy of issuing the mental command, he reconsidered, laying down on his bedroll with a smile. This was his new life, a life of adventure, and limitless possibilities. He breathed in the pine scent around him, it had a slight musky hint to it from the compies and Shura being in the enclosure. "Maybe Toris was right, maybe the wheel will push me forward." With a smile on his lips, he logged out.

———

Matt drained one of the food tubes as he cracked his neck. The comm unit on the coffee table was blinking, but he avoided looking at it. There were only a handful of people that would have actually left him a message, and he didn't really want to talk to any of them. He pulled on his shoes and went for a run. The view panels in the complex displayed a fantastic lightning storm; the rumbling thunder could be felt through the cheap glass.

Which left Matt trying to remember the last time he had actually been outside. The atmosphere on Earth had become more and more extreme over the last few centuries. Which had prompted a fairly massive escape to the stars. The exodus and improved terraforming techniques had reduced the decay, but humanity had proven themselves poor stewards of their birth planet, and recovery was slow.

Dirty veins of lightning spread across the sky as he ran, and he wondered how much of the planet's current state had framed his mindset. Livia was hardly the first virtual world he had escaped to, but it was the first time that he realized he cared more about the fake world where he was a farmer than the real world. A logical portion of his brain nagged that this was probably a result of his grief.

Opting to ignore that, he decided to do some resistance training as well as running, and by the time he was done working through his emotions, he was covered in sweat. Exhausted in mind and body, he took a quick sonic shower before lying back down on his bed. His comm unit beeped right as he closed his eyes, and with a snort of annoyance, he peeked at the caller id.

Lexie.

With a groan, he accepted the call. "Hey." Matt's voice had an edge of antagonism that he didn't particularly want to be there, and he immediately shifted to a kinder tone. "What can I do for you, Lexie?" He didn't really manage nice, but at least the second sentence was less accusatory.

There was silence on the other side for a minute. "Hi Matt." Lexie's voice was timid, almost scared. "Can you switch to video, please? I haven't seen you in forever."

With a grunt, Matt activated the visual component; Lexie appeared in front of him. She had cut her hair, which was now hanging in a wavy-A-line bob to just below her collarbone. Her nose wrinkled in that way that told him she didn't approve of his appearance. "Bob, you look terrible."

Lexie's father had played an old online game where Bob had been the god of wormholes and had appealed to his authority when other people would just say 'God.' It was a quirk he had passed on to his daughter.

Matt frowned slightly at the phrase. "You, on the other hand, look very nice."

Rolling her eyes, Lexie continued on. "I talked to Jerry. He said you were working again." Her bluntness had been one of Matt's favorite parts about her. "He also said you'd agree to come to dinner."

"Yeah, look, you know how I get when I start something new. I told Jerry I wouldn't be able to do that for a few weeks." Matt ran a finger through his hair, trying to surreptitiously fix any errant locks.

"That's fine. Jerry said you wouldn't tell him what you were working on." Lexie paused there, obviously fishing for a response they both knew she wasn't going to get. She sighed. "I don't know why I still try. Six years together, and you never once showed me a project before it was done. And of course, it's been even worse since…"

"What can I help you with, L? I was just about to go to bed," Matt interrupted her introspection.

"I was hoping you could take a break and have dinner sooner." Matt was already shaking his head. "Fine. Tell me as soon as you have an exact day. Where are you even? It looks like one of the dole projects." Lexie started looking around the room.

"Okay, I will. Gotta go, bye," Matt said, and he cut the line as Lexie started to say something else. Looking around at the room around him, he started punching his spare pillow. The lack of resistance wasn't enough, so he got up and did pushups. Just seeing Lexie again had felt like a punch to the gut. The adrenaline in his system needed an outlet, and he had long ago discovered that working his arms was the fastest way to burn it off.

Eventually, his muscles gave out mid push, and he collapsed onto the floor, his cheek laying against the chilled metal. He couldn't bring himself to get back into the bed, so he just closed his eyes, willing the oblivion of sleep to take him.

Thirty minutes later, he groaned as he rolled over, using his legs to push himself up and then falling onto the bed where he tossed and turned for another half an hour. Finally deciding that sleep wasn't going to come anytime soon, he pulled open his art program and the saved map. Forthan hadn't come to talk to him about the plans like he had said he would, so he decided to figure out an irrigation system.

Ideally, it would be a watermill, since he could also use that to grind up the wheat to make flour. But realistically, that would take too much time and effort away from the rest of his building efforts. A channel that he could use to direct some of the water would also have too much pressure and probably damage the plants. Which left him needing to make a basin of some sort that he could open to regulate the flow.

Using Shape Earth, he could easily make a mostly tranquil pool that he could open up to divert water, but that would just get it near the crops, and he'd still have to use a bucket to water the actual plots. That also wouldn't level up his water magic, which was a pretty significant downside.

After searching the internet for another hour for a better solution, he decided he'd just keep using the Create Water spell until he could build a watermill. That decided, he closed his eyes and finally fell asleep.

CHAPTER SEVENTEEN

The Mine 1

DAY 7

Kas logged into light.

Which was strange because he had been expecting to log back into the wanderer's pine where he had logged off. In the half-a-second it took him to realize where he was, Liv appeared in front of him.

"Greetings, Kastigan. I apologize for bringing you out here, but one of the Unbinders desires to speak to you. If you will wait just a moment." Liv's voice was the same as before, it just felt strange to be in this bright place, and even as he thought that the world around him shifted.

Still bright, but that was because he was above the clouds. On a single mountain peak flattened at the top with a small pagoda. The temperature was a little cold, and the wind felt like it was trying to pull his clothes off. He tried to ask a question but the wind blew his words away.

Liv seemed immune to its effects. "The Unbinder is handling another issue currently, but he will be with you as soon as he is able." Liv was still standing next to him. The wind was loud, but he could hear her perfectly, despite the wind rather than over it.

Somehow the primal rage of the wind grounded him, chasing away the momentary fear that had sprung upon him by the lighted void. "What is going on?" Kas asked, as the wind lulled for a moment.

"The Unbinder will explain it all to you. But the subject I was given was: 'Improper companion allocation.'" Liv answered.

The Unbinders were the lore-friendly name for the game masters of Livia. He remembered reading that there had been a lot of blowback because non-combative classes missed their companions. He got a sinking feeling in his stomach. Were the devs going to take Shura away from him?

The surroundings altered again, and he was in a hallway. A handsome woman wearing a black pencil skirt and white blouse was standing next to a door, and she smiled at Kas. "Welcome, Kastigan. Please come in and have a seat. I'm Cassandra, one of the Unbinders for Western Kiddesh." She moved aside so that Kas could do as she requested.

When they sat down, Cassandra put a hand on her desk's reader, and a display appeared between them. "Sorry for the inconvenience. As you might have heard, there was an issue with assigned companions for non-combative unbound. You were flagged because you were one of the unbound who never met with your assigned companion, and since you're still playing the character, we're here to discuss how to remedy the situation."

"Oh, is that all?" Kas asked in relief. "Also, sorry, Cassandra, but there seems to be a mistake. I got my companion," he responded, relieved. There must have been an error in the script, and he was erroneously flagged.

Cassandra frowned and glanced at her data again. A few quick flicks of her hand, and Kas could see a representation of himself pulled up in front of her. "Hmm, that isn't what this is showing. You hired on Johannes then?" The image of Kas was joined with an older, and very weather-beaten man that he vaguely remembered seeing in Tallrock.

Kas shook his head. "No, my companion is named Shura." As Kas said her name, another image depicting Shura appeared next to the two already present. Cassandra eyed the new data for a moment, taking it in.

"Huh? Oh, I see why you would think that. Wow, yeah, especially since she gave you a blood oath." Cassandra gave a perfunctory smile and dismissed the image of Shura. "I'm happy to say that while Shura is indeed filling a similar role as Johannes was supposed to, she was not the companion you were assigned. As such, we have a couple of options going forward." Cassandra palmed her reader again, and Kas' sheet disappeared while Johannes stuck around, and several more images appeared next to him.

"We can redirect Johannes to your location, and he can fill the role originally intended. Or, you can choose one of a few different boons. Please note that we've decided to extend the subscription of all affected unbound by a month as compensation, and you'll be receiving that regardless of your other choices," Cassandra said, and she gestured to the first option. "First, we're prepared to grant you a free tier three building for your farm." The image she gestured to rotated between a windmill, a watermill, a large barn, and a couple of housing options.

"Secondly, we can give you ten loot crates. Or you can have five increased experience gain tokens. That would be double experience for a week per token."

Kas dismissed the loot crates; he'd never liked gambling, but considered the other three options. "What skill set does Johannes have?" he asked, looking at the man.

"Johannes is an experienced field hand; he can work your fields and do some basic construction, maintenance, and pest control around your property. In return, you would need to provide him with shelter and a small weekly payment or share of the farm's proceeds. Whichever you agree to when you meet him."

"I guess there isn't a way to get another land token?" Kas joked as he looked at the options.

"Oh, let me see," Cassandra said, placing her hand on the reader and rapidly rotating through options in the interface.

Kas blinked. Another land token would be great, but so would some of these other options. Expanding the tier three building options, he looked at the watermill, barn, and housing options.

Building Name: Watermill (3)
Tier: 3
Size: 15m x 10m x 5m
Benefits: Using an external water source, the watermill will generate mechanical power that can be used for a variety of purposes. The tier three structure can provide power to two additional structures. Includes either a gristmill or sawmill.
Upgrade: Watermill (4)

Building Name: Barn (Medium)
Tier: 3
Size: 15m x 30m x 10m
Benefits: Creates a storage location for small to large creatures to keep them out of the elements—works best on domesticated animals. It can also store feed or be used as housing.
Upgrade: Barn (Large), Granary, Byre

Building Name: Longhouse
Tier: 3
Size: 10m x 40m x 5m
Benefits: A large building designed for multi-family occupancy.
Upgrade: Barracks

Building Name: Farm House
Tier: 3
Size: Variable
Benefits: Provides a myriad of rooms for a specialized function. This

*building is modular and comes with a kitchen, bedroom, and bathroom.
Two additional rooms can be selected from the following list: bathroom,
bedroom, cellar, common room, dining room, and office.
Upgrade: Various, depends on rooms.*

Cassandra's voice interrupted his inspection. "I'm sorry, but you will only be able to acquire additional tokens through in-game means."

"Any suggestions on how to do that?" Kas asked as he glanced over the buildings, considering.

"I'm afraid I'm not authorized to do that," Cassandra said with a smile. "Have you decided on your boon?"

Shaking his head slightly, he considered the options. The farmhouse would certainly improve morale, but that wouldn't help him get the money that he needed; the longhouse had the same downsides. Which left the barn or the mill. The barn would be convenient, they could probably sleep inside it during a storm even, but... the mill would make getting all those other buildings easier. If he chose the sawmill, he could create planks for the rest of the buildings much faster, or the gristmill would allow him to grind his grains into flour and sell them for a higher price.

"The mill," Kas said after a minute of thought.

"Excellent, would you like a gristmill or a sawmill?" Cassandra held up a token for each.

Put on the spot, Kas tried to think the pros and cons through quickly. With the mill, either would make getting the other faster, and he would definitely make an effort to get the other one as fast as he could. Which was harder to make? The mechanics behind them were probably about the same, so would it be harder to get a saw or a millstone? He had a smith; he didn't have a stonemason. Would Costache be able to craft a saw? He couldn't shape stone, but with his high earth affinity, he might be able to make a spell that would do it.

"Which would be harder for me to make?" Kas asked aloud, and to his surprise, Cassandra answered.

"The gristmill. Stone Shape is a fairly advanced and taxing magic, and even if you could craft it, you would have a hard time moving the stone into position." She slid the gristmill token across the desk. "Plus, your farm is poorly positioned for a sawmill. Normal procedure is to use the river as free labor to move the lumber, but since you're at the base of a waterfall, you would have to haul the logs upstream, which will require a beast of burden.

"This is a summon token. Using it will allow you to use the placement tool. Once it's placed, it'll take about 24 hours before the building can be used." Cassandra smiled as Kas pocketed the token. "Well, it was a pleasure helping you. Is there anything else I can do for you before I send you back?"

Kas pondered for a moment and then shook his head. "No, I don't think so. Thank you very much."

"It's my pleasure, and we apologize again for the error. We hope you enjoy your time in Livia."

White filled his vision again, and he was suddenly back on the mountain with the dryad.

Liv stood next to him, her face full of radiant life. "There is an old saying." Her voice carried to Kas over the rushing of the wind. "That no good deed goes unpunished." Before he could respond, she bowed slightly and Kas found himself on his bedroll under the wandering pine.

You have lost 500 points of Karma.

Kas blinked. He had lost 500 points of Karma? Wasn't that a bad thing? He distinctly remembered fantasy games created long ago about wandering through a wasteland. In those games, you gained Karma for good actions and lost it for bad. Did that mean the game saw his actions as bad? But then why had the dryad called it a good deed? And why was he to be punished for doing it? And why had she looked so... full of life as she said it? So happy? She had seemed very nice when he had met her before.

The internal debate over the meaning of his loss of Karma was interrupted as Dino and Diane hopped out of their den, the two little compies chirping excitedly as they butted their heads into his hands. He reflexively gave them the scratches and pets they were demanding even as he could feel himself losing control.

Talking to Lexie, talking about Elam to Shura, and the events of the morning all added up to something that he suddenly couldn't deal with anymore. He pulled Diane into his arms and hugged her tight even as tears streamed down his face, discoloring her scales. Diane wriggled in his arms and Dino hopped about, squeaking in agitation. It was clear the two compies could tell there was something wrong but that they couldn't determine what the problem was.

It only took a few minutes to cry himself out, his tears sat in a shallow reserve these days. Kas lifted Diane up to kiss her head and then let her go. "Thanks, Diane." Rubbing his eyes, he went through the well-rehearsed actions to remove any trace of his tears. His Create Water spell allowed him to scrub the streaks from his face. He then pinched the skin on his face to get back some color and cleared his throat. Once he was done cleaning away any traces of tears, he stood up and exited the wanderer's pine.

There was already quite a bit of activity around the camp. Shura was making breakfast while Forthan double-checked his men's gear. The miners sat off to one side; they were hefting the newly-made mining picks that Costache had created the night before, and clutching tight to the utility knives on their belts as they stared around uneasily. Each had a hard hat containing small round rocks in a wireframe that covered their heads. Kas assumed these would be the focal point of their light spells.

There was no sign of Costache or Shannon yet, nor was breakfast ready, so he walked over to his crops and began tending to them for the day while he considered where exactly he wanted to put the mill. His wheat was doing well, it had advanced again and was now classified as a growthling;

according to what he found on the forums that meant it was halfway done. Which meant it took about nine days to grow.

His potato field had been the second thing he planted, but they matured much more quickly and were also growthlings. He would probably be able to harvest them tomorrow. The corn would likely be ready to collect the same day as the wheat, as it was now in the sprouts stage.

Timing on crops was going to be a thing he would need to pay attention to; having a bunch of fields in need of harvest on the same day might be a good thing or a bad. He'd have to see how involved the actual harvesting process was. He dealt with the daily tending requirements for the first five fields, then played the minigame to clear an eighth field. Wanting to take advantage of the new mill he had acquired, he also planted wheat in the first empty field. After watering all six plots, he headed back toward the campfire only to discover that breakfast was already over.

"I saved you some," Shura said, nodding her head towards a plate set aside near where she was cleaning out the pot.

"Thanks, sorry I missed it," Kas said between bites. "Had a meeting with an Unbinder that put me behind."

"An Unbinder? Is everything alright?" Shura frowned.

"It's fine, there were some problems and they gave me a building summon token for a gristmill; I figured I'd place it on the river somewhere before we headed down."

"Ahh, well, that's good then. I thought you were just working on the fields, figured you'd want to get your crops done before you go down into the mine. That way if you have to spend the night, you wouldn't miss a day." She glanced around to make sure none of the rest of the group were within earshot. "I wanted to talk to you about the kobolds."

"What's up?" Kas asked, curious to know what Shura would want to talk to only him about.

"Many people think kobolds are evil. They are not." Shura's voice was cast in such a way that he doubted anyone would hear them over the babble of the river. "They are mischievous, which makes them less than desirable neighbors, but they aren't malicious. I know everyone is getting ready for a fight, and I'm not saying you shouldn't fight back if they attack you. But not every problem needs to be solved by conflict."

"So, you don't want me to kill the kobolds?" Kas frowned. He had been mentally hyping up having to kill them since the day before.

"Well, they might not give you a choice. I doubt you'll have a common language, just keep your eyes open. You are going to be invading their homes; they will be scared." Shura put down the pot, having finished cleaning it. "Put yourself in their shoes and see if you can find a solution that doesn't end in blood."

"Uh..." Kas' brain hadn't entirely caught up with the conversation. "I'll try? I mean, I don't want to kill anyone." Which was true, he really *didn't* want to kill anyone. The whole point of him choosing to be a farmer was so that he didn't have to kill sentient creatures. He would have included animals on that list, but frankly, he found the food in-game far better than what was available to him, in reality, these days.

Shura nodded her head and then walked away, leaving Kas alone to finish his breakfast and ponder. The latter lasted longer than the former and ended only when Shannon sat down next to him.

"So, we gonna do this or what?" she asked, and Kas was glad she had dropped her fake accent. She still sounded vaguely exotic, but he couldn't figure out where her accent came from.

"Yeah, I guess we should," Kas said, and he stood up and quickly washed off his plate and put it on top of the others. Then followed Shannon over the clearing where Forthan was still giving some last-minute instructions to his men. Costache and the miners were listening to him provide some basic weapon instructions, while the tribesmen demonstrated what he was talking about. Occasionally one of the miners would try to mimic one of the movements.

"Sorry about the delay, everyone. I wanted to get the crops tended before we left," Kas said, and there was some grumbling but everyone mostly just started picking up their gear. Forthan made his way over to him and nodded.

"We never did get to talk about where we wanted to put everything, but where were you planning on putting the gristmill?" Kas asked, looking around the valley and trying to determine a good spot from here.

Forthan paused, and then pulled out a thick folded up piece of paper from his pocket. Flipping it open, he exposed a reasonably well-done map of the immediate portions of the valley. "The river gets narrow and deep here; the water flows fast and should provide plenty of power." Forthan frowned as he looked at Kas. "Why?"

"I got a building summon token from an Unbinder." Kas pulled the map out of Forthan's hands. Playing around with his interface to copy the data on the map on his personal map before handing it back. "I'll look through these suggestions and see what I think. You coming with us to the mouth of the mine?"

"Yes," Forthan said with a nod. "I'll do some exploring while you're down there, but I'll see you off."

"Sounds good. We can discuss stuff while we walk." Kas looked around, and seeing that everyone was ready, headed towards the mine, the rest of the group falling in behind him.

The map itself was actually quite well done. There were clear demarcations for fields, housing districts, a central market, industrial sector, and more. The group took a few more minutes to get into motion, and Kas zoomed out enough on the map to get a good idea of where the mine was in relation to Forthan's plans.

"Guys, let's follow the river for a bit," he called out. Some obvious things needed to change, but the location of the mill wasn't one of them. For example, Forthan had taken an excellent plot of land to use as the fighting arena. Kas mentally dragged that over to a small half bowl off to one side of the valley.

Then he rezoned the area around the bowl to act as a

barracks and training yard area, giving the entire endeavor a larger footprint while also removing its centrality. Next, he set aside a large section near the lake itself for a park. Making it bigger than was strictly needed, so that he could add some large buildings on the outer edge of it.

If Miranda Valley ever did become a major hub, this would give him plenty of space for the government areas. He also added a few more tweaks to some of the roads, mostly to widen them. Which had a good bit of ripple effects as he was forced to move the entire thing out a lot more than Forthan had initially set it up.

Unfortunately, a lot of the external areas weren't explored yet, so it was speculation, the map in that area fuzzy instead of the details that it held in places they had actually been to. He made a mental note to search for herbs in the less explored areas, even drawing a few routes onto his map to save for later.

Ten minutes along the rough path alongside the river brought them to the location the mill was planned for, and Kas told everyone to wait a minute while he took out the token.

A holographic green outline of the mill appeared in front of him. Next to the mill were a series of numbers, listing how many newtons of force the river would produce with the current configuration, as well as the total square footage, and something called displacement index.

A quick search of the help menu told him that the displacement index was just a measurement of how much dirt would be moved to a pile on one side of the building by the summoning. After playing with the location for a few minutes, he found a spot that he liked and mentally accepted the structure's position. Immediately a dense fog appeared on the riverbank.

The tribesmen and miners all called out in alarm, some of them having been relaxing inside the area the fog covered which was nearly twice as big as the green hologram had been. A few hasty retreats, and everyone was safely outside the building's zone.

"Sorry about that everyone, I got a building token and I

wanted to put it in before we left, since it's going to take a day for it to finish summoning." Most of them lost interest when they discovered that it wasn't likely to improve their housing situation. But Shannon asked him a few questions about how he got it. When he told her about his morning meeting with Cassandra, she frowned.

"I wonder if that means I wasn't designated as a non-combat class," Shannon said with a slight pout. "Not really fair. If I had made my build a little less combat-capable, I'd be able to get a companion. Wish I would have known that going into it. Could have gotten a few more of the things I wanted."

"What sort of build are you going for?" Kas asked as they started back on their way to the cave.

"A bunch of ranged stuff, and stealth and survival skills. I figured I'd be off on my own a bunch, and that would give me the best survival chance. Now I wish I would have picked up animal bonding like Shura has. I think it would be handy to have a bunch of animals following me around," Shannon groused.

"Well, you can always get it with an upgrade. What are your affinities?"

"Major affinities in divination and earth magics, and then cartography, archery, and magitech. Minors are all over the place; I took a recommended package. There are a ton of prereqs for doing the whole dowsing thing well. I won't even be able to do most of them until I get a bunch more affinities, so trying to do animal bonding too would delay a lot of those pretty far." She swatted a tall reed out of her way with a bit of waspish anger.

"Well, part of the whole point of this is creating something for other people to take advantage of. Give it a bit of time, and I'm sure we'll have some beasts that will help you on your travels," Kas said with a shrug. He knew Shura was looking for more helpful creatures, but from the sounds of it, selling bonded animals would be a great addition to his sales. He mentally added a larger ranching area for Shura to the list of changes he needed to make to the valley's layout.

"Tell you what, when we have something you want, I'll give you a good deal on the first thing you buy."

"First thing? Assuming I'll want to buy more than one?" Shannon quirked an eyebrow.

"Oh yeah, Shura is gonna find some awesome stuff. We're gonna try for a cloud wolf when we level up a bit, and some other mounts and beasts of burden too."

"What's a cloud wolf?" Shannon asked, and Kas told her about their first time in the valley. The two talked about what sort of creatures they would like to have as a mount, each time their choices got more outlandish until they arrived at the mouth of the mine.

CHAPTER EIGHTEEN

The Mine 2

Kas wasn't sure what he was expecting, but the mouth of the mine was not it. It was a dark hole a little wider than his shoulders at its narrowest. In all, it wouldn't be hard to get in or out of the cave, but he'd have to basically crawl.

"How did you even find this?" Kas asked as the miners went around handing out light stones to everyone.

"The dowsing rod led us straight to it," Shannon said as she tightened all the straps on her armor; everything lost all the looseness it had. When she saw Kastigan's gaze, she shrugged. "Don't want to get caught on a rock or something."

Everyone else seemed to be making preparations, but Kas had no idea what he would do. His own armor was already reasonably form-fitting, and he didn't have weapons that needed to be secured. He did re-familiarize himself with his spells, though. Death Blast was likely to be the most useful; it was a single target spell and did the most damage by far. Frostbolt or Poison Spray might be helpful as well for the slowing and area damage, respectively. Decay might be useful for crowd control. Rock Shard if he needed to cut something, maybe? In movies, the hero always cut chandelier ropes so that they would fall on the mooks. Perhaps he could do that.

Kas had been keeping his mana just under full since they started the walk; it had allowed him some progress on his various skills, but not much.

"Everyone ready?" Damae asked. The sword and board tribesman was in charge of the entire expedition. However, Bliny was going to be calling the shots when they actually got into combat. He had traded his longbow in for a short bow that he said would be easier to use in the caves, with a thin short sword as his backup weapon. Kas was pretty sure it was called a gladius. Tryry had a similar setup to Bliny, although he was dabbing a viscous red liquid on his arrowheads.

The two miners each held a newly crafted pickaxe as their only weapons. Kas wasn't sure they would get much room to swing them but assumed they didn't have any other weapons. Shannon and Costache each held more traditional arming swords. Costache held a round shield that wasn't nearly as large as Damae's heater shield. Wyk was the last of the group, and he had traded in his long spear for a shorter one that would be easier to use in confined spaces. He also had a gladius in case even that was too long for the situation.

Kas, of course, had his knife, but he really hoped he wasn't going to need it. Damae had him in the back of the group since he had some of the weakest melee attacks and solid ranged combat. That meant that Kas got to watch as everyone lowered themselves down until they disappeared. Taking one last look up at the sky, he was reminded of an ancient video his grandfather had forced him to watch about a kid descending into a mine.

The morning sun disappeared as he clambered down a narrow shaft that descended at about a 70-degree angle. Going down at least three times his height, the tunnel opened up again, coming down on one side of a large open space. Dripping drew his attention to a small pool near the center of the cavern. A stalactite and stalagmite were just a hands-width from touching in the middle of the basin. A thick droplet caught the light and fell from one to the other.

The rest of the group had spread out. There was only one other exit from the area: a large, jagged hole wide enough for Shura to walk through it, leading deeper towards the Spine of Aktrosha. The tunnel's floor was uneven and slanted down, rubble-strewn across the ground making it anything but flat. Damae gestured him forward. Costache was already working on something near the mouth of the tunnel. A large boulder had been moved aside, and the man was tinkering with some kind of mechanical device.

Damae held up a finger to his lips to indicate they should be quiet. "This is our kobold evidence. Closer than it was yesterday. Not sure what that means, but it's probably bad." Damae's tone was low-pitched, not a whisper but designed not to carry very far, pointing to the mechanism which connected to dozens of thin strands. "Touch any of those, and this pulls a cable that leads further into the system. We assume it is a warning system."

"They're that advanced? I was sort of expecting... I dunno, pit traps, or something." Kas tried to replicate the quiet method of talking Damae used as he looked at the device curiously. It wasn't exactly rocket science, just a series of gears and pulleys really, but it was far more intricate than he had been expecting from the reports last night.

"Oh, they are mechanical geniuses," Costache answered in the same manner from where he knelt next to the device. "Thankfully, these ones don't seem to know any magitech, just pure engineering. All this sets off a cable which probably rings a bell or something back in their village." He carefully pulled a gear out, and most of the other gears sprang into motion, each rapidly cranking as all the threads slowly fell to the floor. "Got it!" Costache exclaimed in excitement.

Everyone froze as Costache's words echoed eerily down the tunnel. From somewhere much deeper, they heard a single boom. By unspoken agreement, everyone held their breath, straining their ears to hear anything else, and covered their lights.

After an agonizing moment in the darkness, Shannon spoke into the quiet. "I can hear something, it's far… sounds, it sounds like the sea?" She uncovered her light and looked around. "Only one source, it sounds like waves crashing." Her half-quinthan nature gave her much better hearing than everyone else. Kas idly wondered how the game actually interpreted that, did it make everything louder, or did it filter things out somehow?

"Alright, we're going to keep moving. Costache, you're with me at the front," Damae said as he too uncovered his light. "You're probably hearing some version of 'vik. Kobolds speak a broken version of the holy tongue."

Kas discreetly called up the help file on 'vik.

'vik is a common slang for either Ssar'vik (high draconic) or Ar'vik (low draconic), the languages spoken by Dragons. Few beings can replicate them, having neither the vocal capacity or range of hearing to understand all its intricacies. Context addition: Kobolds speak a simplified version of Ar'vik, usually creating a pidgin of Ar'vik combined with the most common local languages in the area they occupy. Understanding either draconic language (restricted to Dragons and Drak) or the local language will allow you to understand some of what a kobold says.

"Great, anyone speak…" Kas trailed off, trying to think of what the local language to the frontier would be. "Kiddeshan?" Looking around, no one gave him a confirmation. "Well, I guess we can cross that when we get there, I assume some of you at least understand Ssar'vik or Ar'vik?" The last was directed to the tribesmen who were standing near the tunnel entrance.

After looking at each other for a moment, Damae gave a half-half gesture with his hands. "Most of us can sort of follow a conversation in Ar'vik. None of us can speak it, though."

"Can Forthan and Shura speak it?" Kas asked, frowning down the tunnel.

"Forthan only knows the lesser Ar'vik, Shura most likely speaks both," Damae said, and there was a twinge of... guilt in his words.

Kas frowned; he knew that Forthan's family hadn't really participated in the Dragon War. Was that some kind of shame on his family tree? Drak culture was very confusing. He had read a few accounts from people who had opted to play one, and almost all of them made the cultural differences a significant part of their commentary on playing them.

There were significant advantages to playing a drak, mainly if you wanted to play a combat class. They had barely any talent for magic; in fact, you could only put a single minor affinity into magic during character creation. The upside was that they got more weapon and style affinities than any other race by a fair margin. They also got an extensive range of pseudo magical racial talents they could invest in, like their breath weapons.

With a shake of his head, Kas then nodded. "Alright, we'll burn that bridge when we cross it. Shall we?" He gestured forward; Damae nodded, and he and Costache took the lead. They had to stop a few more times to disable traps. Luckily, Costache was far more capable on the subject than Kas would have assumed him to be. It made him wonder just what sort of life the blacksmith had lived before coming to the frontier. Had he come here voluntarily, or was he one of those they took from the prisons?

Not that it really mattered, he supposed. Costache wasn't someone he could build his farm without. Kas had plenty of time to think, though, as they moved slowly through the narrow crack. If they did manage to turn this into a mine, just getting this central passage functional would be a task that would probably take a few days. He would also need to build some minecarts and a track, or at least have his people make them. It would take some time, he imagined.

But they had all the skills they needed to make it happen, just needed to start getting a good supply of metal and then figure out a way to start turning all the logs they were getting into better quality boards.

For a moment, he regretted picking the gristmill over the sawmill, but he forced those thoughts away. What was done was done, and there was no point in worrying about actions that he could no longer change. Besides, he could have his people build a sawmill, it was just a matter of time. Everything came down to time, where he wanted to spend the one resource he would never have enough of.

A poke from behind and a grunt told him that he needed to focus on the task at hand rather than his future thoughts. And he realized he had fallen behind quite a bit, holding up the entire rear of the group. With a sigh, he jumped from the rock he was standing on to the next, landing on all fours and trying to keep himself from slipping down into the small pit between the two. Besides, it would take them days to clear out all the rubble here and make it into a pathway.

The next few minutes were a quick scramble as he tried to catch up with the others, only managing to do so when Costache spotted another trap. While the stout cian worked on disabling the kobold's newest mechanism, Kas looked around. They had just entered another small expansion area. The rest of the group could actually spread out a bit instead of staying single file. Kas looked over and saw that the two miners had their heads together and were discussing something with some level of animation.

Making his way over to them, he patted Simeon on the shoulder. "What's going on?" he asked, interrupting their quiet conversation.

"Oh, sorry, sir, I didn't see you. We decided to take a moment ta look at what sort of rocks were in the cavern, and Gus found this," Simeon said, handing a small rock over to Kas.

Curious, Kas called up the information prompt on it.

Item: Sedimentary Rock
Composition: mostly ferrous

Description: Sedimentary rocks are formed when pressure compresses multiple types of earth. This particular sample contains significant traces of iron. Using a smelter, you can refine this mineral-rich rock into more useful parts.

The information wasn't entirely helpful, but Kas assumed that was because he didn't have any ranks in mining. In fact, he probably only got as much as he did because of his high earth affinity. Handing the rock back to Simeon, he smiled. "Well, that's good news. Have you seen any other likely spots to start mining?"

"Oh, yes sir, indeed, sir. We've found ourselves some tin, zinc, and copper. This is the best bit of iron that we've found, but we imagine that it will probably become richer the deeper into the mine that we delve. We could probably do everything you need of us with the mine up to right here for now. But you'd need to block the passage at least, and maybe still hire some guards. I'm afraid neither Gus nor myself fancy the idea of having kobolds near us."

Kas ran a hand through his hair, or at least he tried to. The thick leather helmet he wore didn't let him through. He looked around the small cave. Earlier he had taken off the helmet and been yelled at by Damae. "It's okay, Simeon, we're already here, and I'd like to delay blocking off the mine. We'll keep that as a last resort, I suppose, but a little bit of effort upfront here will pay dividends down the line, I think."

"Very good, sir. I can't say I'm looking forward to it, but Gus and meself will be right there with you," Simeon said, hefting his pickaxe with a wicked-looking grin.

The fact that if they were right near him they wouldn't be anywhere near the melee combatants where they could actually do some good with their pickaxes didn't escape Kas' notice though. He opted not to mention it for now, though, since the two really were such a valuable portion of his team. Without someone like them to supply the many mineral needs of the farm, they would need to spend a lot more money on tools and materials.

"Well, keep at it, gather as much as you can store without weighing yourselves down. We can pick up more on the way back, but I don't want you loaded down in case we need to retreat," Kas said with a smile at the two miners.

Gus and Simeon glanced at each other for a moment before coming to an unspoken agreement. They began emptying rocks out of their bags into a neat stack on one side of the room. Kas kept himself from laughing at the two's blatant fear of combat.

Which, of course, reminded him of his own fear of combat. He didn't want to hurt anyone, especially after Shura's statements about the kobolds. He spent the next minute deep in thought as he considered how best to use his spells to deal non-lethal damage. When Costache finally announced the passage as safe to travel, they began again, only to stop a few minutes later as the tunnel branched. Kas was called forward.

"Which way do you think?" Damae asked him, and Kas blinked.

"Shouldn't we ask Shannon?" Kas said, turning to the other unbound and casting his voice so that she could hear it. "Shannon, can you sense life or anything?"

Shannon tapped her chin thoughtfully for a moment. "I could look for water sources? The kobolds would probably have some in their village... or lair, or whatever it is that kobolds live in." She pulled out one of her magitech devices and began fiddling with settings on the side of it. After a moment, blue dots started appearing on several sides of the ball, the brightest dot pointed up and in a direction opposite the direction they were traveling and elongated.

"That's the river," Shannon said, and with a few more deft maneuvers, that dot disappeared. Another dot began to glow brighter, this one pointed down and to the 'left' of where they were currently heading. It was roughly in line with the larger of the two branches. It was twice as big as the original tunnel, while the other tube was slightly smaller than the one they were currently in.

"Alright, let's go for the bigger one," Kas pronounced. "Should we leave guards or something on the smaller one?"

"We'll scout both," Damae said, after a moment of thought. "Won't matter much if the tunnel is too small to travel down or dead ends. Wyk and I will scout, you lot stay here."

"Shouldn't Shannon or I go?" Kas asked; the two unbound could respawn, after all.

Damae shook his head. "We'll just scout a bit ahead. You will be plenty close enough for us to help if it comes to a fight."

"What about the traps?" Kas pushed the tribesman.

"None of the traps thus far have been designed to kill, only entangle or warn," Damae said and Kas glanced over to Costache who nodded in confirmation. "They should be safe enough, and you two are some of the weakest melee combatants we have."

Unable to come up with any other reason to not have the two tribesmen go, Kas shrugged.

Seeing his consent, Damae gestured for Wyk to take the smaller tunnel while he ventured down the larger one. They were both supposed to go down the shaft and be back in five minutes.

Kas wasn't sure if it was the sheer weight of the rock above him, the darkness, or the not knowing, but everyone sat in uncomfortable silence, their imaginations playing out the worst possibilities in their heads.

Multiple times, Kas was sure he heard something coming from one tunnel or the other and prepared to cast a frostbolt only for nothing to appear. The others would also seemingly randomly clutch their weapons in response to something they heard. The first few times, there were chuckles, but after a few minutes, no one thought it was funny anymore.

Five minutes stretched out to six before Wyk appeared back. "Damae not back yet?" was the first thing he asked when he returned. When everyone shook their heads, he frowned. "We'll give him another minute…" Wyk said, but he was cut off as a heavy smashing sound came from the tunnel Damae had walked down, followed by a loud curse in Pinthan. A second loud impact was heard, and Kas waited for more cursing. The silence that followed was somehow more terrifying.

"Alright, Costache, let's go down that way, sounds like Damae hit a trap," Wyk said, and the cian began cautiously moving forward, jumping to the next boulder. The group followed behind. Kas' thoughts raced. Had Damae been coming back, or had he kept going the full five minutes?

"By the King's tits," Costache said as the cian man seemed to disappear in front of Kas.

It was difficult to say precisely because Wyk was between them. Wyk jumped into motion, his spear knocking against a boulder as he moved to get a good look at whatever had happened to Costache.

Even as he did that, Kas heard curses from behind him and then felt something heavy fall on top of him, forcing him to fall down to his knees before buckling backward from the weight. A thick net or blanket had been thrown on top of him, the burden preventing him from moving.

Finally, he heard muffled warcries and curses. Craning his neck to get an idea of what was happening, Kas just saw half a dozen shafts of light going off in random directions as light sources were either dropped or were moved as whoever was holding them tried to fight off whatever had attacked them. Kas' own light had fallen near his head, shining up at the ceiling, his eyes followed the beam cast. On a ledge that had been hidden above stood two kobolds.

It was clear they had been the ones to throw whatever it was that was keeping him from fighting. In the light, he could see blue scales, the figures themselves were the size of children, perhaps more stretched out, with thin limbs and a long neck.

He struggled to get free so that he could use his hands, but the two kobolds added weight by the simple expedient of jumping onto the net. What little movement he had achieved before that was stopped. The two kobolds seemed to hiss at each other before one bent down and shoved a cloth into Kas' face. Almost immediately, he felt his body go lax, his muscles not responding.

Unable to keep his head up anymore, Kas laid it down on the rock. Some part of him knew that the sharp material should bother him, but he couldn't bring himself to care. Only able to see half of the battle, he watched as the last of the tribesmen finally fell. He saw a number of the kobolds begin the complicated process of moving the much larger creatures. His own net was picked up by six of the little things and carried away from the light. They traveled in the darkness for a while, the kobolds making quick time over the rough terrain.

They stopped twice to rest, the kobolds dumping him on the ground rather than trying to keep him in any position where he would be comfortable. At the second stop, he had a bowl put to his lips, and he was forced to drink. He tried not to choke as the cool liquid ran down his throat, the chill numbness that had begun to recede came back in full force. It was even stronger this time, and he found he couldn't even keep his eyes open. Kas tried to think, but it felt like he was trying to climb uphill in a snowstorm. Two steps backward for every step forward. It was a comfortable darkness he existed in.

The fourth time they dropped him, they didn't pick him back up. He slowly regained enough control over his movement to open his eyes again. There was a light source off to the side, and after several attempts, he managed to move his neck slightly so that he could see it. It took a few more minutes for him to be able to focus his eyes on what he was seeing. The entire process of being numbed slowly wearing off. He was tied up in a small cave; it was difficult to tell, but he assumed the dark shapes next to him were the other delvers.

Moving his mouth, Kas tried to say something; a low gurgle came out. There were small movements that he could half-see out of the corner of his eyes, he wasn't sure if that was because of the relaxant or the darkness. His eyes steadily gained focus, and he could see that there was a gate of some sort covering the entrance to the cave, and the cave itself had a thick layer of sand along the bottom, which made it all the more difficult to move. At least, he really hoped it was sand. The alternatives weren't things he wanted to consider.

A pressure on his shoulder motivated him to slowly turn. Two kobolds had approached and were in the process of tying his hands and feet. Once satisfied with their knots, they pushed him until he was lying on his back, staring up at the ceiling.

A thick bone was inserted between his arms, and then they slid it between his legs. Four more kobolds then used it to pick him up. They took him through a hole in the darkness. His head lolled around, and he could feel it brushing against the ground every now and again.

In one instance, his head actually smacked against the ground—he could feel a bump form—but the kobolds didn't seem to care. The area they were in was dark so Kas had no idea if it would happen again; he tried to tuck his head up closer to the bone without much success. Luckily the first bump was not repeated, and the room grew lighter, as thick strands of glowing green, blue, and red started floating in his vision. It took him several minutes to realize they were bioluminescent plants. With a start, he realized he could even smell the greenery, thick and pleasant odors that reminded him of falling rain.

The bone was lowered more gently than previously, his head was turned so that he was facing a slightly larger kobold. He tried to speak, but only a low moan came out of his mouth. The kobold hissed and waved his hands, causing a flurry of movement behind him. The kobold's scaled feet made a shuffling sound as they leaped to do whatever the chief told them to do. Since he couldn't talk or move, Kas took the opportunity to study the kobold.

It was difficult to tell by the angle, but he assumed it would stand a little over a meter tall, with a thin, almost snake-like body that moved in a slightly hypnotizing manner. The thick curling whiskers on its snout made him look like an unusually small oriental dragon. His, at least Kas assumed it was a male, scales were the same dark blue as Shura, and he wondered how closely they would be related. Strange feathers hung off several leather straps across his body, clearly more for decoration than protection.

The chief had taken the time to study him as well. He closed his eyes, two separate lids closing in sequence, and then began to hiss. Kas could feel the magic in the chief's words and mentally reassigned him as a shaman. After a moment he opened his eyes, the shaman hissing again, only now he could tell what he was saying.

"Why do the scaleless come to the cave of the Amniwatu tribe?"

CHAPTER NINETEEN

The Mine 3

Kas forced himself to focus on the shaman, there was a ticking in his head that made it hard to concentrate. "We came here hoping to forge an alliance that would be mutually beneficial for both our peoples," was what he intended to say. To his horror, that is not what he said though. "We came for your metal."

"Ah-ha, knew it!" the shaman proclaimed with glee. He jumped around while he pumped his wiry arms up and down. When he had calmed down, he hopped back over to Kas, his fu manchu mustache quivering on his face tickling Kas' cheeks. "Tell me, scaleless, what you intend to give Tu'kar for da gifts of Aktrosha?"

Every syllable caused the thick mustache to tickle his face, which was the only thing that prevented the horror of realizing that he must have been under some sort of serum that made him tell the truth. By a twist of fate that was both boon and bane, the shaman turned slightly, sending his mustache into Kas' nose which immediately caused him to sneeze. Right into the shaman's face. The shaman recoiled immediately in horror even as Kas felt compelled to answer.

"Grain, fruits, and other foodstuffs, possibly animals, and

labor," Kas answered as soon as the sneeze was out of his mouth.

The shaman hurried over to one side of the room, where he ripped up a leaf and then began smearing it all over his face. The faint smell of mint filled the air as he did so. It took him several moments to clean himself to his own satisfaction.

In the meantime, Kas' vision had improved considerably. If he wasn't scared the kobold was going to kill him, he would have been very impressed with the room. Thick stalks of bioluminescent plants filled a cavern that was twenty meters wide and double that long; the ceiling was a perfectly smooth dome above them.

In the middle of the room, a bubbling pond flickered with reflected light, a nearly endless array in every color of the rainbow that sent scintillating flickers of light across the room. Creating an ever-changing kaleidoscope of images on the round dome.

"How *dare you!*" the shaman shouted from a much more distant spot in the room. His glare at Kas was anything but kind. "You come to the home cave, intent to steal and plunder the gifts of great ancestor. To enslave my people and—"

The shaman's tirade was cut short by a gentle snort, which silenced him immediately. A second kobold stepped out of a dark patch in the foliage which had perfectly hidden him. This one was also skinny, but where the shaman was wiry, this kobold was lithe.

The lithe kobold stepped forward with a serpentine sway that was almost hypnotic to watch. "K'ark Na'Tan, the human not say he came to steal. Under the water, he said he came to trade with us."

The shaman's blue scales seemed to whiten a little across his chest and legs, taking on a milky texture. "He has much mana, could be immune to da water."

"You know it take more da'n mana t'defeat da water," the lithe kobold said before turning back to Kas. "Tell me, scaleless, do ye know we were here?"

"Yes, although you're not what I was expecting," Kas blurted out. "And my name is Kastigan."

"We not be interested in the name you take. Yer soul be not connected to this body. Ye be unbound, that name a lie. We call you scaleless," the shaman said, poking Kas' chest with a thin finger. Unlike what he expected, the thick nail on the end of the finger felt more like a callous rather than a talon.

Kas realized that there was some element of truth to that fact, he hadn't told them his name was Matt. This was all part of the game, and somehow that was very comforting to him. He straightened out as much as he could while still being restrained. "What are your names?" he asked.

The two shared a quick glance and then the smaller one answered first, "Dis one be Yazhira, chief of da Tu'kar." The kobold did a strange head bob that seemed to indicate that they pointed with their snouts rather than their hands. "And dat be Na'Tan, our bone speaker," Yazhira said even as he moved to untie Kas from the bone he was attached to. It only took a few minutes but Kas immediately sat down, still not sure if his legs would support his weight.

The freedom allowed him to get a better look around him. The entire pool in the middle of the cavern was surrounded on all sides by the strange glowing foliage. Even to the point that he wasn't sure where they had brought him in. Either they had some sort of illusion magic or they had very cleverly disguised the exits to the room. Given the complexity of the traps they had encountered on the way in, Kas was putting his money on the latter.

"It is a pleasure to meet you Yazhira and Na'Tan." The two kobolds had sat down next to him, with Yazhira taking the more prominent position. Clearly, he was now here to discuss the terms of the trade agreement. However, since that had not been part of the plan, Kas was somewhat at a loss as to where to begin, and the two kobolds were more than happy to let him begin the discussion. Kas wished that Shura or Forthan were here; he hadn't exactly ever participated in the creation of a trade route.

"If I may ask, before we begin discussing a trade agreement, are my companions alright?" Kas asked.

"Yes, dey are fine. You bond wit one o' da great ancestors. Da magic work better on you," Na'Tan answered.

It took a minute for Kas to process that. Somehow his bond with Shura was seen as being bound to one of the dragons? "I see." He paused, trying to stall for time. "Might I be able to see your village?" Kas asked, hoping that seeing the state of their village he might be able to better gauge their needs.

"No," Yazhira said without thinking.

Kas blinked, unsure how to respond to the refusal. There wasn't much he could do without more information and it seemed the Tu'kar had no interest in allowing him to gather any.

"Well, let me start by telling you what we want then," Kas said after collecting his thoughts. "We're building a farm in the valley above this cavern. We are requesting access to mine the minerals in the cave system. Particularly copper, tin, and iron. Although if there are any precious metals, we would also be interested in trading for access to those as well."

"How much?" Yazhira asked.

"How much… are we wanting to mine?" Kas asked, and when Yazhira pounded his chest in agreement, he paused to think about how much metal they would need. "I have two miners with me. As much ore as they can mine in a day. I'd also like to make allowances for additional miners, should more arrive."

Yazhira glanced over at Na'Tan and the two hissed at each other, clearly discussing their terms. After a few exchanges, Yazhira answered, "Each miner will give us one part in twenty of all dat dey mine. Der will also be a payment of fifty units of raw foodstuffs, preferably vegetables or grain, to be paid on da first day of each turning. We allow you to mine in the outer reaches, we mark areas dey no allowed to be."

A popup had given Kas the exact details of the deal.

You have entered into trade negotiations with Chief Yazhira of the Tu'kar tribe.
Current offer:

- *You will pay: 5% of each miner's daily yield, 50 units of food every 90 days.*
- *You will get: Access to the outer reaches area of the Tu'kar Tribe Cave under Miranda Valley.*

Kas had no idea what sort of yield his crops would give him. During the beta testing, a field would usually return anywhere from three to five units of food. Kas was pretty sure his Enrich Soil spell would give him a higher yield than that, but until his first harvest he wouldn't know. Still, knowing that he would only have to pay it every ninety days allowed him to do some quick mental math. A crop took at least four or five days to mature, and if it gave a minimum yield of three units per harvest then that would mean a single crop plot dedicated to feeding the Tu'kar would pay for the miners with some left over.

Now, obviously that was the worst-case scenario, but he could easily do it with just corn and still have a full harvest left over. And that was assuming minimum yield. Sure, it was a bit of a pain to have to dedicate an entire plot to keeping the mining operation going, but if that was the price... Or was it the price? This was a negotiation, and while Yazhira had been fairly upfront with him, what if the kobold was actually trying to fleece him? It was entirely possible that he was being upfront, and trying to negotiate would offend the kobold.

There had to be a way to probe the chief to determine which situation it was. Looking over the notice again, Kas focused on what he would get. "I have a question about this outer reaches area. By the name, I assume it is on the edge of your territory. Is that correct?" The kobolds gave him an affirmative. "Do monsters wander in that area often? I know we often have monsters up above; I assume it's the same here."

The kobolds both shifted uncomfortably. "Yes, monsters are der sometimes," Yazhira said after a moment.

"Which means that I'm going to have to hire guards to protect my miners. Not only that, but you'll be getting free protection since less monsters will wander into the inner sections of the cave." Kas paused, watching the two kobolds. Haven't spent so long with Shura and Forthan he could tell that the two were uncomfortable with this line of thinking. "I see two solutions to this problem. Either we can lower the costs…" Kas paused again, watching Yazhira closely. "Or you can promise that your people will protect my miners."

"It not that way," Yazhira answered slowly, clearly trying to think of a good argument he could use. "Your miners be making much noise; more monsters will come than normal. We may not be strong enough to handle the horde."

Kas frowned slightly, considering. It was entirely possible that he would be able to hire adventurers to clear out the caves. Actually, if he framed it right, he could have them paying him for the privilege of delving into the cave. Which might bring less desirable players out to the settlement. Plus, he had decided to travel so far from Tallrock in an attempt to discourage other unbound from coming out here.

He thought back to his experience with Himmler and his gang on the tram; he really didn't want those kinds of people in the settlement. What he needed was a way to attract the right sort of unbound to the settlement. People like Shannon, or… Dave.

Dave would actually be the perfect solution to this, and he was someone that Kas trusted. The only problem would be convincing him to make a character in Tallrock. His current character was all the way over in Middar. If he couldn't convince Dave, he'd have to figure something else out, which would be less than ideal.

"How many entrances into the outer reaches are there?"

Kas hated not having the information that he needed. "Can I see a map?"

Yazhira hummed for a moment before nodding his head rapidly. "It will cost you. One mana crystal."

At two silver a pop, a mana crystal wasn't exactly expensive, and since Kas could create them, it was really just a bit of opportunity cost and the price of the cooldown. With a shrug, Kas held out his palm and concentrated on his Crystallize skill. He quickly played the minigame by connecting the dots. It was such an easy one and he had done it so many times by now that he didn't even really have to think about it. The rainbow crystal appeared in his palm and he held it out to Yazhira. "Done."

Both kobolds stared at the crystal with a sense of awe. Yazhira went to pick it up but Na'Tan's hand shot out and grabbed the crystal as quick as lightning. The shaman held the crystal to his chest like it was a favorite stuffed animal.

Yazhira and Na'Tan hissed back and forth at each other for a moment, and then Yazhira turned slightly and shouted over his shoulder. Kas watched the scene with a smile, even as he wondered how the spell knew when to translate their words and when not to.

The reaction the shaman had to the creation of the mana crystal told Kas that he had another very valuable bargaining chip on the table. Clearly the kobolds had a need for the crystals and no supply. A short, thin kobold parted the leaves behind the shaman, carrying a roll of leather in its hands. The new kobold handed the map to the shaman who unrolled it and glanced at it. After a quick study, they nodded their heads and then handed the map to Kas.

As soon as he touched the map another popup appeared in his view.

Would you like to add the Tu'kar tribe's outer reaches map to your own?

Selecting yes without even considering it, Kas pulled up the new map of the cavern. The outer reaches were drawn with dimmer lines, showing that he hadn't been there yet himself. It consisted of four main caverns, each about 100 meters in length, although they varied in width and shape. Each of the main caverns connected to at least two of the others, with the one nearest the inner reaches being the only one that connected to all four. It also connected to the inner reaches, although there appeared to be some sort of gate between the two.

Mentally labeling the nearest cavern A, while the second closest was B, he arbitrarily named one C and the last D. The map was updated with his mental declarations and he pulled the map out to create a 3d wireframe. There were three passages from D into the space beyond the outer reaches, while B and C only had a single exit each. Cavern D connected to both A and C. The connection to C was close enough to the exit from C that the guards could easily defend both, assuming they weren't attacked at the same time.

Actually, depending on sight lines, he could station a lookout in D with the rest of the force in C, and be able to cover all of those exits, leaving only a smaller guard in B to handle the exit there. Either way, he would probably need to keep all of the tribesmen in the mine, which wasn't exactly ideal.

He would either need to find additional guards for the valley itself, or trust in the draks to handle everything. Neither of those options sounded like a good idea to him. He would have to see about sealing some of the exits and focus his efforts only on the most profitable caverns.

"Alright, here is what I propose," Kas said, turning his attention back to the two kobolds. "We will give you 5% of the yield, or 50 units of ore, whichever is smaller. Additionally, we will ensure that this gate," Kas indicated the gate between A and the inner reaches on the map, "is not attacked while we are in the mine. Additionally, we will supply you with 30 units of food per 90 days, and 20 mana crystals.

"I would also like to trade for some of those darts that you used on us earlier."

The kobolds hissed at each other for a few minutes after

that, the shaman and chief clearly debating the value of the trade. It would be a big win for Kas, since 20 mana crystals were worth considerably less to him than 20 units of food were.

If market prices stayed where they were anyway. It was a bit of a gamble. If mana crystal prices soared due to lack of players creating them, then he might actually end up paying more than he could with his crops. But something told him that there would be more players making mana crystals than farming, which gave him pretty high confidence that he would come out on top of the arrangement.

After some rather heated debate the popup about the negotiations changed.

You have entered into trade negotiations with Chief Yazhira of the Tu'kar tribe.
Current offer:

- *You will pay: 5% of your daily yield or 50 units of metal, whichever is less. You will also pay 30 units of food and 20 mana crystals every 90 days.*
- *You will get: Access to the outer reaches area of the Tu'kar Tribe Cave under Miranda Valley. +10 Karma. 500 reputation with the Tu'kar tribe.*

Your current reputation is too low to trade for Dirt Wyrm Tranquilizers. Tu'kar tribe reputation must exceed 2000.

The poison darts being locked behind a reputation gate made sense to Kas, they were pretty powerful. What was surprising was the last two additions to the trade. Karma showed up again, what exactly was it? What was it about this particular trade deal that made him gain it? He still wasn't even sure if more Karma was good or bad. Last time he had lost Karma. He tried to remember anything new about Karma, and a phrase came into mind: Karmic dirt.

The idea was that you gained Karmic dirt when you did

bad actions, and lost it when you did good actions. That would mean that he was doing something evil by accepting this trade, and had done something good with the GM earlier.

Liv's whispered words were another mystery. What did 'no good deed goes unpunished' actually mean? Shaking his head, he mentally readjusted the food back up to 50 units, but kept the mana crystals at 20. The Karma change switched from +10, to -10. Well, that sealed it, Karma was bad and he didn't want it. He mentally accepted the -10 Karma agreement and he watched as the two kobolds stared at him in confusion.

"Why would you do dis?" the chief asked, clearly confused.

"I don't want us to be enemies. I don't want to have to worry if you are going to stab my people in the back. I'm willing to make some sacrifices to ensure that our people both have a very long, and mutually beneficial relationship. If that isn't to your satisfaction, then I'm sure we can go back to the original agreement," Kas answered with a smile.

"We must discuss dis with the council," the shaman announced and the two rushed off into the trees beyond the pool, leaving behind the one small kobold that had brought the map.

"Hi. Don't suppose they cast the spell on me and not on themselves?" Kas asked the left behind warrior.

The clear look of confusion on his face made it clear that the unnamed kobold could not understand him. He added learning their language—or a spell that would allow him to communicate with them—to the list of things he needed to acquire. Still, he felt like this was going in the direction he wanted it to. Those two kobolds clearly had not been expecting his last counter offer, and that could only mean good things for Miranda Valley.

Kas took the time to really look around the pool area. The highest the ceiling got was about three times his own height, with more than a dozen hanging stalactites breaking up the surface of it. The plants around the outer edge of the room had been cleverly designed to hide a number of very small paths that twisted almost immediately, making it impossible to determine where they went or what mysteries they hid. Kas didn't think the kobolds would take him exploring these paths kindly, so he turned and circled the pool.

The pool itself looked deep, although it was nearly impossible to tell with how much it bubbled. A thick pillar of rock just barely connected right above the surface of the pool, having narrowed down to something as thick around as two finger lengths. The rock had a bulbous smoothness that gave it an unreal appearance. Thick bands of red streaked through both the upper and lower sections, which was a good sign for his future mining operations.

Finding nothing else of interest in the pool, he turned back to the plants on the outer edge. Instead of looking at them as a whole, he started focusing on individual plants. One particular plant had a strange purple pod with what looked like red tufts sticking out of a central line. As he studied the plant, the identification minigame popped up, and he shot seeds at the bugs as they tried to eat the pod at the center. The timer ran out and the health of the flower at the center still had a few slivers of HP, which meant he was able to successfully identify the flower.

A prompt showed up, giving him the option to name the plant. After a moment of consideration he called it the Grotto Pod.

Congratulations, you have discovered a new botanical species. You have been granted bonus experience to your herbalism skill.
2/10 conditions met to earn title: "Gogland Explorer"

This was followed by six other plants that counted towards his Gogland Explorer, bringing him up to a total of 8/10. His ability to name things was somewhat lackluster, thus: A hanging moss got named Kobold's Beard, two different kinds of fern like plants were named Red Grotto Fern and Blue Grotto Fern.

He had tried to call a thick three-leafed bush the Three Leaf Cave Bush, but the system gave him an error saying that the name was already taken. Which honestly made him feel better about his naming sense. He instead called it Tu'kar's Flower. The last two were flowering plants that he called Yazhira's Boon and Night Feather, both of which were approved by the system without complaint.

There were still a number of plants to identify, but Na'Tan and Yazhira had finally returned to the grotto, interrupting and cancelling his attempt to identify a dark purple flower that reminded him a lot of an orchid. The chief and bone speaker both bowed in greetings. "We greet you, scaleless. Da elders have spoken, and dey agree, we will enter into dis agreement with da people of Miranda."

Kas was confused for a minute trying to figure out when he had told them about the name Miranda, but realized it must be what the system had called his side of the negotiations.

The chief continued, "As an expression of our thanks, you have free access to dis cavern." The chief gestured around him in an expansive manner. "We, da Tu'kar, accept this alliance."

Another prompt popped up in front of him, telling him that his trade negotiations had been successful; it also gave a counter for when he would need to begin upholding his portion of the contract. Thankfully, it would be a full tenday before he was expected to begin guarding the outer reaches.

After a few more pleasantries, the two kobolds escorted him back to the chamber where he had originally been kept. The tribesmen, Shannon, and Costache were all present and there was even a small area where the kobolds had clearly attempted to provide food for their captives. Costache was the only one taking advantage of it though, the cian happily crunching into some sort of baked beetle.

"Hey everyone," Kas said with a half wave as he was led back in. None of the group looked any worse for wear, and he wondered if part of what they had been doing was returning everyone to this room while they waited. "I managed to sign a deal with the Tu'kar tribe here, and we're free to come and go as we desire. I'm sure there are a lot of questions, but we should probably report back to Shura and Forthan before I tell the full story."

With a small amount of grumbling from the tribesmen, they all picked their things back up. The chief escorted them as far as the edge of the main village caverns, pointing to the tunnel that would lead to the outer reaches. "Dis is as far as most of you will need to come into da main tribe lands. The scaleless can come further, but that be your portion of the lands." From there he led them back to where they had been captured before bidding them farewell.

Kas left behind the miners and two of the tribesmen to gather as much ore as they could on the way out, but the rest of the group headed up to the surface. As soon as Kas reached the surface he sat down, giving everyone a chance to rest. He used the time to create another mana crystal, and then layered it. Pocketing the death crystal in his inventory, he looked around. The tribesmen were all giving him sidelong glances as they rested. Shannon sat down next to him though.

"So, glad we didn't die. But what exactly did you do back there?" Shannon asked.

"I just... talked to them," Kas said with a shrug.

"But, they were..." Shannon trailed off, trying to explain what she meant. "Evil?" she questioned.

"Were they?" Kas asked. "Because they trapped the way into their home? I mean, think about it. They didn't kill any of us, and we were invading them. I don't think I would do the same if someone was invading Miranda. Does that make me evil?"

"But..." Shannon said, trying to articulate why she was uncomfortable with the kobolds. "They drugged us."

"Yup, and they didn't apologize for it afterwards. But, again, I don't think I can blame them for that. They are physically pretty small, and I don't think they have any great destructive magics. That puts them on the back foot here in a world where people are going to try to take what you have. They have to find... alternative solutions to problems. I think we sometimes get in the habit of assuming there is a 'right' way to do things, based on our capabilities. We don't often really think about what other people are capable of, and how that changes their problem solving," Kas said with a shrug.

"Besides, as cunning as those little guys are, I think we're much safer having them as allies than enemies."

CHAPTER TWENTY

The Mine 4

Kas stepped away from Shannon as Damae called everyone to get up and head back to the farm. They passed by the mill on the way in, and it was still covered in a thick fog with strange sounds coming from inside it. He checked the timer and realized they had only been inside the mine for five hours. Which meant there was plenty of daylight left to do some of the other things he had on his ever-expanding to-do list.

The farm was empty when they showed back up. Damae had the tribesmen start doing their usual chores. Kas walked over to the half-completed house and got started. With the tool he had discovered the night before, things went much faster, as he was able to copy the existing structure onto the new one.

There was actually some ability to change what he was copying too. After a little bit of playing around with the system, he found he could change the anchor points by up to about an arm's length of distance. This allowed him to slightly alter the slope of the roof. He was curious what the best angle would be. And having a couple of different options would enable him to see what people liked best. He managed to get all but the last two sections done before Shura came back to camp.

A commotion drew Kas' eyes over to where the large drak was entering the camp; in her arms was a large creature. Its fur was short and heavily matted by thick chunks of mud, three thick tusks protruded from both sides of its elongated snout, while a fourth had clearly broken off, leaving a jagged stub. The creature's eyes had the glazed over look of someone that had taken a few heavy blows to the head. Upon seeing him, Shura made her way over to Kas.

"Greetings, Kastigan. It seems your time in the mine did not last as long as I thought it would." Shura gave him a once over. "And was less violent than we feared it might become."

"Yup! I managed to form a trade agreement with the kobolds," Kas said, brushing off his hands. "What's this?" he asked, pointing to the creature.

"This is what ruined your corn field. It must have been abandoned by its family because it was injured; I wasn't able to find any more." The drak put it down with a grunt. It was clearly still stunned, and the creature just slumped to the ground.

Now that it was outside of Shura's arms, Kas was amazed that the drak was able to carry it at all. About a meter and a half long, it would have come to Kas' shoulder if it had been standing up. The matted fur had initially appeared brown, but Kas thought it might be gray under the mud.

The entire creature looked like someone had crossed a wild hog with an elephant. The lack of injuries led Kas to believe the skin was thick and resilient. The eyes were beady and looked to lack intelligence, but that wouldn't matter if they bound the creature.

Kas idly wondered if they would make for good eating as well. There was plenty of meat on the body. If he could create some kind of bacon out of it, that would be ideal. He focused on his husbandry skill for a minute to see if that would give him any further information about the beast.

The long-nosed hog is a creature native to Gogland. They are numerous and can be considered pests if found in large numbers. Their quick breeding and maturation cycle can make infestations of the beasts challenging to control. However, their hides and meat are generally accepted to be delicious.

The Kiddeshan tribes use them to train their younger hunters, giving them practical experience in selective hunting as well as providing the tribe with their primary supply of leather and meat.

With your husbandry skill, you know that this is a juvenile male. It will reach maturation in fourteen days.

"Looks like he's still a juvenile. Did you want to bond him? Or were you thinking of trying to keep them wild?" Kas asked Shura.

"I think it is a good idea to bond the alpha of any pack or herd which, with proper training, he could become. We can keep the rest of them wild; as long as the alpha has enough control over them, I think we will be fine," Shura said, even as she pulled another bonding crystal out of one of the pouches on her harness. "I thought you might like to see the bonding process at work, though." She held the crystal up to the hog's forehead.

"That would be great. Do I need to do anything?" Kas asked as Shura pressed the crystal into the hog's forehead. She removed her hand a second later, and the gem seemed to have sunk into a thick ridge of skin around the forehead. Her hand hovered over the crystal, a strange blue glow bathing the crystal in light. There almost seemed to be a laser connecting the gem and the center of her palm. The hog's eyes narrowed, and he grunted loudly.

That was the first sound the beast had made since Shura arrived, and it took Kas by surprise.

Tripping backward, he could see Shura's frill expand in amusement as he stood back up. Dusting off his hands and his pants, he resumed watching. He had clearly missed some of the process, but the hog was now completely frozen, his eyes locked on Shura's. It seemed like there was a battle of wills going on, Shura doing her best to overpower the hog's limited mentality. Kas unconsciously held his breath, not wanting to disturb Shura any further.

Without looking away from the hog, Shura gave verbal instructions to Kas, "There is a pouch near my left ankle, inside are beast crystals. Spread as many as you can in a circle around the hog, no closer than one of your arm's length apart."

The big drak's entire body spoke of intense concentration, the air taking on an almost electric aura. Kas could swear he could smell burnt ozone as the two continued their unseen conflict. To his surprise, Shura's blue scales actually began to crackle with electricity. Starting between her horns then running down her body, he could see the sparks of electricity flickering between her fingers, seeming to build up a charge before suddenly creating an arc of brilliant white light that struck the gem, and then traveled into the hog.

Kas moved to act on Shura's orders, finding the pouch and spreading gems around. The first one he placed burst almost immediately with an electric pop and then collapsed into dust, so he replaced it. Static crackled in the air, and the hog's muscles, previously stock still, began to twitch. The hog's fear was a palpable presence, the thick musk pushing the scent of ozone out of the air. The hog's neck muscles were straining to escape. Kas replaced two more crystals after they popped.

With an almost painful abruptness, the tension in the air disappeared. Both Shura and the hog collapsed, exhausted even as four more crystals surged out of existence. Kas reached out to Shura but knew there was nothing he could do to support the thirteen-foot tall drak. He watched as the crystal embedded in the hog's forehead sunk deeper into his flesh, and then disappeared. The bonding process complete, the pig laid his head down, and soon the whistle of his breath could be heard as he fell asleep.

"Are you alright?" Kas asked Shura, who looked up wearily and bobbed her head.

"Yes, I will be fine. One of the reasons I wanted to come back first was that I knew this creature would be at the limit of my powers. Still, it was a very good experience. I improved my beast tamer skill twice." Shura gave him a drak equivalent of a smile and sat down. She gestured to the pig. "I think I managed to impart some of my electrical affinity to the beast as well."

Kas looked at the long-nosed hog and saw that the ridge along its back had turned a bright yellow under the mud. Shura almost immediately transferred the bond to Kas, who accepted it with a mental command. And, of course, that was when the prompt to name the beast showed up.

Kas groaned, "You're making me name him?" He glared at the drak, who he was absolutely sure was giving him a shit-eating grin, even if that was an emotion that he wasn't sure how draks expressed.

"Fine," Kas muttered under his breath. Two could play at that game, and he named him 'Thunder Pig.' As soon as the name appeared above the pig, he could hear Shura start to laugh. He ignored the drak and focused on his new pet.

This particular long-nosed hog has been blessed with the meta element of lightning, which is a combination of air, fire, and life.

With your husbandry skill, you know that this is a juvenile male. It will reach maturation in seven days.

Some new information there; lightning was a meta element that was basically the exact polar opposite of his own elements. He wondered if water, earth, and death formed a meta element? It would probably be poison or something, if his spells were any judge. Did that mean lightning was super effective against his spells? Or was it one of those things where every-thing canceled each other out? He asked his question of Shura, who shrugged.

"I do not know. I haven't found that my breath is more or less effective against anything..." Shura trailed off, thinking.

"Actually, no. It is weaker against things with high concentrations of earth element, and stronger against things of the water and death elements."

"Which would imply that it is more life and fire than air?" Kas mused aloud. That was a problem for another time, however, and he focused on the last line of Thunder Pig's entry; it now said he would reach maturity in half the time it had before. Was that a function of the bond, the new elemental attribute, or his own husbandry skills? Since there was no way to know for sure until they had at least a few more test cases, he put that line of questioning aside for the moment.

"Where are we gonna keep this guy?" Kas asked, looking at the massive sleeping pig at his feet.

"I think you should probably build a pen or a stable or something?" Shura said.

With a groan, he added another thing to his to-do list. Which was growing quite substantially out of hand at this point. "He'll have to deal with being out in the open for a bit; I don't think we should prioritize animals over people. And I'm not sure what we would feed him if we penned him up, anyway. This way we can get him to forage for his own food. I assume he can do that?" Kas eyed Thunder Pig again, considering.

"I mean, he has survived this long on his own, I imagine he'll be fine. Just need to make sure he doesn't get into the crops," Shura recommended.

"Right..." Kas glanced over at his fields and gave the pig a mental command to avoid them. As he did so, he heard a couple of chirps from the forest line and saw Dino and Diane making a beeline for him. The two stopped short when they saw Thunder Pig, then rushed forward and began jumping around the slumbering form of their new bond mate. Watching the three, Kas turned to Shura. "Is there a limit to how many bonded companions I can have?"

Shura was watching the two compies as well but just shook her head. "No, there is no limit, although the more you have, the less likely a bond will transfer properly. I would imagine your husbandry skill also affects how many bonded companions you can have, especially if they aren't used for combat."

"Makes sense, I guess," Kas said as the two compies curled up on Thunder Pig's flat skull, which was plenty big enough for both of them, although Dino kept having to push himself back on as he slipped off. "Well, it looks like those three will be fine."

"Indeed. Have you had any luck milking the compies for their numbing venom?" Shura asked.

"Oh, I haven't really had time to try to be honest," Kas answered, and he went to scoop up Dino.

The little compie had solved his falling off problem by wrapping his tail around one of the horns, and he gave a chirp of annoyance when Kas shifted it around. When Kas held him in his hands instead, the little lizard was happy enough to burrow his head into Kas' elbow. "Do I need a vial or something?"

He focused on Dino.

The Compsognathus was long thought to be extinct. Fossils have been found on just about every continent. It wasn't until Kingdom Explorers reached the Spine of Aktrosha on Gogland that live specimens were discovered.

A strange mix between predator and scavenger, the Compsognathus has a numbing venom that it uses to lull weakened creatures to sleep and then eats them. The venom is sought after by alchemists to create sleeping droughts.

With your husbandry skill, you know this is an adult male.

Nothing new there, although he was pretty sure that was the first time he'd ever actually inspected either of the compies. He scratched Dino's exposed belly as he searched through his interface for any hints as to how to harvest from domesticated animals. After thirty seconds of searching, he found it, but it required a sub-skill of husbandry that he didn't have.

"There is a sub-skill of husbandry that I'm missing. I'm not sure I want to try doing it unskilled on their venom, though. I need to make another trip to Tallrock soon anyway, to get more guards for the mine. I'll try to find someone who can teach me the skill there."

Shura bobbed her head, clearly a little disappointed. "I suppose that makes sense. I wish we did not have to go so often, though."

"Yeah, I know. I'm afraid we're going to have to try to recruit more unbound too, hopefully a friend of mine." Kas explained the agreement he had made with the Tu'kar kobolds and how he would need to get more combatants. "I'm not sure how we're going to get them to come out here, though. Shannon was easy enough; she had her weird class that needed to go out into the wilderness. What we're gonna need are people who are willing to do dungeon dives pretty much constantly. Maybe even have them camp down there."

Shura reached over and scratched Diane's head, causing the little compie to sleepily chirp in pleasure. "I think you are underselling yourself. Many will leap at the chance to have some normalcy in their lives. If you can get a group that will delve deeper a few days a week, but otherwise travels out into the mountains or forest. You can find a bound that will keep the camp itself. If we can bring Forthan's cook here, we can even promise them good food."

"Oh, yeah, that's a good point." Kas thought back to the meals in-game. They had all tasted delicious. If the man was that much better than Shura, then it would be a real bargaining chip to get the unbound to come. But that would also mean he would need to make an inn or something. They weren't likely to stick around if they had to sleep in a tent. And the cook had basically said he wouldn't come out here until he had some sort of proper kitchen to cook in.

Glancing at his list of things to do, Kas rearranged a few things. Getting the sawmill up and running would be first priority. Once that was done, he would work on getting an inn, building the kitchen first, if at all possible. "Guess I need to talk to Costache about what he needs to get the saw built." Kas slipped Dino back onto his porcine bed and went in search of the blacksmith.

Costache was in the spot he had designated the smithy to be built. It was on the far side of the waterfall from his farm. The cianese man had begun building what he assumed was a smelter. A waist-high circle of rocks had been piled up, and the cian was using a limestone mortar that he had mixed up in a bucket.

"Hello, Costache."

The cian grunted but didn't turn away from what he was doing. After finishing the immediate task, he turned to look at Kas. "What can I do you for?" he asked even as he began searching for the next rock he wanted to use.

"I was wondering how long it would take you to forge up a saw blade? I think that's what is holding us back the most right now." Kas watched with fascination as the cian carefully applied the mortar and then stuck the next rock onto his smelter.

"I'm hoping to get the smelter and forge done today. If'n I can do that, I should have some usable metal by tomorrow morning. Setting up the anvil will take another hour or so, and the blade will take the rest of the day to finish up," Costache answered, adding another rock.

"Hmm, tomorrow evening then." Kas glanced in the direction the mill had been built. "I should be able to get at least a frame up before then. We'll be using the power from the waterwheel I started earlier today. Not sure if that changes your plans at all."

"Shouldn't change much," the cian muttered. "Might need to build some smaller pieces for the connection, but I'd need to look at what the current building provides before I make any decisions about that."

"Alright, I can't really start working on it until it's finished anyway. Which should be some time tomorrow morning. I'm just gonna get materials ready until then."

Kas' statement was met with another grunt from the cian, which he took as the conversation being over.

Finding Max was the next task on Kas' list. The lumberjack proved more challenging to find; he wasn't near the tree line of the clearing. Which was where Kas had initially assumed the old man would be.

Enlisting Shura and her pet falcon's help, they found him on a small rise half a mile away from the farm.

Kas made his way there, seeing the older man sitting on a log overlooking the valley. He climbed up to the top of the small hill, finding himself slightly winded by the time he got to the top. He sat down on a rock next to Max.

The view was one of the most picturesque Kas had yet discovered. Around the valley, dozens of different colors stood out. A downward slope still carried a thin thread of pristine white snow, shrouded on both sides by a tall cliff; only the barest hint of the narrow canyon could be seen. Bright green leaves covered most of the valley floor, broken here and there by a few trees with leaves that were a purplish-blue. A single grove of golden trees off to one side, taller than the rest of the trees by a considerable amount. Completing the color spectrum were steep shrub-covered hills, the red dirt outshining the still brown bushes.

"This is an amazing view," Kas said after giving himself a few minutes to catch his breath and take it all in.

Max grunted in response. In his hands, he held a small block of wood that he was carefully carving. It was unclear what shape it would eventually take, but his practiced ease was apparent.

"Just taking a break, and appreciating it all. You've got a beautiful plot of land here," Max said, flicking a piece of wood off the carving before he considered his next cut.

"Thank you." Kas let the wind ruffle his hair, and he smiled. "I've been so busy trying to get it all up and running, I think this is the first time I've really had a chance to take it in."

"More to life than just making money. It took me a long time to figure that out, wouldn't want you to make the same mistake," Max said as he made a final cut then carefully stowed his carving and knife away. "Now, I know you didn't come here to shoot the breeze with an old Thel'kan like myself. What can I do for ya?"

"Ahh, I was wondering if you could cut down some trees in a slightly different spot," Kas said, his eyes following the river to the foggy area where the gristmill was being created.

"That fog there your doing, then?" Max asked, following Kas' line of sight.

"Yeah, I summoned a gristmill there. We'll be building your lumberyard next to it to take advantage of the wheel's power. I guess I should have asked you if that was alright first, but... a little too late now."

"You... summoned a gristmill?" Max blinked rapidly for a few seconds as his brain tried to catch up with what his ears had heard. "Right, unbound are different. Sometimes I forget you are unbound. I'm a practical man, mister Kastigan. I assume you put it there because that is where it worked best for the wheel?"

"Yes, Forthan told me that was the best place for it."

"Hmm, I'm not sure you should listen to everything that Whitekin tells you to do. Something in my bones tells me he will always look out for himself first and foremost. That said, at this point, what's good for your farm is what is good for him. Bind his fate to you close enough, and you might be able to trust him, but I'd be worried he might seek to displace you." Max snorted slightly. "Although it's no easy task to displace an immortal being."

"Immortal being?" Kas hadn't really considered the repercussions of the unbound being effectively immortal. Sure, one could kill an unbound, but that wouldn't get rid of them, just make them go back to their spawn point. "I guess. Not much I can do about Forthan either way. We need him and his men right now. But making myself less reliant on him is definitely on my mind.

"Now that we're alone, anything more you can tell me about that argument with Costache?"

Max sighed, looking down at his hands. "It was… nothing really. Just a heavy-handed attempt to manipulate me."

Kas tried to figure out to what end Costache would try to manipulate Max. Was this related to Forthan?

Max interrupted his musing. "Well, I assume you'll want me to start clearing the trees near that?" He looked over at the fog.

"Yes, the plan is to get the sawmill up and running in the next two days. I'll be building at least the basic framework for it as soon as the fog clears," Kas said in agreement.

"Alright, I'll start clearing some of that." Max paused. "Although you might be able to do it better than I can. Cycle mages are often called up to do that sort of work."

Kas blinked and then looked over his spell list. "Well, I suppose I could kill the plants. With my death spells, would that be helpful?"

Max laughed. "Oh yeah, I'm sure we can figure something out. Tell you what, I'll go down there with you and tell you what I think we should do, and we can try out some of your spells, figure out what works best." The old man got up and then stuck out a hand to help Kas up.

"Thanks, Max." Kas accepted the hand and the two made their way down the steep hill. "Oh, and if you want, I'm sure we could build you a house here."

Max just grunted. "Oh, no need for that. I'm just glad to be out from under the legion's foot. Not sure I want to settle down anywhere just yet."

"Offer still stands. You're a good man, and I'd be happy to have you work with me to build this place into something great," Kas responded, and he thought he saw a smile flash across Max's face before it disappeared, the old man returning to his normal leathery stoicism.

CHAPTER TWENTY-ONE

The Mine 5

Decay didn't work, since it specifically targeted creatures. Poison Bolt proved very useful if he was trying to kill a specific plant. Death Blast was another single-target spell. The real winner for the task was Poison Spray, which allowed him to target multiple things at once. It also turned the ground into a muddy mess, so he rotated between the single target and the AoE spells.

In the end, he would cast his single target spells at the largest of the plants, then Earth Stomp to break up the ground and painstakingly pull all the plants out of the dirt. He wished he had a pitchfork; he was using a spare pick axe as his primary method of removing the detritus. An hour of back-breaking work later, and he had collected a mound of weeds as high as his waist, but had only managed to clear a few meters of land.

Taking a moment to rest from the back-breaking work of clearing land, he glanced over at Max, who had already felled one tree and was cussing under his breath as he cleared the branches.

Sitting down on a large rock, Kas considered his options. The wall of mist sat a dozen paces away, downriver from where they had opted to start clearing the land. But based on the last hour of effort, he was convinced that the best part of the summoned building was that he hadn't had to clear the land.

"This is going to take too long," Kas muttered to himself. Clearing the land was important, sure, but he needed something that would do it faster.

"Just wait 'til we have to try clearing some of the stumps out."

Max's addition startled Kas, who had been focused on the task and missed that the lumberjack approached.

"Yeah, I think I'm going to need some new spells. If I had a spell like Decay that only worked on plants, that would make this much easier." Kas shook his head, glancing around. Poison Bolt was particularly useful; casting it at the root of a plant would quickly kill the entire plant, even drying it out and turning it into a husk.

"Might be able to find someone with a spell like that in Tall-rock. Hard to say, really. A low powered one would probably be pretty cheap too, since it has such a narrow application," Max mused aloud. "Especially if you found one that couldn't be used in combat."

"Yeah, something that would kill it over a few hours, maybe?" Kas asked. His own spells had killed the plants quite rapidly, and it had been decent skill grinding.

"Yeah, like I said, you might be able to find something like that in Tallrock. But if not, you could use one of the spell altars instead. Depending on how much the legion is charging to use it."

"Sorry, what's a spell altar?" Kas frowned. None of the forums had mentioned anything about this.

"Well, spell altars are how you create new magical spells. Never used one myself, but in Thel'kan, they were used regu-larly. The Kingdom has them a lot more restricted than we did at home. They claim it's to support the war effort, but I'm pretty sure that's just an excuse to keep magic out of the hands of the peasantry. Tasdel has always been worried about an uprising," Max added, even as he got back up and began hacking at the tree again.

"Well, I'll put it on the list of things I need to do when I'm in Tallrock again. Which looks like it's going to be sooner rather than later," Kas muttered as he got back to clearing land. The two didn't work in silence, but they didn't continue the conversation, most of the noise grunts and curses.

It took Kas nearly four hours to finally clear all the land in a ten-meter square area. He sat down and pulled out a canteen. Filling it with water, he poured half of it over his head to cool down a bit, then drank the rest in one long pull. Leaning back against a large rock, he pulled up the notifications of his gains.

Assault I: 13/100 -> 34/100
Area of Effect I: 6/100 -> 33/100
Single Target I: 5/100 -> 41/100
Earth I: 14/100 -> 26/100
Shaking I: 13/100 -> 45/100
Water I: 15/100 -> 27/100
Filling I: 27/100 -> 48/100
Death I: 6/100 -> 23/100
Decay I: 2/100 -> 29/100
Poison I: 4/100 -> 32/100
Mana Manipulation I: 6/100 -> 22/100
Meditation I: 3/100 -> 14/100
Mana Circulation I: 2/100 -> 5/100

Pretty much the best rate of improvement he had ever had. He wondered if there was something about using the skills to actually accomplish tasks gave more experience than just casting them to burn his mana. That was the only explanation that he could think of.

Then there were also his spells, which had also vastly improved. Poison Bolt had reached level three and was 87% of the way to level four. Earth Stomp was level two, 73% of the way to the next, and Death Blast went from level one with zero experience to level two with 18%.

Deciding that was enough clearing land until the building finished summoning sometime the next day, he left Max cutting and clearing branches. Hopefully, there would be enough lumber by tomorrow for him to get at least the foundations of the sawmill completed and a frame put up.

As he walked back to camp, he tried to figure out when he should go back to Tallrock. Ideally, they wouldn't need to go back until he had some crops to sell. There wasn't much point in making the trip often; it was too long and dangerous to be convenient.

He would need to take at least one of the draks with him—probably Forthan so he could keep an eye on him, leaving Shura here to tame more beasts and protect the village. They could possibly leave a few of the guards here, although if there was anything Shura couldn't handle, he didn't think the tribesmen would be much help.

They could bring back the rest of Forthan's people. No, that wouldn't work; the cook had explicitly said he wouldn't come until he had a proper kitchen. Which meant he needed the sawmill up and running. Kas kicked a small rock in frustration. Everything was coming along too slowly, and he was already beginning to regret picking the gristmill over the sawmill.

He sighed and did a mental exercise he had been taught after they lost Elam. He breathed in and out, focused on letting go of the past, forcing himself to focus only on those things he could do something about.

Alright, so what were his priorities? He needed more time. Shy of discovering magic that allowed time compression to work, he wasn't going to get more time. The only way around that was to start delegating tasks more. There wasn't anyone in the camp that was idle though; everyone was working as hard as he was trying to get everything up and running. Which meant that he would need more people. To recruit more people, he was going to need more money.

There was a chance he could generate more income if he went adventuring into the mountains. But there was a chance he wouldn't be able to find anything valuable, plus he didn't want to fight, and that was what he would have to do if he went adventuring. That left him with his farming, which would take days before he could get anything, and even then, he would need to make a trip to Tallrock to sell it. Plus, he hadn't figured out a way to move large quantities of material all the way back to town. What he needed were small, high value items to sell.

Glancing at his skills, his eyes focused on the one set of skills he hadn't really done much with. Alchemy.

If he could use this time to make some healing potions, poultices, or anything else adventurers would want, he could supplement his spending money by a considerable amount. With that thought in mind, he stepped off the partially-created path that led from the mill back to the farm.

Stepping deeper into the dense foliage of the tree cover, he began searching for more herbs he could harvest. It took him another hour to get back as he took a meandering path through the valley, but he managed to acquire a bag full of herbs.

The new materials ranged from a crumbly bark he had gathered off of a tree called a Thundering Willow, black leaves off some kind of ivy that, for some reason, were called Rocky's Tears. Several types of mushrooms, and a red and orange flower called Retribution of the Dawn. Clearly, whoever had named these plants had a better naming sense than Kas, and he vowed to put more effort into any future plant names he found. The rest of the plants were repeats of things he had already seen.

Getting back to the wanderer's pine, he read through the prompts on the plants and hung up a few that said they needed to dry out. Thankfully, some of the plants he had already set up to dry were finally ready to be used. He spent two hours grinding up plants. His first attempt to grind plants ended in a brown powder that wasn't usable for anything. His next three attempts managed to produce a minimal amount of pink powder.

Inferior Pink Alchemical Powder. The product of any number of plants. Pink powder can be used to create alchemical concoctions that boost health regeneration.

The black ivy that he had gathered earlier was called Rocky's Tears. The process of getting useful materials out of it was much more complicated than the grinder. The help file said he needed to bruise the leaves and then steep them in pure water; after that, he needed to distill the water down into a crystallized form.

Kas opted to play the minigame instead, since he didn't really have the right tools and set up to do any of that. This particular game involved bouncing a melon-sized ball ten times in a row. Kas wasn't entirely sure why that game was picked, since it was so vastly different from all the other games he had to play, but managed to accomplish the task on his second set of leaves. The resulting crystals were an inky black that seemed to glow darkness. Which was... a most disconcerting effect, and he couldn't look at them long.

Inferior Black Alchemical Crystal. Harnessing the power of darkness, this crystal can be used to augment your stealth skill, critical hit chance, or create an invisibility potion.

Kas figured that using crystals would to require more advanced skills than he had, so he put it into his pack to sell at Tallrock. He told himself that was why and not because looking at it was giving him the creeps.

The next group he tried to deconcoct were the mushrooms. Most of them required he harvest the small gills underneath the cap, the spores and gills were then mashed together with a bit of water to create a thick yellow paste.

Inferior Yellow Alchemical Paste. This paste can be applied as a salve to reduce swelling, improve circulation, or relieve pain. Applying the paste to a bandage will create a longer effect duration. 11 hours 59 minutes until this product loses potency.

That was beneficial, although not quite what he was looking for. He really wanted to find something that would restore HP immediately or regenerate mana. The pink powder had been an excellent first step towards a healing potion, but he felt like he needed something else to make that really work. He turned his attention to the rest of his ingredients. Silki grass grew in shadows, and he had a feeling it would help with his other efforts. The dawn lily and river lily's both seemed like they would work, but they both needed to dry for a longer time.

Wanting to make sure he wasn't missing out on something, he did a quick help search on inferior alchemy items.

Inferior alchemical products are a designation of quality; they are usually created by using basic skills or low level resources. Improving the quality of either or both will improve quality. Product grades are as follows: inferior, weak, common, superior, strong, and potent.

Kas mentally added a dedicated drying area to his list of things to build, then with a sigh added a dedicated builder to the list of people he was trying to recruit. It was one of those time things. He couldn't build a drying area and kitchen. Hopefully Max would be able to keep up with their lumber requirements, but for some reason, he doubted it. With a shake of his head, he looked back at the other herbs he had. Finally, his eyes settled on the thunder willow bark.

It was another mortar and pestle task, and he felt confident enough in his skills to start working on it immediately. The flaky bark ground up into a very appealing deep red dust. Which Kas actually found very attractive. He wondered if it would work as a spice, and he tasted a dab of it. He tried to spit out the bitter dust, but his mouth was too dry. A swig of the canteen washed it down but filled his mouth with an electric feeling that faded quickly, leaving his mouth slightly numb.

"Whew," Kas exclaimed, but his tongue seemed fat in his mouth. A few more swallows of water and the feeling returned to his jaw. "That was weird." He inspected the powder when he realized he hadn't done that already. Wait, had he really tasted something without inspecting it? That was an incredibly stupid thing for him to have done.

Inferior Thundering Crimson Alchemical Dust. Crimson dust is used to create healing potions and salves. The thundering variant can also improve your lightning damage or increase resistance to lightning damage.

So there was something special about that particular strand of willow trees that had caused them to get the thundering quality. He opened up his map and made a quick notation of the location. With Shura and now Thunder Pig, he was bound to find a use for something that augmented the lightning attribute. He hoped the bark was something he could acquire regularly. The question now was if he could combine the crimson and pink dust to make a healing potion.

The problem with any actual alchemy was, again, his circumstances. There were undoubtedly applications of alchemy that could be done 'in the field,' so to speak, like applying a paste to a bandage, or preserving certain herbs that needed to be dealt with directly after they were harvested. Most alchemy should be done in a lab, though. Or at the very least on a table.

Kas did not have either of those things. So he found a rather large, mostly flat rock and spent ten minutes reshaping the ground underneath it so that it would lay mostly flat. It wasn't perfect, and there were several uneven sections, but it gave him enough room to actually set up the alchemy gear he had gotten as part of his starter kit.

First, was a large glass... decanter? That got put on a magitech burner, which was powered by mana crystals. Thankfully it didn't need any typed crystals, and the consumption seemed to be pretty low. Next to that was another glass vial that appeared to connect in with the decanter. And a third vial that had a second heating unit on it. Lastly, there was a small cauldron; the game helped him set it up, creating ghostly outlines of where everything needed to go. When the entire thing was set up, a prompt appeared in his vision, giving him a list of available actions.

Unfortunately, none of these options were 'create healing potion.' Instead, it looked like Kas would have to do some intermediate steps, from 'mixing the solutions' to 'distill secondary flask.' There was an action listed 'finalize the result.'

With a sigh, he looked for any hints as to how to progress his alchemy. This would require some out of game research. Looking at the clock, he decided he didn't have time to do that now; dinner should be served shortly, and he wanted to talk to the entire group about his deal with the kobolds.

On his way to the dinner pit, he found a lazy-looking Thunder Pig nosing at his crops, and with a growl, Kas chased the hog away from them. "No! You don't eat my fields." He sent another mental command to the pig to ensure that he wouldn't come anywhere near his precious fields. The pig grunted and slowly turned away from the crops, beginning to munch on some of the shrubs near the edge of the clearing instead. "Now, that, you can eat. If you wanna clear the ground around the camp, that's all yours."

The pig turned slightly to give Kas a stink eye, and then returned to eating the underbrush. "I also need to figure out a place to keep you at night, don't I?" The wanderer's pine Kas and Shura had been staying in wasn't going to fit the meter and a half creature.

He glared at the pig for a while longer to ensure it didn't plan on going back before continuing on his way to the firepit. The tribesmen and miners were already back, while he could see Costache still tinkering around with his forge and smelter over on the far side of the waterfall.

The area they had taken to eating in was near where the small lake flowed down the valley, but around a low rise that blocked most of the tumultuous roar from the falls themselves. A thick copse of thin river trees blocked off most of the spinward view, but there was a small clearing that they were quickly outgrowing.

Several large logs had been dragged over near a central firepit, and trampled grass off to one side was used for various games of chance or skill when not being used to train or practice. The river provided an accessible location to wash their dishes after the meal, as well as an easy source of clean water.

Shura was already serving up the first portions when Kas arrived, so he got in line to grab his own bowl of stew. The compies were happily fighting over the entrails Shura must have given them. From the feathered portions, it looked like Shura's contribution had been some sort of bird; there was also a number of the wild tubers he had found a few days ago.

Kas wasn't sure what else went into the stew, but found it to have a very interesting spicy aftertaste. About midway through his meal, Shura sat down on the ground next to him. The drak didn't often use even the rustic furniture they had in the camp due to how large she was.

"What is this?" Kas asked, holding up a spoonful of meat.

"Tryry took down some sort of feathered land bird. It was pretty big; actually, I think he called it a Wellbeter. Pretty aggressive and dumb, though, said it wouldn't make for a good pet," Shura answered between bites of her own stew. The massive pot of stew in her hands was five times the size of Kas' own bowl, but it looked small; it didn't look out of place in the drak's hands.

"Well, they're pretty good. Maybe we can cultivate them for food, at least," Kas said, enjoying the tangy taste of the meat.

"Yup. How is Thunder Pig doing?"

"He's alright, had to shoo him away from the fields already." Kas sighed, glancing over to where he had last seen the pig. "Need to build a pen or something for him. Think we can get a mate for him? I know he's immature right now, but he should be an adult soon, and I'd like to see if that thundering nature of his can be passed down."

"It should be able to," Shura said and then frowned. "I can't bond an adult yet, but if we find another juvenile, then I should be able to bond them. I think it would be better to just let Thunder Pig mature a bit, then have him take over a sounder as the alpha. With the bond and his new thunder ability, he should be able to do that. And then we don't have to waste stones on a sow. I'm still looking for something small and useful, as you suggested."

"Yeah, the compies are cute, but we need something furry to sell before we can really rake in the dough, and even then… we'll need enough to keep the supply line going," Kas said after a moment's thought. "Although I think Thunder Pig could be used as a mount or maybe a beast of burden. We'll have to see if he'll take a saddle once he grows up."

They talked more about other animals Shura had seen around the valley as Kas kept an eye on everyone's bowls. When the first tribesman finished up his bowl, Kas set his own aside and got up. "Hey, everyone, I know most of you know this by now, but I just wanted to give you all a rundown of what happened in the mines today."

Kas went on to describe his negotiations with the kobolds, although he only described the final agreement, not the dickering back and forth.

The miners had a few questions about how that would affect them, but since they were already getting a flat daily rate, they weren't too upset by the production tax. Costache was the most upset about it, muttering about how they would need more miners to keep up production.

Kas made a mental note to give the miners additional rewards based on how much they produced. He had long ago realized that people worked better when there was something in it for them.

Next, Kas talked about what he planned to do with the rest

of the village. How he would need to hire additional guards and other high demand professionals. He actually got a cheer when he mentioned bringing aboard a dedicated builder, since it meant everyone's living conditions would improve at a much faster rate. After he answered a few questions, everyone got back to their food and whatever other entertainment they could find in the rough camp.

The executive council—as Kas mentally started calling Shura, Forthan, and himself—met shortly afterward, the draks having more detailed questions about building locations and timelines. The biggest issue was figuring out a mutually benefi-cial priority queue.

"A kitchen first," Kas said. "I know Shura is doing her best, but I'm sure there are better uses of her time than cooking for all of us. And getting Adel and the rest of your crew out here will help a lot. I think I want to delay heading back to the city until I have at least some crops to sell. I have a feeling we'll need the income to hire the unbound."

"I'm not sure how much I like the idea of trying to convince more unbound to come out here," Shura muttered. "You and Shannon seem nice enough, but the unbound have… a reputa-tion. It would also be incredibly difficult to regulate their behav-ior. At least until we are more settled. I think we should focus our efforts on getting bound guards for the kobold caverns, then once we get a few more facilities prepared, we can start worrying about how to deal with the unbound…

"I'm still worried about what happened to the legions and whatever these mysterious dwellers are. Until we know more, I'd like to keep our Minotaur poking to a minimum." Shura glanced over at Forthan, who nodded his head.

"It's true, unbound are much harder to guarantee loyalty. I think it would be wise to ensure we have a strong infrastructure here before we start bringing them on," the white drak agreed.

"Okay. I'm just not sure how easy it will be to get combat-ants who are willing to leave Tallrock and come out here. We don't exactly have much to offer them," Kas said, gesturing to the logs and campfires around them.

"You forget two things," Forthan said, holding up two claws. "First, we have Shura Blueblessed. There are quite a few who would be willing to come out here if it meant being trained by the Lightning Dervish." Shura looked unhappy when he mentioned that nickname but said nothing as Forthan continued. "And second, Tallrock is a legion outpost. There are enough Kingdom dissidents, particularly among the non-humans, that we should be able to find plenty of people just looking for a chance to get out from under Tasdel's minions."

"I knew that the Kingdom wasn't well liked, but I don't think I realized it was quite that bad," Kas responded with a frown.

"Well, take your cian friend, for example. Do you know how well blacksmiths are paid in legion towns? It's significantly more than we're paying him, I assure you. The legion always needs work done, but yet he was willing to come out here into dangerous land just to get away from them." Forthan's white snout had pointed at Costache, who was still working on his forge. "You make this a place where non-humans are accepted, and we'll have plenty of people willing to come."

CHAPTER TWENTY-TWO

Recruitment Drive 1

After that, the conversation petered out, and Kas eventually begged his leave; he had a lot of research to do before bed, and the physical labor had left him exhausted. A whistle called the compies over, and he set Diane on his shoulder, where she happily nuzzled into the hair behind his ear. Dino chirped around on the ground, pawing at Kas' leg until he picked the little guy up and cradled him in his arms, heading towards his room in the wanderer's pine.

Before ducking under the branches, he turned and really looked at his farm. The crops had all started flowering, thick blue-green stalks of wheat that would eventually turn golden brown. Yellow and purple flowers grew on the potatoes. Kas looked forward to having them in the stews rather than the wild tubers they had been using lately. The yellow flowers on the corn looked odd to him, but the tiny flowers would eventually turn into a light purple.

Beyond the farm, he could see Thunder Pig, who was sniffing around various trees. With a start, he realized he hadn't built anywhere for the pig to sleep for the night, and he set Dino down, approaching the hog and patting his flanks. Thunder Pig turned to look at him for a moment before flipping his thick ears back and returning to his task of sniffing at the base of the tree.

"So, what should I do about you?" Kastigan asked as he considered what kind of shelter the big animal would need. He certainly wasn't going to dig something large enough for the creature to sleep in. He glanced around the clearing again and saw the second barracks house, which was only half-finished. "I guess you could sleep in that for tonight. I'll have to build you something better for tomorrow." As he said that, the pig turned to look at him again then eyed the building warily.

Turning to look at the half-complete structure, he huffed in annoyance. Walking over to it, he grunted at the two-foot hole he would have to step down to get into the rest of the dugout. With a groan, Kas used Earth Shape to gather up loose dirt to create a ramp down. The pig turned to examine him more closely as he worked his magic, the long nose prodding his arm. When Kas was done, the pig snorted and then gingerly stepped down.

Stepping into the rest of the structure, he hooted softly as he turned around a few times. Kas was a little worried that the pig would brush up against the walls and break them. Still, he actually seemed very gentle with it all, and on the third turn, settled into the floor, his head leaning against the rock wall at the back of the dugout, and he hooted again in satisfaction before closing his eyes.

Kas rolled his eyes. "Well, I'm glad it meets your standards."

His words caused the pig to open one eye; he focused on Kas then snorted once, his long nose flaring out in a clearly dismissive gesture.

"Yeah, yeah, sleep well," Kas said, turning back to the wanderer's pine and sitting down. The two compies eagerly swarmed him, fighting for space and attention. Their antics made Kas laugh as Diane pushed around the smaller Dino to get the most preferred scratches and perches.

Separating the two of them to either side of his lap, he

rubbed their bellies to happy chirps. The little lizards pushed against his stomach to rub their backs into his thighs. He sat there longer than he had planned to, just being with the two small, affectionate lizards.

After a moment, he began humming one of the nursery rhymes he had memorized when they were expecting Elam. He had been looking forward to moments like this with his son. Watching him fall asleep in his arms, peaceful and calm.

Stopping to brush the tears out of his eyes, he sighed heavily.

Diane peeked open an eye when he stopped petting her, but when she saw his face, she trilled. Sitting up, she put her paws on his chest and butted her head against his cheek.

"It's okay, baby girl. I'll survive, just a little broken still."

Dino joined in, hopping up onto his head and wrapping his tail around his neck, clutching tight to his scalp. The absurdity of the whole thing made Kas laugh.

"Alright you two, that's enough of that for tonight. Sleep well, and make some eggs of your own soon, okay?" Kas said, gently pulling Dino off his head and setting him down. The two looked at him, curious and then chirped.

Would you like to breed Dino and Diane?

The system prompt caught Kas by surprise, but he happily mentally selected yes, and it disappeared, the two compies quickly running off into their den. "Well, I guess I just had to ask." He laughed softly, still in a somber mood he logged out, ready to do some research.

———

Sitting up, Matt breathed out a sigh. "Well, that was a day," he muttered to himself even as he went about the task of getting a real dinner and pulling up the forums. First, he needed to do some research into how people were doing alchemy. He found a couple of recipes that could work with pink and crimson powder. What was interesting was that despite using the same materials, all four of the recipes he found had different methods of creating it. There was actually a bit of a competition between the alchemists.

Several of them had posted their methods and what their results had been. Other comments called their methods idiotic or belittled them in different ways. As Matt dug deeper into it, he noticed something unusual. All the most knowledgeable posters had a small dot in the bottom left of their profile pictures. It was almost impossible to see on typical images; Kas wouldn't have noticed it except that three posts in a row had it on three different avatars.

Pulling up a larger version of the image, he zoomed in on the dot and frowned. What he had initially thought was a dot was actually a small, black smiley face. He spent a minute isolating the face and then did an image search. It was the symbol of a group calling themselves the Praetorians of Knowledge. That was the only information he could find out about them. There was no member list, just a single landing page listing their name with the smile. What was even more curious was that the site was hosted by Livia, the company that ran the game.

Was this some sort of secret organization that exceeded even the bounds of the game? It was clear that whatever they were, they were much better than the average run of the mill characters that were posting their alchemy formulas on the forums.

He spent the next few minutes scraping the forums for more posts with the dot, focusing mainly on the crafting professions, and he found them. Dozens, maybe even hundreds of different accounts, all people that were clearly a step above their peers.

Taking another ten minutes, he set up a detailed search that would go through these known members, find people they associated with, and figure out where they were located. Matt stretched and decided he needed to go for a run.

When he got back and cleaned himself off in a sonic shower, he looked at the results. The first instance of Praetorians was well before launch. A group of three artisans had gotten together and were talking shop, and mentioned the need to share information as they discovered that the further along they got, the more they needed the other crafting professions to hone their own craft. The leader of the group called himself Dancing Dan, and he was deep in Thel'kan, which meant that there was almost no chance Matt would be able to find him.

Looking for locals, he didn't find any of the members posting in the Tallrock thread, but three of their members were in the next community to the north. Pulling up a map that someone had made, that looked like a three-week trip at least. Most likely more since it was going to be through unbroken territory. He might be able to get a message to them, but their interests weren't aligned to his, one being a smith, and the other two being carpenters.

None of the three were interested in alchemy or farming, though, although one of them was also a leathercrafter. With a sigh, Kas went looking for the closest alchemist. He didn't have regional data for most of them; however, only about a third of the confirmed members posted in their local forums. None of them were even on Gogland, all either in Thel'kan or back in the Unified Realm. Or, in the case of a guy named Lupin Dal'ray, the deep rimward territory of the beastkin.

The next search was to try to figure out which of the Praetorian alchemists seemed the most helpful, and he found one named Kanudawn. He typed up a message to her, asking about some different methods of preparing healing potions. Before sending the message, he pondered how to advertise that he was looking to join the Praetorians. He ended up putting the smiley face in a box and grouped it with a question mark.

Glancing at the clock, he decided that he was tired enough that it was time to get to bed. Hopefully, Kanudawn would have responded before he entered the game tomorrow.

Waking up to his comm unit going off, he glanced at the

clock on his wall—it read 03:00, and he cursed. It was too late for anything even closely resembling a good call, but it was Lexie on the other end. So he slapped the comm unit and answered it. "What's wrong?" he asked.

"Matt? Is that you?" Lexie's voice on the other side of the line sounded raw, haggard, and slightly slurred.

"Lexie, are you alright?" Matt repeated. Lexie had never been a regular drinker, which made those irregular times when she drank much worse than they could have been.

"Matt, I just need to know why," Lexie said after a minute. "Why do you hate me so much?"

"Lex, are you at home?" The concern in Matt's voice was unmistakable.

"Yes. No. You can't do this," Lexie slurred out. "You need to be angry. Why aren't you angry?"

Matt tried to search for an answer. He never had gotten angry about anything with Elam. How do you get mad at the world ending? "What should I be angry about?"

"Me, fate, anything," Lexie pleaded.

"We can talk about this later. You need to go to bed now, Lex." Matt pulled up the house's interface and queued up the hangover routine. "Take some of the pills the house is giving you, they'll help with the hangover. Will you go to bed for me?"

"No, you can't take care of me. You can't just ignore all your problems! You left. You can't love me anymore!" Lexie shouted into the mic and then hung up.

With a sigh, he sat and watched to make sure she didn't try to leave the house. He also instructed the house not to give her any additional liquor. Then he leaned back in bed, closing his eyes. After exhausting himself in the game, he wanted to sleep. But Lexie's call kept running through his head.

Should he be angry? Matt wasn't sure if that would help anything. It wasn't anger that he felt, just... regret? Like there was something more he should have been able to do and didn't. Some part of him realized that he had been running ever since Elam died. First from the job, then Lexie, and now from life itself. He was becoming one of those people who lived in virtual reality. While the stigma against that kind of lifestyle had disappeared over the years, there were significant issues with people who lost themselves and never reintegrated back into physical society.

Never before had he seen the appeal, but Livia and his life in Miranda Valley were so much better than the physical reality that he currently lived in. Tossing and turning, he couldn't get back to sleep; he checked in on Lexie a few more times just to make sure she was still at home, but was unable to drop off into unconsciousness. Finally, another beep on his comm unit told him that there was a private message from the Livia forums. Checking it out, he saw that Kanudawn had responded.

The original request had been for a basic primer on how alchemy worked, and she sent him to an obscure link on the wiki, which contained much more information than he had been able to find on his own. For some reason, the wiki had almost purposefully been hiding the info. He read about the underlying ideology and thought he understood a bit more about what he needed to do to make a healing potion.

He could make a healing potion by doing several easy steps. This would create the most basic and worthless potions and require more basic components than using a more advanced method. By distilling, de-concocting, heating, cooling, or several other procedures, Matt could make a more effective product and use fewer resources to do so. Even opening up the option of allowing the ingredients' secondary effects to take place.

This was where the thundering variant on his powder became relevant. A typical method would never actually take advantage of these augmented powders. The benefit was that it was much faster to make the easier products that didn't rely on the individual skill and skills of the alchemist. He decided that he had no interest in being one of those alchemists that just created base products. Unless he could come up with an easy way to mass-produce potions with something he could grow.

Looking into how to cultivate herbs led him to believe that it wasn't possible for most people to ever get to that point. It required several skills that were buried deep in the farming and herbalism skills. However, with significant affinities in both, he was uniquely suited to be able to do that particularly tricky task. He just needed to find the right seeds or plant clippings and find the right place to grow the plants. Which meant he would need to build a greenhouse.

Pretty sure he had no desire to look at the massive list of things that were on his to-do list at this point, he sent a quick thank you to Kanudawn and finally got to sleep.

DAY 8

The next morning he did some basic stretches as he checked the forum. He also decided to send a message to his friend Dave that wanted to be an adventurer, telling the guy that he had a pretty permanent need for an adventurer group to go into a dungeon-like setting. To his surprise, Dave sent him back a message as he was finishing up his breakfast food tube.

Dude, are you kidding me? You have a dungeon? Where is it? What level is it? How many people can get into it? I've had a little bit of luck finding some wandering monsters, but having a dedicated dungeon? What level is it?

Matt chuckled at Dave's excitement, which was followed immediately by a full visual call from him. Dave was a shorter guy, skinny with a dark complexion that had nothing to do with spending time in the sun. "Hey, Dave."

"Dude, do you really have a dungeon?" Dave asked.

"I'm not really sure, to be honest." Kas went on to quickly explain his situation with the kobold cave.

"Hmm, so, there might be a real dungeon underneath all that, but that just sounds like a high-density monster spawn." Dave put a finger to his lips as he considered. "Might be hard to sell it to the group, but honestly that beats what we're doing right now. We got thrown into an area near the shieldwall in

Thel'kan and man, the barrier is causing a lot of tension. It draws so much mana that it takes ages for the casters to regen.

"Tell you what, I'm gonna talk to my group. Not sure how many of them are gonna be willing to restart, but I think most of them will. We start in Tallrock, right? Man, I wish we could just fast travel over there. The game really needs to add something like that."

"Yes, Tallrock. You have a little while; it'll be a few days before we head back to the town and we're a ways from there, so amenities are scarce. But we're working on that," Matt answered.

"Dude, that's not a problem. Real monsters make an inn totally irrelevant, plus, like you said, that's just for a little while." Dave frowned. "I've been getting a bit sick of being a human anyway. I think I found a much better build that would have required I start over anyway.

"Alright, I'll see about liquidating everything here and then make my way over to Tallrock," Dave said with a sense of finality. "I'm sure the others will want to come too. It's not every day you get a chance at dungeons all to yourself."

"Try to keep it only to those you trust. I'm trying to build something here, and I'd just as soon not have every kid on a power trip know I'm out here," Matt urged.

"Dude, I get it. We'll be fine. You said you'll be in town in three days?" Dave asked, and when Matt agreed, he ended the call with a quick, "Alright, see you then, dude."

Matt had forgotten how much Dave used the term dude; it had bothered him when they first met, but it was just something he got used to. He laid back down on his bed and activated the login sequence.

———

Kas was excited to discover that he was still in the tree when he logged in. No repeat of yesterday's GM intervention pending. Sitting up, he looked around for Dino and Diane. Peeking into the den he had dug for them, he caught no sight of either of the two compies nor were there any eggs. With a shrug, he got up and headed out to do his morning gardening.

There was already a field waiting to be seeded, so Kas cast Enrich Soil on it and planted another crop of potatoes. He would need the higher yield they provided to feed all the new mouths that were coming to camp in a few days. He would need to figure out a fair way to charge the adventurers for their board, though. Or at least make that a part of their contract to clean out the mines. That would probably be better, depending on how well his crops actually sold for.

Enrich Soil's 30-day duration meant he would eventually have 30 plots of land that he could enrich at a time. He pulled up a map of the valley, which was getting more detailed every day thanks to all the various wandering that happened from his employees. The parts that Shannon mapped out were particularly detailed, even showing individual trees within a radius of her paths. Kas would have to ask her to map out his entire territory before she left.

Mapping out where the 30 plots would be on the map, he also added the greenhouse and alchemy labs. Kas had already reserved a large portion near the waterfall for his own use, throwing in a large block on a slight hill as where he wanted his own house, and then a few sheds around it.

The next thing was finding a paddock for Thunder Pig; he selected a large portion of land for grazing and made a couple of barns around it. In case there were different kinds of animals that didn't get along and needed to be kept apart.

Glancing up at the sky, Kas looked for the cloud wolf. That would be a sure-fire money maker, but it would require getting Shura's taming skills up. He would have to make do with compies and long-nosed pigs for now. He still wanted to get a couple domesticated chickens or something.

Adding in some areas for coops and some additional housing areas for staff ate up most of the previously set aside land, but there was still plenty left. The gristmill was on the outer edge of that plot, with the sawmill inside of it.

Deciding that it would be better to have the main center of population nearer to the mine and the colosseum, he put the inn halfway between the two, with room for a small garden or park around it. Creating space for a town square near that, where they could set up a market, was next on the list. From there, he borrowed heavily from Forthan's designs, creating a town hall, bathhouse, and other public amenities. Large areas of land were set aside for personal housing areas.

Which left him with another question about how exactly he was going to do that. Owning all the land in Miranda Valley meant that everyone would have to come to him if they wanted to build anything. Did he want to sell land parcels to people to build houses? The unbound probably wouldn't settle for renting. Maybe he could structure it as a renewable five-year lease? So he couldn't kick them off of it unless they opted not to renew, but it would still be his land, and they would have to pay him for it. That was probably the best way to deal with Forthan's landgrab attempts too.

There was a delicate balance that needed to be maintained. Kas needed to give people enough freedom that they felt like they could buy into Miranda, but he didn't want to give up his ultimate control over it. Which meant he needed to lay the foundation for how he wanted the valley to develop before Dave and his friends got here. Forthan was going to be the big sticking point. He needed to figure out a way to negotiate with the drak. Their verbal agreement wasn't going to cut it forever.

Would Forthan accept a rent-controlled lease? Hard to say unless Kas actually proposed it to the white drak. How did the indentured servitude with Shura affect that? Could he even accept a contract in that state? Shaking his head, he made a note to go talk to Shura about the whole thing and ask for her advice.

Pushing the issue aside, he tried to focus on finishing up his daily obligations to the farm. The smell of breakfast caught up to him before he started on the last field, and he decided to take a short break.

Starting into the morning hotcakes and kababs of meat, he took his usual spot on the log. To his surprise, it was Costache that came and sat down next to him first.

"Kastigan, are the miners allowed down into the first part of the mine today? I was hoping to get another couple loads of metal in today, and they'll never get enough just wandering around looking for nodes."

"They should be. They can't get into the main cavern until we can fully man the place, but they should be safe with a group going down and clearing to that fork and then having one or two stay down there while they work. Maybe they can start clearing up the path once the ore is done?" Kas asked.

"Aye, was hoping for a bit more ore than that, but it'll have to do," Costache said with a sigh.

"Will we have the blade ready today?" Kas asked, looking over to where the cian had set up his shop yesterday. Already smoke was trickling out of the forge's chimney.

"Depends, I was gonna head down to the mill in a bit and look at what we'll need to transmit the power. That will dictate how I build the saw." Costache rubbed his forehead. "Probably be tomorrow, to be honest."

"That's… probably fine, I doubt we would be able to use it today anyway. Thanks. I'll head out to you after I finish up on the farm and get the miners sorted."

CHAPTER TWENTY-THREE

Recruitment Drive 2

Tracking down Damae since Forthan had gone off somewhere with Shannon, he asked for a group of three to go down with the miners to at least ensure they were safe.

"Hmm. I could send Blinall and Wyces. I was hoping to get Tryrynall out hunting, and I was gonna see about helping you with the sawmill," Damae said after a moment of thought.

"Oh, good points. I doubt they'll be in any real trouble. Maybe just send them to clear out the tunnel and then leave Wyk down there?" Kas frowned. "I'm more worried about stuff that wandered in during the night."

"Fair enough. Tell you what, I'll go with Blinall and Wyces just to clear the place out. Wyces can set up some traps while he's down there. Have him show the two how to reset them and all. That way, we can just trap the place when we aren't using it, and we don't have to keep sending folks down."

"Sounds good to me. Hoping to get the sawmill up and running by early tomorrow, so more building to be done after that," Kas said as he and the tribesman separated to their various duties. Shura was finally done with breakfast, so he went to chat with her. She agreed to walk with him to the mill after she cleaned up from breakfast.

"Any chance you know where Forthan is?" Kas asked the drak.

"He and Shannon went off early this morning and told me they would be back late," Shura said before taking another bite.

"Okay, what direction did they go?" Kas tried to think of what Forthan would have needed the surveyor for.

"Towards the mouth of the valley," Shura answered with a shrug.

"Okay, I'll see you when I finish the last plot then," Kas said, heading back to finish weeding and watering the last crop plot. As he worked, he called out to Dino and Diane, but neither responded to him. Assuming that they must still be off in breeding mode somewhere, he wondered if they had made a different nest somewhere. Perhaps the hole he dug wasn't in the right conditions? Or maybe they were stockpiling food or something.

The entire process was a little weird, and he wasn't sure what 'breeding' the two creatures seemed to mean. Shura arrived right as Kas was finishing up, so he dusted himself off and waved at the drak. "We need to grab Costache as well, but I was wondering if you could answer some questions about Forthan's... sucker?"

"It is sukar, not sucker," Shura answered automatically. "What would you like to know?"

"Well, Forthan has a lot of money, and he's helping us a lot. I would like to get him to buy into Miranda Valley. I just don't think I want to actually sell him land. How do you think he would respond to a lease of the land instead of him buying it from me?"

Shura hummed softly to herself. "It would be improper from him to buy land from you currently. A lease for the duration of the sukar is required. As for after that..." She trailed off, considering. "I think it would be wise for him to lease the land from you. I do not entirely trust his motivations; I think he will rechallenge Sh'kar as soon as the current sukar has ended. That will give you another ten months and a day. That is how long you have to figure out a way to bind him to yourself.

"If you do not, I am not sure what he will do, but it will not be good news for either of us." Shura sighed. "Forthan is unfortunate; he excels in ways that are not important to the drak. That is what will make him so dangerous to us."

"Alright, so how do I do that?" Kas asked, Shura's words having scared him considerably.

"You will need to gain power of your own, independent of him. I know you do not like to fight, but neither does he; this is a war you must wage on a battlefield I am ill-equipped to fight." Shura's frill flattened in disappointment.

"It's okay, Shura. I don't intend to lose." Kas fell into deep thought as they left the farm and went to the central campfire, where Costache met them. The cian clearly was confused by the muted greeting but didn't seem interested in ending the silence himself. The walk to the mill with Shura was interesting, whereas before there had been plenty of small animals and birds throughout the forest, now they moved in a muted silence. He hadn't noticed it before, but clearly, the animals responded to her presence like they would have with any large predator.

When they got there, they saw Max working on a downed tree even as Kas inspected the fog, which still surrounded the building. "Fifteen minutes until completion," he told everyone else. Deciding not to waste any time, he picked up where he had left off the day before in clearing undergrowth, killing the plants and then casting Earth Stomp to break up the dirt. Shura stepped up next to him, pulling the weeds from the ground with much more strength than he could muster.

Keeping one eye on the fog and the other on his work, he stopped when there was just a minute left. Already the mist was beginning to disperse, thick patches of mist dissolving into the surrounding forest. Through the gaps in the fog, Kas caught his first sight of the structure. Over the next sixty seconds, it entirely disappeared, leaving behind a large stone building. It looked like it was made of local materials, various shades of dark granite making up the lower half of the building's exterior, giving it a solid looking foundation.

Black beams stretched from the granite several meters up to the vaulted roof, which was tiled with dark slate. Between the darkened oak support beams were slats made out of what looked like pine; the individual boards had some sort of treatment on them, however, and had been whitewashed to create a contrast with the rest of the darker building materials.

One large bay door took up a goodly portion of the visible side of the building. Near the top of the roof were several narrow windows. Still, the only other external fixture was a bulbous covering that Kas assumed was how other structures could take advantage of the wheel's power.

Stepping up to the large door, Kas opened it, and it swung quickly, evidence of some sort of mechanical assistance. Inside, more of the dark beams crossed the room at surface level, with a line of the same going down the center. The underside of the roof was exposed, leaving a gap in the attic. Several large boxes sat along one wall, while the center was occupied by the mill-stone itself, covered by another layer of boxes, with access hatches near the center of the room.

A set of stairs led into the underside where Kas assumed the actual mechanics of the building were held; this upper floor was mostly for storage and manipulating the mill. Several large levers were set up to one side, allowing him to control the mill without having to go into the dark half-level below. A few glowing stones lit up as the door opened, augmenting the natural light from the windows, creating a warm and inviting workspace.

Glancing down the stairs, Kas could see more unlit stones that would presumably light when someone descended. All in all, there was plenty of room to store bags of powder, even though he didn't think he would need to worry about building a grain silo or anything like it soon.

The ceiling was tall enough that Shura could come in,

although it clearly wasn't made for someone of her height. She looked around for a bit and then ducked back out to where she actually could stand up. Costache, on the other hand, had made a beeline to the mechanism connecting to the next area. He had already removed the cap and was muttering to himself while he figured out how to interface with whatever the system generated.

"Well, I guess we could have a few people sleep on the floor in there for now," Kas said, glancing at Shura, who nodded.

"Not much use until your crops grow up," the drak acknowledged. "Until then, we have work to do."

Max had already gotten to work clearing out some of the larger trees that would need to be removed to put up the sawmill. But with Shura lifting all the heavy things, they made quick time on clearing the rest of the land they would need.

Kas finished up clearing out the underbrush while Damae took the finished logs and began setting up the foundation. Kas got called over to create the holes for the large logs that would be used as the main beams of the project.

When they took their midday meal break a little while later, everyone was looking forward to a rest. The work had been proceeding at a breakneck pace. Already the skeleton of the structure was visible; Costache had disappeared a few hours ago to begin working on the connecting mechanism, telling Max that he would need a single large beam to be set aside. The next portion was going to rely heavily on Shura's height and strength as they set up the cross beams, and everyone had decided it would be good to come at the task with a full stomach.

Not that the food was particularly filling. Lunch had been dried rations since they arrived in Miranda, and today was no different. Everyone was looking forward to the cook showing up at the camp.

Damae also recruited several of the other tribesmen for the more difficult task of raising the cross beams. The heavy lengths of wood needed more raw strength than they could muster alone. Kas wished he knew where Forthan had gotten to; he would have helped a significant amount.

With the help of Shura they got it into place without incident, though, which was a relief to Kas, who went to work fastening it while everyone else held it in place. From there, they raced to get the rest of the frame up and going, Damae and two tribesmen against Shura and Kas. The drak's strength again proved to be invaluable, and Kas finished his length of wall a few minutes before Damae's team. By then, it was nearly sunset, and everyone was ready for a hot meal.

Two of the tribesmen, Wyk and Damae, decided they wanted to sleep on the hard floor of the mill for the night when Kas opened it up for people to sleep there until other accommodations were ready. Simeon and Gus both volunteered as soon as they discovered they wouldn't be alone.

Dinner continued with good levity after that, everyone excited to see the rapid growth in the valley. There was a moment of tension when Thunder Pig made his way into the middle of the camp. When he sat down next to the fire to soak in the heat, everyone calmed down.

Kas offered him his own spot, and he went to sit down next to the hog but paused when he got downwind of the thing. "Hey you, come on, we're gonna go get you clean," Kas said, prodding Thunder Pig's rump. The hog gave him a long-suffering sigh before shambling to his feet and following Kas to the river. The cold winter runoff didn't seem to bother the thick-skinned hog, but Kas was soon shivering as he scrubbed the muck out of the thick fur.

Discovering that there was a better method, Kas started using Water Spray to blast the sides of the hog clean. Thunder Pig actually seemed to enjoy that, snorting in pleasure and moving so that the jet could reach more itchy sections. In conjunction with his shape earth ability, he managed to clean off the pig in just under half an hour. Quite a bit faster than he anticipated, given that the porcine companion was nearly as tall as he was now. A shivering Kas walked the pig back to camp where the still-soaking pig plopped down in the same spot next to the fire and went to sleep.

"Sorry, everyone," Kas said, hip bumping the pig aside, glad that the area around the campfire hadn't quite been turned into dirt yet, the flattened grass at least not turning into mud under the pig. He turned around in front of the fire to dry off, even as he pulled off portions of his clothing. To his pleasure, he discovered the game actually dried clothing much faster than reality, and he was dry again within a few minutes.

Forthan and Shannon arrived just as the light was dying. Shura had set aside portions for the two, who looked like they could use baths themselves.

Shannon took a seat next to Kas, happily digging into the lukewarm meal.

"Heya," Kas greeted the other unbound.

"Mm." Shannon nodded, eating hungrily.

Kas chose his next words carefully. "Y'all look like you had fun?"

With a shake of her head, Shannon pulled up her interface and then sent an updated version of her map to Kas. Figuring it would give her time to chew, he pulled up his own. To his surprise. Shannon and Forthan had ranged quite a distance up into the mountains around Miranda Valley.

Several notable features were marked, from valuable mineral deposits to unusual trees. Of special interest to him was a section of land above the waterfall. There didn't appear to be an easy way up, but once you got to the top, it flattened out and created a sizable secondary valley.

Right near the waterfall was an almost unnaturally flat plot of land, next to the river. Unnatural was obvious because where it intersected the river was a large, partially-buried disk of a strange black metal. "What is this?" Kas asked the dowser.

"Source of the blockage on my abilities. Everything near that point is nearly impossible to dowse; the further away you get, the easier things become," Shannon said before taking another bite. With her mouth full, she continued, "We cleared off some of the grass, found some stone underneath it. It's got some very, very old writing on it that Forthan says he thinks is from around the time of the War of Blood."

Kas frowned. "Any idea what it does?"

"No idea, but whatever it is, it's big, old, and still super powerful," Shannon said. "Forthan tried to do some tests, but draks can't do any magic at all except for their bloodline breath stuff. You're probably the best equipped to figure anything out. Although we'll probably need to find some cipher for the language. I was gonna check online tonight to see if anyone has found anything similar anywhere else. I'll send you the images."

"Do me a favor, don't post anything about it on your main account?" Kas said with a frown. "I don't want everyone coming out here before I can adequately lock the area down."

"Sure thing, bossman," Shannon teased with a smirk.

"Ugh, don't call me that," Kas said, and the talk turned to more mundane matters. Kas kept looking at the image of the disk on his map, though. Thanks to Shannon being there, it was drawn in exquisite detail. He estimated that it must be at least dozens of meters across based on the lack of trees or anything with deep roots in that area. Of course, since it was Shannon, the fact that they were unable to determine what the actual material that the disk was made of was another mystery.

The dowser should have been able to figure out most substances, although the fact that it was blocking her divination magic might be part of why she was having issues determining what it was made of. Adding a trip to the top of the waterfall to the list of things to do when he had a free minute, he opted not to share too much with everyone else. There wasn't much to share currently anyway; it could just be a relic of the Blood War, something they had made to block divination attempts.

An ancient relic of the Blood War has been found on your land. Find out more.

2000 experience. Additional rewards based on success.

It was the second time Kas had been given an actual quest prompt by the system, and this was far less specific than the first had been. The game didn't seem to want him following a specific quest prompt. If someone wanted to go out and stop the necromancer, they just went out and killed their minions until they could kill the evil creature itself.

This must be something big; he would be checking the forums to see if anyone else had found something similar. He glanced over at Shannon, but it didn't look like the woman had gotten a similar prompt.

Kas assumed that was because she didn't own the land the relic had been found on. Which was a bit of a relief, since that meant at least no one else would be getting a notification that there was an ancient relic on his land. Which would give him some leeway introducing new people to the disc, whatever it ended up being.

Kas spent an hour just enjoying his time with the group. Thunder Pig seemed content enough to stay near the fire, but Kas prodded the animal to his feet and led him over to one of the areas that was destined to become a stable. Twenty minutes of labor later, and he had an improvised shelter created. Mostly this had been a function of getting the pig to work for him; using the bond, he was able to issue simple commands to the pig. He had started it off by having the pig pick up a tree with its nose.

Unlike an elephant trunk, which his nose partially resembled, Thunder Pig's nose was only about a foot long, but it served a very similar purpose. By bracing the log between his snout and tusks, he pushed one side of the log into a nook high up in one of the trees. Then, with a lot of effort, Kas was able to aim the other end of the log into a similar spot and have Thunder Pig shuffle sideways until it was securely resting on either tree. Using that as primary support, he dragged several other branches over, creating a one-sided lean-to that would act as a windbreak and stay relatively dry.

After a few toots and snorts, the pig carefully prodded the

structure with his nose, pushing here and there before curling up under the lean-to and closing his eyes again. Kas considered the whole thing a success; he hadn't really explored the limits of the bond yet, but he had been pushing them to get the task done.

Sitting down with his back to the pig's neck, he looked up at the stars and smiled. Now that the pig was clean, he emitted a slight ozone smell. It was far too faint to be unpleasant, but Kas found it odd that the affinity would change such a simple aspect of the creature. Other than the ruff of yellow fur down its spine, there were no other indications of a change.

With a start, he realized he still hadn't seen the compies for the day and went looking for them. His hunt was unsuccessful, and he ended up in the wanderer's pine forty minutes later. Shura was already sleeping, and he realized he had stayed logged in later than usual. With a sigh, he sat down and logged out.

———

Stretching his arms for the first time in hours, he heard bones creak. The technology behind the implants meant that his muscles did still move small amounts while he was in the simulation. Enough that a vigorous day of work left him feeling just as sore out of the game as he had been in game. A quick sonic shower to get rid of a day of sitting mostly still left him feeling clean, so he pulled up the forums as he ate his dinner nutrition tube.

First, Matt went looking for any other references to War of Blood relics. There were dozens of well-known ruins, the ancient populations that built them a mystery, but their building techniques were ages beyond the ken of the current world. Several of the most defensible points on Livia were once out of the way outposts during the war. Out of the way, because that was the only way anything survived. There were several other well-known battle sites, and the same indestructible materials were used.

Except that in the ruins they clearly weren't indestructible. Small portions of foundations were all that remained, jagged and fragmented by forces that were beyond understanding. The more Matt dug into the War of Blood, the more he realized that no one knew much about the it; they didn't even have real names for the sides.

They just called them the Lagit and the Tagit, which meant Builders and Destroyers in one of the oldest languages on Livia. No one even knew which side won. Just that, eventually, the war had ended.

Matt frowned, considering this information for a bit. None of the ruins looked like discs, though he did manage to find some examples of their languages. But so few pieces remained of the language that no one knew what they meant at all. It would take finding a Rosetta Stone to really delve deeper, although people were collecting scraps of text to see if they could begin the decryption process.

Next, he went looking for sites where divination magic was blocked. Here he turned to the dowsing forums; most of it was locked behind a wall that required you to prove your skills as a dowser before you could get to them. There was an open section, and here he found what he thought was an answer to one of his questions. There was an interaction between a newbie asking why his skills were giving him inaccurate results in an area outside one of the main starting zones in Dragoria.

What was interesting about the post was that another player told him to just ignore that area; a few miles away, his equipment would work just fine. That led him to a string of other complaints, usually from new dowsers who claimed their skills were broken. Matt wasn't sure, but it sounded to him like at least a good portion of the starting zones had these divination blind spots in them. What if these discs were placed all over the world, and he just happened to be lucky enough to find one where a river kept a portion of it uncovered?

With that knowledge, he created a new forum ID and then posed a question to one of the newbies that had complained about a divination dead spot, asking if he could pinpoint the exact location of the interference. Matt even went so far as to tell him the method Shannon had used to pinpoint it, which was easy enough to see from her map.

Each time Shannon did an active query, the discovered map ballooned around her, making it easy to see where she had been actively dowsing. Unfortunately, he didn't know why she had opted to go in a specific direction after doing a detection; sometimes it seemed completely random. And there were a couple of bubbles that nearly overlapped like she was trying to compare relative strengths of various directions. His respect for the dowser went up a bit; actually, the more he examined the map, the more effort he realized she had put into her discovery.

The realization that these discs were probably all over Livia settled at least part of his unease with the whole subject. If his disc was one of many, then it was less likely that anyone would try to take it from him. With that weight off his mind, he checked up on Lexie; seeing her at home was another relief. Then he closed his browser down and got into bed, exhausted. Sleep came much easier than normal.

CHAPTER TWENTY-FOUR

Recruitment Drive 3

There were three messages on his comm device. Matt tried to decide if he needed to check on them. With a guilty sigh, he clicked over to check. The first was from Dave, it said he had managed to convince four of his group mates to switch. The other two might give it a shot, but weren't going to try to liquidate their assets like the first four.

Livia allowed you to make as many characters as you wanted, but Dave wanted to buy some better gear and skills immediately, rather than trying to grind up the gold to get it.

The second message was from Larry, his lawyer, telling him that he had received finalized papers, but they were being held in trust until after his dinner with Lexie. Which had apparently been scheduled for two weeks from now.

Matt frowned when he saw the date: his birthday. Was she planning on throwing a party? Matt had never been very interested in birthdays or holidays. They just had never felt important to him, something that had driven Lexie crazy.

The third message was from Lexie herself, and it included the official invitation to the dinner. It gave him directions on what to wear, but it amounted to what he used to wear daily anyway, so he wasn't too worried about it. He would have to stop by the storage unit though, as there wasn't a ton of space for him to store most of his old life.

He sent a reminder to Dave that he wouldn't be back in Tallrock for a few more days still, then a thank you to Larry. It took him longer to respond to Lexie's message, but he eventually just sent a confirmation that he had added it to his calendar.

With a sigh, he laid back down and logged in.

DAY 9

Logging in, Kas immediately checked to see if the compies were in their den. There weren't any new signs of habitation, and Kas frowned, wondering where they could possibly be. Making his way out of the pine, he checked over the crops. To his delight, he discovered that the first field of potatoes was ready to harvest. Hoping to get them included in the breakfast meal, he pulled out a few plants and shook the dirt off the roots. Quickly cutting the tubers off, he gathered them in a bag.

Good Yellow Potatoes - Ingredient, Consumable - A root vegetable, the potato has been the staple starch of many cultures throughout history. These potatoes have been grown in good soil and have been carefully tended. Additional stat buffs will be given to food or drink prepared with these ingredients. Five kilos of potatoes are one unit of food for settlement purposes.

Consumable? Who ate raw potatoes? Kas sniffed the potato but decided to leave that for some other, more desperate time. Rinsing them off, he set a baker's dozen down next to Shura, who glanced over at him curiously.

"The first fruit of my fields. I think we should celebrate by eating it!"

Shura's frill fluttered as the drak laughed. "Well, I think I can figure something out, although I doubt we have the facilities to really showcase these." Shura looked the potatoes over for a bit, then peeled the golden-brown skin off using the claw on her thumb, revealing the white flesh underneath. She then pulled out a knife and quickly diced them, throwing them into the pot where she was cooking the breakfast meat. When she caught Kas' glance, she winked. "Got some more rabbit this morning from the snares."

"Well, it smells delicious. I'm going to go back to work. I look forward to seeing what you make," Kas said and then headed back to finish harvesting the potatoes and tending to the other crops. As he pulled the last of the potatoes out of the ground, he got the XP notification.

For growing and harvesting your own field, you have received 200 experience. You have received 1000 bonus experience for harvesting Potatoes for the first time.
You are now level 4.
You are now level 5. New spells received: Life Drain, Life Fusion. New skill received: Transference I.

To his surprise, he actually leveled up twice, reaching level five. He hadn't been paying a lot of attention to his levels lately, more just doing all the work that needed to be done. Two levels was a considerable bump, though. Also, the bonus experience from harvesting a crop for the first time almost made him regret having planted multiple fields of wheat. Still, the steady experience to be gained by harvesting fields was nothing to scoff at. With thirty fields going all the time, he could rake in experience much faster.

Although there was probably a point of diminishing returns; at level five, the experience he needed to get to level six was at 3200. If he recalled correctly, that would mean every level the amount of experience needed would double.

Hopefully, harder to raise crops gave more experience, or he would fall behind pretty quickly. Granted, that wasn't his only means by which to get experience, and it was impossible to say right now how the game would play out at higher levels, but he was enjoying what he was doing right now.

Deciding that he wasn't going to worry about levels until it became an issue, he pulled up the information on his new spells and character sheet.

Name: *Kastigan* **Race:** *Human* **Origin:** *Pinnocian-Capital*

HP: *85,* **Mana:** *205,* **Stamina:** *127*

Level: *5,* **XP:** *1650,* **XP TNL:** *3200*

Attributes:
Intelligence 22, Dexterity 14, Strength 17, Wisdom 19, Agility 14, Constitution 17.
Unspent: 6

Regen Rates:
HP Regen: 25, Stamina Regen: 6/m, Mana Regen: 6/m, Combat HP Regen: 0/h, Combat S Regen: 3/m, Combat M Regen: 3/m.

Most of the stat increases had been from using his abilities, deciding to roll dexterity and agility up to 15, wisdom up to 20 and intelligence up to 25 used up all six of the stat points he had just gotten.

Spell Name: Life Drain
Prerequisites: 75 death affinity, Death Magic I 5, Attrition I 1
Cost: 10 mana
Cooldown: 30 seconds
Description: Drains vitality from a touched helpless lifeform. Drained vitality will be stored for 24 hours in your vitality pool.

Spell Name: Life Fusion
Prerequisites: 75 death affinity, Death Magic I 5, Transference I 1
Cost: 0 mana

Cooldown: 12 hours
Description: Transfers vitality from your vitality pool into the touched target.
Vitality used in this way has a variety of effects.

Kas blinked. Those were very potent spells. The need to have it be helpless made Life Drain less good, but it said life-form rather than a creature. Which meant he could use it on plants, and there weren't a lot of plants that could resist.

He decided to test it out, and walked over to one of the bushes he wanted to remove at the edge of the clearing, touching one of the leaves. Casting the spell took just a thought, and immediately the leaf began to shrivel. The entire plant, previously healthy and vibrant, began to look like it was dying.

The bush was still alive, and nothing was preventing it from recovering if he left it alone, though. Kas waited the thirty seconds and cast it on the same plant. Four casts in total and he had drained all the vitality out of the bush; it was now a dried-up husk that had collapsed in on itself. Checking his interface, he saw that he now had 18 points of vitality in his pool. The first three had given him five vitality each, while the fourth killed the plant after only giving him three points.

After his little experimentation, he turned his mind back to his farming and realized he had a slight problem. There were A LOT of potatoes. Far more potatoes than he could comfortably carry back to Tallrock.

There would be another crop of potatoes, the two fields of wheat that would hopefully be turned into flour, and the partially-damaged field of corn. There was no way they would be able to move all that material in their bags, even if Shura and Forthan could carry it all. It was just too bulky for what they had. If Max and Costache worked on making a cart, could they have Forthan and Shura pull it? Something told him the two draks wouldn't take kindly to being used as beasts of burden.

A hoot came from behind him and he looked back;

Thunder Pig had found his way into the clearing with the crops and was giving the potatoes a look Kas didn't appreciate.

"No, Thunder Pig!" Kas yelled even as the pig gave a final snort and charged towards the potatoes. He had gobbled up a handful before Kas could stop him, shooing the big hog away with all the force he could muster on the bond. Thunder Pig turned away, but not before grabbing three more potatoes in his mouth. He parked himself over at the edge of the clearing, happily munching away at the tubers.

Which was why Kas had to spend the next while moving the potatoes to the completed house. Every time he took a trip, he glared at Thunder Pig, who had rolled onto his side, idly chewing weeds. When the potatoes were secured, he was already late for breakfast. With a glare at Thunder Pig and a reinforced order to stay away from everything in the clearing, he went off to eat his rabbit and hash browns. The food gave him a buff to his regeneration rates, the first time anything Shura had made did so.

Spending the rest of the morning tending to his crops, he decided to plant peas to replace the potatoes and in the new field. Until he could figure out a way to transport them, the bulky produce was going to take a back burner to some of the lighter products. After that, he headed to the lumber mill, where Costache, Max, and Damae had been laboring most of the morning.

The connector between the two buildings was in place, and Costache had managed to create most of the machinery they needed, although the cian was clearly annoyed by the quality of some of it. The three of them were currently lifting one end of the heavy crosspiece into the bracket that was sitting on the ground still. Kas moved to help, and the four of them managed to settle it down even as Damae began hammering some notches down to lock the bracket in place.

"Sorry it took so long for me to get here, had to hide the potatoes from Thunder Pig," Kas said to muted laughter. Looking at the work they had done, it seemed like the lumberyard was almost ready to go. The base structure that had been built yesterday had been built up somewhat. Several large logs had been laid crosswise, to where two larger beams were resting just off the ground. This created a channel to drop logs into the cutting mechanism.

The cutting area itself looked to be run by several levers that connected to a set of gears. The gears, in turn, were connected to a set of pulleys that would push the log through the area where the saw itself was set up. A second set of gears were connected to the saw, allowing it to rise up and down as the log moved forward, eventually getting dropped out the far end where it could roll down a small ramp, built of more cross-wise logs, into a collecting area.

"Looking good. Although, it looks like it's gonna be a lot of work to move logs into position." Kas remarked.

"Yeah, we'll rig up another set of gears that will help us elevate the logs from that pile over there," Max said, pointing to where a few trees were already waiting. "But it's gonna take more metal than Costache had available until after the miners get back tonight. It'll probably be a few days before it's running at full efficiency, to be honest, but just having the ability to use it will help a lot."

"Good, I was hoping to build a cart or something after this was functional. There is no way we're going to be able to bring all the harvest to Tallrock without one," Kas said, glancing around and trying to estimate how much work needed to be done on the sawmill.

"I think I could rig something like that up if you can get Thunder Pig to wear a harness," Damae said. "Might be diffi-cult to move it down the switchback, though."

Kas blinked, of course! Using Thunder Pig was a much better option than trying to convince the draks to do it. "I'll see about it; he's still not fully grown yet, but we might be able to use him." He hadn't even thought to check how much longer it would take to get the Long-Nosed Hog to become an adult, but if they could use him... Kas was reminded of a movie he had watched a long time ago, where a tribe of smaller people called Nelwyn used pigs to farm.

"I guess we could figure out some sort of lift like they have in Tallrock, but that's probably more expansive of a project than we're really willing to take on just yet," Kas mused.

"Yeah, I think we could get most of the lads together to take it down the switchback at least. I'll see what I can do about maybe building two, one to take it from the farm to the switchback and the other at the base to get through the forest. Although without a proper road through the forest, I think we're probably better off just creating a harness for him and strapping as much stuff on as we can," Damae said after a minute or two of thought.

"Yeah, the river, in particular, is going to be a challenge to get across. I'm not sure Thunder Pig can even get across that fallen tree that we've been using," Kas said with a frown.

Max glanced at a couple of the logs in consideration. "I think we could turn that into a small bridge pretty easily, but you'll want to build a full-sized one before we start carting stuff through the woods."

Kas hadn't really considered how the distance from Tallrock was going to complicate his plans, but it was going to be a struggle to get his goods to market. Maybe there was some sort of hot air balloon he could use? That was probably more expensive than just building a road, although it didn't come with all the attendant risks that having a road through the woods would have. "We'll figure something out, probably just the harness on Thunder Pig for now."

Assuming that the pig would allow himself to be harnessed. Kas wasn't sure how much weight the adolescent pig would even be able to carry. Looking at his new spells, he wondered if he could cut some of the time until Thunder Pig was mature by feeding him vitality. A morning of work had given him another 238 banked vitality. The spell description had been vague, and the 12-hour cooldown meant he hadn't yet used it for anything.

Kas turned back to working on the last few finishing touches for the lumber mill. Once the second bracket was in place on the log, they had to lift them both into place—four sets of hands made the task much easier than it had been with three—and the mill was ready to go. Well, except for the backbreaking labor of lifting the logs into place so that the mill could use them. Kas helped Max load the first couple.

It took about five minutes per log for the machinery to run, and Kas had managed to rig up a system so that Max had a few logs held in reserve. He would need to find another lumberjack or two though; Max couldn't run the mill and do all the other tree-cutting activities. "Would you rather run the mill or cut logs?" Kas asked, leaning against the post after having just lifted the last of the heavy logs up into position.

"I think I'd rather run the mill. But if you're looking to hire on some help, I have a few friends that I'd suggest hiring," Max said after a moment. "Some good lads back in Tallrock that might be interested in steady work away from the legion."

"Sounds good. Did you want to approach them yourself or just give me the names?" Kas asked. "We'll be heading back to Tallrock with a load of produce in a few days."

"Probably best if I ask 'em in person." Max said, pursing his lips in thought. "I warn you, they might not look like what you're expecting though." When Kas gave him a confused sigh, he shrugged. "They're not human is what I'm saying."

"That's fine," Kas answered. "Miranda is open to anyone who wants to work."

"Well, you might want to go slow on that. I don't have a problem with it, and yer unbound so you can get away with more than others can…" Max trailed off, trying to think of the best way to say this. "But you keep taking on the non-humans, and you'll find it's hard to recruit the humans, particularly if you put 'em in positions of power."

Kas frowned; one of the reasons he had picked a human was because of the racism that existed in Pinnoc. Given that most of the population of Tallrock was from there, it made sense that a lot of that would transfer over to the bound in the region. "Well, at this point, beggars can't be choosers. I'll take anyone willing to work. It's not exactly a glamorous life here, but if you want to work, we'll have room for you."

"Fair enough," Max said, although it was clear he didn't think it was the smartest decision.

Kas wandered back to the fields, draining plants and gathering herbs; he discovered that the larger the plant, the more vitality he could drain from it before it became an issue. A tree could handle a single drain without showing a sign of wilting, but smaller plants couldn't handle a single drain before they died.

By the time Kas got back to his farm, he had several herbs and 587 vitality stored up. Thunder Pig was still sitting on the edge of the clearing around the farm snoring. After an inspection, he saw that he would mature in five days. A frown crossed Kas' lips as he realized that another line had been added to the pig's description.

Due to the consumption of high-quality food, your bonded animal currently has a .5% increased chance of gaining boons upon reaching maturity.

The few potatoes that Thunder Pig had eaten were enough for a .5% chance, which wasn't much, but... would eating more increase the chance? What was the current chance? How much of an improvement was that exactly? What exactly was a boon?

Thunder Pig's affinity didn't seem to register as a boon, which meant that boons must be something else. Would boons be inheritable? A dozen more questions were floating around in Kas' head, but he realized he needed to focus on the immediate problems. Five days to maturity was too long. Kas needed the pig to be an adult within the next three days if he was going to use him as a beast of burden to take the crops to Tallrock.

Walking over to the pig, who was leaning against a tree that didn't seem to appreciate the weight. The pig lifted one lazy eye and stared at him, even as he leaned down next to him. Kas had no idea where the pig would like to be scratched and didn't think his attentions would even be felt through the thick hide anyway. He scratched the pig's head for a moment, then ran a hand down the tuft of yellow fur along Thunder Pig's back. He could almost feel the static charge building up, his hand even starting to tingle.

Shaking out the hand a little to regain feeling, he began scratching the head again and then cast his new spell. 587 points of vitality were transferred directly into the pig, who snorted wildly and then stood up. Thunder Pig started rubbing himself against the tree wildly, which creaked dangerously. Figuring that the pig was somehow itchy after the infusion, he began casting a Water Spray. Thunder Pig realized quickly that there was more comfort in the jet and moved closer to Kas so that he could aim.

When the spell ended, the pig snorted angrily. Kas looked around the clearing and then had an idea, commanding Thunder Pig to head over to the waterfall. The pig looked at him for a moment and hooted, moving at a brisk pace until he was sitting under the falls. The loud hoots of enjoyment were quickly drowned out by the sound of the falls. Kas watched to make sure the pig didn't get pulled into the river, but even as young as he was, Thunder Pig was plenty strong enough that he was in no danger. The hog left the falls a few minutes later, his itch seemingly satisfied.

The pig shook off a little, then headed for a patch of rocks off to one side that had been sitting in the sun all morning, laying down on them to soak up the sun himself. Kas examined the pig again, this time with a Cheshire cat sized smile. Thunder Pig only had 4 days left until maturity. Another infusion or two would hopefully have him maturing just in time to make the trip to Tallrock.

Feeling a reward and a small apology was in order, Kas went back and grabbed a shirt-full of potatoes, laying them down near Thunder Pig's mouth. Kas watched as the pig's nose twitched once, twice, and then his eyes shot open, and he scarfed the potatoes down. When they were done, he nosed at

Kas' shirt for a moment before determining that no more food was imminent, and went back to his sunbathing.

The last inspection showed that the percentage had increased to .7% chance of a boon. Did that mean Kas would need to feed different types of food, or was it just a smaller amount of potatoes? What would happen if the animals had better food from birth? More experiments for later.

Taking a few minutes to get the herbs he had gathered on the way back set up so that they could dry, he then went in search of Shannon. The dowser was eating lunch near the campfire. She had made a salad and topped it with some of the leftover rabbit meat.

Kas' own meal was more dried rations. Sitting down next to Shannon, she nodded to him. The first few bites of the dried rations had him asking where she had gotten the leaves for her salad; he was getting sick of the current cold rations.

"There are a few patches here and there, I had to dowse them out, I'll mark 'em on your map," Shannon responded and shared her map again. Kas made a note of seeing if he could get seeds from some of them; they didn't look like normal lettuce.

"Awesome, thanks. You busy after lunch? I was hoping you could help me find the compies. They've been missing for a bit," Kas said between bites of his lunch.

Shannon frowned. "I guess I haven't seen them around for a bit. Something wrong, you think?"

"No, they sort of disappeared after I got the prompt to breed them."

"Really? I'm kind of fond of them. What would it take to get an egg?"

"I'm not sure how many eggs they are going to lay, nor how many will be viable." Kas vaguely recalled reading that a lot of lizards only had half or less of their eggs actually hatch.

"Hmmm, fair. Alright, how about this? If more than four eggs hatch, you have to give me a chance to buy one. This close to that disc, it's going to be nearly impossible to find anything, gonna be a lot of work for me," Shannon counter bid.

"Fine," Kas said. He wasn't sure if that was a good deal or not, but losing one hatchling was better than the whole batch if he couldn't find Dino and Diane. They finished up their lunches after a few minutes, and Shannon began fiddling around with her dowsing orb, muttering under her breath as she tried to account for the disc. She kept squinting up at the cliff and then facing away from it to do her tests, slowly turning in a circle away from the waterfall.

"This way," Shannon said after a moment, pointing away from the camp and waterfall on the trailing side. They walked a hundred meters or so, and Shannon repeated the process from earlier. This time it looked like it went a bit faster, and she led them closer to the valley walls. In the middle of the third dowsing, the thing sparked, and the lights it had been showing disappeared. Shannon gave a grunt of displeasure; she opened a port on the bottom and shook out the dust that was inside it.

"I hate it when they burn out in the middle of a dowse. I really should be using higher quality crystals this close to that disc," Shannon muttered as she cleaned out the last bits of dust from inside the device, then she turned to him and held a hand out.

Kas grunted and created a crystal, holding it out for her to take.

She gave him a smile and a wink. "Thank you." She gave a final glance to make sure there wasn't any more dust in the device. "If you mix crystals from different creators, it causes a lot of strain on the machine; even the residual dust from a crystal can throw off the readings." She then inserted the crystal into a holder on the bottom of the port and then raised it into the bottom of the dowsing orb.

The device took another thirty seconds to warm back up, and then Shannon repeated the previous process of turning in a circle, this time, she moved back and forth a few times. "I think…" she said as she slowly turned, and then the device lit up blue, and she smiled. "Yeah, that way. Getting a clear reading on it now."

Following the new heading, they had to cut through a patch of unusually thick pine trees. Kas knew they were there before he could see whatever was on the other side, however. Dino ran up to his leg, hugging him at the knee with his two upper arms and chirping happily. Kas reached down and picked the compie up, holding him against his body as he struggled to get through the last of the tree cover. When he did, he stopped in confusion. A foot-tall mound filled a small natural cavity in the trees.

The shade from a large white pine cast the whole place in shadow. In the center was a large mound made of dirt and plant detritus. Diane was sitting near a small hole at the base; she chirped tiredly when she saw Kas, but didn't move. Telling Shannon to hold there for a moment, he approached the tunnel, Dino clambering down when he saw the destination to butt his head against Diane's before turning back to Kas to chirp happily.

Leaning down to scratch Diane, he saw that behind her was the glimmer of dozens of eggs.

CHAPTER TWENTY-FIVE

Recruitment Drive 4

It was clear that they couldn't move the eggs. Diane's angry chirps when Kas tried to move one of the eggs made that clear. He did manage to get close enough to the eggs to inspect them, however.

Compsognathus Eggs. These small eggs are laid in a mound nest and mostly covered. This provides most of the heat needed to incubate the eggs, as well as protection from adverse weather effects. Only about half the eggs are viable, as a protection against predators. These eggs should hatch in two days.

Alright, so he shouldn't expect dozens of new compies, but there were still plenty of eggs to distribute to at least the people currently in Miranda. He would have to see about getting them some wild mates to facilitate genetic diversity. He wasn't sure how closely he could mate things—that would be another task to research later; he wasn't sure how close to real-life the game was. Perhaps there was some sort of in-game library? Another job to see if he couldn't delve into when he was in Tallrock.

Looking deeper into the nest, he pondered how best to

protect it. They could leave meat here for Dino and Diane so that they wouldn't have to scavenge for food, which would at least give them some protectors. Maybe he could convince Thunder Pig to stick around; the massive beast might drive off any of the smaller things around that would prey on the compies' eggs. Of course, that might just bring more big creatures who were interested in eating the adolescent pig.

Was there such a thing as warding magic on Livia? Something else to research. Kas dropped off some food for the two compies and then left them alone, making sure to mark down where the nest was on his map.

Both mills were at the point of self-sufficiency and his crop plots had already been tended to. What he was really worried about was being able to earn enough gold. At this point, the only thing he could think of that would make a significant dent in his bottom line was his alchemical products. They were small enough to easily carry, and hopefully worth enough to make up for any deficiency in his crops. So, the rest of the afternoon was spent working on his alchemy. Despite implementing some of the knowledge Kanudawn had sent his way, his first few attempts were unsuccessful.

Looking at his notes, he tried to figure out where he had gone wrong on the most recent procedure. If he let it steep for a little longer in the third stage, that would give him time to stir the bonding agent a little longer, giving it a thinner consistency. Maybe that would allow the second powder to dissolve into the solution better. It had felt just a bit too gritty last time. Deciding that would work, he made a few more notations and created a new instruction set.

Getting distracted about halfway through the fourth stage—when a bug landed on his face and he had to wipe it off—created an entirely unexpected boom of air that blew his hair back. Kas checked his eyebrow to make sure it was still in one piece. Relieved that there didn't seem to be any adverse effects to the minor explosion, he went back to work, doing things the same as before but trying to avoid any distractions created by his less than ideal workplace.

The fifth attempt ended up actually creating a product. It was better than most of the reported potions but not as good as Kas knew he could do. Already there were things that he sensed could be improved, and he went back to trying to finagle the best quality of potion he could get out of the ingredients that he had on hand.

Mid-afternoon, he actually had to stop and grind up the rest of his ingredients, so that he had enough powder for more attempts. Even so, with just a few hours, he had blown through what amounted to almost a day's worth of gathering herbs. This meant that a full-time alchemist would need dozens of harvesters working for them to supply them with enough raw materials to keep up with their demand. Realizing what the bottleneck in the process was led him to believe that there must be a way to cultivate at least some part of the process.

The price jump from the base ingredients to the finished product might allow for an alchemist to buy from herbalists, but the margins would be reasonably small. The only real reason to do that was to grind up skill levels, which... wasn't actually a bad idea. There also might be enough profit in it to make a modest living that way, and as he got better, the margins might improve considerably. Putting the profitability of full-time alchemy aside for a later time, Kas inspected his finished products.

Inferior Healing Potion: This potion was created using untested methods, it provides 38 points of healing.

That was the first potion, and by the time he had managed to refine the process until it was crafting at around 44 points, he had created 17 potions. Several ideas he tried to implement actually hurt the final product, so there was a fairly even mix between that range. When Shura finally called out that dinner was ready, he was more than prepared to take a break. He packed up the rest of his alchemy tools, hoping that the next time he got to actually use them, he would have a better place to do so.

As an unbound, he didn't really need a comfortable bed, although the better his sleeping arrangements were when he logged off, they would give him a buff to his stats for a little while the next day. So he decided that rather than building himself a house, he would focus on getting a proper alchemy workshop built, and then he could just sleep on the floor there. The buff wasn't nearly as important to him as it would have been to someone who was spending their days adventuring.

Dinner was another pot of stew filled with some kind of gamy dark meat. When Kas saw the skins, he realized that whoever had hunted, had probably caught a few more wild compies. Hopefully they weren't damaging the local ecology to the point that Shura wouldn't be able to tame more.

He spent a few moments trying to decide if he wanted to eat the stew or not; he made the decision to not let it affect him. Eventually, he would be butchering a lot of the animals that he raised on the farm. Getting over this aversion was something that he needed to do to be a farmer.

After dinner, Kas realized he hadn't yet created a new plot for the next day. He spent two hours creating four additional plots. Looking at the four plots, he pondered if it was worth it to try to work these fields without them having the Enrich Soil buff cast on them. He decided to give it a shot.

When he had harvested the potatoes earlier, he had also gotten two bags worth of potato seeds. One of them was labeled as just regular seeds, but the other had a good quality attached to them.

Deciding that it was worth an experiment to see how much the soil buff was actually affecting the growth, Kas planted the regular seeds in one of the empty fields and then watered it. An inspection told him that it was poor soil with insufficient nutrients, but he decided to test to see how much that actually affected the results. He refrained from planting the rest of the crops until he had a better idea of what it would actually do to them.

With what little light he had left to him, he started working on the rest of the housing, knowing that he was going to need something for Dave's crew to sleep in once they got here, not to mention the rest of the tribesmen and any other craftsmen he managed to recruit when they went into Tallrock. Ideally, he would make a longhouse shortly so that everyone could at least be inside, but he needed to give Max a few more days to get enough logs cut for that.

The last thing Kas did before logging out was to check in on Dino and Diane. Diane looked less tired this time, but she still curled up on his lap while he tried to teach Dino to fetch. The little compie didn't really seem to understand the concept but would chase down the twig Kas threw, bite it in half, then run back to Kas, excited. It was close enough that he kept doing it until he ran out of convenient sticks nearby. The compie didn't seem nearly as interested when he switched over to dirt clods and rocks.

Scratching them both behind the ears for a few minutes, he put Diane back in the tunnel, gave them both some dried meat he had taken from the camp, and then headed back to the wanderer's pine. Shura was already asleep, which told him he had stayed in-game longer than usual, and he logged out.

DAY 10

Logging back into the game after sleeping for the night, Kas checked the experimental field first. It was a full day behind where he thought it should have been, but he wasn't sure if that was due to how late he had planted it or some other factor. The additional fields were healthy.

Kas was quickly running out of seeds, especially since he didn't want to plant too many more potatoes until he had a better way to transport them. He still had one pouch each of corn and peas. As well as the good potato seeds.

Deciding to do the peas as being the closest thing he had to a lightweight crop, he planted and cast Enrich Soil on that crop plot. By his estimation, he would be able to harvest both the corn and his first wheat field the next day. This meant that he should hopefully be ready to go back to Tallrock the following day, assuming that he could mill the grain that afternoon. Today, he needed to cut time off Thunder Pig's maturation and build a harness for him to carry the produce in.

At breakfast, he announced his intention and asked both Bliny and Shura to see if they could find some bigger game. It wouldn't be as good as treated leather, but he could hopefully rig up a harness from the rawhide. There were plenty of smaller skins that he took with him and started turning into bags, but that would require sewing, so he planned to do that after dark when he felt less confident gathering vitality.

The first stop after his fields and breakfast was back with Dino and Diane, giving them some of the meat from breakfast. Deciding it was best to gather vitality by making the trail to the switchback more established, he drained plants along what was mainly a game trail now. Since Forthan's group had come, they had posted guards at the top of the switchback; the path to and from had become at least slightly established. He worked to expand that into a proper road.

Walking up and down the path and draining some of the more significant impediments earned him just shy of a thousand points of vitality. Mostly from a bush called the Western Purple-Leaf Strangler, named after its tendency to kill nearby plants with its extensive root system.

The roots stored an immense amount of vitality; Kas was able to harvest two or three dozen points from each waist high bush. When he got back to camp, he initiated another transfer of vitality to Thunder Pig and saw that he would now mature in two days.

Both Shura and Bliny were successful in getting larger game, Shura some kind of hornless elk that weighed half as much as her, and Bliny managed to take down a six-armed bear.

There was plenty of meat for the pots, and Kas assumed there was some method of preserving it, although he left that for other people to worry about.

That was a good point, though; he hadn't seen a freshness meter on any of his crops. Did that mean they wouldn't spoil, or that it was just so far away from spoiling that it wasn't included? Would he need to make some sort of silo or cold storage area?

The hides from both the elk and bear were plenty large enough to create a harness for Thunder Pig, and Kas set to working on it. While he had no sub-skill for tanning, since he was just working on rawhide, he was able to bring his leather-working skill to use. He cut the elk skin into a large central piece to go over the hog's back and ridge, with flaps along the sides to act as straps. He cut them long so that it would fit Thunder Pig's frame as he got larger.

After that, Kas spent far longer than he wanted to sew straps onto the central portion of the harness. Costache saw what he was doing and told him he would make some buckles to secure the harness and hooks to hang bags off of.

The rest of the night was spent creating bags from the plethora of smaller skins they had saved up over the last ten days. It quickly became apparent that they weren't going to be able to take anywhere near the amount of produce he was able to create.

Which meant Kas had to make a decision about what to bring. He was reasonably sure the flour would be more valuable than the potatoes, but he might be able to bring some of those as well. If the meal auto-generated with a bag like he was hoping it would after going through the gristmill. Maybe it would be better to make a litter they could attach to the harness somehow? The river would still be nearly impossible to get across, but that was going to be an issue until they built a proper bridge.

Deciding that was the best course of action meant that Kas then had to figure out how to make a litter that would hold enough weight to be worthwhile. He logged off, frustrated at his lack of progress. There had to be a better way to transport stuff.

———

Matt searched the forums. There were a few spells that would work, but he didn't have the right elements or skills to learn them. Some magitech devices would allow it as well, but they would be expensive to buy and maintain. He sent a message to Dave and asked him if any of his people had the affinities needed for the spells. He fell asleep dreaming about hot air balloons, trains, and bridges.

DAY 11

With three days left before Kas needed to make enough money to quit his job, he ran some numbers. He had a relatively large stockpile of crystals, he estimated they would net him around 60 gold, 65 after today's crystals. Including the 55 gold he had already in the bank, that gave him around 120 gold total. He needed to make 200 gold to pay for his living expenses and such, maybe more like 205 depending on the taxes and transfer fees, plus keep at least 10 gold in the bank to keep that open.

Which meant Kas needed to make at least 130 gold a month off of his crops. No, he was looking at it wrong, he could just about pay his rent off selling his mana crystals. So, if he could make 50 or 60 gold off the crops, that would be more than enough to keep him going.

Inspecting one of his potatoes, he found that he couldn't pull up any detail on how much it was worth. With a frown, he focused on his mana crystals and discovered that they also didn't have a cost on them anymore.

It must be because of his distance from the town; the only time Kas remembered items having a price on them was when they were close to Tallrock. Which made the decision of what to bring a little harder to determine. After a few minutes of consideration, he logged quick to send Dave a list of items to price check in Tallrock.

It was going to be a busy day; two fields were ready to harvest today, which meant three plantings, and another eight that would need to be tended and, of course, putting the wheat through the mill.

The first half of the day passed by in a quick blur as he harvested the wheat and corn and then tended to his other fields. Just like with the potatoes, he got new seeds from planting the crops; for the grain, he got both good and excellent seeds, while the corn only got him a single pouch of regular seeds. Deciding to replant both fields with the same crop, he planted the excellent wheat seeds and more of the regular corn. In the new plot, he planted the good wheat. Figuring that with the mill, the wheat was bound to be his best-selling product.

After that, he went to check in on Dino and Diane; the meat from the night before meant that no one was going to begrudge them some, and he gave them enough for the day. After that, he spent time building a litter that he could easily break down to its component parts. Cutting down two long but thin trees, he made three cross beams, one to go over Thunder Pig's shoulder and attach to the harness. The second just behind Thunder Pig to keep it steady, and the third at the far end.

Kastigan's bedroll was then commandeered to act as the net between everything; after that, he went to work getting the harness ready for Thunder Pig to wear. During all of this, he had been stocking up on more vitality to be used to power-level the pig so that he would be an adult before they left. The first test of the whole thing was when he loaded all the wheat onto the back of it to transport it to the mill. A few pounds of potatoes were fed to the pig to coerce him into wearing the harness and working as Kas intended, but since he had more potatoes than he could possibly move, that wasn't much of a sacrifice.

As an additional treat, he fed the pig some corn and then used the sweeter vegetable to lead him to the mill, where another few ears were sacrificed. Kas considered this a good investment, since Thunder Pig's chance to receive a boon rose all the way up to 1.4%. The mill itself was pretty self-explanatory; he didn't have to thresh the wheat or anything to get the chaff out, and was able to throw the starting product directly into the mill's opening. A popup told him it would be ready in an hour.

With that going, he took the harness and litter off Thunder Pig, and went collecting vitality from things along the trail to the mouth of the valley while also gathering herbs. By evening, he had managed to fill up almost a thousand vitality, which he transferred into Thunder Pig.

Your bonded animal is growing up! Thunder Pig has reached maturity! For raising an animal into adulthood, you have unlocked its characteristic menu.

You are the first character to raise a Long-Nosed Hog to maturity, you have received the Hog Wrangler badge.

You are the seventh character to raise an animal with a special boon, you receive the Boon Breeder badge.

You are the third character to raise an animal on Gogland, you receive the Advanced Gogland Breeder badge.

You are the first character to raise an animal with an elemental affinity, you receive the Greater Affinity Breeder badge.

You are the fifth character to raise a bonded animal, you receive the Bonded Breeder badge.

You have received five breeding badges. You are the first character to reach this milestone. You receive the First in Show title.

That was far more than what he was hoping for! Pulling up his character screen, he looked at the badges and title.

Hog Wrangler: All Ungulates you raise will have 5% higher stats.

Boon Breeder: All creatures you raise will have a 2% higher chance of receiving a boon.

Advanced Gogland Breeder: All creatures you raise on Gogland will have 2% higher stats.

Greater Affinity Breeder Badge: All creatures you raise have a 1% chance to gain an affinity.
Bonded Breeder Badge: All bonded creatures you raise will have 5% higher stats.
First in Show: All creatures you raise will have 5% higher stats.
Note: Bonus stat gains are only applied once to a particular bloodline.

That meant that every animal he raised from here on out would have 17% higher stats, 2% higher chance of receiving a boon, and 1% chance to get an affinity. The restriction of it only affecting a bloodline once was interesting; if he merged two bloodlines, what would that do to the bonus? It would require a lot of experimentation with breeding lines to make it all work. It would also require getting a lot more animal stock, but he needed to do that either way.

Thunder Pig - HP: 148 AP: 15.8
Strength: 23 [3.9](A)
Constitution: 14 [2.3](B)
Intelligence: 4 [.68](F)
Cunning: 4[.68](D)
Potency: 10[1.7](C)
Skills known: Beast of Burden, Charge, Gore, Static Load.
Boon: Natural Leader

The letters next to each statistic were probably a growth rate or potential. The brackets were the bonus statistics granted to Thunder Pig by Kas' badges. Beast of Burden was a passive that increased his carry weight. Charge was an active skill that cost 5 AP, which gave a temporary bonus to Thunder Pig's movement speed and attack power. Gore was another active skill, costing no AP, that did damage, while the static load was an active ability that gave all his attacks an electrical component for 30 seconds, but cost 10 AP to use. Depending on how long it took to regen AP, he could use both charge and static load once per fight. More things to try out; hopefully not in the near future, though.

The natural leader boon gave Thunder Pig a boost to his control over other long-nosed hogs, which would be helpful if they started a pack.

Going back to the mill, he discovered that the flour was done, and it had been placed in a thick fabric bag which Kas assumed weighed about 20 kilos. The field had only generated enough for one bag of flour, which didn't seem like a lot. Inspecting it told him it was at least good quality, which was actually a step up from the regular quality wheat he had managed to gather. Was that because he had a higher tier mill?

Realizing he had never inspected the mill, he focused on it and brought up the menus for both the gristmill and the sawmill.

Grist Mill (Tier 3): This water-powered gristmill's milling mechanism is highly sophisticated. Effects: 25% chance of increasing the quality of products ground within the mill. Inputs must be below tier three.

Saw Mill (Tier 0): This water-powered sawmill is barely functional. Effects: 50% chance of reducing the quality of products created. Inputs must be tier one or lower.

Kas frowned; he really needed to get the sawmill up to at least tier one, which he assumed would be when they had completed the entire structure. Damae had made some progress on the mill during the day, but it was only about three quarters finished.

If he had to guess, tier one would make it a 25% chance of reducing the quality, tier two would remove the reduction chance entirely, and anything tier three or above would improve the benefit. He didn't even know what a tier three product was. More questions, more things to test and explore. Kas was amazed at how much depth the game already had.

The rest of the night was spent making adjustments to the litter now that Thunder Pig was at what was hopefully a full-grown state. The large long-nosed hog's head was above his own, the thick yellow fur on his spine crackled with electric energy that shocked Kas even through the thick leather hide he used as the base of the harness. The hog himself didn't seem to mind the harness, although he disliked having the litter attached; he kept turning his head to look at the bulky contraption.

Loading the flour was easy, the bag made it easy to contain. The potatoes and corn were a different story; the few bags he had made were moderately useful. However, most of the produce was just piled onto the blanket in a big pile. When he got as much of it as he thought they could quickly move, he looked at the piles of food yet to be moved and frowned. Only about half the corn and potatoes were able to fit on the stretcher, both of them being bulkier than he would have liked.

Feeding some of the excess corn and potatoes to Thunder Pig seemed to placate the beast, and he accepted his burden. Shura had to help him attach the harness, the large drak easily holding the poles in place while he strapped them onto the pig.

"I'm really hoping I can figure out a better method for moving all this stuff soon." Kas eyed the whole thing before beginning the process of removing the harness.

"I'm sure that you will figure something out," Shura reassured Kas.

"We need to, this is going to be a pain," Kas said, helping Shura move the entire litter under a tree and then covering it with another blanket. With that done, he logged off for the night, hoping for a message from Dave.

CHAPTER TWENTY-SIX

Recruitment Drive 5

Matt spent a few hours researching. Badges were easy to find information on, they were awarded to players for doing certain activities. From what he could discover, the first person to do something got the best reward and then staging down at three, ten, and hundred. After a hundred people had done something, the badge downgraded to an achievement, and you no longer got the bonus associated with it.

Titles were like advanced badges, and usually required that you get a collection of badges or achievements to gain them, they also always gave rewards. Although some, like Kas' First in Show, seemed to be limited in number. Either way, he didn't think that chasing badges was going to be worth doing. He would either get them and reap the benefits of their acquisition, or he wouldn't. 17% was massive, but since it was a one-time bonus, others could get to the same point he was, it would just take longer.

Being the best of the best didn't interest Matt. There was too much competition, too much in-fighting to get that title. What he wanted was to be able to build something that had meaning and substance. Sure, there would always be people who wanted to tear down anything anyone else made. Those people were different than the ones that wanted to stomp out all competition, though. Deciding that it wasn't worth telling anyone about his badges and title, he moved on.

There wasn't much on the forums about husbandry. What little there was actually came from Dancing Dan, one of the leaders of the Praetorians, who seemed to be focusing on alchemically improving creatures. He still hadn't gotten very far in the actual breeding line, but he had made some very meticulous notes about some of the processes he was using. Matt made a note of a couple that Dan said would improve an animal's strength score; they seemed within the realm of things he could achieve with his own alchemy skill.

Checking the new account he had created to talk about the Blood War Relics, a few dowsers had said they would check it out. He responded, telling them he was looking into his own and would share when he had more information to post. This would hopefully have them post information too. By the time he'd sent a dozen replies, he felt tired enough to get to bed.

Tossing and turning, sleep eluded Matt. Tomorrow would be the make or break day, being able to harvest multiple fields of wheat. If he could sell the flour for at least ten gold a bag, he'd be set. But what if it was less than that? Until he figured out a better transportation method, he was stuck selling small amounts of everything but the flour. He couldn't afford to spend a day traveling to and from Tallrock every time he wanted to sell a field's worth of corn or potatoes.

Sitting back up, he checked his messages. Dave's only response to his request was to say that he would ask. That had come in right about the time Matt had logged out for the day; Dave might not even be planning on logging in again to ask until tomorrow morning.

Matt sat back down, flipping his pillow over so that he could use the cold side. Moving through his breathing exercises, he tried to calm down his mind enough that he could get some sleep. When the alarm went off the next morning, he wasn't sure if he had actually slept more than a few minutes here and there. Before logging in, he sent a message off to Dave telling him that he should be in Tallrock by later that evening and would meet him at the Church of the Seven. Then he logged in.

DAY 12

Waking up early gave him enough time to finish tending to the crops before the others had woken up for breakfast. He only had corn and potato seeds left, and he opted to plant corn. The second field of potatoes was ready to harvest, earning him two hundred XP, two pouches of good potato seeds, and a larger pile of potatoes in the finished house.

At this point, he let Thunder Pig eat as many of them as he wanted; he figured they might give the creature a boost at the very least. He had far too much to move in any reasonable amount of time unless one of Dave's people could transport stuff, and that was days away. Either way, it was better to get some benefit out of the materials, especially given how much work he intended to put the pig through later that day.

While Kas was finishing up his daily farming chores, the rest of the group had already harnessed Thunder Pig and made the first leg of the journey. From the farm to the switchback out of Miranda Valley was probably the most straightforward portion of the trip.

After that, they had removed the litter, and Forthan and Shura had carried it down the switchback. The two draks were able to move the weight, although there was a close call as Shura, who was on the downward slope, took a misstep on the narrow path.

The two draks were resting at the base when Kas finally caught up to them. Thunder Pig was grousing around near the edge of the clearing, munching away at the greenery. The rest of the group consisted of Max, Shannon, and Tryry.

Leaving Costache, the two miners, Damae, Wyk, and Bliny

in the valley. Damae was working on getting the kitchen up and running, while the two guards patrolled around, and the three metal workers went about their regular business.

The trip back was uneventful; the slow rate of Thunder Pig through the forest made the trip take a few hours longer than previous attempts. The two draks were kept busy trying to keep the path clear for Thunder Pig, while Shannon and Tryry escorted Max and Kas to the log they were using as a bridge. The lumberjack felled a few small trees, and the four of them managed to debranch them enough for Kas to build a less narrow bridge across the river. There were no rails, and it was just barely wide enough for the pig to walk across without fear of falling, but Kas was glad Max had thought to bring several boards with them to use.

The resulting bridge looked unsafe but was actually quite sturdy. The group took a break when they got to the river. Shura and Forthan carried the litter across, but it took several ears of corn for Kas to convince Thunder Pig to follow him across. Still, once on the other side, the pig gave the bridge one more speculative glance before condescending to allowing Shura to reattach the litter. They made it to Tallrock a few hours before dark but had to wait almost an hour to receive approval to bring Thunder Pig up onto the plateau.

Other groups came and went, the lift having enough traffic that it would make the traversal at least once every fifteen minutes. Kas was actually surprised by how many unbound there were. Last time he had been in town, there had been considerably less idle chatter while they were waiting and they told him that it was mostly due to the undead base towards the rim.

No one had managed to bring down any of the actually powerful monsters, but large groups managed to farm some of the smaller undead by baiting them into a trap. This gave them pretty good experience, based on the fact that most of them were now above level ten.

As soon as he reached the top of the lift, Kas received a prompt.

You have established a trade route between Miranda and Tallrock.
You are the first player to establish a trade route to Tallrock, you received the Tallrock Trader badge.
You are the ninth player to establish a trade route on Gogland. You receive the Gogland Trader badge.

Kas didn't want to spend the time trying to figure out what the badges did while he attempted to get Thunder Pig off the ramp, but he managed to bribe the pig out of the loading area. That was when most of the party split up.

"We'll be meeting up here again at 8 tomorrow morning." Kas announced.

Forthan begged his leave to go and do some business in the town, while Max just bobbed his head, silently excusing himself. Shannon waved, telling Kas she planned on heading back alone tomorrow. Which left Kas with Shura and Thunder Pig.

Making their way to the fort and the auction house contained within, they stepped outside, there was a small building that looked like it was designed to house visiting wagons and other mounts. The interface told him he would be able to sell or store anything in the stables while he was in the fort, so he left some food for Thunder Pig and, realizing that the legion wouldn't let her in, had Shura stay there to guard the goods. Taking the time while they were stabling Thunder Pig, he pulled up the info on the badges he had just received.

Tallrock Trader Badge: All trade goods sold in Tallrock will be worth 1% more.
Gogland Trader Badge: All trade goods sold on Gogland will be worth .25% more.

Nothing huge, but 1.25% more on everything Kas sold would eventually add up to quite a bit. It would be interesting to see what the system classified as a trade good, though. If he sold livestock, would that count? Armor or weapons? Shaking his head, he waved goodbye to Shura and headed over to the fort.

Getting into the queue to enter the fort, he heard a commotion from the other side of the walls.

"Where is he?" The anger in the voice had a familiar ring to it, and Colonel Holzer stormed out of the fort's entrance. When his eyes landed on Kas, he pointed. "You! My office now!" Before turning on his toe and returning to the fort.

Two guards came forward. "Pardon me, sir, if you would please follow us."

"Am I in some sort of trouble?" Kas asked, and the guard that hadn't spoken just snorted in laughter.

The first guard glared at his companion before answering with a shrug. "Not exactly sure, sir, just know that the colonel wants to talk to you." Not wanting to make a scene in front of the other dozen unbound that had queued up to go into the fort, Kas followed along, unsure what exactly to expect.

They ushered him into the main garrison building and up a flight of stairs. Near the top, they took a turn into a more austere area of the fort. Holzer's office was spartan, a few broken weapons lined the walls, a large desk took up most of the room with several long windows along the far wall. None of the chairs looked particularly comfortable, including the one that Holzer sat in.

"Come in, unbound Kastigan," Holzer said, pointing at a chair. "Please sit, the legion would like to talk to you about your trade route."

Kas sat down, frowning slightly. "How can I be of service to the legion?"

Holzer glared at him for a moment and then turned slightly to look out the window. "Tallrock needs food. Every day the king sends me more soldiers and worthless adventurers, but fewer supplies. Our ability to grow is limited due to the nature of the fort's position. Half our bondsmen have turned to banditry, the undead menace to the south means that few of the unbound are hunting, and what food we do get comes in the form of meat. Greens and vegetables are in short supply. As such, the legion will have first refusal on any sales you make within Tallrock."

"Is that a request or a statement?" Kas asked with a frown.

"That was a statement," Holzer said, his eyes narrowing.

"At what price?"

"Five percent less than the average of all sales of that quality for the past tenday," Holzer answered.

Kas considered. He wasn't averse to helping the legion and Tallrock in general. It would also mean that he got paid immediately, rather than waiting for an auction sale to get paid. The five percent was the same as the auction house cut, so it was a pretty negligible trade-off.

"Cash on delivery?" When Holzer nodded in agreement, Kas shrugged. "That's acceptable. Depending on your demand, I have a bunch more produce, but I don't really have a way of transporting it here..." Kas trailed off while Holzer considered.

"Unfortunately, Miranda is too far away for me to send legionaries, but I would be willing to create courier contracts for the unbound," Holzer responded, managing to keep the vitriol out of his voice for everything but the word unbound. Kas wasn't sure why the colonel hated unbound so much, but it was clear he did.

"I'm not ready to open the valley en masse for the unbound, unfortunately."

You have entered into trade negotiations with Colonel Holzer of the Unified Realm's 76th Legion.
Current offer:

- *Your obligations: Present your trade goods to the 76th Legion first.*
- *You will get: Pass to Fort Tallrock, 500 reputation with the 76th Legion, all purchased goods for 5% less than the tenday average in cash, upon delivery.*

They signed an agreement after that, and Kas was awarded a direct pass into the fort. The colonel then directed him to the quartermaster, who would handle all the actual transactions. The quartermaster's office was located in a warehouse within the fort's walls, but in a separate building from the one Holzer's office was in. It took Kas a few minutes to get there, but when he did, he was greeted by a dour-faced quinthan.

"You the trade route manager?" The quinthan frowned through his immaculately groomed handlebar mustache.

"Uh, yes, I'm Kastigan." Kas pulled out the pass Holzer had given him.

The quartermaster pulled it out of his hands impatiently, giving it a thorough inspection, even holding it up to the light. Kas assumed that was to make sure it wasn't counterfeit. Finally, the quartermaster harumphed in satisfaction and handed the pass back.

"We'll take all the dry goods you have in the stable," the quartermaster said after a moment. "The 20-kilo bag of good wheat flour we'll buy for 12 gold, 32 silver. We'll give you 98 silver for every 5 kilos of potatoes, and 73 silver for the same amount of corn. Total is 32 gold, 67 silver, and 5 copper. I'll have some of my men unload your… 'wagon.'" He even put finger quotes around the word wagon, clearly showing how valuable he thought that was.

The wheat had taken up only a small portion of Kas' cargo space and made up more than a third of the total value, making it by far the most efficient thing to transport. He had to leave nearly three times as many potatoes as he brought, and he only brought about half the corn. In terms of sheer value per field, the wheat was probably lower in value than the others, but its ease of transportation made it leaps and bounds better for Kas currently.

"Is there anything, in particular, you'd like me to grow?" Kas asked the quartermaster before leaving.

The quinthan frowned then looked around. When he was

sure no one else could overhear he whispered, "I miss aspara-gus." Tapping his nose, the quartermaster turned away.

Walking out, Kas did some math. 32 gold from the crop sales, with another 20 or 30 gold worth of crops harvested but not transported, plus all the mana crystals he had created, and the bounties... he had earned more than 155 gold in 12 days. Wait, no he couldn't count the bounties, that wasn't a sustain-able source of income.

He glanced at his alchemy items. Hurrying over to the auction house he started looking through prices on the potions he had made. What he found was a bit discouraging. Similar products were selling for large values, but the auction house took a huge cut from alchemical products, a full 40% of the sales price.

He also discovered that his potions and powders were not included in his deal with Holzer. While he was there, he checked on his seed auctions. Several of his bids on seeds had won. Kas placed a few more bids on unknown types of seeds. None of them were costly, although he had to go up a few silver more than he had before. He also put some bids on a few spell-books, but he didn't really have any hope that he would win those after glancing at the bidding history.

Glancing through the seeds he had acquired, they had been listed as unknown, but Kas' farming skill allowed him to identify them. They fell into two basic groups: herbs and crops. The herbs had much more delicate growing conditions than the crops did, but he had acquired: ash sage, dilo reed, fire lotus, burnt hasper, and drowned man's bane. He assumed most of those had come from some sort of fire dungeon since the first four all had fire elements attached to them.

The crops were simpler. Kas had acquired oats, barley, rutabaga, pumpkins, and butternut squash. He was also able to pick up a packet of asparagus seeds from the quartermaster for cheap. He looked into getting cotton, coffee, or tea, but all those auctions had started at several gold per pouch, which was a little out of his price range.

Selling off his excess mana crystals was simple enough. He made sure to keep the ones he needed for the quest from the leatherworker. He was left with just under 145 gold.

The bank was closed for the day when Kas tried to visit. In typical banker fashion, they closed well before sunset. With nothing else keeping him in the fort, he headed back to Shura and Thunder Pig in the stables. Shura had removed the litter and harness, leaving them leaning off to one side of the stable while the pig was content to sleep.

"How did it go?" Shura asked.

"Alright. I still need to sell my alchemy stuff, but I think we're in good shape. I still have enough to recruit a few more people, but I figured it'd be best to go meet up with my friend and see what skills they have before we look elsewhere." Kas was pretty sure he hadn't stopped smiling since he realized he had made his goals. "I guess we better figure out a place to stay for the night," Kas mused as they made their way to the Church of the Seven.

"We could stay with Forthan's group, although I think I would rather not," Shura answered.

"Yeah, me too. I'd like to rely on him as little as possible. I wonder if the church would allow us to stay there for the night again." Kas sort of wanted to talk to the old priest again anyway, having enjoyed all of his conversations previously.

"I will just find an inn, I think," Shura said.

"Do you need money? I haven't exactly paid you for any of your help," Kas said, looking at his gold value on the interface and feeling a bit guilty.

"Oh no, it is fine. I managed to sell a few of my drops to merchants while you were inside the fort," Shura answered.

Kas blinked, he didn't realize that Shura had been getting drops from all the animals she had hunted. "Oh, are you sure?"

"I'll be fine, use your coin to grow Miranda," Shura said, giving the drak equivalent of a chortle.

Stopping near the downtown area, Kas found a shop that was willing to buy all the potions and powders he had brought for another 30 gold. Which was almost double what he would have gotten trying to sell it on the auction house.

He stepped outside and walked towards the edge of the plateau. Taking a seat on a rock overlooking the vast forest below, he did some figuring. He had 60 gold worth of crops, plus almost 30 from the alchemy, another 6 gold in crystals.

That was a good start, and it would only increase as he got more fields online. Kas had only managed to harvest four fields of his eventual thirty that he could keep up with Enrich Soil. There was still a lot of work to be done, not the least of which was trying to figure out a way to get everything back and forth to sell it, but it would work. He could feel it deep in his bones that this was a life he could live.

A weight slid off his shoulders. He had done it! He had enough money to quit his job and stay in the game. He closed his eyes and felt the wind blowing past his face; this high up it was fast and cold. Sitting in the wind, he allowed himself to just be; calm and unconcerned for the first time in what felt like forever. Shura put a single finger on his shoulder breaking him out of his reverie.

"Shall we go meet your friend?" the large drak asked from her hunched over position over him.

Kas smiled back at her. "Yes, let's."

They arrived at the church a few minutes later, finding a group of six adventurers loitering near the entrance. Dave was obvious once Kas saw the names; he had gone with his old standby of Wulfgar. What was a surprise was the fact that Wulfgar was actually a wolf. Sort of.

Dave had apparently chosen to play as one of the wolf beastkin; there were a couple different varieties. Wulfgar had the gray and black fur of a timber wolf, sharp incisors, and an elongated snout. The fur on his head extended back, creating more of a bristled mane than hair. He was bipedal, but his legs had three joints in them, with a slightly hunched over posture that was only possible due to a long tail.

Next to Wulfgar was Dave's husband, another timber wolf

beastkin with a more muscular build, named Drengar. Neither had much in the way of armor, but Kas didn't think they would need much with their thick fur. Drengar held a long spear while Wulfgar's only visible weapons were his sharp claws. They were joined by a quinthan in tight leather named Dokejin. She had several knives strapped to her body, and Kas assumed she was some sort of rogue.

Next to Dokejin was a tiny drak named Samu-an-el. Well, he was tiny by drak standards. Samu was only about seven feet tall but built like a brick, a large shield adorning his back while a morningstar hung from his waist. The drak was still adorned in drak fashion, his black scales showing under the harness, but his harness offered much more protection. Thick iron plates, and chainmail covering large portions of his body where his scales were the smallest, clearly marking him as the party's tank.

The other two members of the party seemed almost normal by comparison. A human named Ryab was decked out in magitech, at his side was a thick stick that vaguely looked like a rifle, and a wire extended from the rifle into a heavy backpack he wore that hummed softly.

The last human was wearing a divided skirt in green that set off against her bright red hair and a brocaded vest that left her slim arms bare. Her name was Gwen, she was reading from a book, and he saw the symbol of Talin, the goddess of learning, on her shoulder.

"Wulfgar!" Kas shouted across the square, and the two beastkin looked up, giving him a terrifying grin of sharpened teeth.

"Matt?" Wulfgar asked, looking him up and down, and then turning his attention to Shura. "Who the heck is the muscle?"

"Wulfgar, this is my companion, Shura. Shura, Wulfgar is my friend. You can call me Kastigan here."

They went around and gave introductions. Wulfgar had evidently chosen to be something called a Packcaller, which sounded like it was a wolf summoner. Drengar was a ranger; Kas had apparently missed the big bow. Samu introduced himself as a scale guardian but was eyeing Shura with awe. Dokejin introduced herself as a treasure hunter, but the wink told him she was following the age-long tradition of thieves calling themselves that.

Ryab glared at Kas when he asked what class he was. "You ask too many questions." Everyone else laughed, so Kas assumed that was some sort of inside joke. Gwen smiled at him and was, in fact, a priestess of Talin and the group's healer. They seemed like a good group of people.

"So, Wulfgar, any of your guys able to cast those transportation spells?" Kas asked once everyone was going back to getting used to their new bodies. Apparently, it took some getting used to, especially for the two beastkin and the drak, and they had spent the last few days just putting their new bodies through their paces.

"Oh, yeah. Dokejin and Gwen both can do some variant of them," Wulfgar said while almost tripping over his tail as he turned too fast, and it got caught in his legs.

"Dokejin?" Kas asked, eyeing the rogue speculatively.

"Yeah! Couldn't stand the idea of leaving good treasure behind!" the quinthan said with a grin. "Asked the AI how to get around that. Only have a bit of magic, but it's almost all involved in making me move silently or lift heavy things."

"Awesome, I have a lot of heavy stuff that needs moving back at Miranda." That turned into a discussion about skills and what they would be getting at Miranda. They seemed more than happy to help around the valley in exchange for meals and, of course, were more than happy with the idea of delving into the kobold's cave. At this point, just having them ferry stuff back and forth was more worth it for Kas, so he felt like he was getting a good deal out of it.

They had retired to a tavern just down the street from the inn while everyone got to know each other. It was a few hours later, as Kas sat at a table, watching Shura arm wrestle both wolves and Samu at the same time that he realized something. For the first time since Elam died, he felt alive.

ABOUT XANDER BOYCE

Xander is a USCG veteran and lifelong sci-fi/fantasy reader. Having begun creating worlds for his pen and paper roleplaying games more than a decade ago, he has always been fascinated by what can be done when people are pushed beyond normal boundaries. He was drawn to science fiction as a way to explore the human condition, and his debut book, *Advent*, is an extension of that desire.

Connect with Xander:
Facebook.com/AuthorXanderBoyce
Patreon.com/dmxanadu
Discord.gg/h243Sg4